PLUSH

A Novel

Pamela Gates Laux

Plush

A Novel by

Pamela Gates Laux

Copyright ©2013 by Pamela Gates Laux
Cover copyright ©2013 by Jodeen Gates Simmons
First paperback addition,© September 2013 by Pamela Laux
Printed in the United States of America
www.pamlaux.com
ISBN: 978-1-892357-03-8

Cover Design by Jodeen Gates Simmons
Cover photography by Joseph Ray Photography,
model Chasity McVay

Beau Ridge Publishing

This is a work of fiction. While, as in all fiction, the literary perceptions and insights are based on experiences, all names, characters, places, and incidents are either products of the author's imagination or are used fictitiously. No reference to any real person is intended or should be inferred.

I dedicate this story to the memory of
Greg Gates and Jack O'Donnell,
my brother and brother-in-law who left us too early in life.

ACKNOWLEDGEMENTS

I am indebted to the following people for their contributions
   to this book:

To Duke Pennell and Dorrie O'Brien for their editing talents.

To my fantabulous team of beta readers for their insights to making the
   story better; Jay Falconer, Jodi Olson, Lee Laux , Natalie Nicodemus,
   Mike Peevy, Ernest Leonard, Jody Simmons & Marilyn O'Donnell (my sisters),
   Connie Gates (my mother), Kalle Karu (who picked the title),
   and Kyle Moll (who helped me stay on course).

To Tom Gates (my brother) for his creative insights.

To Joey Ray and Chasity McVay for the cover photo.

To all my family and friends for their encouragement and support that assisted
   me through the journey, from the bottom of my heart, thank you.
   (Tami, Diane, Jamie, Coach, Veronica, Vicki, Tim, Dad...
   you all know who you are).

To Jody, my sis, who put up with my constant changes to the book and cover
designs.

And finally, to my three kids; Lissa, Ben and Courtney Laux
   — my life and greatest champions.

One

Texas

June 17, 1998

SUE PRAYED the stranger hadn't ripped off Hollis's legs or, worse, popped his eyes out or mutilated him beyond recognition. She trusted that the hawk would be in perfect condition. She needed it to be perfect. It just *had* to be.

It had taken her months of searching to find Hollis. Now she was stuck in a hot car behind a Mexican restaurant, waiting for the contact – her heart racing, her silk blouse stuck to her back from sweat. Only a few hours remained before her deadline. She scanned the dark, deserted alley – no sign of him yet.

She rolled down her window. The combination of diesel fumes and greasy tacos made her gag. "Phew!" She closed the window before turning up the air conditioning.

Thank God this heat eases up after midnight, otherwise my Suburban might overheat.

Sue looked at her watch. *I hope he doesn't have a change of heart.*

She checked her cell phone . . . no missed calls. She fidgeted with the seat controls before focusing her gaze to the far end of the narrow street. The moon played shadow games with the steam rising from a pair of storm drains guarding the entrance to the alley. The cracked pavement flickered in the moonlight, highlighting the river of trash overflowing the dumpsters.

A late model sedan drove slowly into sight. It crawled toward her with its high beams on, their brilliance blinding her to the interior of the car. She heard the stranger's engine knock, like the heart pounding in her chest. The red glow of brake lights flamed the alley.

The car pulled in close to her front bumper, stopping inches away. She felt trapped, her car pinned between the stranger's grille and the taco shop's door behind her. All she could see were glaring headlights and a body-sized dent across the sedan's hood.

She took a deep breath, opened the door and stepped down onto the gravelly road.

Why am I so nervous?

The headlights went dark and the engine died. A thin, middle-aged man in jeans and a wrinkled white shirt popped out of the car, taking several long menacing steps toward Sue, carrying a brown grocery bag puffed out as if it contained a bowling ball. She could feel him staring at her.

She knew the man only by his internet name of Rospi. The stranger's expression said she looked good enough to eat. Her face flushed as he leered at her.

"Do you have the money?" Rospi asked, eyeing her up and down.

"What, no small talk?" She regretted the comment as soon as she said it. Her wit trying to mask her nervousness. She didn't like the look on his face.

"Huh?"

"Sorry, never mind." she leaned against her car and looked him over, business-like in her pencil-straight skirt and sticky-in-the-back purple blouse. She couldn't see the color of his eyes but his breath smelled like an overworked brewery. His olive skin was peppered with warts and dark spots, reminding Sue of her son's frog, Stitch.

"I have it. But let me see him." She nodded toward the swollen sack, ignoring Rospi's gawk.

He scanned the alley and eyed his car like he was inspecting it. He hesitated, then he slowly opened the paper bag.

Sue peeked inside and a smile crept across her face.

"Come to mama, "she crooned, her ordinarily commanding voice soft and velvety. She removed the twelve-inch stuffed hawk.

"Hello. You're a hard toy to find." *Wow, this hawk is fabulous. So real, so bold. Strangely compelling.* She ran her fingers through the deep, soft pile of the velveteen fabric. It was in perfect condition. She tried to read the tag sewn to the butt of the stuffed toy, but the streetlight was too dim. She turned toward the moon. It wasn't bright enough.

Rospi reached into his back pocket, catching her attention. She saw the flash of a silver handle in his fingers. For a moment, Sue froze. The thought of her lying dead in this alley – her three young kids at home in their beds, orphaned – raced through her brain, dumping a jolt of adrenaline into her bloodstream.

"Do you need a light?" He grinned as he slid out a small flashlight.

Thank God, it's not a knife. She nodded, aware of a prickle of sweat rolling down her neck.

He turned on the penlight and ran it over her body, lingering at her breasts. "Nice."

"Where are your manners?" she said, her uneasy feeling persisting. His comment grated on her nerves more than she wanted him to know. He'd seemed like a smart person in their correspondence on the internet, not like this fool standing next to her.

She snatched the flashlight from him and examined the tag, matching the serial number with the one she'd memorized. The light reflected off the glowing holographic figures on the tag as she confirmed the blood-red numbers. *Yes!* It was the one – the only one.

She held Hollis up, admiring the hawk and its realistic design. Its wings were an iridescent orange, variegated color, complemented by a brown breast and a downy red tail and its gray hooked beak, the signature identification. She turned the toy over. The talons looked so real she could picture a bloodied rabbit trapped in them.

"Where's my money?"

Her concentration broken, Sue glanced at him. *Idiot.* She shook her head and squeezed the hawk's midsection. It was stuffed solid, like all the Yorkston toys. It felt heavier than the other bird line toys.

This is the real thing.

She could read designs like an accountant understood balance sheets. There was nothing forgotten, nothing left out. Every detail revealed a lifelike bird that collectors would love. She ignored Rospi's heavy breathing as he stood beside her, and ran her hand over the soft featherlike fur. She was ecstatic, even jealous of his creator.

"Stop taking your sweet goddamn time. It's the real hawk." He pulled a mint out of his shirt pocket and popped it in his mouth.

"I'm just making sure it's not a fake." *Geez, it's not his breath that stinks, it's his attitude.* She felt a nervous premonition, but she wouldn't let it overshadow the reason she was there.

"Listen, chick, we ain't got all day."

"Okay, renting him for six hours was the deal." Sue gave him a wad of bills and a deposit check for five thousand dollars. She wanted to get the hell out of there. She hugged the stuffed bird of prey close to her chest.

"Yep. That's the deal. But I'd rather sell it for five grand," Rospi said.

Good lord. She had already said, 'No way'.

"We've been through this. You agreed to a rental. The five thousand is just a deposit check, and if I don't return the toy you can cash it." She didn't intend to keep Hollis. She needed its photo for the catalog. That was all. If her estimates proved right, just the photo of this feathery soft plush alone would help her sell over two million catalogs.

He counted the bills. "Six hunnert," he said. He jammed the crumpled bills into his back pocket and scanned the check. "This check says Logan Designs. Where's your name?"

"I'm Sue Logan. I'm the president. Hold on." She spun around, opened her SUV's back door and grabbed a toy collector's catalog from the backseat. She returned and handed it to Rospi.

"This is me on the back cover." She tapped her finger on her photograph, the one with her blonde hair down to her elbows, not up in a twist like this morning.

He stood close to her, examined the photograph, then looked at her and then back at the catalog.

"Hmmp, okay. Well, if you work for the toy manufacturer, why don't you get your own damned stuffed animal?" A piece of the mint flew out of his mouth as he talked, hitting Sue's hand.

She jerked her hand back, grimaced.

"It's complicated," she mumbled under her breath. "I don't work for Yorkston Toys, I just make a collector's catalog of their collectibles. Look, I don't have to explain my business to you."

"I could care less about your business with some stuffed toy company." He crossed arms.

"It's a *plush* toy. Designer stuffed toys like this one, using a soft, cuddly fabric are often called plush."

"Plush. Stuffed. Whatever." Rospi shook the check at her. "Okay, I'll take the damn check and hold it until you return the *plushie* later this mornin'. "

"My assistant will meet you back here to return the hawk as planned. We *will* get that check back."

Sue climbed back in her car with Hollis tucked safely under her arm. She set the hawk on the seat beside her.

"Don't fail me, a lot of people are counting on us."

She needed the Yorkston catalog to succeed, but it was her own secret toy launch that would save her company. She had worked hard since her husband, Jonathan, died. She had saved and scrimped and the plans she had carefully laid out for this coming year would make or break her.

TWO

ANTHONY ROMERO, SPRAWLED OUT in the back seat of the Dodge, heard Rospi crunching on gravel as he approached the car. Rospi opened the driver's door and collapsed in the front seat.

"That bitch was hot," he said, as a cloud of cigarette smoke filled the car. "I wanted to tip her a twenty, but I doubt she would've given me much of a lap dance."

Anthony laughed, though he'd heard that same joke from Toad a dozen times before. He waited until the white beams from the headlights were gone and the alley went silent. He sat up, brushing grit from Rospi's car seat off his shirt. "She didn't see me, did she?"

"Nope. She was too in love with the toy, couldn't keep her eyes off it."

Good. He hoped she carried it everywhere. "What took you so long? It's hot as shit in here."

"You should've waited at your ride." Rospi turned on the car, flipping the air conditioning to full blast.

Anthony held his hand over the back seat. "Well, Toad, did you get the check?" Rospi meant toad in Italian – Anthony had given him the nickname because of his nasty complexion.

"Yeah, Chief, got it."

"Let me see it."

Rospi gave him the crinkled check. Anthony used a cigarette lighter to read it. He smacked the back of Rospi's head.

"You dumb son-of-a-bitch! This is a business check."

"So?" Rospi rubbed his head.

"So, you freak show? You were supposed to get a personal check!"

"You didn't say nothin' about that," Rospi said.

"Just take me back to my car." At least she took the hawk, and that was more important than the check. He wanted her personally buying the collectible, but that Sue Logan was a smart one, keeping it a business transaction. "Did she give you cash? Three hundred dollars?"

"Yep, got it."

"Keep it for your trouble."

"I'm planning on it." Rospi smirked at him in the mirror and drove the Dodge from the alley, crossing the bridge to the public access area beside the river.

"Do you want me to meet her to pick up the plushie?" Rospi asked.

"Plushie? What are you a fucking connoisseur now? No, I got it covered. Don't contact her anymore." Anthony shaking his head, got out of the car and leaned against Rospi's window. "You understand?"

"Yep."

Anthony walked over to the waiting white stretch limousine.

"See ya later, Tony. Nice doing business with you again!" Rospi yelled out the window.

"It's Anthony, you asshole. In fact, it's Mr. Romero to you."

Anthony settled into the limo and, with a shaky hand, he picked up the mobile phone and dialed Nathanael Yorkston's number. "Yeah, Boss, she took it. Toad delivered the goods."

Anthony hung up the phone and said to the empty backseat, grinning with his crooked teeth, "Yes, indeed, that hawk is a rare bird. It's one of a kind." He just hoped Sue Logan would give them what they wanted now.

He tapped his gold ring on the glass that separated him from his driver. The limo pulled out of the parking lot and within minutes they were on the expressway. A minivan wandered into their lane. The limo driver swerved to avoid it and Anthony was whipped forward, his face pushed up against the dividing window. He scowled out the window at the soccer bumper sticker-covered minivan. The interior lights were on and the woman driver was swiveled in her seat, her neck craned, yelling at a backseat full of kids. Anthony punched the seat with his fist. "Damn, I hate these Texas women. They drive like hell."

The driver glanced in the rearview mirror, but didn't comment.

"What're you lookin' at?" Anthony said.

The driver shook his head.

"I can't stand suburbia and that whole lifestyle . . . soccer moms and carpooling and all that crap."

From his research, he knew Sue Logan fit that suburbia profile. Soccer moms made his skin crawl. He smiled, as he wondered what else was planned for her.

Anthony knew his boss was greedy, selfish, demanding, and would stop at nothing to get what he needed from Sue Logan; even if it meant becoming her worst nightmare.

THREE

SUE WAS LATE. But it was worth being late. She sped down the expressway in the breaking dawn to the photo shoot location where a crowd waited for Hollis, the star of the catalog. She glanced at the hawk perched on the passenger seat.

Maybe he should be in a seatbelt. If I get in an accident, will my insurance cover this gold mine of a toy once he's road-kill?

Sue retrieved a chocolate Krispy Kreme doughnut out of a white box, her favorite indulgence, took three big bites, and hit the speaker button on her cell phone. She pressed the 2.

"Did you get it?"

"I'm fine, thanks," Sue said with a mouth full of sticky donut.

"Well?"

"Yes, Mary Jo, I got him. I'm glad to see you're not worried about me meeting a chat room lurker in a dark alley."

There was a few seconds of silence from the speaker. "Was the guy creepy? Did anything happen?"

"He was a bit odd, to say the least, but everything was fine. I still can't believe my luck in finding Hollis after searching for months at collector shows and on the internet."

"Yep, somehow you've managed to accumulate all of them now, even Hollis! Woo hoo, you've got the complete dozen!"

Sue smiled. "Yes, we do finally have all twelve of the October Yorkston bird line. I can't believe how the collectors pounced on the Yorkston's newcomers – including the pink penguin and the oh-so-popular Hollis the hawk. I can't wait to see the completed catalog.

9

Is everyone set?"

"Yes, we'll have the whole team there ready to shoot the mock Halloween scene. This is it. This will be the last shoot before the publishing deadline."

"I know. I know. Talk about being under the wire."

"Nobody wants an out-of-date collector's catalog."

Not to mention the millions in revenue at risk, Sue thought.

"What's he like?" Mary Jo's voice rang through the car.

"Hollis?" Sue glanced at the passenger seat. "He looks great. Authentic. I'm impressed by how detailed his talons look. And the tush tag is real. You'll see. I'll be there soon."

"Great. We need the director here before it gets too hot, and the kids' painted faces begin to melt off."

"Try to keep the crowd under control."

"Okay, boss. See ya."

"All righty. Bye, Mary Jo." Sue clicked off the phone and accelerated into the fast lane.

Soon it was stop-and-go congestion along the gridlocked freeway. She was thankful that her offices were only a few blocks from her house and most days she avoided traffic. Sue turned up the radio and sang along to the Dixie Chicks as she watched the bright sun crown over the horizon like a golden tiara. She was happy to have Hollis and the makings of a great catalog edition in the works.

Within the hour, her SUV came to rest in front of a sprawling colonial house, the backdrop for the photo shoot. Her black patent Christian Louboutin high heels made four-inch divots in the soggy dew-covered grass as she teetered across the manicured lawn. Sue had selected the model house in a gated neighborhood because she wanted to avoid the press and the Yorkston groupies. It was hard enough to get good catalog shots without having a crowd of onlookers and the media getting in the way.

The child models, their parents, and several neighbors were milling about. Sue saw a table stacked with acrylic boxes, each one about the size of a human head and each one occupied by a furry, plush animal. She looked around; Grady was the only photographer on site.

Thank God. No media.

"Hi Sue. I'm Joanne, Kaitlin's mom." A lady rushed forward with a catalog. Sue recognized the cover photo; it was her last year's edition. "She was in your catalog last year. I have that edition and wanted to see if you'd sign it." She shoved the catalog at Sue.

"Sure. Kaitlin's a sweetheart. She reminds me of my daughter, Maddie, with all those curls."

Joanne beamed at Sue. "Maybe with a note to her, so I can keep it for when she grows up. I figured the catalog may be worth something in the future, since the toys are worth so much now." She handed a sharpie marker to Sue and balanced the catalog on her forearm. It was folded back to a page with curly-haired Kaitlin holding a Yorkston stuffed dog. "I was thrilled to see you had the Yorkston lab puppy in this issue in her photo."

"I own and use all your collectors' catalogs." Joanne talked while Sue scribbled the note. "When I buy a new Yorkston collector toy, I circle its number in your catalog so I won't make a mistake and buy it again. And all the new releases I buy, I circle in green, so I can tell at a glance whether I bought it before or after the date it gets retired. It's weird, I know."

Sue smiled at her. *What's weirder, collecting the catalogs or collecting the toys in the first place?* Sue reminded herself that six years earlier a Louis Vuitton teddy bear was auctioned off for $190,000 to an avid arctophilist and the first comic book sold for $185,000. Sue knew that many families invested life savings into the Yorkston plush thinking that someday, like rare coins; they would be worth a fortune. Even a popular day time soap opera TV star had invested $100,000 into the Yorkston plush.

"Hey, is that Hollis?" Joanne asked, pointing to the toy in Sue's left hand. Several onlookers heard the comment and came toward them with their eyes on the gray-beaked hawk.

Sue felt the crowd getting hyped up and she felt nervous. Sue held up her hand, motioning them to stop, and some retreated. "Please, later. We need to get the shots."

A heavy lady twisted her head and ooohed at Hollis as if he were the hottest rock star. She grabbed Sue's arm. "Can we see that one? And take pictures of it? Look at the claws on it."

11

Ouch, take your claws off me. Sue tightened her grip on the red-tailed stuffed bird. "Not yet." She pulled her arm away.

"Jeez, I wish I would have thought of the software program that tracks these numbers," a large woman with a puffed, red face commented.

Sue stared at her, half-smiled and took a few steps backwards. Out of nowhere, Grady emerged from the crowd. He towered over the women and sported his signature yellow bandana do-rag, overalls and raggedy flip flops. "Well, you didn't invent it and she did. Let's give this young lady a chance to get to work." He parted the gathering women, grabbed Sue's free hand and navigated her past the groupies to the tripod camera.

Sue whispered in Grady's ear. "Thank you." She felt a glow of pride at his powerful actions.

"My pleasure boss. And hello."

She turned toward her photographer. "Good morning, Grady. Is everything set?"

"Yep, Mary Jo has everyone in position. We're waiting on you."

In a low voice Sue asked, "Have you seen any other shooters here?"

"There was one old man disguised in baggy jeans and a ball cap. He pretended to be a groupie, but I spotted his Nikon."

"Really?"

"Yeah. I called the security guard at the gatehouse. They dragged his ass out of here. He snuck in through the backyards."

"Thanks for handling that." Sue had heard on the news last week about several near-riots occurring at a local mall where crazed adult collectors shoved and trampled the shop owners to get the newest toys. The addicting success of the Yorkston stuffed animals could be daunting at times. People who bought her catalogs were mostly mothers and young adults. The main reason most adults, like Rospi, collected the soft toy was to make a quick buck reselling them as collectibles for higher prices. "Let me get Hollis set up and we'll be ready to go." Sue smiled at him and she saw a trace of a smile in return. She walked gracefully up the brick steps, approving of the vast Colonial's porch colorfully crowded with children in costumes and the Yorkston rare birds. The scene was poetic. She stood spellbound at the staging of her final shoot.

This is it. Showtime.

Sue could sense all the eyes on her. She smiled when she saw Mary Jo rushing over with a large ceramic mug of steaming java.

"Hi, Sue. Nice outfit." Mary Jo handed her the coffee.

"Thanks. I could use some coffee in my veins. Oh, before I forget, I have doughnuts in my car for you and Grady." Sue took a sip and returned the mug to her.

"Minus a few chocolate ones, I'm sure." Mary Jo set Sue's mug down, picked up her own Styrofoam cup and sipped.

A little girl's hat slid down her head. "Here, let me help with that." Sue wrestled with a witch's wig under the pointy hat squashed atop the head of a chunky girl.

"Mary Jo, look at that." Sue pointed. "The Godzilla monster is wearing pink high top sneakers."

"That's okay, I can Photoshop them out."

"That's cool."

"Yep, I've been using Photoshop since I picked up my first mouse." Mary Jo followed Sue.

"You're definitely a better designer than administrator." Sue said teasingly.

Mary Jo rolled her eyes up and stuck out her lower lip. Sue acting as if she didn't see her, while adding the final touch by propping the hawk center stage on top of a pumpkin. Mary Jo following her, brushed the fingerprints off the pumpkin.

Sue thumped the large pumpkin with her finger. "Firm and real." She grinned at Mary Jo, nodding her approval. "It sure was a challenge locating pumpkins in June. But I love to use genuine items in the photo shoots. Luckily you came across them at that nursery."

"Yeah, I can't believe they harvest the pumpkins in a greenhouse. Who would of thought? Such a rare find in the Texas summer."

Sue swept her hand over the pumpkin. The greenhouse pumpkins were bright orange like a marshmallow circus peanut. "Ironically, they look like fake foam pumpkins."

"The nursery is awesome. However, I still think we should

use fake ones. Most food photographers do," Mary Jo replied.

"I like real versus fake. It's more natural." She grinned and walked back to Grady.

Mary Jo said after her, "Are we still talking about the pumpkins?"

"It's perfect! Grady, let's start shooting." Sue gave him a thumbs up and Grady bent over his tripod. "It's our last shoot. Let's make it the best."

"I plan on it." He said.

She patted his shoulder and then paced behind Grady as he shot.

Sue yelled over to Mary Jo, "Can we get the children to look happier?"

Mary Jo brushed her red bangs off her sticky forehead and rolled her green eyes. Droplets of sweat rolled down her face and gathered on her chin. She swatted a fly buzzing her as she shouted at the kids.

"Come on kids, I know it's hot out here, but I need you all to smile! Can I get the three of you up front not wearing masks to look more excited and smile? After all, you *are* trick-or-treating."

Mary Jo continued to coax the kids standing on the front porch. "Remember, Ms. Sue is going to let each of you pick out your favorite stuffed animal to take home."

The enticement of picking out one of their favorite squishables got the children excited. A little fairy princess with a red, runny nose had been sucking on the tag of a pink plush. She held it up and gave it a kiss, smiling ear-to-ear.

An amused, approving smile formed on Grady's lips as he peered into his camera and started snapping photos.

Mary Jo nodded as she looked over at Sue. "This photo will complete the month of October and the catalog." She had a saucy voice, a quick smile and skin that the sun had left freckled until they all ran together and made a tan.

"Good job. Thank you everyone. Let's get the children out of their costumes as soon as Grady is finished. It's melting hot out here." Sue dabbed her fingers on a drop of sweat forming on her brow, walking over to Grady with the perfect picture highlighted in her mind. Grady glanced up and winked as he purposely clicked the frame.

Thirty minutes later, Grady and Mary Jo packed up while the children picked out their gifts. Sue watched several of the kids search through the plastic bin of the Yorkston animals. Mary Jo had set aside the off-limits toys including Hollis the Hawk.

A skirmish broke out between a teenage boy and a young girl. Sue watched the two kids with amusement, reminded of her own three kids.

"Hey, I saw PT first!" The boy tugged on a flipper wing of a pink Penguin named PT.

"Noooo, you didn't!" The little girl pulled the other wing taut. "I had my hand on it before you."

"I saw it first! Stop before you tear it!"

"Why do you want a *girl* Penguin anyway?"

"I don't have *that* serial number," he said. The little girl let go for a second, allowing the boy to take control of the toy. He held it above his head and out of the girl's reach.

"But I like him! Mommmy!" She jumped up and down thrashing her hands at the Penguin.

Mary Jo stepped in. "Hey, sweet-pie, I have another pink PT in my car."

The little girl stuck her tongue out at the boy. "Woo-hoo! Let's go get it." The girl clapped her hands in excitement, her rainbow flip-flops smacked against the cement as she skipped behind Mary Jo toward the car.

The boy ran to his mom showing her the guerdon penguin and its inimitable fabric label. They smiled, nodding in excitement. The woman looked at Sue and waved. "Thank you."

The cloth tag was the attraction, not the toy. The Yorkston's holographical fabric tush labels sewn to the critters doubled as a lottery ticket for kids and adults.

Mary Jo wandered over to Sue and handed her a stack of papers. "This is the last of the signed model release forms."

"Thanks, Mary Jo." Sue crammed the papers into her leather briefcase. "I won't miss this part of the catalog shoots this summer." Sue pointed at the kids pushing, shoving and grabbing at the stuffed creatures. She scoffed at the success of the plush animals. "Yorkston could put a prize winning tush tag on a stuffed Escherichia coli and collectors would fight over the digestive tract bacterium."

"Stuffed E-coli. Right? The sweetest kids turn into twerps when it comes to those flippin' varmints." Mary Jo watched the children groping the toys. "It reminds me of Wonka."

"Who?"

"You know, the crazy guy Wonka and his chocolate factory?"

"Hmm. Like Chocolate?" Sue had watched the show when she was a kid.

"The toys are scrumdidilyumptious," Mary Jo mocked in a deep, singing voice. "But no, they're not like chocolate."

"Let me guess. Nathanael Yorkston reminds you of Wonka?"

"Ha ha. Not physically like Willy Wonka or that actor, Gene Wilder. But I guess nasty Naty Yorkston does resemble him with his big hooked nose and his styleless, klutzy bookworm appearance. But I meant the tags are like the golden tickets."

Sue chuckled at Mary Jo's description of the creator of the stuffed toys. "The golden tickets?"

"The phenomenon of the Yorkston animals reminds me of the Wonka mania that hit the world because everyone was hunting down those five golden tickets hidden inside packs of the chocolate bars. Remember?"

"Yeah. And the toys remind you of—"

"No, not the toys, but the tags on the Yorkston animals are like the golden tickets."

"Ah. The serial numbers on the tags are like the tickets." Sue made the connection. On one side of the fabric label was printed the registration number, meeting all legal requirements, but on the reverse side of the woven sewn tag, in holographic lettering, was the name of the toy and a unique serial number.

"Yep, that Yorkston dude, Nathanael, is like Willy Wonka. He is boosting the plush animals by tying them to special games and then controlling the distribution."

"I get it. Just like selling the chocolate to get to the golden tickets. On top of that, Yorkston only makes a small number of certain animals, like Hollis. The toy's shortage combined with the unique numbering concept captures the adult collectors."

It was true. The internet had become a quick source to buy and trade the collectibles for inflated prices. A series of the plush tripled the value over a solo toy. A collection of five consecutively numbered tags was the equivalent to a royal flush in the World Poker Championship. There was big money in it.

"I'll stick around for a few minutes to make sure all the kids get picked up. Go ahead back to the office before you return Hollis. I'm hoping to see some of the proofs by tomorrow night," Sue said.

"I know. I know." Mary Jo mocked a parting salute to Sue, and when Sue gave her the evil eye, she pretended to be mopping sweat from her reddening forehead.

Sue grinned as she watched Mary Jo gather up the remaining props and toss them in her trunk. Retrieving the folder that Mary Jo had left her, she flipped through the model release forms, signing the bottom of each. When she got to the bottom of the stack, she found a spreadsheet listing hundreds of the Yorkston plush animal line and their associated tag numbers. As she looked at the chart she was reminded of the many hours she had spent logging and researching the serial numbers of the stuffed toys, unlocking the secret code to the system. She had discovered a lot about Yorkston. She found the unique mystery of the Yorkston toys because she had thought of the idea herself, over a decade earlier.

Sue was convinced that Yorkston's success was based on her long-lost designs – the ideas stolen from her that could have changed her life forever. Yet there was a nagging problem … an issue with the product she had created.

How did he solve it?

FOUR
Indianapolis

EVAN TAYLOR, the only reporter in the country – or perhaps the world – with a press pass to interview Yorkston Toys, turned his blue Taurus into the tight parking spot. The car's bumper hit the visitor sign and it wobbled.

"Crap." He threw his cigarette butt out the window, withdrew a small tattered notepad from his briefcase and looped his press ID badge around his neck. His rumpled khaki pants stuck to him and a line of sweat ran along the small of his back.

The shadow of The Yorkston Building shaded his car and gave a small relief from the Indiana sun. He glanced at his reflection in the rearview mirror and ran his fingers through his salt-and-pepper shoulder-length, wavy hair.

He strode through the building lobby, indifferent about his meeting with Benjamin Baggett, Director of Marketing, but excited to see Tori.

"Hi Charlie." Evan approached the security desk.

"Good morning, Evan." The elderly guard replied. He looked at his watch. "Well, it's almost afternoon."

"Yep, I have an 11:45 appointment with Benjamin in Marketing."

"You can go up."

"Thanks." Evan signed the logbook. He flipped through the visitor pages, looking to see who else had been in The Yorkston Building.

18

"I read your latest article." Charlie peered at Evan through wire-rimmed glasses with thick lenses

"The business section of the IndyStar?" Evan replied.

"No, Gift World News. Nathanael doesn't get quoted much. And you've been quoting him in the papers a lot lately. I mean a lot. My wife opens the IndyStar, and there's Nathanael Yorkston, predicting that the Yorkston plush will likely be the number one toy for several more years. Then I leaf through this business rag, and there's Nathanael again. Shoot, it's frontline news across the country, and on TV." Charlie paused and removed his glasses. He rubbed his red eyes. "How'd you end up being the only reporter allowed in this building?"

"A little work and a lot of luck." *And a college alum that thinks you know a secret about him.*

For Evan, the Yorkston luck began two years ago. At age forty-three, he had joined the freelance writer pool at the IndyStar. *I was just a reporter in search of a good story.* He took a few steps toward the elevators.

As it happened, Nathanael Yorkston had also been in search of a reporter that could write his stories the way he wanted them, the kind that would put his stuffed animals on the map. Together, Evan and Nathanael Yorkston created a media frenzy that leaked the newest releases to the public. Nathanael Yorkston controlled the press.

Evan had to give Naty credit for his thinking. He manipulated the supply and demand. Evan, guided by Naty, would announce that a toy would soon be retired. The price would skyrocket and the collectors would go fanatic, hunting down all the plush before it retired. He soon became the only reliable source who could foresee the toys' changes. Upon such a foundation, Naty's empire was built. Today Evan's Gift World stories were the top-read articles, but he would love nothing more than to have the Wall Street Journal or the New York Times ask him to sell his articles to them. He dreamed of being read around the world.

"Do you have any worthy news for me?" Evan asked.

Charlie scowled at Evan and pointed his finger at the elevator door as it opened. "Go."

"Okay. Okay. Don't have me arrested. See ya, Charlie."

Evan pushed 49 and smiled at the guard as the shining metal doors closed. Once settled in the elevator, he winked at the camera in the corner. He knew Brandon would be slouched at the security desk in the basement, sucking on salted white pistachios, reading the paper and staring at the bank of TV monitors.

Evan checked his watch, eleven thirty-five. In a few minutes he would slip into the private office of the chief executive officer of Yorkston Toys.

Victoria Romero, Naty's Executive Secretary, had said the CEO would be out of town until the next day. Evan had been reliving their call all morning.

"Tori, I have an hour to kill before my meeting with Benjamin. I can meet you for coffee before I leave town."

"I dunno. Why are you going to Texas?" she asked.

"It's no big deal . . . just some interview with a company. Can you meet?"

He heard silence. Her hesitation on the other end of the phone worried him that he hadn't been keeping their relationship interesting. At twenty-seven years old, she was nineteen years younger than he was. What started out as a rocket-fueled hot romance was starting to sputter out.

"Hey, I have an idea Tori. Naty's gone. Right?"

"Yeah, he's back in a few days. Why?"

"Why don't you meet me in Naty's private office? I've heard office sex is exciting."

He had worried she would think he was too bold, but in the end, she agreed.

It was at a party where Evan met Tori. Her father, Anthony, and Naty had been college roommates. Both were divorced men and often attended parties, hunted, and vacationed together. Naturally, Evan tagged along whenever he could. Meeting Tori had been an especially lucky break, and their relationship had been a nice perk this summer. Not only did he get inside information, but the sex was great too.

He had scheduled an interview today in The Yorkston

20

building with Benjamin regarding their new line. But the meeting would wait. What he really wanted was a nooner.

Stepping out of the elevator on the forty-ninth floor he glanced over at Victoria's small wooden desk perched outside Naty's office, empty. The narrow lobby hallway running the length of the west wall was also empty. He didn't see a soul as he walked down the hall to the first door; his sweaty hand on the brass doorknob slowly opened the heavy mahogany door. Once inside the executive conference room, he took a deep breath, thrilled of the idea of a quickie in the CEO's office.

The conference room was empty and in a couple of strides, he was at the door to Naty's private, well-appointed chief executive chambers.

Naty's office smelled of leather and a musky, spicy scent. The room was chilly. Evan's gaze swept the unadorned office like a heat-seeking missile targeting on Tori. She sat on the edge of the rosewood table, her deliciously long bare legs crossed, a stiletto-clad foot swinging back and forth. The table with elaborately carved legs served as Nathanael Yorkston's desk — no drawers, file cabinets or credenzas.

Wow, she looks hot. His hungry gaze traveled over the gorgeous, voluptuous young woman in front of him as he walked toward her. A low grunting sound came from deep in his throat and his legs felt wobbly. "Hey baby, I'm so happy to see you," he said.

"Come here and show me how much." Her hands grabbed his shoulders, pulling him toward her. She uncrossed her legs and pulled him between them.

"Tori, you're smoking hot. I love your eyes."

"I get them from my father's side of the family, from Valencia." She fluttered her lashes at him flirtatiously and formed a salacious smile.

Evan stared into her black shimmering eyes, thick lashes and graceful eyebrows. "They're gorgeous."

She repeated the batting and fluttering. "Come on, you're a writer, you can do better."

He hesitated. He wasn't good with romancing women. *Maybe that's why I'm still single at forty-five.*

21

"Your beautiful eyes conjure up a fable of black-eyed, topless maidens of Paradise every time I fantasize about you." *God, I love how she wants me to tell her stories while having sex.*

"I love that you're a writer." She planted a tantalizing, wet kiss on his lips then backed away. "Do you like me better with my natural auburn hair or this Marilyn Monroe platinum blonde?" Her long hair fell haphazardly as she flipped it off her shoulders.

"I loved your dark hair, but you're a foxy blonde." Keeping his eyes on hers, he ran his hand up her velvety smooth leg.

"I have that to thank from my papa's family too. At least I change my hair color often."

Evan did love her blonde hair, except it now sprouted her dark natural color at the roots. "It is amazing how much you look like your dad."

Tori looks bizarrely like her dad. It makes it a kinda creepy reminder for me, since he's head of Yorkston security.

"You look wonderful." They were nose to nose as he pushed his mouth full on top of her red lips.

"Evan," she barely breathed as he slipped his hand under her jacket, rubbing the silk camisole.

"Come on, dark-eyed maiden, let's get you topless." He pushed her down on the large desk. Her jacket fell open and he cupped her breasts, under the garment. "I love when you go braless," he said, while brushing his fingers over her repeatedly. As he caressed her, he could feel her responding to his touch under the thin silk.

"Mmmm," she moaned approvingly as she gazed up at him.

When he slipped her jacket off, it fell to the floor. He bent down to retrieve it and noticed the desk up close. "Wow, look at the legs on this table." A bare woman's bust was carved into each of the four table legs, displaying full breasts with two high peaks, a shapely waist and sculpted stomach. "These are crafted beautifully, like something you'd see on the front of a pirate's ship."

"I've heard that the table cost Nathanael over a hundred thousand dollars. It came from a church in Italy and he has been known to rub his hands over the bare chest for luck," she giggled.

"That's an odd rumor. I can't see uptight Naty doing that in a meeting, like he's stroking a magic lamp to summon up the Genie inside." As he said it, he made up and down motions with his hand over Tori's breasts.

Tori let out a laugh, shaking her head. "Yeah, maybe it's the little genie that helped him be so successful with those stuffed animals."

I don't think luck had anything to do with it, nor did rubbing the ladies tits. "What other rumors have you heard?" Evan liked that she fed him gossip about Yorkston.

"Later." She grabbed his hand and put it under her skirt, on her panties. As she did, the jacket drifted from his fingertips, and he emitted an oscillating groan.

Even as he kissed her hard on her lips and continued to run his hand between her legs, he wondered what rumors she had for him. He was hungry for dirt on Yorkston. Evan purged his mind of work, to make way for the ensuing ecstasy.

"I'm so glad I met you at your dad's party," he said breathily. His fingers fumbled with the tiny buttons on her camisole. When she didn't object, he continued by slipping the camisole off, leaving her with her skirt and five-inch heels.

Kissing her neck he whispered, "You're gorgeous," then moved his lips to her breasts. His hands roamed over her slim waist, which gave way to her well-rounded hips. Moving over her, he unzipped her skirt, sticking his hands inside, caressing her hips, then pulling it down along her smooth trembling legs, her skin warm to his touch. He stepped back and quickly removed his shirt. His hungry eyes rummaged her panty-clad body, drinking up his fill of her.

Tori stood up, trailed her fingers over his chest, stomach and rib cage. She moistened her lips with the tip of her tongue.

"Hmmm," Evan groaned.

He closed his eyes, ready to explode as she reached down, taking an eternity to undo his pants.

"Let me help you baby." His trousers were off in seconds, followed by his briefs. He maneuvered his body up against the desk facing the wall leading to the conference room. Wild desire flooded him as he responded to her touches.

"Tori, you are so beautiful," he repeated, his hands fondling her breasts. He ran his hand up her leg, feeling the creamy, soft skin of her upper thigh.

He loved the excitement of being in a forbidden place. Passionate and hungry, but somewhat nervous at the idea of getting caught, he wanted to hurry the pace. He took her hand, resting it on his lower stomach.

Her cheeks rosy in her ashen face, she knelt in front of him and moved her hands familiarly over his flat stomach and across his hips. She swirled her hair back and forth, brushing it over his erection, sending tingles throughout his body.

Evan was lost.

She ran her wet tongue across his stomach, dipping it in his navel. While his body responded for more, he wanted his turn. Evan started to pull her to him, when — voices!

He froze and looked down at Victoria.

Her eyes were wide with panic as she stared up at him.

Dark eyes. Big, dark eyes.

She had heard it too! Voices coming from the adjoining conference room.

Oh shit! He had been so preoccupied he didn't hear the door open in the next room. Evan reached over and turned off the light on the desk. He put his index finger to his lips. Victoria was rigid, still in a squatting position, under the desk looking helpless, holding her breath.

Crap! I can't get caught with my pants down and my tongue in Nathanael Yorkston's assistant's ear, especially not in his office! I'll be screwed. He felt stifled, but a vital part of his body was not.

Humiliated, he stepped into his trousers and briefs in one motion. Victoria scrambled on all fours over to her camisole. Hastily, she slipped it on, pausing to fasten one button in the middle.

The sun's rays peeking through the cracks of the shutter gave Evan a vision of Victoria that would have done justice to an ad for an erotic magazine – her hair tousled, her cheeks flushed and only one button fastened, exposing part of each creamy, voluptuous breast. Unconsciously, he shivered as his passion began to stir and he felt his body responding again.

The voices in the next room got louder and clearer. Evan swallowed, trying to rein in his libido. His body wanted one thing, but his mind wanted another.

24

Focus. I have to focus. The door! Had he remembered to lock the adjoining door?

He sprang toward the conference room door, like a cat pouncing on an unsuspecting mouse. He clicked the deadbolt into the locked position, the clack of the lock as loud as the hammer of doom to him.

Victoria's dark eyes went wide in her pale face, making her look like a life-size, inflatable rubber doll.

He stared at the door, as if watching a car accident, waiting for a response. Nothing. The conversations on the other side continued without hesitation or interruption.

Thank God!

His teeth gritted together, his nerves were fried and he needed a cigarette. Evan lowered his head as he tried to listen to the conversation on the other side of the wall. He recognized two of the three voices; both were Yorkston lawyers, Cecil Pennington and Stuart Masson. The third voice sounded like Benjamin Baggett. Evan caught fragments of the conversation. They were talking about Logan Designs, the Texas outfit Naty had ordered Evan to go see, posing as a gift magazine reporter.

Jesus. This is unbelievable.

He could hear some of the meeting, but needed to fill in the blanks.

"That Logan Designs woman . . . the hawk." Pennington's voice was identifiable, but soft.

"Are you sure it can't be traced back? She can't find it, can she?"

"We sent Romero. He knows what he's doing," said Masson.

"I don't . . . we'll have her ass in a sling." Was that Benjamin's voice? Could this be possible? He could have a story — a big, juicy story.

For fifteen minutes, Evan sat quietly in the dark office with Victoria, trying to hear the intruders next door, afraid to leave and risk being caught, anxious to get all the information he could. By now, both were fully clothed and put back together.

After the conference room had been quiet for ten minutes, Evan turned on the lights. He pulled Victoria close to him and gazed into her dark eyes. It was difficult to see where her iris stopped and her pupils left off. She blinked furiously as her pupils begun to dwindle in the full light. Oh, how Evan loved those sensual eyes.

"That was close. Are you okay?" He whispered in Victoria's ear, inhaling her sweet perfume.

"Yes." She giggled and blushed.

"Can I come to your place Thursday night when I return from Texas and finish what we started?" He kissed her mouth with force, his fingers caressing her satin top.

"Yes. Eight o'clock," pushing him away. "Right now, I'm starved. Let me grab my purse, hit the ladies' room and head to lunch. Do you have time to eat? With Nathanael gone, I'm taking a long lunch." She tugged at her top and combed her fingers through her hair.

"No, I have to get going." Evan gave her a long, wet kiss before leaving.

Evan waited for the elevator. Damn, he was disappointed they were interrupted. He saw Victoria return to her desk, retrieve her purse, and head toward the ladies' room. Seconds later, he stepped into the first elevator, feeling deprived and frustrated like a horny teenager. As the door closed, he heard the adjoining car open.

Nathanael Yorkston walked off the elevator. Rolling his luggage across the marble floor, he was pleased he had cut his trip short by a day. A waste of time, in his mind.

He was unlocking his office doors when he noticed Victoria was still at lunch. He made a mental note of the time. She should have been back at her desk by twelve thirty.

As he entered his office, his brows narrowed. His office smelled faintly like Victoria's perfume.

FIVE
Texas

AFTER AN ONEROUS meeting at the bank, Sue stomped into the lobby of the Logan offices hauling her briefcase over her shoulder. Her foul mood dissipated somewhat when she spotted a small egg-shaped virtual pet sunk to the bottom of the lobby water fountain. She smiled at Mary Jo.

"I was enlisted to babysit and feed the little cyber-creature today. It's beeping drove me nuts, so I decided to give it a bath," Mary Jo said when she caught Sue looking at the Tamagotchi toy.

"You're daughter's not going to like that."

Mary Jo shrugged. "I can buy her another." She squinted, shielding her eyes from the sun's glare shining through the front door. Mary Jo's reception desk sat to left of the front door in the lobby. "How'd your meeting go at the bank?"

"It was productive, but I still believe Jennifer liked dealing with Jonathan more than she does me."

Mary Jo shrugged. "Who knows? I always say single women in business have a tougher time than their male counterparts."

"It seems that way in this business. Hey, did you return Hollis as planned?"

"I tried, but no one ever showed up." Light danced on the large constellation of freckles on Mary Jo's cheeks as she continued to squint.

"Really?"

"Yep, I arrived early and waited for thirty minutes. I looked in and outside the restaurant but no one ever showed. The hawk is in your office." Mary Jo pointed toward Sue's open door.

"Let me send this guy an email. I don't want him to be able to cash the check. Will you stop payment on it? What a crook."

"Yeah, what an asshole, thinking he could get away with keeping your five thousand by not showing up. Yes, I'll do that now, and I'll keep an eye on the account and see if he tries to cash it." Mary Jo picked up a stack of phone memos.

Sue noticed a small tear in the overstuffed peach colored leather sofa that sat in front of the foyer picture window. She walked up to the couch.

"Take a look at this. I'll need to have this repaired. It makes our lobby look cheap, which it most certainly is not." Sue rubbed the offending gash with her fingers, wondering if her own children had caused the rip.

Turning back from the couch, she took the stack of memos from Mary Jo and walked into her office, tossing her briefcase on the floor next to her desk. Sue noticed Hollis was staring at her from his acrylic box perched on the top shelf.

"That hawk seems a bit scary now, sitting up there," she said through the doorway to Mary Jo. Sue had seen a hawk flying over the creek behind her house last week. "It's like an aerial predator, not a stuffed toy." The plush hawk's glass eyes made Sue feel as if she was a young mouse Hollis wanted for dinner. She'd have to find the owner soon or sell the thing.

"You forgot this one." Mary Jo walked into Sue's office and handed a small note to Sue.

"Is Grady in? Or any of the marketing reps?"

"No. everyone's at lunch. I'll have the new month's layout for you to see in a few hours. Grady did a fantastic job with the photos. They turned out wonderful," Mary Jo said, not moving from the front of Sue's desk.

"I look forward to seeing them." Sue slouched in her chair.

"Any messages from Daniel?"

"Afraid not. Are you looking forward to spending time with him?"

"I hadn't really thought about it that way. This trip is all about the meetings. He's a consultant escorting me to China. This is a crucial trip to secure manufacturing for our products."

Could Mary Jo see her smile when she talked about Daniel?

"I know you have meetings while you're there, but you said yourself when you returned from New York that you had met a nice-looking available man."

"I didn't say *available*," Sue said.

"You said something like that. He is single, right?"

"Yes, but I'm not going to China to 'date'. This is all business."

"I just thought in the evenings you may go to dinner, and –"

"Look, what are you, my mom now? Geez, you, my sister Dee, my mom, it seems the three of you are always on me about men. I'm a working girl, and a single mom. Three kids keep me busy and I'm fine with that."

The phone rang on Mary Jo's desk and she ran to answer it.

"End of discussion. And I want to see the October proof by end of day!" Sue yelled out the door.

She looked around her small office. The walls, like the ones throughout the building, were adorned with framed Logan magazine articles, product photos, plaques and awards for best products and showroom. Sue took time to concentrate on the frames, hoping their reminders would calm her worries about the finances. The warehouse down the hall had shelves overflowing with her products and prototypes. The walls throughout the building were peppered with children's crayon drawings of themselves with Logan toys.

I just pray that my hard work is rewarded.

She smiled and pushed the bank meeting to the back of her mind.

Sue was returning emails when Mary Jo walked in her office.

"You have an interview with a magazine tomorrow. And don't forget to call Mr. Winston regarding your meeting place in Hong Kong," Mary Jo said. "Have you eaten? Do you want me to bring you back lunch?"

"Yes, lunch would be great, thanks. What magazine interview is this?"

"Um . . . it's either Gift World Magazine or the Texas Women's Magazine. And the reporter's name is Evan, I think. Or Taylor. I'll check. Three soft chicken tacos?"

"Yes, thanks. Maybe I'll tell the reporter about the Millennium Kids," Sue said.

"Well . . . hopefully it isn't too early to let the cat out of the bag."

"Yeah, the Millennium Kids plush has that new functionality, and we've managed to keep the design secret for so long." Sue looked around the office. "Maybe when I return from China with a final product I can talk about the new line in interviews." She decided to wait to mention her new toy line, like a secret lover she wanted to leave undiscovered.

"I'll be back with lunch in a few." Mary Jo left the office.

Sue unlocked the bottom drawer of the antique credenza, wrenching open a false wood panel inside. She retrieved a faded cloth bag and untied the frayed cord. She pulled out a small doll. Sue flipped the doll over and examined it — her first prototype. She ran her hand over the facial features, the tiny sewn threads of a lip and the overstuffed dimpled cheeks. Turning it over, she fumbled with the fabric tag, and stared at the red numbers written on it from so many years ago. The other side of the tag had an inscription that read *To Grandma, Love Sue.*

She slipped the doll back into the bag and hid it in her drawer. She picked up her phone and called Daniel, getting his voicemail.

"Hi Daniel. I'm all set for our trip Saturday. I wanted to confirm that we are meeting in customs after your arrival. Oh, and try to stay away from the peach martinis Friday night before you get on your long flight over."

The manufacturing meetings were important to her company, and the anticipation of going to China added an additional level of significance. Whether it was ascending the career ladder, saving her company, or anything in between, this well planned trip was an important part of her launch strategy arsenal.

SIX
Texas
Outside Logan Offices

ANTHONY REMOVED the earphones from his head. "When is she going to China?" he asked his two security men.

"Beats me," Eddie, a rotund and intimidating man said.

"When's the last time you showered, man?" Anthony shook his head.

"We've been on surveillance," Eddie replied pushing his black, matted, straggling hair off his forehead.

"I think she said in a few days," Brick, the Asian man with a cobra tattoo on the nape of his bald head, replied to Anthony.

"Good. I'm glad Evan will be there before she leaves."

"Yeah, Taylor masquerading as a toy magazine reporter. Should be interesting," Brick said.

"Her success has been attracting media attention. Setting up the fake interview was easy." Anthony stuck a toothpick between his slightly crooked and overlapping front teeth. "Evan's supposed to be there tomorrow."

"That's what I heard. The assistant confirmed it," Brick said.

"Are there any more tapes for me to listen to?" One of Antony's talents was hiding mini spy devices strong enough to capture voices from a long distance effectively from inside a toy or object. "Her assistant mentioned the plush design and its new functionality, but that was it."

31

"Nope, this is all we have. She's been out all morning." Brick said.

"We should be able to get the interview tomorrow. Maybe she'll take the eavesdropping bird into the warehouse or her design room."

"We'll get more information tomorrow," Brick said. His strong neck tendons popped as he spoke. "Do you want another smoke?"

Anthony shook his head. "Let's hope Evan gets the information. Let's follow her home in case she brings the hawk to her house."

Anthony took off his headphones and put them on the seat next to him. He rubbed his eyes, and bent his neck to the left, then to the right, hunched his shoulders and tried to stand, feeling his muscles stretch out. He turned up the AC and pointed a vent toward him. It was caked with dust and dirt. Cigarette smoke and ashes blew around the small windowless van.

"Surveillance sucks. I can't wait to get back to the limo," Anthony said.

But first, he needed to get some information. And he needed it soon. Sue's Millennium doll rollout was looming closer with each day and his boss wasn't a patient man.

SEVEN
Atlanta

DANIEL WINSTON WALKED out of the stockroom of his flagship store, paused for an instant, then spun back the way he'd come, bumping into this brother. The sagging, scuffed hardwood floors in the long hallway had endured over thirty years of the two Winston brothers. They had raced the newest scooters and trikes down the narrow hallway when they were kids, jockeying for position, and passing when one of them slowed. Today their wide shoulders made it impossible for them to stand alongside each other in the hall.

"What are you up to?" Harry asked, moving aside and pressing his back against the adjacent wall.

"Counting," Daniel said. "You're looking dapper."

"You know I like to dress professional while in the office." Harry held up his silky striped tie and flipped it at him. "I have to keep up with you. Even if I'm not the most sought after single man in town like you bro — us married dudes can look good."

Daniel cracked a smile. "All rumors." He looked at the spreadsheet in his hand. "I have to get back to the numbers."

"The thought of you physically counting in the stock room reminds me of the times Dad had us spend our weekends here climbing ladders, opening every sealed box, taking count to make sure the vendors didn't short us."

"Yeah, when are you going to put your kids to work?"

"When are you going to get married and have kids?"

Daniel ignored the comment.

A serious look crossed Harry's face. "Are you checking inventory before you leave for China?"

"Yes, I'm on my way to run the report. I'll update the computer and be out of your way." Daniel slapped Harry on the shoulder. "And thanks for helping the buyers last week. You did a super job, as always."

"Hey, thanks. No rush on the computer. Dad's already left for the day."

"He shouldn't come in at all."

"Try telling the old geezer that. He'll be here until they take him away in a body bag or a straight jacket. Man, when I'm seventy, I plan on being on the golf course every day, not at this office." Harry didn't wait for Daniel to comment. "Did you hear about Yorkston's new releases?"

"I heard the bird line is doing well."

"In the first week on the shelves we sold over three thousand units—a Winston store record. We can't even get the hawk or the penguin. They've been on backorder for months."

"That's incedible. Any winning tag numbers from our stores?"

"I hadn't asked. By the way, the new glass Dream Fairy line is off the charts."

"That's surprising. Whose idea was it to carry a bunch of glass fairies anyway?" Secretly, Daniel had worried about the bold move his brother made in purchasing a large inventory.

"Yours truly. And I know it may have been risky choosing this new product line to promote in our stores, and even riskier ordering containers full from China. But who knows, it could be the next fad if my predictions are right."

"Yeah, fads come out of nowhere, sweeping the country, and then – poof – vanish overnight." Daniel flashed his hands in the air to demontrate.

"But not before making us a buttload of money. And then we count on you to discover the next new fad." Harry put his arm on Daniel's shoulder and guided him down the hallway, stopping at the manager's office. "We're counting on you to keep the stores' revenues growing."

"You can always count on me, Harry." Daniel reached for the doorknob.

Harry turned to walk away. He stopped after a few steps, turned back and said, "Enjoy China. Find us something new and exciting."

"Thanks, I will." Daniel was always excited to find something new. The truth was, he felt he had already found it. A meeting in New York last month had connected him with an incredible inventor. He looked forward to meeting up with beautiful, blue-eyed Sue Logan again.

He stood there and watched Harry wander off down the hallway. His older brother had been the general store manager of Winston's for twenty years. Daniel knew the family-owned business was fortunate to have such a loyal employee, and he was lucky to have Harry for a brother and a friend.

Daniel Winston's family had owned the chain of gift stores bearing their family name since 1941. The chain numbered over five dozen locations. The Winston Corporation holdings included the store chain, two four-star hotels — one in New York and one in Atlanta —and other stock investments in the novelty gift manufacturing industry.

His father, Harrison, had given Daniel extraordinary executive powers to run the business, however it was the manufacturing side Daniel loved most. He sat down at the computer in the back office, typing several numbers into a spreadsheet. His cell phone beeped, indicating he had missed a call. The number displayed was from Texas. He smiled as he dialed his voicemail.

He listened to Sue's message, chuckling at her last comment, reminded that he had told her about a restaurant in Atlanta that concocted a famous peach martini.

Daniel's design and manufacturing consulting was his passion. He had only consulted for a few other manufacturers because he loved the thrill of the hunt for that perfect next big hit. The consulting money wasn't an issue to him. And he was picky who he helped. When he volunteered to assist Sue Logan, it was on a whim. He liked her. And he would have helped her for free, but his accountant wouldn't let him. So he charged a fee.

35

Typing Sue an email message, he confirmed he would meet her at customs when he arrived in Hong Kong. He was excited about working with her on her designs. She had awakened something new in him, with her eagerness to be successful. She had awakened something powerful.

EIGHT
Texas

MUNCHING ON A CELERY STICK smothered with peanut butter, Mary Jo stood in the doorway of Sue's empty office. She flipped on the light switch. Sue's office, located in the interior of the building, had no exterior windows and the only daylight filtered in from the open door and the lobby beyond.

Mary Jo's administrative assistant title was a perfect cover for her snooping obsession. While straightening papers on Sue's desk, she saw an email prompting her from Sue's inbox. Since Sue traveled a lot, she often retrieved Sue's emails. Mary Jo opened it and read it.

"Okay, Mr. Winston, let's see what you've got lined up for Sue in China."

She was tidying up a few more papers when she heard Sue's high heels clicking down the foyer hallway. She took a few steps away from the desk.

"The meeting was great. The marketing reps have an aggressive forecast." Sue said, walking in the door and sitting down behind her desk. "What's up?"

Even after her meeting in the alley and the sticky humid photo shoot, Sue looked impeccably attired in her outfit and matching shoes, her blonde hair firmly twisted in a bun. But then, Mary Jo thought, Sue always looked groomed, elegant and smart. "Daniel called."

Mary Jo thought she saw a ghost of a smile in her expression.

"Why didn't you get me?"

"You were with the reps and I didn't want to disturb you. He said he'd email."

Sue looked at her computer. A quick frown at Mary Jo, then a look of amusement, yet puzzled.

I can't believe I read his email. She felt disloyal and held her breath.

Sue picked up a pencil and tapped it against the screen a few times and nibbled on the eraser. She finally smiled at Mary Jo. "He wants to meet in customs."

Whew. "Oh, I think that's a good idea. That way you can ride to the hotel together. You two are going to have fun. Wow! China with a hunk." She shook her head.

"It's business." Sue murmured, a hint of glee in her comment.

"I know. You just seem happier since you met him last month. How did that go? You never gave me details." Mary Jo remembered how excited Sue had been when she returned from the New York Toy Fair.

"I was displaying the products at the convention at the Javits Center, as you know, hoping to get new buyers. I was in my booth when Daniel stopped by."

"Had you met him before?" Mary Jo sat on the overstuffed couch in front of Sue's desk. She liked seeing Sue relaxed and happy.

"I had heard a lot about the younger Winston. He has an older, married brother. But Daniel's reputation preceded him. The retail industry is a small world. Everyone knows everyone."

"What did you hear about him?"

"Typical southern gentleman, born with expensive champagne in his bottle, a real party boy chasing skirts, who hadn't strayed far from his family business. I expected him to be a bit bigheaded."

"So was he?" Her tone was more forceful than she felt.

"He was nothing like that." Sue shook her head and smiled warmly. "He wandered around the booth, seeming uninterested. I watched him as he inspected my products."

"Is he tall?" *I need details.*

"Hmmm. Yeah, I guess. I think he used to play football is what I heard."

38

"Soooo, what happened?"

"Well, another buyer stopped in, and he left."

"What? No way!"

"Just kidding, while I helped the retailer, I watched Daniel out of the corner of my eye. He was flipping through my catalog. He had the cutest grin and the greenest eyes, oh my God, the broadest shoulders…." Sue trailed off.

"Did he know you were spying on him?"

"I wasn't. I mean, I suspected he noticed me in the corner. How could he not? My eyes were locked on him from the moment he entered the booth."

"Right, how couldn't he?"

"He wandered up and asked if I was the rep for the line."

"That question had to amuse you." Mary Jo knew Sue was asked that a lot at the shows she worked.

"I said 'yes.' "

"Yeah, but you wanted to say, 'No, I'm the Owner, Creator, President, Head of Manufacturing and Quality Control, VP of Marketing and oh yes, the rep'. "

"Don't forget the janitor."

"No, that's my job," Mary Jo said.

Sue and Mary Jo both laughed.

"I had my show badge dangling from a lanyard around my neck. He read it and said, 'So you're the owner? Hi, Ms. Logan, I'm Daniel Winston,' and I have to admit I loved his touch when we shook hands." She smiled at the memory.

"I know he talked to you about the pricing of the catalogs for his hundred stores."

"Winston chain of stores has about four dozen."

"Forty eight, a hundred, whatever, I know they're huge. But he said he'd help you in China and didn't you meet him for drinks too?"

She nodded.

Mary Jo saw something in Sue's deep blue eyes. *Yes, oh yes, she met him.*

When Sue didn't reply, Mary Jo prompted, "Where did you meet him?"

Sue looked at her watch.

"Didn't you meet at his hotel to discuss him helping you as a consultant in China?" *Geez, she just won't let me get close. Ever since Jonathan died, she seems so closed.*

"Yeah, we did meet a few hours after the show closed. At the lobby bar of the Broadway Winston Hotel."

"His hotel? His idea?"

"No, my idea. I knew his family owned a couple of hotels in New York. It just made it easy to meet at one of them. Turns out he was staying there." She smiled amusingly.

Mary Jo sat up more. "And what was he like?"

"Mary Jo, it wasn't a date! It was a business meeting."

"I know, right. But you had to be wondering how old he was, what his deal was, and so on? Right? Details. I need details. And why is he consulting if he's so rich?"

"I know he works with his brother. His dad started their empire. Sources have him valued at twenty million. But shit, technically, that isn't correct. That's his family's net worth, which he shares with his father and his brother. And I guess Daniel to be in his early thirties. He looks around my age, but then knowing his background in the industry would make him at least thirty-five.

"He grew up in the southeast and you can tell that from his southern drawl. He's cute and I could tell he isn't one of those guys that's preoccupied with his looks."

"See, now we're talking. What about his shoes?"

"His shoes?" Sue's mouth curved with amusement.

"You can always tell if a guy is a fixer upper if you have to take him shoe shopping," Mary Jo said.

"No, there wasn't a lot to fix." She took a deep breath. "You know, we have work to do."

Mary Jo leaned forward on the couch. "I'm sorry boss, but you're going to a foreign country with this guy. I don't wanna sound like Thelma and Wilford, but I gotta know more."

Sue laughed at the comment about her mom and dad.

"Well, at first, I was suspicious but curious why he would help me. But I checked him out. Mike and others have used him in China, and paid him to go there."

"You didn't tell him about the new line?" *I hope she's not letting too many people know.*

"I told him enough."

"Like what?" Mary Jo asked boldly.

Sue looked her sternly in the eyes. "I told him it's been a long process. It's a toy I created when I was a teen. I've spent years perfecting it. And the functionality of the doll is so unique that it would be perfect for this generation of kids."

"Did he question the functionality?"

"No, not really. Just the design. I told him I couldn't get the facial features on the M Kid toy right and I had so many versions with different eyes, noses, cheeks, eyebrows. And I have this exciting technology I'm building into it that has to be hidden inside . . . and how the fabric colors are challenging since the dolls are all races and ethnicity."

"And he can help?"

"He said he'd love to see them and to help me. And said we would get it right when we go to China."

"Did you share with him the technology and what it's used for?" Mary Jo worried.

Sue looked around the office and toward the open door. She leaned in closer across her desk and lowered her voice. "I said I'd wait to show him, but it's designed to follow kids as they grow."

"And he was okay with that?"

"He looked disappointed, but said it was fine."

Sue stood up, signaling the end of their meeting.

Mary Jo stood too. She could tell Sue liked Daniel and she worried that Sue might leak too much too fast to him. They hardly knew him. And what if he worked with their competitors?

"What about the advertising? Are we set to go with our big splash in eight months? I want Kim to stay on top of it." Sue said, very businesslike.

"She's all over it." Mary Jo was disappointed Sue shifted gears, but not surprised. Sue wasn't much of a talker.

"I want a huge rollout. Lots of advertising." Sue's eyes were wide and she looked proud.

"Seems like advertising can be a waste. Other toy companies these days can't seem to get their share of the market since Yorkston Toys sure have covered the advertising gambit."

"I know, every time my kids turn on the TV there's a new commercial out there for their plush. Not only are the toys popular, but the products they have chasing the kids attention range from pjs to fruit chews." Sue crossed her arms.

"That egomaniac Nathanael Yorkston guy really knows how to create strong brand awareness," Mary Jo said.

"That's what I plan to do. They won't know what hit them." Sue nodded and a small mischievous smile appeared on her lips.

"I have no doubt you've something creative planned."

"I do." Sue ran her hands smoothly across her tight blonde chignon.

"What about approaching Yorkston? Maybe a joint partnership?" Mary Jo said.

"What?" Sue shouted. "Are you kidding?"

Mary Jo heard something other than anger in Sue's voice. Fear? She swallowed and put on a smile.

"Yeah. Just kidding."

"God, I hope so. You have crazy ideas sometimes." An almost imperceptible smile played on Sue's lips.

Mary Jo hoped Sue didn't see her disappointment.

NINE

A WALL CLOCK CHIMED six times, dragging Sue away from her PC. She thought of her kids at home and decided to call it quits for the day. Mary Jo had left an hour earlier.

Sue got behind the wheel of her car, leaned back with the radio blaring, and smiled at her reflection in the mirror.

"I could use a new adventure." The blonde in the mirror smiled back. She was looking forward to her trip to China.

Within a few minutes of leaving the office, her cell phone rang. The display indicated her older sister, Goldevia, was calling. Sue flipped it open. "Hi Goldie," she said.

"Hey. Did you get the hawk?" Dee said, ignoring Sue's loving nickname reference.

"Yep. The shoot's done and we've completed this year's edition of the catalog."

"Awesome," Dee said.

"Yeah, and we got to keep the hawk."

"Shut up! You're keeping Hollis?" Dee sounded excited.

"Yep. The owner never showed up to reclaim him after we rented it all day."

"Who cares anyway . . . oh, but wait, it's a *Yorkston*. I bet his feathers will fall out after a few months."

"You're just jealous because he's mine and you can't get your grubby hands on him." Sue could never understand why Dee always disliked the creator of the Yorkston toys. Dee had once told her Nathanael Yorkston was a creepy twerp – 'a real nerd.' He wasn't a nerd in the mismatched clothes sense, but his mop of hair always looked unkempt and he had a pockmarked face. Dee hated that Sue manufactured the Yorkston catalog.

"Sell it before that hawk is as worthless as the chipmunk head my cat spit out this morning."

"What is it with you and that Yorkston guy?"

"He gags me with a spoon," she chuckled. "So you have all twelve plush from the bird collection. That's worth thousands."

"Yeah, I guess."

Dee started singing in the tune the Twelve Days of Christmas. "On the 12th day of Christmas my true love gave to me; *A dozen plush birds, two turtledoves, and Hollis in a pear tree.*"

"I'm plugging my ears. Don't sing to me, Dee." Although her sister went silent, Sue swore she could hear a smile coming through the phone.

"Hey, did the producers of the Jay Leno show get back to you?" Dee asked.

Eager to change the subject, Sue replied, "Yes, they want to present my products as gifts to the Tonight Show guests in the green room baskets at the end of next year for the new millennium."

"That's wonderful!"

"I know. Thanks." Sue pumped her fist in the air.

"Are you looking forward to China? I hope your new *friend* will keep an eye on you."

"Don't *you* start on me."

"Geez, you're snappier than bubble gum today," Dee said, animated and excited.

Sue laughed. Dee always made her smile. She could picture Dee sprawled in her Toyota's backseat with a pair of binoculars and camera at her side and a pile of ding-dong wrappers. The private investigator job fit her sister perfectly. Her wacky-chick persona would not camouflage well in a conventional workplace. Corporate America could not handle Dee's fabulous ebullience and her Whoopi Goldberg off-colored jokes.

"I just don't want to discuss Daniel," Sue said.

"Why? You know something you're not saying?"

Sue didn't reply. She watched a white van fly behind her and

44

get on her tail, just inches from her SUV. She turned swiftly into her neighborhood, and the van hit the brakes, but kept going straight.

"Sue, are you there?"

She drove through the neighborhood entrance, passing a dozen houses and turned down her street. The Logan's home sat in a cul-de-sac in the Estate section of a desirable neighborhood in Francis. It was a casual Tudor with a slate roof sitting on a secluded street, backing to the golf course and creek.

"Hey Dee, I hate to be rude, but I gotta run. I'm pulling in my neighborhood now and the kids will attack me when I walk in the door. See ya."

"Tell them their best Aunt ever said 'hi'. "

"You're their only aunt."

"Exactly. Hugs and kisses to all," Dee said, and the phone went dead.

Sue hung up her phone. "Yep, hugs to you too Goldie." She thought maybe she should send Hollis to Dee as a joke, like the time she sent her a carton full of Quaker Oats.

Dee McCray, Sue's older sister, was called Goldie before her parents even left the hospital nursery. Dee was short for Goldevia. Their parents had different stories about how they named their daughter. Daddy said the name was after the meaning "a good life." While Mom said she had always liked the name Godiva, meaning "God's gift." Mom was crazy about the rich Godiva chocolates and Dad claimed she almost bankrupted them during her pregnancy with Dee because she ate the expensive chocolates like raisins. Their Hispanic housecleaner called her mom's chocolates "Goldevia." Sue's mom had just assumed Goldevia was the Spanish version of the English Godiva.

Neither Dee nor Sue believed either of their parent's explanation for the name. They knew their parents had an amazing sense of humor. When they named their daughter Goldevia, they had to know the curly blonde-haired baby would end up with a nickname early in her childhood. Sue and Dee's maiden name was Lockes. Goldevia Lockes's nickname through her childhood was "goldie-locks." As a result, Dee hated oatmeal and to this day, she refused to eat anything remotely close to porridge.

Sue pulled in her front entry garage and as the door closed, she saw a white van cruise slowly by. The driver shot her a despicable, evil look causing a chill to run down her spine.

TEN

"MOMMY, MOMMY!" the kids yelled as Sue entered the family room.

Colt and Maddie jumped up, ran at her, and wrapped their arms around Sue's legs. Sue picked up her youngest daughter, giving her a hug. Maddie, with rosy cheeks and blonde ringlets, resembled a toy porcelain doll and was as fragile.

"Hi sweeties! How was your ice cream with grandpa today?" She kissed them both.

"Hi, Mom." Elizabeth, her oldest daughter, was sitting at the kitchen table working on homework. She looked up, a blonde braid coiled on top of her head, and waved.

Sue walked into the kitchen with Colt and Maddie in tow.

"Hi babe. What are you working on? And where are your grandparents?" Sue eyed the mess sprawled across the table.

Sue put Maddie down, barely listening to Elizabeth rattling on about her cheetah project. She peered out through the family room windows to see Grandpa Wilford scraping the side of the pool with a brush; beyond the pool was the undulating green of the golf course.

Sue picked up a stack of mail, casually thumbing through it.

"Mom, did you know cheetahs are the fastest mammals in the world?" Elizabeth asked.

"Granddaddy is out back pleaning the pool," Maddie chimed, tugging on Sue's free hand.

Elizabeth gave her little sister a malicious look. "Clean-ing,

47

not pleaning. And stop interrupting me, Madeline Logan."

Colt had returned to the floor, sitting cross-legged in front of the television, watching a giant Purple Dinosaur singing, "I love you, you love me, We're a happy family . . . ."

"Mom, did you know cheetahs are the fastest mammals in the world?" Elizabeth repeated.

"Mommy, what's a nammal." Maddie pulled at Sue's skirt.

Sue absent-mindedly smiled at Maddie as she continued to look through the mail.

"You're a mammal, Maddie," Elizabeth said.

Maddie's lower lip protruded and her big blue eyes began tearing up. "No I'm not!" Maddie placed her small hands on her hips.

"Yes you are." Elizabeth stuck her face close to Maddie's face. "You have blood in you. You're warm. And you have hair on your skin. That makes you a MAMMAL!" Elizabeth shouted.

Colt jumped up, running over to see what was happening to his sister. He looked puzzled as he inspected her from top to bottom. Sue wondered if he was looking for blood, or hair on her, or both.

Maddie's eyes were wide with fright; she looked like she would burst out crying any second.

"Moooom, Izzie said I'm a nananal," Maddie whined.

Sue listened in amusement, but before she could intervene, her dad walked in the back door.

"What's all the commotion in here?" Wilford looked concerned. "Oh, hi Suz, I didn't hear you come in." He walked into the kitchen.

With the entrance of their granddad, the two younger Logan kids scrambled into the family room, settling in front of the next pre-dinner kid's show featuring colorful overstuffed characters named Dipsy, Tinky Winky, Laa-Laa and Po.

Sue strolled over to her dad and gave him a peck on his crinkled, tanned cheek. She noticed that one of his loafers and white socks were soaking wet. "Dad, take your shoes off. I'll give your sock a tumble in the dryer."

He shrugged. "No, it's fine. I slipped on the pool step."

"Did you walk over?" She looked out the front window searching for his car.

"Yeah, I walked over, but your mom's here. She drove the caddy over like she was stalking me. She's always worried about me crossing Golf Street. I tell her we only live a stone's throw away, but she still worries about me walking across that street."

"I worry too, Dad. But I love having you all close, especially after Jonathan …." She trailed off, not completing her sentence. "The kids love it too," she added with a big smile.

"Well this old bag of bones, at sixty-five years old, is still pretty active."

"Yeah, active in the local Lions chapter and drinking beers with your Sunday golf dates. But I love it." Sue reached up and gave his white handlebar mustache a tug.

Elizabeth gave Sue a warm, loving look. "Mommy, we're glad you're home early, but we were going to surprise you."

"Oh, you were." Sue looked up from her mail, smiling. "What's the surprise?" She ran her hand through her daughter's bangs.

"We were going to make your favorite meal, but you beat us home before we could go to the grocery store," her dad replied.

"That would be wonderful. What's the occasion?"

"We want to make you a special *American*—" Elizabeth stopped, and corrected herself. "*Texas* food before you go to a foreign country."

"That's so sweet."

"Colt has a soccer game tomorrow night, and Elizabeth has a birthday party Friday night and then you leave. So tonight was your lucky dinner night," Wilford said. "It could wait, if you're starving now and would rather go out."

Sue frowned when she thought of her son's soccer game. He had just started the sport and it was more like a battlefield than a soccer field. The other teams' coaches and parents came for blood.

Elizabeth piped up. "I'm starving and could eat anything."

"How about pickled mosquito tongues?" Wilford teased.

"Ew, Granddad. Gross." Elizabeth wrinkled her nose and returned to her project.

"Have you started it yet?" She walked into the high-tech kitchen. There was a pile of coloring books on the granite counter and a pan on the stove with a few swollen pieces of macaroni and cheese stuck to the sides. The air smelled faintly of this morning's coffee.

"No," he said. "In fact, your mother is about to go out and run an errand. We can have her pick up barbeque instead."

"That would be my choice." She winked at her daughter. Elizabeth returned a wink.

An elderly woman with platinum gray hair twisted in a knot at the back of her head came down the back staircase carrying a laundry basket. "Hi honey," Thelma said.

"Hi, Mom. You don't need to do the laundry. I'll get Maria to do that Friday."

"It's no trouble. Besides, Maddie dripped ice cream on her dress today and I wanted to wash it right away." She walked into the kitchen. "Wilford, take your shoe off. You're tracking water in the kitchen."

Wilford gave his wife a cantankerous look and walked toward the back door.

Thelma dropped the laundry basket on the sofa. She pulled a jade and ivory comb out of her white hair, releasing the bun. She ran the comb through the short hair then secured it with the comb, leaving a few loose curls, as curly as a standard poodle. "Did you wear that to work today?"

"Yes, Mom."

"You shouldn't wear one hundred percent silk in the summer. Sweat will stain it and you look more rumbled."

"Well at least I don't look like a school girl with pressed chinos and that immaculate white starched cotton shirt and your dark socks and penny loafers." Sue gave her mom a light slap on the arm. Her mom rolled her eyes. "Besides, no one really saw me. Just me and Mary Jo and a few marketing people in the office today."

"You had a photo shoot, correct?"

"Yes. It went well."

Thelma looked over at the kids and back at Sue. "Did you get it? Did you find him?" She said softly.

Sue glanced in the direction of the kids and then whispered, "Yes, I finally found Hollis."

50

Later that evening, Sue was lying in bed reading when Elizabeth came in and sat near her.

"Are you okay?" Sue sat upright. Of all her children, Elizabeth was having the hardest time adjusting to the loss of her dad and often came to Sue's room at night.

"I can't sleep."

"C'mere." She patted the empty spot on the bed next to her. She put aside the spreadsheets she had been reading. Elizabeth didn't hesitate. She climbed in and slid under the covers.

"Now, what's keeping you awake, sweetie?" Sue smoothed her daughter's hair while holding her hand.

"I am afraid for you to go to *China*." She emphasized China as if it was a deadly disease.

Sue looked at her oldest daughter's translucent blue eyes. She had anticipated that Elizabeth would have concerns.

"You know Hong Kong is one of the most important places for shipping on the entire continent of Asia because of the major port and its easy route for ships and it's important for me to go there to make some of my products."

"I know, but Daddy went away too, and didn't come home."

Sue had known the root of Elizabeth's concern was the fear of losing her, like she'd lost her daddy. Sue's heart ached as she tried to reaffirm to her daughter that she was always going to be there for them.

"You know I'm not going to ever leave you alone, right?" Sue said.

Elizabeth didn't look reassured. "I know."

"You can sleep here tonight, if you like."

Elizabeth smiled, snuggling deeper under the covers.

Sue turned off the light on the nightstand. "I love you."

"I love you too, Mommy." Elizabeth drifted off to sleep, breathing her soft child-snores.

Sue didn't fall asleep as easily. She turned her head away from Elizabeth. Tears welled up in her eyes as the overbearing weight came down on her – the sadness of Jonathan not being there when her dream came true. Losing Jonathan had nearly driven her crazy, but the time dedicated to her kids and her company had helped her to sew closed the ragged wounds the loss had left. She still cried occasionally, like tonight with Elizabeth so close. She still ached, but she had learned to go on.

ELEVEN
Indianapolis

NATHANAEL YORKSTON SKIMMED the five morning newspapers fanned over his desk, the business section of each paper stacked directly in front of him. He flipped through the Texas paper and then folded it and threw it in the empty trashcan. The elevators to his floor dinged. He scooped up the other papers, setting them aside.

The heavy wood blinds shut out most sounds of the rush hour traffic from the street below but a car alarm overpowered the honking horns. Nathanael shut the blinds behind him. He could see the world passing by, withdrawn within his air-conditioned cocoon, but the world couldn't see him. This was the way he liked it.

Anthony Romero entered his office. Nathanael stood up, walking around his desk, cupping Anthony's hand in both of his, "Hello, Anthony."

"Hey, Naty."

Nathanael Yorkston, often called Nat as a kid, signed his homework *Nat Y,* so the nickname "Naty" stuck throughout school but only a handful of close friends called him that today.

"Do you want a Scotch?" Nathanael asked.

"No, I still haven't had my morning coffee yet boss," Anthony chuckled.

"Cigar?"

"Nope. Can't smoke in here. Charlie will have my ass."

"Hell. I own the building. You can do as you please."

Anthony sat in a leather tucked chair across from Nathanael, who sat down at his ornate desk. Anthony slid low in his seat, stretched his legs out in front of him, crossing them at the ankles. He locked his fingers overhead, resting his head in the cup of his hands. His jacket flipped open, revealing a hint of his revolver in the shoulder holster.

"Tori can get you coffee, if she's here," Nathanael said. "But I know how you like a Scotch in your hand when we talk business."

"No, no, this won't take long. I don't want her to know I'm here. That's why I suggested we speak at eight."

"Yeah, that's right. She won't be in 'til later this morning."

"You're looking lean. I swear you must have lost ten pounds while I was in Texas. You running?" Anthony said.

Nathanael didn't answer. He hated those people that were up at dawn every morning to run six miles. He wasn't a runner; he wasn't an athlete at all.

When he didn't reply Anthony asked, "Did you have trouble getting in the office this morning?"

"Not a problem today. Got in early, while it was dark. Brick parked the limo in the lower level where no one will see it." He hated how the fans approached him at the shows, constantly asking how they could get one of the plush toys. "I hate the fans."

"I know. I know. Brick is good. He's my best man. He'll keep the fanatics away."

"We just announced the new line on TV yesterday with hefty prizes. The fucking maniac fans always track me down. Just leaving my penthouse to go to the office these days is an ordeal. They're always stalking me."

"That's why I have Brick driving you. If I need to put another guy with him, I will." Anthony smiled. "The inconveniences of stardom, boss."

"Have Dyno work with Brick this week."

"You got it."

Nathanael was embittered by the years of acrimony the collectors displayed to one another while they chased his limo. The white limo was a marketing ploy initially used in his early days. He had dressed up in a white tux with tails and a white top hat and drove around in a white limo selling his plush. During the first few years, he had a decent relationship with the collectors. He tipped his hat and became a popular guy. But over time, his conscience couldn't handle the stardom.

"How was your trip?" Nathanael asked.

"Texas is hot as hell. But we delivered the goods."

"Anything yet?"

"I'm waiting on the tapes, but in short, hell no."

"We only have a small window of opportunity. We have to find this out soon."

"I'm on it, boss." Anthony's smile was still there but Nathanael could see the hint of strain.

"I wanted to be clear. I won't let anyone, no one, outsmart me in this business, especially a small-time redneck. You're making sure she doesn't find us out?"

Anthony didn't blink.

Nathanael leaned forward in his chair. Anthony was gazing at him steadily, coldly, his expression like a sin on Naty's mind.

"That little Texas chick won't know a thing," Anthony said.

"Yeah, make sure of that."

"I'll look after you, boss. Bizness is bizness, Yorkston-style. We'll get everything. We don't want to kill the goose that gave us the golden eggs."

Nathanael grabbed his glasses and glanced over a piece of paper on his desk. "We have another problem."

"The leaks inside? I have Jason looking into it." Anthony ran a hand through his dark hair.

It irritated the hell out Nathanael that Anthony, his own age, still had a full head of hair. At fifty-four years, Nathanael had wiry graying hair and piercing dark eyes. His elongated pockmarked face was a backdrop for his prominent hooked nose.

"Let's call Jason."

Nathanael had used faithful employees to spy on other employees. Since every imaginable kind of stuffed toy was discussed in Yorkston's highly guarded office, he was concerned that employees would leak new design ideas out before they were introduced or, worse, steal his design ideas. His spies kept him informed. Eventually, he feared that his spies were conspiring with other employees. He had Anthony and his security team watch the spies.

He pushed the speaker button and dialed Jason Gombac, the VP of Human Resources, one of his most trusted spies.

"HR," the voice on the other end said.

"It's Nathanael."

There was a pause. "Sorry, Mr. Yorkston, I didn't catch the extension. What can I do for you?"

"Have any intel?"

"We know it's internal. The warehouse guys have been talking."

"You need to make it right, or I'll be firing warehouse staff every day until we find the leak."

"We think it's Markham."

"Why do you think it's him?"

"We know he visits a chat room. He uses a fake user name and email from his home computer, but IT traced the IP address back to him."

"Fire him."

"You want me to fire him?" Jason said. "Okay, you just tell me what the bullet costs and I'll pull the trigger."

"Give him two weeks." Nathanael tightened his fist.

"He's been here seven years."

"Did I or did I not make it clear to Markham and all employees that if they talked about our private information they would be terminated?"

"You did."

Nathanael's mind was set. He had rules about what his people could or couldn't talk about. This was a clear breach.

"Two weeks, no more."

"Okay."

"Then dismiss him in the warehouse, in front of everyone,

replace him with Rupert. You can easily find a replacement for Rupert."

"Will do. See you at the board meeting."

Nathanael clicked off his speakerphone and looked at Anthony. "What else?"

Nathanael thought about how his success as a toymaker had changed Anthony's life. They had known each other since college, but Nathanael always felt like he had made Anthony into what he was today. Anthony had what power Naty gave him. And to think Nathanael had been a simple, small town schoolboy with pimples and a paper route. Today he was a tycoon.

Their freshman year in college, they ended up as potluck roommates. It was Anthony's wild influence and his completely opposite persona that attracted Nathanael. Anthony was a partier all through college, even dragging Nathanael into the deeps of Satanism, which they both loved. They parted after college and Nathanael lost track of Anthony for ten years.

It wasn't until his late twenties that Nathanael started dating, eventually marrying his first wife. That ended poorly. He was divorced within one year. He was married to his second wife when he reunited with Anthony. Anthony, still rambunctious and into all sorts of criminal mischief, hadn't settled down even though he had a wife and a young daughter. Nathanael hired Anthony and his company, Romero Security Group.

They became closer through both of their divorces. Anthony worked discretely to make sure Nathanael's second divorce and other indiscretions escaped the scrutiny of the scandal- hungry press. Their business endeavors deepened. Nathanael paid Anthony handsomely to run his security group and to manage any problems that couldn't be handled in a traditional manner.

Anthony and his team worked overtime keeping Nathanael Yorkston's whereabouts in obscurity. The floor to his office was as secure as the pentagon. There were no marquees on the high-rise building indicating Yorkston headquarters. Monitored security cameras pointed in all directions.

Since the introduction of his plush animal line, Nathanael Yorkston was methodically guarded whenever he was in public. The success of the toys had catapulted him from boredom to stardom in the bat of an eye.

Changing gears, Nathanael dropped the discussion about Markham and focused on the reason for the meeting.

"Did you get the information on the bank?"

"Yeah, got it yesterday." A twitch fluttered across Anthony's eyebrows as he leaned back into the chair.

"Good. Can we accomplish our endeavor by year end?"

"We could use more time, to make sure." There went his twitch again. "Naty, your reputation in certain circles is well known, and we are trying to do this covertly. It's a small Texas bank, no corporate owners or out-of-state investors. It's important your name isn't linked."

"We're running out of time. I want the announcement next spring."

"Will do."

"What about our other defector? Our scientist buddy?"

The tic passed over Anthony's brows, as he absentmindedly brushed his forehead. "I'm watching him, too. And got a backup plan to cut him loose."

"You'll do what needs to be done to keep him quiet, right?" Nathanael glanced at Anthony's jacket. Nathanael didn't like Pete Shapiro and looked forward to the day he disappeared. They didn't need him anymore.

Anthony nodded and patted the side of his jacket. They studied each other for a moment, each understanding the other, and coming to an agreement without exchanging words. This was why Nathanael Yorkston dubbed Anthony as his one-man cleanup crew.

TWELVE
Texas

"BUT I HAVE an appointment with Ms. Logan, what do you mean she isn't here?" Evan Taylor asked.

"Like I said," Mary Jo, the flame-haired pixie assistant explained with a trace of irritation in her voice. "She was called into another meeting today."

Evan stifled his disappointment. "I thought we had a meeting set for an interview. It's imperative I see her today. Crap. My boss will kill me if I don't get this interview with her." *This is probably truer than it sounds.*

"Oh please. It's not that big of a deal that she's not here."

Evan stood in the Logan lobby. The walls were crowded with black frames with wide white mats surrounding colorful crayon drawings and paintings.

"Jeez, there's got to be hundreds of drawings on these walls." Evan's gaze roamed up and down the tall foyer walls and down the various hallways branching off the lobby.

"Sue likes to frame a lot of the drawings kids send her. She says it inspires her."

"Sure looks like she is a kid fanatic and an art addict." Evan walked over to a Lego table filled with partially built ships and buildings. "Do her kids play here?"

"They do. But she has kids here to test her toys."

"Well whatever her obsession, she's done good. What's she like?" Evan hoped he had warmed her up and Mary Jo would launch into a laundry list of adjectives. He could always discover a lot about a person he was investigating by what their employees said about them.

"Sue Logan, my boss, is beyond fabulous. She is a big fan of her people and proud of her products and I am a bigger fan of hers. I design the products after she thinks them up. She tells me what her vision is and I make it come to life. She is an awesome seamstress as well."

"Do you have any information on her new designs? Any samples of what she's working on?"

Mary Jo eyed him suspiciously. "I don't think I should share the new designs with you. We just met, and I can't possibly know what you're looking for. I'll let Sue be the one to help you there."

"Are there other employees here I can talk to?" Evan walked toward one of the open hallways.

"We only have a dozen people here. We outsource our warehouse and marketing and sales. We sell our products through marketing companies that have reps. They don't work for us. The reps carry many vendors' lines, including Logan products."

"Can I talk to the reps?"

"They're not here. They're located in all the world trade centers across the country. We have a showroom in the one in downtown Dallas. I really need to get back to work." She turned her head and leveled her burning-green eyes at Evan. He cringed.

"Where are the products manufactured?"

She turned toward him. "They're all made here in the US. Why?"

He shrugged. "Just wondering if any were made in China."

"Not yet."

Evan raised his eyebrows. "I don't blame her. They say piracy is rampant."

"I don't think she's worried about that, as much as she is worried about not overseeing the products. That's her passion." Mary Jo looked at her watch. "Sorry, I need to get back to work."

"I understand. Where can I meet up with her?" Evan let it drop. He didn't want her to become suspicious.

"She left me a note saying she had a brochure photo shoot at our other warehouse. She asked if you could reschedule in a few weeks." Mary Jo flipped the calendar pages looking at dates.

No, goddamn, NO! I need to talk to her. Shit! Evan flipped open his cell phone. Under the watchful eye of Mary Jo, he stepped into the adjoining room and whispered into the phone.

After a few minutes, Evan slammed his phone shut. *Dammit, all these powerful connections and I get screwed over by a brochure photo shoot.* What the hell! He had to get to her, but how?

"I talked to my office and they really wanted just a few quick quotes from her today, if that's possible," he lied. "I can talk to her at the warehouse. Can you tell me where she'll be so I can go meet her?"

"Well. Let me see," Mary Jo spat. "She has written here; 2:30, photo shoot, at the warehouse."

"Okay, good. I'll go there then." Evan checked his watch. Two o'clock. No, make that one o'clock, Texas time.

"Your choice." She exhaled impatiently. "She can't meet with you next week because she'll be in Hong Kong."

"Of course, if I get to her today, we can run it in our next issue," he lied again. "Can you give me directions to your other warehouse?"

"Please?"

"Please," he spouted. He was already thinking of Plan B.

Plainly miffed, the redhead scribbled the directions on a slip of paper shoving it at Evan.

"It should take you about twenty minutes from here." She muttered in exasperation, rolling her emerald green eyes.

"Thanks." He walked toward the door and swung it open.

"Good riddance," Mary Jo replied as Evan strode out the door.

Evan had time to kill before the photo shoot but he decided to drive directly to the warehouse. He sat in his car in the parking lot reading the newspaper. He decided to wait for the brochure photographer to arrive so they could walk in together. The photographer would be easy to spot walking in the door a few minutes before two thirty with an arm full of photography equipment.

His car's air conditioning was set on high, all vents pointing at him, and he was still sticking to his seat.

Man, how do Texans stand the heat? It isn't bad in spurts, but it goes on and on and on. I'll take my snow shovel any damn day over this insanity.

He looked out the window. "Hey, wait a minute," he said. He saw a photographer coming out of the warehouse not going in. Evan verified the time on his dashboard 2:02.

Shit.

Evan crushed his cigarette butt in the ashtray and flicked it out his cracked window. Before he could turn off the car and grab his notepad, he saw a slim blonde come out behind the photographer. He had seen photos of her. It was Sue Logan. Damn it! The shoot was over.

What the hell? I won't let this trip be fucked up.

He would go to Plan C. Which was?

Evan hesitated too long. She was in her SUV within a few seconds. Sue didn't even look his way as he held up a hand to signal her to stop. He tried to get her attention, but she kept driving.

"Damn." Evan grabbed his cell phone, mashing his tobacco-stained fingers on the dial pad. "Hello, Mary Jo, right? This is Evan Taylor," he cleared his throat, "um, no, I missed meeting up with Sue at the photo shoot. She did? An hour earlier, of course. Well, I'd still like to send her the questions. Can you tell me where she is staying in Hong Kong?"

"Un-huh, Hong Kong Inn, Kowloon. Un-huh. Oh, the Saturday evening flight. Okay, I see."

He hung up, forgetting to say good-bye.

THIRTEEN
Suburb of Indianapolis

"HAVE BRICK PICK UP Cherry at the club and take her to Naty's penthouse," Anthony said into his cell phone. "Yes, now."

"I don't care what time it is." Anthony raced his car up his winding driveway. "And pay her 10 bills to keep her mouth shut, or else." Anthony worried about Naty's infatuation with young girls. Cherry claimed she was eighteen, but he knew she was younger.

Anthony gunned his black Porsche into his garage, pressed the remote lowering the door.

"Yes, I heard Evan didn't get the interview. Worthless shit," Anthony pressed five numbers on the alarm keypad and opened his door from his garage.

"Just keep reviewing the tapes. The receiver is good from her office and her house." He threw his keys on a side table.

"No, I'm not going to fire him. I might kill him, but I'm not going to fire him." Anthony walked toward the dark living room and spotted an overturned plant. He froze, slipped the phone silently into his pocket, and pulled his Colt.

Anthony felt a jolt between his shoulders and sharp pains on his neck. He hunched over, but before he could turn, a large yellow cat jumped from his back to the stair landing over Anthony shoulders.

"Crap, Chubby! You scared the shit out of me!"

He bent over to brush up some of the dirt on the floor. "I'll make Victoria replace this plant. I hate when she leaves you here without telling me."

The cat purred and bounded up the stairs.

Anthony yelled up after it. "Chubs, I'm not pissed at you. I'm just angry 'cause I have a couple of shitty soldiers to deal with."

He walked up the twelve white deep-pile carpeted steps to his master suite, threw his shoulder holster on the bed and unzipped his pants. Chubby sat in the corner, flipping his head back and forth.

"Whacha got there big fellow? You find a mouse?" Anthony bent down to see what the cat was chewing on.

"No. Shit! Let go of that. What are you … trying to kill yourself?" Chubby arched his back, hissed, and bolted under the bed. Anthony scooped off the floor a chewed up Yorkston stuffed hawk. He flipped it over and saw the tush tag was chewed off.

"Damn, Chubby don't go getting sick on me." He forgot he had left the bird on his desk. He had used it as his model for the one he gave to Sue Logan.

He thought of Sue and the stuffed bird. Yes, he was going to get what he needed from her one way or another. God help her.

FOURTEEN
Hong Kong

SUE SMILED as she gazed out the window of the Boeing 777. In fourteen hours, she would be landing in Japan where she would change flights to make the last leg of her trip to Hong Kong. Butterflies of anticipation crept into the pit of her stomach. The success of this trip would take her company to new heights.

"Ms. Logan would you like water, coffee, or a drink before we take off?" the flight attendant asked.

"Yes, water please. Thanks."

The attendant came back with a glass of ice water.

"We have a representative meeting you in Narika, and she'll take you to the airport club to freshen up while you wait for your connection to Hong Kong." She took Sue's blazer, hanging it behind her in a closet.

"Thank you," Sue yawned.

Sue drifted off into a blissful nap while the rest of the passengers boarded the plane.

"*Hi, this is Captain Long and my copilots, Chad Decker and Kristine Woodard.*" Sue woke to the overhead announcement. She viewed a floor of fluffy white clouds out the window. "*I'll let you know it's safe to get up and move about the cabin when we reach our cruising altitude.*"

She was truly excited.

For the first time in my life, I'm thrilled at the direction my product line is going.

She reached under the seat pulling out her briefcase and setting it on the empty seat next to her. The only other passenger in First Class that she could see was sleeping, his snores almost concealed by the distant hum of the plane's engines.

She focused on her doll line and retrieved drawings and prototypes from her briefcase.

Why is this design so difficult?

Studying one of the prototypes reminded her of the few dozen versions prior to this one. Pinching the mid-section of the plush doll, a nickel-sized chip popped out of the opening in the back seam of the doll.

"Are those for your children?" A flight attendant stood in the aisle looking at the four Logan Millennium Kids sitting on Sue's tray table.

"No. I'm designing a new plush." She held one up for her to see.

What harm can a random flight attendant do? She isn't taking photos or anything. The uniqueness of my designs is vital to success.

"These are so cute! But what's up with this one's face?"

"I'm still working on that. I'm on my way to Hong Kong to work on the molded rubber faces to fit the bodies."

"Oh, I see. They're all so different!"

"Yes, that's the idea. A unique doll that fits a kid's unique personality, and grows with them as they grow. An interactive one."

"Oh my gosh. Have you heard about Furby's?"

"Yep, Furby's were quite the rage. They interact with other Furby's through infrared."

"These dolls are cuter."

Sue smiled to herself. She knew they weren't quite there yet, but being in Hong Kong, close to China where all the parts were made – the hair, the face, the stuffed torso, and maybe even the chip – would help her make her deadline.

"Miss," a voice from a few rows back called. The flight attendant smiled at Sue, nodded and walked away.

Sue worked for several hours on the designs, ate a light

dinner and read sales spreadsheets on her other toys until her eyelids became heavy.

She woke to the bright sunlight streaming through the window, the beautiful Sea of Japan below her, and a foreign land just beyond.

"Welcome to Narita, Miss." The young Japanese woman greeted Sue as she walked off the plane.

"Thank you. I'm glad to be here. When is my flight to Hong Kong?"

"You follow me please, lady. May I please see your passport and ticket? I get your boarding pass in the club. Okay lady?"

Sue's escort was a plump, smiling lady and nodded every 20 seconds. Sue followed her, catching a glimpse of a familiar face in the distance. Where had she seen that man before?

"Can we stop a minute? I think I see someone I know."

Her escort smiled, nodded, and kept walking. "Follow me lady, please."

"Please can we stop for one minute?" Sue pleaded, trying to drop her southern drawl. "I think I see someone I know, can we wait up a second?"

Plump, nodding woman kept walking. "Follow me please. Okay?" She grabbed Sue's arm, guiding her in the direction of the club.

"Okay." Sue turned her gaze from the bald man in the distance. *Damn. I wish I knew Japanese.*

Her flight to Hong Kong had taken longer than she expected, but the wait was worth it. The view of skyscrapered Hong Kong Island was one of the most stunning urban panoramas Sue had ever seen. The runway extended out into the bay, past apartments so close she felt she could reach out and touch the laundry fluttering from the bamboo poles.

She had arranged to meet Daniel Winston outside of customs. She was arriving before him so she made her way through customs and found a seat.

"Daniel, over here." Sue stood up and waved at him as he passed through the customs security gate.

"Hello, Ms. Logan." Daniel approached her. "Did you have a nice flight?"

"Absolutely." Sue noticed he had a radiant bronzed tan face, and he wore his auburn hair shorter than she remembered. Though not handsome in the movie star sense, he was one of the most attractive men she had seen. He was in great shape. When he came over to shake her hand, he towered over her.

"I am so excited to be here," she beamed.

Daniel sized her up as she gathered her luggage. She raised her eyebrows at him.

"Sorry. I remember you being a bit shorter, but maybe it's the boot heels that account for a few more inches."

"So you don't like the boots?" Her golden hair was long and loose, framing her face. She wore a flowing skirt and cowboy boots. She raised her skirt to reveal their high tops.

"Not precisely Hong Kong attire," he said jokingly.

Sue cocked her head at him, and mocked a pout.

"But on you, hey, they look right." Daniel quickly added, "Better than right."

"Let's head to Kowloon and get settled into our hotel." He grabbed her luggage and his bags, with the casual grace of an athlete and a quiet air of authority.

They walked out of the airport and it finally hit her.

"Wow! I'm in Hong Kong!"

I'm so wound up to be here, especially with my ally, this enigmatic, young Winston.

As if reading her mind, Daniel smiled. He helped load the luggage into the taxi, keeping one eye on Sue as she climbed in.

They arrived at the Hong Kong Inn within minutes, situated in the heart of Kowloon's bustling city center.

Sue stepped out of the taxi, feeling the warm night air on her face.

"I just love the energy I feel here. This is so amazing, Daniel. It's after midnight and the place is just packed with people." Even the air smelled foreign to Sue, a mixture of spices and tropical breeze.

They walked inside.

"I love that you're excited." He smiled warmly at her.

She returned a smile, and tried to reply but her words were tangled in yet another yawn.

Daniel laughed. "You look tired."

She nodded. Her body was stiff from sitting for hours on the plane.

"Me too. We'll have other opportunities to enjoy the night life." He stood by her in the lobby. "Get some rest tonight." He hugged her and she hugged him back.

"Good Night."

She dragged herself to the elevators, sweaty and beat after being on the road twenty-two hours. Sue smiled, once inside, saying hello to the other riders. She heard responses in several different languages and dialects; definitely not in Texas anymore.

She peeked out her window, after settling in her room. She had never been in any city where the proximity of the next building was so close. She felt she could reach out and touch the apartment building next to hers.

She saw a man in the window across from her. He looked familiar, like the man in the Narita airport.

She closed her drapes. Drowsiness took over; she took a quick shower and collapsed in bed.

FIFTEEN
Michigan

DEE'S PHONE RANG. Caller ID said it was Wilford Lockes. Why was her dad calling her now? He always seemed to catch her at the worst times! She'd have to call him back. *Sorry, Dad.*

Dee Lockes McCray positioned her tiny body, cramped under a blanket in the backseat of her own car, using her female urinal. She had it pressed close, trying to relieve herself in a reclined position. The price she had to pay for having a second Coke three hours earlier.

"Ugh, leak proof seal, my ass," Dee said to the empty car. The red digital clock on her dashboard read 02:39. She'd been sitting in her car since six this morning, watching the front door of her target's house. Just when she was about to leave and find a bathroom, she saw activity inside. She decided to stay and wait.

I hope Dad isn't calling about Sue or her kids. Her sister would have landed in China by now.

The front door of the house opened and a middle-aged, portly man walked out.

"Oh crap! Oh crap! Oh crap! He's walking. I need my camera!" Dee squealed, as she scrambled back into her gym shorts.

The man glanced up the street and Dee ducked, but he paid no attention to her car.

Was he walking without a limp, not even a cane, to the garage?

She grabbed a pair of binoculars from the front seat and verified his identity with the photo.

Wait, what the hell is this?

70

The portly man went inside the garage and returned carrying golf clubs. He threw the bag in his trunk while Dee took a series of photos with her high-powered lens.

She tossed her camera on the seat, waiting for him to leave his driveway.

Dee looked at her file, studying two days' of surveillance notes. The man's employer and their insurance company had paid her private investigation company to catch him walking. The file showed he had been shamming them for unemployment insurance and workers comp resulting from a fall he had in his employer's plant. The pictures showed him in a wheelchair. And the notes stated when he walked he used a cane.

She followed his car out of the neighborhood. She dialed her dad and got his voicemail.

"Hey Dad, sorry we missed, I was on a stakeout watching some scam artist. Call me later. Hugs and kisses. Bye."

Dee was five years older than Sue. However, she was often taken to be the same age, despite that she commonly wore her curly blonde hair back in a bun and covered her blue-gray eyes with granny glasses. At five foot even, she was built like a gymnast and as spunky as a cheerleader.

She dialed Patrick's number. He picked up on the second ring.

"Hey Babe. How's the job?"

She was silent a moment, unsure which direction the man was turning at the light. He was three cars ahead of her.

"Dee, are you there?" Patrick said.

"I caught him. I'm pretty sure he's headed to the golf course," Dee replied.

"Geez, I thought you'd never get him out of the house. I was going to park my squad car in his driveway and crank up my howler. If the siren didn't get him out, I was going to fire a few rounds from my Glock. I wanted you home by dinner."

"You're out of control. And *that* would make the insurance company happy. That's why they choose me for stakeouts over you. You have cop written all over you. Plus, I don't think a hydrogen bomb blast would have budged him from his couch.

71

"You wanted the stakeout 'cause you just love the thrill of hiding in your car all day. You didn't drink a Coke did you?"

"Two."

"My God, a rebel. Don't you remember anything from training? Or do you just like using the pee jar?"

"I'm not ashamed of it. Tease all you want."

"Go on. Get the bastard before I fly the ghetto bird over your car and proclaim my love for you and blow your cover."

"See you in a few hours."

Dee was smiling as she hung up the phone. She fell back several car lengths behind her quarry's car. Within ten minutes, he pulled into the Kalamazoo Lakeside Country Club.

She reached for her camera, feeling a tingle of accomplishment run through her.

Dee had been home for a few hours, completing the paperwork for her client. Her cell phone rang and she snatched it up.

"Hi Dad, sorry we missed talking earlier. What are you up to?"

"Hi honey. I'm up to six foot, same as the last time you asked." He didn't wait for a comeback from his oldest daughter, instead he turned serious. "Dee, I want to fax you a letter Logan received today from an anonymous person. Sue is in China and is unaware of it. Her assistant, Mary Jo, gave it to me."

"What's it regarding?"

"You'll see. After you and Patrick read it, let's talk. I want you two to investigate this."

"Okay, Dad, anything for Sis." Dee was curious but didn't push her dad, wondering if the letter had to do with one of Sue's employees or manufacturers.

"Hey Dad, did she take any cute sundresses with her to China?" Sue had said that Daniel, her manufacturing consultant was handsome.

"I've no earthly idea, that's your department. I'm not the matchmaker."

"Well, maybe the trip abroad is just what the Love Doctor ordered. Hugs and kisses. 'Bye, Dad." Dee hung up and scooted to her basement office and her fax machine. She waited for the punch from Texas to arrive.

72

SIXTEEN
Hong Kong

IN THE SILENT HOTEL ROOM, Sue switched on the light to read the clock. *Five a.m. Hong Kong time and I'm wide wake. Ugh.*

Doll prototypes scattered the desk. "This is a pivotal point in my manufacturing," she said as she witnessed the first morning's light strike the tallest building, turning its mirrored windows gold.

A few hours later, Sue spotted Daniel having breakfast.

"I suppose breakfast tacos are out of the question," she said, approaching him. He sat at an impeccably set table minus the silverware.

He smiled as he looked up at her. She decided she loved that smile.

"I agree, I think decent Tex Mex food is hard to find in Asia, but today's buffet has bird's nest, fresh abalone and crunchy choy sum," he replied.

"Coffee is good for me."

"Good morning," he said as he stood to pull out her chair.

After breakfast, they had a brisk stroll to the Shuhua Toys building providing Sue's aerobic workout for the day replacing her morning run.

"Slow down, will you." Daniel rushed in the doors behind Sue.

"I'm just so excited I could burst. I can't wait to see what

73

they've done." Today she hoped to see her creations come to life.

They entered a brown brick high-rise building with Chinese letters etched on the glass doors. Before Sue met Li-Chieh-Yu, the young Chinese woman, manager of Shuhua Toys, she envisioned an oriental lady, delicate, quiet like an exotic lotus blossom. Li wasn't any of these stereotypes. Li was overpowering, plain, and smooth as jade.

"This is Mao-Tun. He oversees the manufacturing."

Sue and Daniel shook hands with Mao-Tun. He bowed at Sue. He was a slender man with a lot of dark hair neatly parted in the middle and spots of gray at the temples.

"You understand English?"

"Yes, we do. We will translate what you say to everyone else. Please follow us."

They led the two Americans to a conference room the size of a large classroom, where one end of a table was littered with stuffed animals and plastic toys. There were several crude prototypes of the Sue's Millennium Kids set to the side.

"This is Mr. Wang. The plant manager in mainland China." Li said.

"Nice to meet you," Sue said, bowing her head.

"He no understand English. Please sit." Li pulled out a chair at the head of the table.

The windowless room had bare walls with the exception of a large silver wall clock displaying nine o'clock.

Sue sat down, surrounded by her prototypes. She didn't wait to open the meeting. She picked up a doll and examined it.

"Oh my. A blonde curly-haired one. With green eyes. I love it. Maddie will too."

She set it down and picked up a tan doll. "This fabric is great. This could be American Indian or Hispanic, subject to interpretation. I love the fabric feel." She smiled at Daniel and then at Li.

Sue put it down and examined a few other dolls with different fabric colors. She picked up one with a slightly protruding tummy. "Is this from the pattern I sent you? Pattern C?"

"Yes," Li replied.

"This appears to be the body and the pattern that was done last week."

"We can take it apart to show you the differences." Mao said.

"No. This is fine. I can just look at this and see the shoulder line is different. This is a softer edge, more rounded."

"I have the written instructions and pattern you sent. We make the pouch inside for the chips."

"Can I see that?" She hesitated and glanced at Daniel. She had briefed Daniel over the phone about some of the chip functionality. Just like the Furby's chips, this one could store and repeat certain words kids said. This allowed parents to capture their kids favorite foods, sports, colors — the potential for the line was huge, not to mention the draw of the plangonologists.

"It's okay, Sue. This is a confidential meeting. They all have signed a non-disclosure agreement. Everyone you meet with this week have signed NDAs," Daniel said.

Sue put the doll down and reached in her briefcase. She withdrew a file and a drawing. "These prototypes with pattern C were originally developed with the internal pouch because of the dolls I designed non-commercially. The doll's chip can capture a lot about a child over the years, and then later the software we have developed will allow parents or kids themselves to design their next generation doll.

"I want a natural-looking human kid, starting as a baby, but growing as the line and collectors grow. The unique thing about the M Kids is that they are filled with a special fiber like batting that allows the chip to be hidden. And this unique fabric, Cira, replaces the material popular today in the Yorkston plush called Volboa. And, ohhh, it's much softer."

"Can you notice the chip?" Daniel picked up the blonde doll.

"No, because of the combination of the Cira material and the special fiber batting. Whereas Volboa that Naty uses is a very soft material that you can feel the stuffing or pellets through it."

"But his plush animals have been very successful with that fabric." Daniel set the M Kid doll on the table.

"Yes, but it won't work for M Kids. There are no dolls on the market today or that I can remember made to sit up and be moveable like the M Kids in a soft plush fabric."

"Yes. Nice. No injection molding." Li said.

"I know. Right. The only doll I can recall with a plush body today is the Raggedy Ann. Everything else was injection molded." Sue looked at Daniel. "Meaning plastic or vinyl."

"I know. I did my homework. Mattel and Tyco have that market sealed up with the Barbie line and Girly Girls lines."

"Let's work on the face. I want a boy face and girl face that every kid in America is going to pressure Mom or Grandma to buy. But let's start with the body first."

She fixed her attention on the dolls for hours. They went through all the changes, while Daniel took copious notes on his laptop.

"Is the arm size okay, Ms. Logan?" Daniel asked.

"I am okay with the arm size and shape," Sue replied.

Mao translated to Mr. Wang. He smiled and nodded. He understood.

"What about the hands, Ms. Logan?" Daniel asked.

"I would like to see stitches where the knuckles should be."

Daniel made notes while Li translated to Mr. Wang. She held up the doll's hands and translated for a few minutes. Mr. Wang wasn't smiling and was concentrating on her explanations. He replied to Li. The buzz of Mandarin flew by her.

"He said he would need to make a different hand pattern," Li translated.

Sue brought out her drawings and went through her ideas of the separate thumb and the stitching for the four digits. Mao and Li translated to Mr. Wang.

Eventually they decided on a compromise. Mr. Wang would take the train back to his plant in China, with all their notes, and have his development team make the changes. He would return to Hong Kong the next day with the new prototypes.

Daniel and Sue took a break and ate lunch with Mao and Li. After lunch, Sue escorted by Daniel spent the rest of the day at the plastic and puzzle manufacturer's offices. Tired after their long day, they returned to the hotel to freshen up. They planned to meet for dinner later that evening.

"You look great," Daniel said, grinning when Sue entered the lobby. "I'm glad you ditched your boots for sandals. We have a lot of walking to do through the crowded streets."

"Thank you sir," Sue said. "And I'm glad you ditched your tie."

After dinner, the two Americans wandered down the peninsula into the traditional districts of Yau Ma Tei and Monk Kok.

"I've never seen so much ivory, jade, and paper flowers," Sue said as they walked among the street vendors and the thronging crowds.

"And you can buy a Rolex for twenty bucks," Daniel said, pointing at a cart they had just passed.

"I've seen all sorts of wheeled carts of cheap designer knockoffs from purses to watches." Sue strolled alongside him.

"They keep the knockoffs in carts because there's a spotter looking for police. When they see a cop, they whistle and all the carts fold up and are wheeled away before the police walk up," Daniel said.

"Nice." Sue wasn't a shopper. If she wanted a designer item, she would not buy a knockoff. However, she did want to bring back authentic Chinese souvenirs for her kids, parents, and Mary Jo.

They seemed to be in an endless maze. The outdoor markets ran parallel to the streets on either side of them. The crowded streets were packed end-to-end with shop fronts or street stalls, every inch dedicated to making money.

Everywhere they went, they attracted stares. The staring was pure uninhibited curiosity.

Sue stopped to watch an old Chinese man with white hair and a skinny pointed beard fold colorful paper to form an origami bird's nest. The old man placed his paper nest in her hand. He took a green palm frond, split the wide leaf with his brown long fingernail, and begun to swiftly weave it. He formed a bird and placed it in the nest in Sue's hand.

"Very nice. Thank you."

Daniel reached in his pocket, retrieved a few bills, and handed it to the man.

Sue expected a smile or at least a nod of thanks, but the old man promptly sat down and continued his work.

Sue watched an oriental street dancer, which seemed to specialize in seductive hip twitches and lizard-like movements of his neck. Sue couldn't help herself, she laughed at the man's quirky gestures. Daniel, following closely beside Sue, laughed too. Even his hearty laugh disarmed her. It was deep, sexy and full of promise.

"This is so amazing, watching the frenzy of all these vendors pushing their wares at us. And to see all these dancers rolling right in the street," Sue said. "Not something you see in Texas."

"It is astounding what they do for a buck," he winked.

"I'm sure they enjoy the dancing too," she teased back at him. She turned to watch another dancer spin by them.

Daniel stared at her with a slight smile. Sue felt his strong gaze and enjoyed it. But, despite his charm, she had no intentions of getting involved with him.

He must have sensed her uneasiness. "Come on. Let's go back."

Sue passed a young Chinese girl, sitting quietly on the curb. Sue handed the paper nest and bird to her. At first, the young girl looked cautiously at Sue, then she smiled, warming Sue's heart.

The two were quiet in the cab.

"I could go for one nightcap and maybe dessert when we get back to the hotel, if you're up for it," She raised her eyebrows. *I hope to learn more about Daniel. Things couldn't be better in my life right now.*

"One nightcap and maybe an Irish pudding it is."

Yep, things couldn't be better.

SEVENTEEN

THE IRISH PUB across the street from their hotel attracted Westerners longing for a taste of home. Any night of the week, the bar was filled with Europeans, Australians and Americans in search of English-speaking cohorts. The bar was bustling and raucous.

Sue and Daniel sat in a corner booth, the ebullient couple chatting freely about working together. She sipped an Irish whiskey, dipping her spoon gingerly into a bowl of green tea ice cream while Daniel looked on with a wry smile. "So you really thought black pudding was a dessert?"

"Yes. I had no idea it was blood pudding, or made with animal blood. Sounds like a true gastronomic test to my cardiovascular system."

"I'm not a fan of it either. By the way, where did you say you grew up?"

"Texas, I've lived there my whole life." She drank the tepid liquid gingerly, feeling giddy from the whiskey as it warmed her insides. She really liked Daniel and felt comfortable with him. "Silly. You knew I grew up in Texas."

There's his wonderful smile.

He looked knowingly at her. "Ah, yes. And you went to college in Texas, right?"

She nodded. "Yes, my life was unexciting . . . a peaceful and normal childhood. After college, I married. I had a nice, decent, wholesome husband, wonderful kids, a beautiful home, a great business, and then . . . ." She trailed off and never finished her

79

sentence. She felt her face turn cold. She stared thoughtfully at her coffee.

Daniel reached across the table and took her hand in his.

She looked at him, feeling comfort for a moment.

Should I share with him my feelings? Would he understand that some of my life has been tragic, and that was a part of me?

She toyed with her drink in front of her.

Could he read it in my eyes, a flicker of pain?

"About five years ago my husband was killed in a hunting accident."

Daniel sat still and squeezed her hand hard.

Slowly she shook her head, holding his eyes with a firm look of her own. She felt her eyes glistening with moisture.

"It's okay. Tell me about your children again."

She nodded slowly appreciating his concern for her privacy. They talked about her kids and then eventually back to business.

"My concern is that the Millennium Kids get copied or, worse, it's a flop," she said.

"If an idea is a good one, you know more than one person will have it as well."

"I know. I can't freak out over that. I consider it marketplace validation of my concept."

"With superior execution, it's not about being first, it's about lasting."

"My biggest fear is that someone will beat me to the punch. Every day that slips by seems to make it more likely someone else will come up with these similar designs and features. It's important I have the plush kids available on the shelves for the millennium. Everyone is racing to get their products to market first."

"Once a product is released here, you have a bigger risk of it getting copied."

"I know. Well, then it's a race. Together, we get this product completed and announced by next spring. Deal?"

"Deal." They clicked their glasses together and then sealed it with a handshake.

After the shake, Daniel held on to her hand. She loved how he didn't let go.

"I really like your point of view. And you've done a great job with the product line. I like your smile too…and I'm talking too much." Daniel picked up his glass, took a swig of his drink and before Sue could answer he continued.

"I know this may be out of place but I'd like to ask you. Would you like to grab a bottle of wine and finish this talk at the hotel?"

"I'm not sure. I'd like to, but—"

"But do you feel this is anyway wrong because we're working together?"

"Well, I have my concerns," she said without hesitation. She had her rules about dating her manufacturer reps or her colleagues in the trade.

"There may be a day that you don't pay me." He had a firm look of resolve on his face.

"I'm okay. This is fine here, if you don't mind?"

"Not at all."

Sue debated her continued silence about her husband's death and found no reason to not share with Daniel. She enjoyed his company. She reached for her Irish coffee and took a slow drink.

Why not tell him? I trust him as a friend.

"Jonathan had gone on a combination golfing and hunting trip with our banker Marc Gambino to the Gokarnac resort… compliments of our bank." She stopped and looked into her coffee. It was true, she thought, the bank had given them use of a resort suite for the trip. But after Jonathan's accident, the bank ended up paying Sue for the whole trip and more.

They were probably afraid I would sue them.

She never did. What good would it do to sue anyone; the hotel, their guide, the park? It would not bring Jonathan back.

"Were you with him?" Daniel held her hand lightly tracing circles with his thumb on her palm.

"No. No. He wanted me to go, but I was busy with the kids."

"It's okay. What happened?" He had a concern, caring look as he watched her.

"He was with three friends that day. They were hunting and made their way to the western peak, the outer fringes of a steep mountain terrain." She paused, looked down and rolled the corners

81

of the paper napkin with her fingers. "The area was rough and unsteady along the cliff edges. Heavy rains the weeks before their hunt caused erosion."

"Did he slip?"

She nodded her head. "The local papers called it a 'mishap'. Really? A mishap? A *mishap* is a misfortune that happens to you when you miss an airplane; but not when your husband slips and plummets to his death off a fifty-foot cliff and his body gets washed out to sea, never to be recovered." She physically shuddered.

"I'm so sorry Sue. I can't imagine the pain you've went through. Was he alone when it happened?"

"Gamby, Mike Simmons and Jeff Elliott were the last three to be seen with Jonathan. And they say he wandered off to take a photo."

Daniel took her hand out of his, studied it, and returned it to his clasp.

She smiled. Oh, it felt so good.

"Jonathan died at thirty-one. We were married six years. The children were so young when they lost their father. Elizabeth was only four, Colt two, and Maddie only one." She paused and then barely whispered, "I was a widow at twenty-nine."

"You have a lot of great people in your life and a wonderful business . . . which you love."

"I do love my work and my family are great supporters. I don't think I could have done it without them. And I'm so glad you are here to help me."

They got back to the hotel after ten, and Daniel was extremely polite when he left her once again at the elevators, kissing her softly on the cheek. Just as he had the night before, he left a warm glow inside her and the ticking awareness of him as a man, of herself as a woman, not just colleagues.

EIGHTEEN

SUE, ACCLIMATED to Hong Kong time, still woke up before dawn. Last night's revelation about Daniel still at the forefront of her thoughts. She lay in bed and thought about Daniel and how he had been such a good listener. She thought about the tender kiss at the elevator when he said good night.

She made several quick phone calls regarding work and then called her family.

"Hi Daddy."

"Darling, how is everything going?" Her dad's soft voice across the miles made something in Sue's eyes sting. She blinked the feeling away. She was there to make the doll design work.

"The designs are coming together." Sue wondered if this was true. The designs were close to completion but still lacking pizzazz. She continually worried about the market's acceptance, despite the endless hours spent designing all the unique features of the toy.

"That's great. So they're looking good? Are you pleased?"

"Yes, we're getting there," she said quietly. "But I feel the doll's facial design is lacking."

"You'll get it figured out. Anything else? Is everything okay?"

"Fine. I'm just tired that's all."

Tired of running an uphill race. Tired of trying to get the product out while the concept is hot and the deadline is looming. Tired of being the only one with all the company's responsibilities on my shoulders.

"Well is there anything else you want to tell me?"

Her dad could always tell when she was holding something back, so she said firmly, "No."

"Are you sure, sweetheart? How's the consultant? How's that working out?"

Did she hear something in the way he asked about Daniel? Prying? On the other hand, was he just asking because he was hoping she was having a good time while she was there? He had told her that he felt a trip aboard would do her good. She also knew if her dad didn't ask about Daniel, her sister, Dee, would strangle him.

Sue twisted her hair with her free hand. "He's fine. Tell the kids I love them, and we'll talk tomorrow around the same time."

"Okay, sweetie. Talk to you soon. We love you." His voice sounded tired and crinkly.

Sue and Daniel's activities were similar to the days preceding; they met at Shuhua Toys and reviewed the new prototypes. They spent hours on the design. By the end of the third day, the toll of the time change and the long meetings had exhausted Sue. She wondered if she would ever make the deadline. She had to have a solid product design soon.

"Sue, you look frustrated." Daniel walked alongside her after the long day, returning to the hotel.

"I just never realized how hard it was going to be to come up with a line that is satisfactory in quality, costs, and consumer acceptance."

"We're almost there. And, no matter how hard you work, there's no guarantee that it will be accepted."

"I understand. I have three young children and I know what it takes to get the attention of the consumer." She struggled to stay on the crowded sidewalk. "Daniel, I have an idea."

He stopped. "You have my attention." A few ladies bumped into him as he moved off to the side.

"How about I go to mainland China to the toy plant in Guangdong?"

He shook his head.

"Daniel, this is the only way I am going to be able to articulate the design. I need to be in the trenches, working side by side, supervising the pattern cutters, overseeing the sewing steps and tweaking the poly filling." She threw her hands up. "And besides I've never been to mainland China." She put her hands together into praying hands. "Purty please!"

"Okay. Okay. I'll see if Mao and Li can escort us into China and be our translators at the manufacturing plants."

"That would be great!"

NINETEEN

DANIEL WINSTON looked forward to the evening and to telling Sue the good news about their trip to mainland China.

Companies hired Daniel because of his expertise in China. Doing business there was different than in the USA. The culture and methods were foreign to most westerners, like Sue. He wanted to take what could be an overwhelming China experience and turn it into a profitable foreign trade transaction.

He had worked for several other small manufacturers like Logan, but none of them led by a woman like Sue. *Who would have thought this little lady had so much gumption?*

They were in front of the Star Ferry when he told her the news.

"Our two translators agreed to go with us to China."

"Thank you!" Sue squealed, and gave Daniel a big hug.

Several tourists, lined up to have their photos taken beside the rickshaws, looked over at the noisy American lady.

"You're welcome. I have to say, I agree with you going too."

Wow, she looks great.

"By the way, if you're trying to look like an everyday tourist, it's not working. You're gorgeous." Sue had chosen to wear a loose fitting sundress and flat sandals.

"Thank you. But tonight I am a tourist and how would you like to be my tour guide?"

"That I can do." It dawned on him how much he liked Sue's

blonde good looks, her lovely manners and the not-so-subtle way in which she did things. "How about a trip across Victoria Harbor, and then we'll return for dinner at the Peninsula Hotel afterwards?" Daniel said.

"That sounds great. I'm at your disposal tonight."

They boarded one of the many ferries at the dock.

"All these," David pointed to the line of massive green and white double deck ferries, "cross the harbor over three to four hundred times a day carrying commuters from Tsim Sha Tsui, central to Wan Chai."

"Wow."

"This way." Daniel led her to the front deck.

Sue stepped out on the open deck and her hair whipped around her face. Daniel liked the way her hair looked when it was free and unhampered. They peered back at the remarkable view of the island. The short voyage to him always evoked a satisfying sense of history and timeliness. He loved the history here.

"The smell of the diesel is making me feel nauseous," Sue said.

"Let's move from the lower deck. You'll get fresh air on the top level." Sue followed Daniel upstairs. "Did you know the two-deck system was originally conceived to allow for the Europeans to travel apart from the Chinese commuters?"

"I'm sorry, what did you say?" She was looking out over the water.

"I said you look lost in thought." He watched her staring intently over the side of the ferry.

"I am just taking in the harbor views and sea breeze," she replied. "This is a nice break, Daniel. Thanks for coming with me. You're not on the clock now, are you?"

It amused him that she watched him log his hours on his PC at the meetings. That was mostly for bookkeeping. He knew this trip would cost Logan Designs close to ten thousand dollars in consulting fees to him, but the savings on her landed costs of the products would be worth a lot more.

"Yes, I'm off the clock. I do have a personal side of me too," he grinned at her. "I've been to Hong Kong many times and there are sightseeing trips I can do over again, especially when it's with a first-time visitor."

"Well what else do you have in mind for this first-time visitor?" She tilted her face up and a spray from the sea splashed on her cheek, startling her.

Daniel withheld a chuckle. He pulled a handkerchief from his pocket and offered it to her. Sue wiped her face. Her eyes caught his and they both laughed. It was good to see her laughing and relaxing. He was concerned with how serious she was all the time.

"You look like you're enjoying the break from the hustle of the business."

"I am. Thanks."

"Hey, I have an idea. Why don't you visit Stanley Village tomorrow? I'm not working for Logan tomorrow and have to meet with another manufacturer in the morning, so you can go alone. We can ask the hotel front desk to write out the Chinese characters for the locations you want to visit, that way the cab driver will know where you want to go. You'll love the shopping and exploring of the quaint seaside village."

He saw a look of disappointment cross her face, and added, "Maybe tomorrow evening we can meet up, if you like?"

"Yes, that would be a nice ending to the day."

Daniel changed the subject and told Sue about the history and culture of Hong Kong.

"I'm impressed you know so much about China's history," she said, listening intently.

He pointed toward the harbor and described the takeover that occurred previous years. He leaned in next to her, feeling their closeness and liking it.

"I was here on business. It was incredible. A huge fireworks display lit up Victoria Harbor that evening in July. While four thousand guests sat down to a banquet in the convention center on that harbor front," he was still pointing out toward the harbor, "five hundred Chinese troops crossed the border into Hong Kong." Daniel imitated a droning guide voice.

Sue applauded after he finished his speech.

He took a bow. "Are you making fun of your Chinese tour guide?"

He thought she looked beautiful standing on the deck under a canopy of tinkling stars and bursting lights in the background.

"No, not at all. I love the history, go on." She leaned in closer to him.

He loved that she enjoyed listening and watching him talk. He just loved about everything she did. And that was beginning to be a problem.

"Do you think Hong Kong's changed much since its return to China?"

The smile that crossed his lips had nothing about business in it.

"I think the locals say 'yes' because of the political and business differences and the changes in the laws. But I don't see a lot of change now. Hong Kong is still the business city it was before the takeover . . . a very cosmopolitan and exhilarating place to do business."

"I guess time will only tell." Her expression was similar to his. *I think neither one of us gives a damn about the take-over.*

At the end of the evening, they were standing outside their hotel. "Thanks again, Daniel, for the great day and evening."

"How about a night cap at our favorite Irish bar?"

"Okay." They took a few steps toward the bar. Sue turned to look at Daniel. "Just one beer and –" Daniel grabbed her arm and jerked her back to the curb as a car swerved toward Sue.

Sue's eyes went wide with terror, as she watched the car that almost hit her turn the corner. She was shaking all over.

"You're not used to looking in the opposite direction before stepping off the curb. You have to remember that in Hong Kong cars drive on the left."

It was a British thing. The traffic lights, road signs and road markings were exactly as they were in the United Kingdom. Being from America, Sue was probably not use to this. But he thought she looked first. Hadn't he looked both ways too? It was as if the driver saw her and kept coming. He spun his head to watch the car.

89

The driver cursed out the window as he shifted gears. Daniel could see he was a bald Chinese man with a cobra tattoo on his neck. The car almost went out of control before swerving around a corner and disappearing.

"Aghh," Sue gasped, as she stood rigidly on the curb with Daniel's arm still locked around her waist. She put her hand to her mouth and closed her eyes. She collected herself, and quietly whispered, "Thank you. You saved my life!"

He held on to her, afraid to let go. He gave Sue a long look. "What about that drink, Sir Churchill?"

Sue leaned forward, drew his mouth toward her own, and kissed him. Daniel took the lead, and his powerful mouth claimed hers, urging her to open to him, to allow him access.

Her mouth was warm and tender. She relaxed, moaned slightly. It was a sweet kiss, long denied. After passionate moments, he heard another honk and, just like that, the magic dissipated and the kiss was over.

Sue linked her arm in his, allowing him to guide her safely across the street. They walked the short distance to the pub.

"So why Churchill?" she asked.

"He was Britain's greatest wartime leader."

"And he reminded you of me, because . . . ."

"Because he died by stepping off a curb and getting hit by a bus."

"Liar, I happen to know a little about history myself. He died of old age. He was like 90 years old when he died at his home."

"Hmm, I think you're right. Well, a bus hit him once. I think. I was trying to make you not feel foolish for not looking both ways before you stepped out into traffic." He glanced at her, feeling the warmth from their kiss and enjoying their close proximity.

"A business consultant by day, tourists guide by evening and now a knight in shining armor; you are multi-talented, Mr. Winston."

"I aim to please, Miss Logan. Come." He took her elbow and guided her through the front door of the pub. A look of appreciation crossed her face.

"Can I get you an ale, stout or lager?" Daniel smiled.

"What are you, a certified cicerone too?"

90

He raised his eyebrows. "A beer sommelier? Nope. I just like quenching my thirst. And happen to know a good array of beers."

"One beer it is. And then I need to call it a night. I could talk nonstop the rest of the evening about the toy business, but we have tomorrow."

"I understand. I'd love to talk all night," Daniel said.

Sue looked into his eyes and smiled.

"Me too." There was an undercurrent of affection in her two words.

TWENTY
Mainland China

AFTER A DAY OF TOURING the markets in the seaside community of Stanley Village, Sue was anxious to get back to her mission. She had hardly slept because of the sheer excitement of going to mainland China.

She called home and explained to her dad how the toy makers traveled by train from Mainland China to meet them every day, returned to their factory with the prototype, worked all night and arrived back the next day with their new versions.

"Dad, they have a special molding plant in China, I have to see."

"But I thought you weren't using injection rubber molds," he replied.

"I'm not. It's a special pattern. The mold is used in a new fabric for . . . ." Sue stopped and was afraid, even across the miles, to discuss her pattern C.

"What did you say?"

"Dad, I have to travel to China to expedite the process. I have to see firsthand the factory that makes the fabric and sews it."

"Be careful honey. It's one thing to visit Hong Kong but quite another to venture over to mainland China. Western women seldom do." Wilford said.

"Don't worry. I'll be fine. Daniel and our Chinese escorts

will be with me. Thanks for everything you and Mom are doing with the kids. I'm sure they love you spoiling them to death."

He didn't respond right away.

"Dad, can you hear me?"

"Yes, I can. We had a special letter delivered . . . ." It was as if he wasn't listening to her. He appeared distracted. After a few silent seconds, he said to her, "It sounds like you're doing great work there so far."

"Yes the trip is going great. I miss you all."

"We miss you, too. And Susannah, there's something I want . . . ." he stopped talking.

"Dad, What is it? I didn't hear you."

Did he call me Susannah?

He normally reserved using her formal name for more serious talks, usually centered on her mom, the kids, or financial issues.

"Daddy, are the kids okay?"

"Yes, everything is fine."

"What did you want to tell me?"

"Never mind, it can wait. Have a safe trip to China."

She realized when she hung up the phone there was something more, something he was not telling her.

Daniel and Sue had met up with Mao and Li their China escorts. They had their China applications that would allow them entry into mainland China. "Entry into Hong Kong doesn't necessarily win you entry into China," Daniel had explained to Sue earlier in the week.

From the moment she and Daniel boarded the train that crossed the Luobu Qiau bridge to China's economic zone, Sue had a flutter of butterflies nesting in her stomach. The train was overcrowded and they had to stand until a seat became available. Daniel stood behind Sue as the train departed. Sue held onto the railing in the center of the passenger car, catching a reflection in the window of several Chinese men and women staring at her. When she turned to look at them, they lowered their eyes. She watched with curiosity while others gaped at her.

She looked at an older woman mesmerized by Sue. Everyone seemed to be staring at the two Americans.

Sue leaned back against Daniel and whispered, "I feel like we're celebrities. The people here are giving us so much attention." Many looked up at her and began to gawk as she whispered to him.

"The Chinese have no social rules about staring. If they find something interesting, they have the right to stare as long as they would like. You are a guest in this culture and they find you very interesting."

"I'm glad you agreed to this trip," she said quietly. She felt special just being with Daniel. Several women whispered to each other and nodded.

"So am I," he said.

"Just for the record, the trip so far has surpassed my expectations. I'm so impressed with the work ethic and the manufacturer's overwhelming desire to get these products right." She decided to finish their discussion later because now everyone on the full train car was staring at both of them.

She giggled and whispered, "The way the Chinese are gawking at me, makes me feel sympathy with the crazed pandas at the Chengdu Zoo."

"Don't let it go to your head."

"Sue, this way." Daniel signaled her to follow him across the packed and chaotic border crossing.

"Where are Li and Mao?" Sue said, as she looked back and forth.

"They divide customs by Nationals and non-citizens."

Sue's eyes went wide when she saw border police armed with submachine guns and shotguns staring down the passengers. She stopped, pulled her camera from her backpack, and took a photo.

A guard yelled at Sue and Daniel in unintelligible Chinese. Sue glanced at Daniel.

"Just keep going through customs." Daniel pushed her on.

They took a few steps but were stopped by a large guard who held up a stick, barring them from entering.

"Be calm," Daniel searched the crowd looking for Mao or Li.

"Damn it."

More security people started to congregate. One guard gestured for them to follow to another part of the station.

Sue kept close to Daniel, looking at him helplessly, like toddlers looking for their mommies, trying to figure out where to go or what to do.

"Nothing is in English," Sue sighed softly. A guard gave her a sideways look, sending chills down her spine.

"Follow them," Daniel nodded.

"Where? No one has even attempted to speak to us," Sue whispered to Daniel. "Why were we singled out and not allowed to go through immigration? Where's Li?" Sue bit her lower lip.

"Just show them your papers and passport."

Sue was impressed with how cool Daniel appeared. She tried to harness her mounting concerns and anxieties

"There they are!" Daniel pointed at Mao and Li coming through the turnstiles toward them.

"Thank God." Sue slumped into a chair and ran her hand through her hair.

Li talked to a custom guard and began the translation. "They want your camera, Sue," Li explained.

"My camera?"

"Yes, they said you took pictures of the guards, like a spy."

"No, no, only for my photo album. I thought the guards were handsome. Please Li, I have photos of my daughter's birthday on this camera, I don't want to lose it."

Li spoke to them in Chinese. Sue and Daniel had no idea what had conspired but after many back and forth discussions, all the officials that had gathered seemed to be satisfied with the explanation.

"Give this to them at customs." Li handed a small slip of paper to Sue.

Several more guards looked over their passports at the customs booth. Sue gave them the paper.

A guard pointed to her camera.

Sue handed it to him.

He took it and dropped it in a plastic bag.

"Wait my photos . . . ." Sue didn't finish her sentence.

"I have my camera. It's better to lose it than to end up in a Chinese prison," Daniel said.

Sue nodded with her mouth downturned, as they stamped her passport. "Not only did I lose the birthday pictures, but I lost photos of my prototypes. That concerns me more, especially if it gets in the wrong hands."

A van waited outside of the train station to drive them to the factories.

Sue climbed into the dilapidated van. The front passenger seat was missing.

"My China adventure has officially begun," she sighed to Daniel.

"At least our driver didn't show up pulling a rickshaw."

Li and Mao sat in the middle section of the van while Daniel and Sue climbed into the back row.

The road was quiet and empty, which was a blessing because their van driver had a fondness for speed and swerving from lane to lane. Sue noticed the Chinese drivers drove angrily and aggressively, as opposed to her small Texas town, where everyone drove as if they had baskets of eggs on their seats. She gave Daniel a nervous look.

He smiled and whispered to her. "China has about three percent of the world's drivers, but about a quarter of all people killed each year by cars."

"Great. That's reassuring. Thanks Daniel," she whispered.

He looked amused before his face went serious. "Remember, we're not in Hong Kong any more. Let's stick close to our escorts."

They looked out the window in silence.

The foreign landscape intrigued Sue. The rich cultural legacy added to the fascination of being in China. They were traveling on a desolate road leading to another border crossing ahead.

Sue saw an old Chinese man zigzagging on a rickety bike with pretzel-like wheels and stick handlebars. He had two baskets on either side of the back wheel filled with rolled up papers. Sue wondered where he could be going since she hadn't seen a building yet.   Sue's face muscle tense up as they approached an armed border patrol. "I thought we were already in China."

"We are," Daniel replied softly. "The patrols here are to keep out migrating workers. They work ten hours a day, six days a week. These jobs are better than the alternatives in their home districts. So many young workers try to get into the Chinese economic zone where they can work."

"And the guards?"

"The guards verify that the people have the proper paperwork. They come from all over China. Among the city's twelve million people, only about four hundred thousand are native. They come here bringing their hopes and dreams with them, begging to work in this area."

"I thought many didn't like this way of life." She turned her head upward to hear his whispering and met his gaze.

"This may be the only work they can get. The passion of people who had been restrained for many years under the planned economy system exploded in this city." Daniel murmured low so their escorts and driver couldn't hear him.

"This area made its fortune on low-end manufacturing, because foreign companies were looking for cheap places to manufacture their goods. The economy here was growing by fifty percent a year. To many, this work is their only salvation." He said softly, meeting her gaze.

"That makes sense." Sue watched as Daniel kept his eyes focused on her and then back to the guard gate. Daniel was trying surreptitiously to watch the guards while he talked to her about the Chinese economy.

The driver of the van and Mao talked to the border patrol. The guards looked in the back seat at Daniel and Sue. They showed their stack of documentation to the guards. The guards nodded at Mao and opened the gate.

After hours of hard driving, through countryside thick with rice fields, Sue began to see buildings as they traveled farther into China.

"Look at the back." Daniel pointed at a building. "Those are generators to make their own electricity, because the government shuts off the power to the plants after a certain hour so manufacturers don't work all night long. The generators keep the plants operating."

"I feel it's still rather . . ." she paused for the right word, "rustic."

Daniel smiled at her choice of words. "Yes I guess that's part of the reason many people hesitate to travel here. The security, the ruggedness, the different languages and dialects — they all mingle together. Did you notice all the different languages around us?"

She nodded. She had seen the different ways people said hello and thank you. Even their greetings were different. It was so exhilarating being in a foreign country. And, right now, she wouldn't have dreamed of having anyone else, other than Daniel, to share it with – raising that guarded concern of conflicting interests.

They turned down a dusty, well-grooved road that dumped into a four story-building complex that resembled a college campus. All the buildings were painted baby blue. It reminded Sue of a scene out of Miami Vice.

Daniel helped Sue out of the van. "Let's go make some dolls!" They followed their Chinese entourage into the plant.

TWENTY-ONE

A SHRINE WITH FLOWERS scattered around a Chinese guardian figurine and the aroma of incense welcomed them into the building.

"What is that?" Sue asked pointing at the shrine.

"An altar…for praying."

Sue stopped and knelt down in front of the altar.

The entourage kept walking but Daniel stopped. He watched Sue with an amused smile on his face.

She stood up and when she walked past Daniel she said, "I'd gladly make an offering if the process brought me good luck."

"You are one crazy woman, Ms. Logan. And you won't need luck. You have talent. Let's put it to use."

"Hello Mr. Wang. Thanks for letting us come to the plant and help make the dolls in the factory. This will save a lot of time. Plus, I wanted to see the operation."

Mr. Wang bowed his head to Sue and gestured toward the plant.

Sue walked into the factory. She stopped dead in her tracks and stared at the plant floor workers.

There were hundreds of young Chinese women sitting row-after-row at their sewing machines, lined up neatly like dominos. Their jet black heads were bent over their fabric working and, as Sue and Daniel entered the room, like a single flick to the first domino, their petite, porcelain faces looked up at them.

In the corner of the plant, Sue saw a chest-high mound of discarded doll body parts left over from production mistakes. The pile almost looked gruesome, scattered with multi-colored doll arms, heads, and legs that seemed to be torn or ripped from the rest of the dolls' torsos. "Are any of those my toys?"

"No. We are working on one of your dolls, here at this machine." Li pointed to the first seamstress.

The iron black sewing machine reminded Sue of the antique one her grandmother Lockes used. Li handed Sue a doll. While Sue examined the stuffed toy, she felt all the eyes turned toward her. Daniel came close to her, observing the doll over her shoulder.

"Are these young women all from here?" Sue whispered to Daniel.

"Most of China's toy workers are young women migrants from the countryside, who often live in dormitories on the factory grounds."

"They live here?"

"Yes, all of these ladies live on-site at this factory. There are dormitories above us on the upper floors. Conditions are crude by our standards," Daniel said in a low voice.

Sue wondered why he whispered since most of the people in the room would not understand English.

"A lot of these workers are from the other provinces in China. They migrate here because they can earn a lifetime of wages in just a few years."

"These women look like teenagers," Sue said quietly.

She felt the warm temperature in the building. The room was noisy and hot. The air reeked of a severe chemical smell, like carpet in a new house. She watched one group of several dozen young women pick up a toy from a box on the right, sew a few stitches and then drop it in a box on the left. Each girl repeated the same motions, over and over. The sewers worked methodically. Their delicate hands performed the tasks like cellists strumming back and forth to create a melody.

"I feel faint." Sue rubbed her forehead with her hand, wiping away perspiration.

"Let us take you to the Research and Development Department. It has air conditioning," Li said.

The research department was in a small room with the floor and tabletops littered with stuffed animals. Bubble-packed role-play kits complete with swords, doctor bags, firefighter hats and accessories covered the gray pegboard walls.

Mr. Wang retrieved a box of Logan stuffed prototypes, setting it on the table in front of Sue. She pounced at the toys, wanting to see firsthand what changes they made to her designs.

They spent three hours in the research room with many trips back and forth to the sewing floor using the new fabrics.

Sue, restless after the continual passing off to the seamstresses, took a big gulp from her water bottle, emptying it. "Li, I'd like to do the sewing, please."

Li's mouth dropped slightly, and then she nodded. "Follow me."

Sue collected several pattern pieces resembling human parts. Daniel lifted his eyebrows and smiled as they made their way back to the factory.

Mr. Wang, Mao, Daniel and Sue plus several young assistants from the research room followed Li to the plant floor. The authoritative Li said something to a teen girl sitting at the end sewing machine. The young Chinese girl eyed Sue, but stood up and backed away and did a slight bow toward Sue.

"Sheh sheh . . . thank you." Sue sat in the young girl's chair thinking if they only knew I learned how to sew before learning how to ride a bike.

Show time! I can do this now.

She took the dolls she collected from the conference table. Familiarizing herself with the bobbin and foot controls, she began to sew the dolls mid-section.

For twenty minutes, she concentrated intently pulling out stuffing, stitching feverously, repeating the sewing over and over, totally involved in what she was doing and oblivious to everyone watching her.

The rubber molded face she chose captured every detail of a young child with wide blue eyes, dimples, and a scattering of freckles but bald as a cue ball. Sue rummaged through the box of doll wigs choosing one in honor of her assistant – a redhead.

She sewed the head to the torso and turned to Daniel. "Do you have the tracker?" She felt a mischievous smile move across her face as she looked at Daniel.

He reached into his pocket and pulled out a small square chip. He returned a playful gleam in his eyes.

Sue took the chip and delicately removed it from the casing. The wafer silicon chip was still a prototype. Sue felt fortunate to have them manufactured in a small electronic instrument plant in Texas. She had brought a dozen with her. Daniel looked wildly around the factory. Could he read her thoughts?

"It's ok. This will be one of the few prototypes." Sue kissed the shiny metal microchip and slid it deep into the folds of the belly of the toy with the fabric in pattern C. Daniel winked at Sue. His wink warmed her and gave her inspiration. "Do you have sand?"

Li left the floor and returned with a jar. Sue poured the beige grains into a cloth pocket she had made. She placed the weighted pouch into the bottom of the doll.

Sue truly enjoyed fashioning the final products and knew no limitations creatively, which had been gratifying this week. She had her artistic gyroscope whirling in a way that gave her a huge breakthrough in her design, one that had always been a roadblock before. She contemplated the doll she had created.

She examined every seam and pitched every dart. She flipped the doll repeatedly. A contented smile settled on her face and a glitter of satisfaction in her eyes. She placed it on the table and the doll sat firmly.

"That's it." She glanced at Daniel and he smiled reassuringly. She held up the doll for all to see, as if she had just given birth.

Everyone within sight applauded, making Sue feel like she was in seventh heaven.

Daniel delicately examined the beautifully crafted doll.

"Very nice, Ms. Sue Logan. I just love your whole look at the designs —from a child's point of view. I think you've nailed it."

He gave her a high five. His approval of her product sent a rush of pleasure from her head to her toes. She reminded herself that he admired her enterprise, not her. But when he slapped her hand, she held on to it, as a tease. He in turn pulled her close and gave her a hug. Sue blushed. The hug lasted only a second, but it felt sparkling.

She was beaming as they passed the doll around to the group hovering over the machine. All the discussions flying around her in Mandarin was mind boggling and she could barely conceal her excitement as she waited for the translation of the dialog.

"Miss Sue, this is beautiful doll. We'll be able to give you an estimate for this style and size of doll, okay?" Mao said to her. "May we keep this one?"

Whoopee! Her creative side was high fiving her talented sewing side. "Yes. Thank you for all your help on this toy. I like what we've accomplish today. I just have one other request."

Everyone waited and she squirmed.

"Where's the bathroom?"

Sue had been drinking bottled water all day and she was about to burst. Her question triggered an ensuing Mandarin conversation between Li and Mao and several of the Chinese people around the room. Sue listened as the uncomprehending Mandarin crescendo around her.

"We must drive you ten minutes to a restroom," Li said.

Sue was bewildered. "This is a dormitory filled with hundreds of girls, surely there has to be a ladies bathroom."

"The girls all share a few bathrooms. There is a long line in the dormitory and it would be better to drive you. If this is okay?" Li replied.

"Can you come with me?" Sue whispered to Daniel.

He nodded quickly. "Of course."

She was pleased she didn't have to persuade him to go along.

They all arranged to meet up in an hour to eat dinner. Sue squirmed impatiently as the van bounced its way to the bathroom in town. The drive was more than ten minutes and on top of that, there was another checkpoint.

Crap!

The guard station wasn't like the previous one. It was less thorough and intimidating, and well-armed Chinese in smart uniforms didn't man it, but instead it consisted of unshaven Chinese men in untucked shirts, smoking cigarettes. Their driver and a guard exchanged a few words and the guard chuckled and waved them through. He winked at Sue as they drove by.

The driver brought them to a modest hotel, but she would have settled for a port-a-potty in the middle of the road. Sue ran into the hotel.

She caught up to Daniel waiting nearby.

"Thank you for coming with me and, for future reference, I don't mind a squatter."

He laughed and put his arm around her shoulder. "I'm proud of the work you've done here."

"Thank you."

"Very driven."

She raised her eyebrows and frowned.

"In a good way." He laughed, lowering his hand on her back to guide her. "Let's go find our driver."

They walked up to the van and Sue saw a man with a strange snake-like tattoo on the back of his neck turn down an alley.

The van was leaning to one side. "This can't be good," Sue said.

Their driver, a Chinese man with a gap in his smile and a bad cowlick, pulled Daniel over to the front of the van and pointed at the tire.

"Flat." Daniel looked at the deflated tire and crossed his arms.

"Well, it looks like we'll be dining at this village. Does Li know where we're at?"

The cowlick driver's cell phone rang and he answered it. Sue couldn't understand what he was saying but he handed the phone to Daniel.

Daniel nodded as he listened. "Okay, Li, no problem. Don't worry, we'll be fine."

Daniel hung up and handed the cell back to the driver.

"Is everything okay?" Sue asked.

"Yes, that was Li. She said they would come to meet us in a few hours with another van. She said we should stay close to the hotel and they'll find us.

We have some time, should we go for a walk?" Daniel raised his eyebrows and grinned an all teeth smile.

"Yes, I'd like that." Sue smiled back. "A walk would be fun before eating."

They strolled from one side of the street to the other, looking at the shops. They explored the labyrinthine streets, walking past the open-air stalls and noodle restaurants. The smell of chou doufo, a form of stinky, fermented tofu filled the early evening market air. The streets were alive with people – buying, selling, walking, working, and just hanging out.

While strolling the shaded alleys several young children in brightly-colored clothing kept staring at Sue. Daniel took out his camera and gestured for them to stand by her. "Come here for a photo."

Sue knew they probably didn't understand the language but they came close and stood next to her.

"Smile," she said.

Daniel took a few photos. Most of the kids weren't smiling, but instead were looking at Sue. One young girl touched Sue's hair.

"You're probably the first blonde haired person they've seen."

"Then why don't you show them the pictures on your camera screen?"

"Good idea." Daniel showed them the digital photos he had just taken. The kids giggled at the camera, surprise and awe written on their faces. They pointed at Sue and at his camera and jumped up and down. Daniel took more photos. They continued on their way, but after a few minutes, a dozen children were following them. The children begged them, not for money, but for photographs, instead.

Sue smiled approvingly as she watched Daniel. He patted their heads and said a few words to them in Mandarin. They were chattering, grinning, and laughing with him. Just like that, Daniel had made friends with a swarm of foreign children. She found herself wondering what her own children would think of him.

"They love having their pictures taken and then seeing it on the screen."

"I can see that." Sue watched as more and more kids showed

up to see the digital photos. It got to the point where they had to outrun the kids. Whenever they stopped, the children would grab at them and pull on their arms. Daniel handled them quite well, despite the congregating masses.

"Daniel, you're a pied piper, if there ever was one." They ran through the streets, laughing and exhausted.

Sue caught a glimpse of a Chinese man every so often. Was he the man she saw back by their van? When he turned around, she saw a snake tattoo winding up the back of his neck ending at the base of his bald head. She was sure it was the man by the van. He seemed out of place in the alley, but he was always there. It seemed like he was trailing them, but at a safe distance. Sue thought maybe it was a good thing children surrounded them wherever they went. She didn't like the looks of him.

A motorcycle pulled up beside the tattooed man. She heard him yell at the driver in Chinese and, hopping on the back, they sped out of sight.

Scurrying through the alleys in the Chinese town, Sue had a fleeting thought of the filthy alley where she had met Rospi to rent Hollis the hawk. The foreign alley they roamed was as dingy, but she felt safe. Daniel's presence made her feel safe.

"Everything okay?" Daniel asked.

"Yes, just hungry." She dismissed her concerns and hoped Daniel didn't see the dark shadow that crossed her eyes.

Sue was exhausted when they found their way back to the hotel and collapsed at a table within sight of their crippled van. "I want to keep an eye on the driver and the van," Daniel said. If he was nervous about their welfare, he didn't show it to Sue.

They sat at the table on the busy street next to the hotel and waited for their escorts.

A tired-looking old man walked past, dressed in a blue Mao jacket and cap with a bamboo pole across his shoulders, carrying a bundle on either end. Sue whispered to Daniel across the table.

"For me this image . . ." she pointed at the man as he walked by, "captures how I had envisioned China. But this doesn't seem to be the norm here, the city is more modern than I thought."

"Yes, he is the exception now. A lot has changed over the past ten years."

106

Several minutes later, a whole fish was staring from a plate on their table.

"You can have the honors." He gestured toward the steamed fish.

A few evenings ago, while they dined at a restaurant in Hong Kong they had chosen their dinner from live fish swimming in a tank. Sue had balked at the sight of an entire cooked fish lying on the plate staring directly at her, until Daniel had explained a fish served whole was a symbol of prosperity and it was always pointed toward the guest of honor.

Sue crinkled up her nose, took her chopsticks and picked at the fish, like a kid poking holes in Play-Doh.

"No, the best part is here, right behind the eye."

He positioned his strong hand over hers holding the chopstick, pulling at the delicate meat located behind the eyeball and placing the fish in her mouth. She felt her cheeks flushed from the simple but ever so erotic gesture.

"Mmmmm," Sue reluctantly swallowed the slippery fish meat, without chewing. She didn't enjoy the fish, but she liked the touch of his hand on hers.

"You didn't even take a bite, you just swallowed it." He poked her with his chopstick.

"I know you've told me that it is an honor to take the most delicate piece behind the eye of the Yu. Today I am wishing for prosperity for the coming holiday season for Logan Designs."

He scooped up another piece of fish from the eye area, feeding it to her.

"And it is believed eating fish helps your wishes come true in the year to come."

She smiled. "This is a nice, un-programmed two-hour intermission."

"We deserve a break. You've worked hard. Are you satisfied with the designs?"

"I'm ecstatic with them and ready to take these versions back to Texas with me."

Daniel considered Sue for a long second. She saw something in his eyes, a mixture of happiness and something else too. For a second, she thought she saw sadness, just a flicker, like a flutter of a hummingbird wing.

"I admire your passion and what you've achieved with Logan Designs. I think your plans for the future with the company are right on."

"Thank you, Daniel. Coming from you, that means a lot."

He raised his water bottle to hers. "As the Chinese proverb says, a journey of a thousand miles starts with the first step."

Sue tapped her bottle to his. "You just gotta start somewhere."

She felt a bond had formed between them. The two Americans.

TWENTY-TWO
Remote China

FENG MANEUVERED his truck along the gravel road, headed to his last stop. He was traveling to a small plant situated in Fuzhou, a thousand kilometers north of the Luobu Qiau bridge leading to China's economic zone. Established six years earlier, the plant was in an undisclosed region of the city with few inhabitants. The plant produced a fabric tag stamped with a US toy registration number.

When he had started the delivery to the plant, Feng's supervisor told him that every stuffed toy manufactured bore two tags. Each toy carried a printed-paper tag that was generally suspended from the ear of an animal or under the arm of a doll, usually connected with a plastic fastener. A second tag, this one fabric, was sewn into a seam of the tail area and couldn't be removed without tearing the toy. This tag was called a tush or butt tag, and was required by US laws. It incorporated the manufacturing location, toy contents and a registration number. Yorkston Toys used the tush tag to include the name of the stuffed animal and a unique serial number.

The small, secluded building's sole purpose was to manufacture the Yorkston tush tags.

Feng knew that most days the tag plant saw only four people; rarely did they receive unsolicited guests. The first visitor was the manager, Xu Guan who guarded and oversaw the workshop.

109

He lived at the factory and could operate the entire production without staff. Another approved employee was the sole female, Mei Li. Feng smiled when he thought of her. She loaded and unloaded the printing apparatus. Occasionally a representative from Yorkston, Pete Shapiro, their scientist, was welcomed there. The last visitor welcomed at the plant was Feng, the muscular deliveryman for the Lo He Dye Chemical Company.

He had heard that bringing everything together in this plant was part of the secret to an American toy company's success. He had seen the toys at the other plant and he didn't understand how the Americans could be crazy over a toy that cost pennies to make.

Feng's oversized rickety truck rambled by the front of the building and around the side, coming to a rest at the back door. On the side of the truck painted in red Chinese characters was *Lo He Dye Chemical Co.*

Feng, wearing a filthy sweat stained undershirt and a baseball cap, got out of the truck and began to unload a large iron drum. He shoved the metal drum and his bicep muscles bulged like a comic book superhero sporting balloon arms.

Xu Guan, the plant manager, exited the warehouse, and examined Feng's identification badge. Every trip for the last five years, Xu Guan had ceremonially inspected Feng's badge to make sure he wasn't intruding on Xu Guan's jurisdiction. Xu Guan lit a cigarette, taking a long drag, and watched Feng unload.

"Feng, do you need the forklift?" Xu Guan asked.

"No. I only have one barrel of DMCY today."

DMCY was the chemical acronym for a combination of dicyandiamide, mordant, and a red dye called cyanurainide. The majority of the dye was made from dicyandiamide, a white, crystalline powder. The exact molecular formula was known by a few of the Chinese employees at Lo He Dye and the Yorkston chemist, Pete Shapiro. Feng knew the Chinese plant had nicknamed it Flo Glow, for its fluorescent, holographic composition. At this plant, the DMCY was combined with a coating gel that contained dichromate.

"How is the printing today?" Feng carefully rolled the drum onto the two-wheeled dolly. The tailgate lift let out a mechanical groan as Feng lowered the heavy drum to the ground. His Popeye arms bulged from his sleeveless shirt as he flipped the dolly upright and maneuvered it through the dirt path to the back door marked Delivery Entrance.

Once inside the building, Feng rolled the drum over to the designated area in the warehouse. He kept looking over his shoulder glancing back into the adjoining workroom beyond, hoping to get a glimpse of Mei Li.

Xu Guan followed him.

"We have to print four dozen pallets of the label sheets by Friday, in order to get them to the cutters and seamstresses by Monday. This high production has me concerned. Mei Li and I need to run the machine all night this week. I hope this'll be enough dye to last us. Do you think you could bring us one more barrel?" Xu Guan asked.

"You know the rules," Feng said.

The machine used to print the fabric tush labels housed in the unmarked building was over 100 kilometers from the Lo He Dye Chemical Co in Tianjen, where the dye was made.

Feng secured the drum. He walked into the other room hoping to get a peek at Mei Li.

Mei Li, the only other employee in the plant that day was working at the tag apparatus. The young Asian woman, who had a face as perfect as a vase of flowers and breasts the size of pink grapefruits, smiled and then blushed at Feng. She was wearing a crimson and white flowered kimono and was bent over the machine.

Feng often wondered if the special dye contained pheromones. Whenever he came to the secluded plant, the smells of the ink positively caused an attraction to this petite lady. It seemed she always wore her prettiest kimono on the days he delivered the dye. He liked the way her dress molded to her soft skin. His hot gaze rested on her for a few seconds.

Feng waved at Mei Li. She nodded her head at him, blushed again. There was nothing but warmth and welcoming in her pale, flower-like face as she smiled as him. She quickly returned to her work, bending over the printing apparatus.

"When are you going to get together with her?" Xu Guan stood behind Feng.

"I can't. We live so far apart and I have my family commitments." Feng thought of his elderly parents.

"You've known her for years. You should make a move."

She fed several sheets of fabric into the tag printer, which resembled a ten-armed octopus.

"I gotta get going. I have a tight schedule." Feng waved and winked at Mei Li.

He tossed the empty dolly in his truck. He drove onto the dirt road, under the watchful eye of Xu Guan.

He looked out his rearview mirror at the dust kicked up from the dirt. The truck's back window displayed a small orange decal in the right hand corner with the Chinese symbol *du*.

Du meant poison.

Du meant death.

TWENTY-THREE
Hong Kong

"THIS IS IT DANIEL, time for me to leave," Sue said. There was a sad tone to her comment.

Sue was right. The Logan work was complete, and Daniel stood heavy hearted at the airport as he saw her off. He still had other clients to work with and, without Sue there, it would be a lonely week in China.

Daniel studied her, as they stood together at the airport. He was treading on perilous ground. In the last week, he knew he came dangerously close to losing his head over this woman and wanting to get intimate with her. Had he crossed the business line on several occasions? They had continued to keep a safe personal distance between them, even after their kiss a few nights ago.

Maybe when we aren't working together, we could pursue more.

He hoped. Or was it the intoxicating combination of this beautiful, smart women and the exotic location? He knew he had to see her again.

"I'll see you in Boston in a few months for the Boston Toy Show, right?"

"Yes, I'll see you there." Sue hugged Daniel at the airport.

"I couldn't have done this without you. When I get back to Texas I plan on ordering the additional containers of the M Kids plush based on the new costs and the feedback from the reps at the summer gift shows. This is the first time I've ordered product from China. All my other products are made in the US. The dolls and my puzzles will be my first import and I have you to thank for the help."

"You have an amazing cost on the plush kids." He handed her a document. Damn, he didn't want to leave the strong and idealistic woman at his side, but it was time.

She took the paper. "What's this?"

"This is the cost breakdown on the products we worked on. I'll email you the spreadsheet I used to calculate this. I'm glad we made the trip to the manufacturing plants."

Sue slipped the paper into her briefcase. They hugged one more time and when she turned her head toward him, Daniel kissed her. She returned the kiss.

Daniel felt an ache inside. They had connected in so many ways on this trip. They shared a bond through the creativity and he hated to let her go. He smiled at her as she looked up into his eyes.

"Thank you for everything. I'll miss you!" She turned to walk away.

"See you in Boston!" He yelled to her.

Daniel had hoped their meeting would be more than a business meeting. She sure was much more than he had imagined. He was impressed with her hard work and dedication, but that wasn't all that attracted him to Sue.

Daniel waved one last time as she walked toward her gate.

TWENTY-FOUR

SUE ARRIVED AT HER GATE just in time to board.

God, he is so handsome and awesome to be with.

She settled in her seat, and reached into her briefcase to look at the spreadsheet Daniel had given her. When she pulled out his document from her side flap, an envelope fell onto the floor.

She held the envelope in her hand and bowed her head. It was sealed but didn't look ready for mailing. No address. No stamp. It felt empty. She held it up to the light and saw the outline of a small slip of paper inside. She ripped the envelope open at the side and shook out a half sheet of ecru stationary paper, folded up the middle. She looked behind her and saw all her seatmates, reading magazines or sleeping. She glanced at the front of the plane. The flight attendant was stacking small dishes filled with nuts on gray trays. Slowly she unfolded the paper. Typed in black block letters were six sentences:

YOUR NEW DESIGNS WILL BE STOLEN. YOUR COMPANY WILL BE DESTROYED. WE KNOW EVERYTHING. YOU ARE GOING TO BE INVOLVED IN A LEGAL BATTLE. YOU WILL BE ASKED TO STOP SELLING YOUR CATALOG. YOU WON'T WIN.

What?

The letter rocked her. It was only five days since the first

115

copies of the catalog had rolled off the presses. The timing couldn't be worse.

Who sent this to me? How did it wind up in my briefcase? Did Daniel know about it? Did he leave it for me to find?

If this was true, she would need Bruce Barrows, her lawyer, to read it.

Sue groaned a heavy sigh. Shock and racing emotions engulfed her. She had to swallow rapidly to keep down the nausea building in the pit of her stomach.

Sue reached for her cell phone. Should she call her lawyer first? The printer? Mary Jo? Daniel? Then she realized it was too late, the doors to the plane had closed.

Sue didn't look out the window. She was uncomfortably aware that she was going to be isolated for seventeen hours with her thoughts.

She opened the note and was teary as she reread every word. She turned it over, searching for any sign of who may have sent it. Nothing.

Sue tightened her seatbelt. "Excuse me," she said to the flight attendant to get her attention.

"Yes ma'am?"

"Can I get a Scotch?"

She smiled at Sue and nodded. She returned quickly with a small glass filled halfway with butterscotch colored liquid, no ice. "Don't worry, the captain is known for smooth take-offs." She winked at Sue.

Sue felt the color drained from her face. She half nodded at her and dumped the liquor into her mouth. The burn at the back of her throat was punishing.

The flight attendant returned for the empty glass. "Can I get you a blanket, Miss?" she asked.

"Huh?" Sue looked at her, not listening.

"Is there anything else I can do, ma'am? A blanket?"

"No, um, a blanket, um, yes, that would be fine."

She was shaking. She felt threatened and cornered, and anger built up inside of her. Tiny shiver spasms besieged her.

Who the hell would be doing this? Daniel? God no. Please

don't let it be Daniel. Who else could've put this letter in my briefcase?

She rubbed her forehead. The sudden flash of anger on her face would've stopped a charging bull. Daniel wouldn't spend the last ten days with her and then tell her anonymously that someone was out to steal her ideas. Would he? Didn't he try to warn her one evening at the Irish Pub that such things are prevalent in manufacturing? Who would admit that there is a company out there spying on her and waiting to steal her designs?

Well, whoever makes it to market first wins.

But who? Who wanted to steal one of her products? Who wanted to destroy the company she had created? She had so many questions for her lawyers.

She read the letter again and pounded her fist on the tray in front of her.

"Shit," she said. Sue rarely, if ever, resorted to expletives. She thought it was inappropriate as an executive of a multimillion-dollar company, but she had to swallow some particularly ripe ones.

She decided to focus her built-up rage in more fruitful directions.

I'll be damned if someone is threatening me. We'll see who is first to get the product to market.

She opened her laptop and began filling out the purchase order request for the containers of stuffed dolls. She would meet with her banker first thing Wednesday morning to finalize the draws against her line of credit. She wouldn't wait to see the results from the next gift shows before ordering the plush.

She worked the remainder of the day and well into the evening, skipping both the lunch and dinner meals. By the time the plane landed in Texas, she was girded for battle.

TWENTY-FIVE
Dallas
Law Offices of Triggs and Patterson

THE RECORD-BREAKING HEAT made the commute from the parking lot to her lawyer's office atrocious. It had been 105 degrees when Sue arrived from Hong Kong, continuing to rise to 110. The famous Texas wind hit Sue like a hot oven opening in her face.

For the fourth time, she checked to make sure she had the letter from China. She kept it with another, similar, letter Logan had received last week while she was in China. Her dad had given it to her when she returned. He said he had been afraid to discuss it with her because he didn't want to inhibit her trip and her inspiration. "I admire how your creativity flows from you like water. And there's no way I was going to let a prank letter slow that process."

The second letter was almost identical to the first with the exception of a threat for her to not "waste her time" on her product because in the end she would lose her market to someone else.

She had been speechless when her dad had showed it to her. He had hardly waited fifteen minutes after the driver dropped her off at the house. She was hugging the kids when he asked them to go wait in the family room while he talked to their mother.

She was startled after reading the second letter, dropping the

118

china doll she had bought for Maddie. Thankfully, her father had caught the doll before it smashed to smithereens.

There was no way Daniel could've mailed this letter to Logan because he was in China when it was date stamped, and the postmark was from Texas, not from Georgia. She supposed he could've asked someone to mail it, but it still didn't make sense.

The threats in the letters made her blood run cold.

She entered the Law Offices of Triggs and Patterson where her lawyer, Bruce Barrows was waiting in the lobby. He escorted her to the conference room.

Matthew Triggs, one of the partners, hurried in to greet her. He was a tall, thin man, with a dark complexion and an impulsive air about him.

"Sue, this is Matthew Triggs," Bruce said.

"We've not met yet." Matthew shook her hand firmly.

"I don't think we have, in all my meetings with this law firm. Nice to meet you," Sue said.

"Please sit down." He pulled out one of the high-back leather chairs for Sue, grinning the whole time. He poured her a glass of water from a silver pitcher covered with condensation droplets, placing it on a brass coaster in front of her.

"Thank you." Sue sank into the chair.

"Let me see these letters."

Sue pulled out the two ecru letters, holding them by the corners as if they were laced with poison.

She handed them both to Matthew. The two lawyers examined the letters.

"Ms. Logan," Matthew began.

"Sue," she said.

"Okay, Sue, first off, until there is any legal evidence that these are true statements about stealing designs, there is no reason to panic. And second, Yorkston is the only company that can sue you on the catalog."

"But how can this be? There are lots of companies who create catalogs using pictures of Yorkston's line. Why aren't they being sued?"

"It's up to Yorkston to decide who to sue. We've researched

and there are a few suits here and there."

"What were the suits?"

" We did come up with a few cases recently filed in the courts of Indiana where they sued a few web sites. Those sites were forced to shut down," Matthew said.

Sue felt a chill run down her spine. Matthew was talking about a giant company. They could squash her small enterprise, like a smashed bug on a headlight.

"Our firm stands behind our original decision that the catalog is used for illustrations that collectors can refer to and it consists of photographs of the Yorkston toys, plus commentary. We refer to this as permitted use of copyright elements, a productive use as distinct from simply a reproductive one. We call this fair use," he said confidently.

Sue rolled her eyes and squirmed in her chair.

Matthew went on to explain some of the lawsuits filed recently by Yorkston Inc. "I'm not saying that every lawsuit was frivolous . . . but a few of them are just plain bullying. We've reached out to some of the lawyers of the defendants, but many of the companies representing themselves have fallen off the face of the earth—"

"Matthew, I've so much invested in the product right now. I moved forward based on your firm's advice on how to cover the copyrighted material and based on your communications with Yorkston several years ago."

"The fifth edition, you said it is in print now, correct?"

"Yes. It went to press over a week ago. The pallets are at the printers ready to ship to us. We'll have a warehouse full of the product." Sue sighed. "I need to know, will I be able to sell the catalogues or not?"

Bruce bounced out of his chair and walked around. "Okay, so we just take this as a practical joke for now. Sue, maybe it's from one of your competitors. Or who knows, maybe just some random jokester. In any case, we won't be alarmed. Right?" Bruce said as he paced.

"I guess I'm okay with that." It didn't explain how the envelope got in her briefcase. "I am still concerned . . . but you're the lawyers. I'm just a creator." She hesitated, adding, "What about the second part of the letters, referring to someone out to steal our product ideas? How do we protect from that? After my trip to China, I ordered product and bought half a dozen containers."

Matthew opened up his portfolio, pulling out several documents. He handed them to Sue. Bruce returned to his chair.

"These are your trademark and patents on your products. This notebook is filled with all of the filings we've submitted on behalf of Logan to the United States Patent and Trademark Office."

Sue saw her drawings of the Millennium Kids, her puzzles and several games. She glanced through the official filings of her products.

"I'm glad to see my money for copyrighting all of my products went to good use." Sue felt somewhat relieved. "Is there a way for people to view all the new filings at the patent offices?"

"Of course, this is public record once filed. Last year the Patents and Trademark Office issued over a hundred and fifty thousand patents and registered over one hundred thousand trademarks. But your products are all copyrighted," Matthew said.

Sue watched her young, collegiate-looking lawyer, Bruce Barrows. He seemed pleased with his superior handling her. He kept bouncing out of his chair like it was made of rubber bands, but he kept quiet.

"But is it possible to find the patent to copy?" Sue asked.

"Sure, it's possible. If someone knew what they were doing, they could spend time in Washington digging through the records in the Jefferson building. You can research the patents you're looking for. A lot of products are developed in research and development departments of large organizations, but it is also the independent inventors, like yourself, who discovered great products. The PTO works hard to make sure that the agency has specialized support for new inventors. You've got great ideas and we've protected them the best we can."

Sue grinned. Matthew was good. He had hit a soft spot. "I have photos of the newly completed products." Sue handed him a thick manila envelope.

"Thanks. Bruce, make sure these get filed with the appropriate offices. We still need to get your stuffed toy registration number. Do you have a sample yet of the fillings?"

"Not yet. Shuhua Toys are sending me a dozen samples. They should arrive any day now."

They spent the next forty-five minutes going through some of the cases they had found. Bruce picked up a pencil, twirling it in his fingers before jotting down something on the pad in his portfolio. That was Sue's cue. He had logged another hour. Ca-ching, goes the cash register.

"Gentlemen, thank you both for the time today. I know you are busy, and seeing me on such short notice is appreciated." She stood up, uncomfortably aware of the price per hour this session had cost her. Nevertheless, this meeting gave her peace of mind. "Thanks again, both of you. I have to run. I have a meeting at the printers and then I need to pick up my kids."

Sue walked out into the blazing Texas sun. Slipping into the driver's seat of her car, she prayed quietly.

I hope that it was only a prank.

After all, she doubted she was even a ping on the toy giant's radar. It smelled like a malicious trick, but it was a warning to keep on her toes.

TWENTY-SIX
Francis, Texas

SUE WAS AT LUNCH with several of the Dallas manufacturer reps from the World Trade Center discussing the new products when Mary Jo called on her cell phone.

"Sue, there's a Deputy Sheriff here, looking for you," Mary Jo said. She lowered her voice to a whisper. "He said he has important papers for you."

"Oh my gosh." Sue jumped up from the table and rushed to the ladies' room. She took a quick look under the stalls. The bathroom was empty, thank goodness. "Can you put him on?"

She heard Mary Jo talking to someone.

"Yep, ma'am, this is Deputy Haralson," a husky southern voice declared.

"Can I help you?"

"Are you Sue Logan, president of Logan Designs Inc?"

"Yes, yes, this is she."

"Ms. Logan, I'm serving you papers in a lawsuit."

"What? What's it for?" This was unchartered territory for her. She hadn't had so much as a traffic violation in the last ten years. Her hand began to shake.

"It's set in the Ninth District Court in the Northern District of Indiana by Judge Barrington and the case is styled; Yorkston Toys vs. Logan Designs. That's you, right?"

"Yes." Her voice wasn't so firm and she was outwardly trembling. She gasped into the phone.

Oh my God.

"Miss, are you going to be back here soon so I can properly serve you?"

Sue leaned against the sink in the bathroom, her reflection in the mirror showed tears welding up on the edges of her long lashes. She let out a small sob and a sniffle, unaware she was still holding the phone to her mouth.

"Uh, Ms. Logan, are you okay?"

"Yes, yes. I, I don't understand." Her voice came out shaky as she struggled for a breath.

"Ma'am, you are the president of the company, right?" he asked in a softer voice.

"Yes, I'm sorry, that's me." She regained her composure. "I'll be back to the office in fifteen minutes."

"Okay, I reckon I can wait that long. And Miz . . . ."

"Yes," Sue whispered.

"If it's any consolation, you ain't nobody until you've been sued."

Sue hung up the phone. Great! She splashed water on her face and dried it off with a paper towel. She ignored the constricted feeling in her chest. She looked in the mirror. Mascara gummed her eyelashes. *Damn it! I'm not a weakling.*

She hurried to the table to grab her purse. Her shoulders slumped a little more than when she had left the table.

"I'm so sorry, something has come up. I've got to get back to my office."

She hoped none of them could see the giant lump sitting in the middle of her throat.

TWENTY-SEVEN

FOR THE SECOND TIME that week, Sue had an appointment with her lawyers. Even though it was early morning, the temperature was already eighty degrees, by noon it would be over one hundred.

She stood in her closet, shifting through hanger after hanger of dresses. She pulled out a blouse and slipped it on.

"Ugh," she said to her reflection in the mirror. She took off the blouse and added it to a pile accumulating on her floor. Selecting a dress, she yanked it off a hanger and squeezed it over her head.

"Dang." She tried in frustration to reach the zipper.

"Hi Mommy, do you want me to zip you up?" Elizabeth stood behind her in the bathroom.

"Sure, please."

"Why are you putting on a pretty dress again?" Elizabeth stepped on a stool and tugged at the zipper.

"I can get it from here." Sue finished dressing. "I have a meeting with my lawyers today. Do you like the dress?"

"I don't like you leaving again." Elizabeth pouted her lips.

"Yes, sorry baby. I go to work every day."

"When you go to work you come home happier. And I thought we were going to the park today."

"I know, babe. I did clear my calendar, but this lawyer meeting just came up."

125

"Pooey." Elizabeth tramped out of the closet.

"Grandma's here!" She heard Maddie yell from the kitchen.

She greeted her mom. Thelma was wearing her curly hair sans the bun today, like a q-tip, with her short fluffy white hair kinked over her head and her skinny stature.

"I want to watch *A Bug's Life*," Colt said.

Maddie wrinkled up her nose and held up her arms. *"No, ion ing!"*

"Lion King," Thelma corrected her.

Elizabeth came over to Sue. "Mom, can I watch *The Parent Trap* upstairs in the game room?"

"Okay, kiddos, quit all the video fuss, everyone scoot your hineys upstairs to get dressed, brush your teeth and make your beds. Then afterwards, Grandma can take you to rent the movie Willy Wonka and the Chocolate Factory!" The kids giggled and turned away. She heard Elizabeth say, "Willy Wonka?," with a bewildered look on her face.

"OK, Mom, what's bothering you?" Sue said when the kids left the room. "You look like a worry doll."

"Nothing darling."

"Come on." Sue walked over and put her hand on her mom's hand. "What's up?"

"Your dad and I are so worried about you, after you told us about your company being sued."

"It will be okay, Mom. I've got my lawyers on it." Sue gave her mom the widest smile because she didn't want her to know how the lawsuit worried her too.

Sixty minutes later, Sue was escorted to the conference room; her two lawyers, Bruce Barrows and Matthew Triggs greeted her warmly. A third man stood next to them.

"I'd like to introduce Carl Patterson," Matthew said.

She sized him up as they shook hands. Carl, an older man of medium height, had silver hair parted to the side and a tan leathery forehead, probably the results of many years on the golf course hatless in the Texas sun.

"I have a copy of the lawsuit. We'd like to go through some

126

options with you and then discuss our fee structure plan," Carl said.

"Do I have to quit selling the collector guides like the letter warned me? I can't yet. I just can't." She sank into the chair.

"We've prepared several responses, but our thinking is still, no, you don't have to stop production or shipments. We feel this is a start of an open communication with the Yorkston Company, and while we are in the process of defining the lawsuit you can continue with business as usual." Carl's bronze thick skin creased up like an old cowboy boot.

Sue was relieved to hear this, but was unconvinced this was what the Yorkston lawyers had in mind when they filed.

After thirty minutes, Matthew Triggs and Carl Patterson left the conference room.

"Jeez Bruce. How much did that meeting cost me? By my calculations, with two partners with their names on the door and an associate in the same meeting, I'd say probably eleven hundred dollars an hour."

"Yes, but we needed you to hear from the partners too."

"And I still can't believe you need a fifty thousand dollar retainer," Sue said, as she stared at the agreement. "You gave me an approval letter before moving forward with this project. I sat in this very conference room. Seems like bad advice now. And on top of that I have to pay you to defend me."

"We discussed that already. We have been communicating with Yorkston."

"Seems a one way conversation, since now you say they never really responded to all your letters and requests."

"We felt a non-response meant they just weren't interested in a licensing royalty. And so many others were using pictures of the Yorkston plush in their magazines and web sites." Bruce lowered his head and looked downward.

"I need you to get me and my company out of this." Sue glared at him.

"I'll try. Can we walk through the lawsuit?" Bruce said.

They spent close to an hour discussing every page of the suit and going through the Logan supporting documentation. Bruce talked while she wore a mommy glaze on her face, one that showed interest in what he was saying, but inside she was thinking about something else.

Back in her car, Sue turned off her cell phone and drove home in silence.

TWENTY-EIGHT

SUE ENTERED her offices, looked around and saw a yellow Post-it note from Mary Jo saying she was at lunch. Sue sat alone in her office on the loveseat, closing her eyes, her head buried in her hands.

"Sue, are you alright?" Mary Jo stood over Sue, looking concerned.

Sue hadn't heard Mary Jo come in. She slowly pushed herself straighter in the loveseat. "Yes, I'm fine. I'm just thinking about a new product idea," she lied.

"Not yet, girl. We need to get the M Kids out." Mary Jo smiled at Sue. "We have to get "C" to work first before any new products."

Sue turned up one corner of her mouth, but a full smile never came out. Mary Jo had nicknamed the M Kid functionality, just "C" because of the chip, chira fabric and Sue's pattern C."

"You look tired," Mary Jo said.

"The last couple of weeks have been trying and have vitiated my energy."

"I know. I know. With your trip to China and the letters. And what's with this lawsuit? Can Yorkston do that?"

"Well, they have. I tried to do the right thing and hired an attorney and now we're being sued. Go figure."

"I think you're being bullied."

129

Sue sat up straighter. She eyed the toy hawk roosting on top of her shelf, as he watched and waited. "What do you mean?"

"Yorkston has to know you're on to something, right? I mean, the World Trade Center reps talk and all."

Sue raised her eyebrows.

"I mean, they don't really know about 'C'," Mary Jo quickly added. "But they have to know you're up to a plush toy, right? So I figure, they send you mean letters threatening you, and then suing you to get you all busy with lawsuits and all."

"I know Nathanael can be ruthless. Bruce told me that Nathanael had his lawyers sue a charity website that mentioned the Yorkston angel toy as an auction item. Yorkston lawyers shut them down."

"See. Bullies."

"Shoot, I hate butting heads with them." Sue slumped further into the cushions, rubbing her temples.

"Don't worry about the catalogs. It'll work out."

"We need the catalog sales revenue to introduce the M Kids."

"Then let's keep shipping."

"Will you visit me in jail?" Sue stood up and walked over to her desk.

"You'll look good in an orange jumpsuit." Mary Jo grinned and left her office.

Sue sat, glancing around the office, blinking back tears. Her designs were scattered all over the shelves, floor, her desk and credenza. She had thousands of laborious hours invested in her company. Would she lose this battle or would her lawyers prevail?

Brick's hands were sweaty when he picked up his phone off the dashboard of the white windowless van. He scanned the parking lot – no sign of the Logan bitch or any of her employees. He flipped open his cell phone, dialed Anthony's number and grimaced. Voicemail again.

"Ya Anthony, it's Brick again. Can you return my calls? All three of them. I have something for ya. Call me back. I'm outside Logan's offices and I got some interesting surveillance that you'd like to hear about. Hell of a lead about the dolls."

130

TWENTY-NINE

"WHAT'S A SUMMARY JUDGEMENT?" Sue whispered into her cell. She was still lying in bed, not wanting to get up just yet. It was Saturday morning. She had wanted another hour of peace, but then Bruce called.

"Are you kidding me? So Yorkston gets to tell their story alone with only a judge? No jury? Some judge in Indiana making an incredulous decision that will affect my company in ways he can't imagine." She stared aimlessly around her bedroom.

"IT'S NOT JUST THE CATALOG AT STAKE !" Sue yelled into the phone. "I know. Okay. Keep me posted. Sorry, Bruce. Goodbye." She slammed the phone down.

She faintly heard the creaking sound of a door.

"Mommy. Are you awake?"

"Yes." She blushed as she turned to see Maddie in the doorway.

"Mommy, are you angry?"

"What sweetie? No. It's fine." Sue blushed deeper, embarrassed by her outburst. She rolled over to view the clock. "Oh my gosh. Look at that. It's nine a.m."

"Are you sick, Mommy?" Maddie asked.

"No. No, I overslept. I needed to sleep in." Sue looked at her youngest daughter with her china blue eyes and blonde ringlets. She could've easily been Sue's twin at an early age.

On Saturdays, Sue's dad usually took the kids to the local

131

pancake house for breakfast while she would go for a long run. It had become a tradition. It was her time alone.

Sue held Maddie's hand as she walked in the kitchen, searching for a cup of coffee.

"Mom, Granddaddy said you needed to rest. Are you okay?" Colt asked.

"Of course, I'm feeling great. Thanks for letting me sleep in."

Her children were playing with one of her new products; a puzzle and a spy game combined into one. She smiled— approvingly. "I bet I know where that goes." She pointed to a corner piece.

Maddie snatched it up.

"No fair," Colt yelled.

Wilford appeared restless. He hadn't smiled or greeted Sue when she came in the room. The sight of her dad's somber face said something was wrong. She knew him well enough to know he was bothered.

"What's up, Daddy?"

"You had a visitor this morning."

"Who?"

"I didn't want to worry you. I wanted you to sleep in," he whispered. "And they tried to serve you papers this morning. You're being sued."

"I know we're being sued. What are these papers? I already got them." Sue whispered back, combing her fingers through her bangs.

"You didn't hear me. *You* are being sued." He walked over to kitchen desk drawer and removed a card. You can call the processor. I told him you weren't home.

She sucked in air and slowly exhaled. "*I'm* being sued?"

She leaned over and read the card. "I . . . don't understand. Yorkston is suing me personally for what? The infringements? Where did he come from?" She bit down on a thumbnail.

Her dad smacked her hand out of her mouth. "Don't bite your nails."

Sue rolled her eyes. "Tell me what he said."

"When I got here this morning to take the kids to breakfast, a county deputy was in a marked sedan sitting in the cul-de-sac. As soon as he saw me, this man looking like Walker Texas Ranger himself got out of his car and came up to me. He asked if I was a Logan. I said yes. He asked me if you were here to sign for the papers."

"And you lied?"

"I didn't want to wake you."

"Good job, Daddy. But damn, they'll be back."

"Yep, you can count on it."

"Can Yorkston do that? I've never had this happen before. Can they sue *me*?" She reached for her cup of coffee, but couldn't bring herself to drink it. Stomach churning, she set it down.

"Hope not. That's why you need to call Bruce right away." He put his arms around her.

Her eyes pooled with tears. "Damn them!" Sue said loudly, pulling away from him.

"Oops, sorry kids." Sue said to her wide-eyed children sitting at the table.

"It's okay, Mom," Elizabeth said.

"I'm losing my patience with Yorkston — with their whole lawsuit escapade, for that matter," Sue said.

"I hope you have the right lawyers for this."

"Me too, Dad." She rubbed her forehead. "I need an aspirin. I feel like someone has just clobbered me over the head with a baseball bat, then turned around and smacked it against my gut."

"Come on, I'll get you some."

"I hope I can swallow it over this lump in my throat."

"Here." Wilford handed her a glass of water and two aspirins he had retrieved from the cabinet.

"Thanks. How long do you think the deputy was sitting out front? Did my neighbors see him? This is harassment. The Yorkston Company is just trying to intimidate me. Those dirty bastards!"

"I'm pretty sure no one saw him. It was early," Wilford said in a somewhat, less-than-reassuring note.

"Daddy?"

"Okay, okay, maybe I did see that nosy Mr. Nelson next door walking his dog. It looked like his terrier had already done its morning business. The mutt was anxious to get back to the air-conditioned house while that nosy SOB Nelson stood around."

"Damn it!"

"Yep, he gave me a wave and a concerned nod 'good mornin'' keeping one nosy eye on the patrol car."

"Oh great. The whole neighborhood will know by sunset. That's all we need is for the kids to go to out to play and hear rumors that the police were waiting for their mom this morning. I can't have them showing up in our neighborhood! They can't do that? Can they?"

"Sweetie, it wasn't the police, it was a county deputy. People probably see it all the time." He tried reassuring her.

"Not in *this* neighborhood, they don't!" She shouted swinging around to see Elizabeth watching them.

"Mommy, can we watch videos?" she asked in quiet voice.

"No, you can NOT watch videos!" Sue threw the card on the counter.

"Sorry." Elizabeth's lower lip jutted out with a quiver.

"It's okay, sweetheart." Wilford intervened, placing his hand on Elizabeth's shoulder while abruptly turning his back to Sue.

Sue gave her dad a dismissive look. Having an argument right now wouldn't solve anything. It never did.

Sue walked out of the room to calm down. She had been so damn jumpy this past week ever since the letters and now the lawsuits.

It took her a few minutes to calm down enough to call her attorneys. Sue talked to Bruce and they agreed to meet first thing Monday. Carl was out of town, and the other lawyers were at their lake houses.

Bruce hadn't reassured Sue as easily this time.

THIRTY
Sunday Night
The Logan Residence

"I'LL RACE YOU HOME," Sue said to Colt. The two were returning from a friend's house after a birthday party. It had been a nice break for Sue to get away from the lawsuit chaos for a few hours.

"I like your sword and dagger tattoo." She was glad Colt had decided against the pirate skull-and-crossbones, but was disappointed when he picked the temporary tattoo he now wore on his bicep, but she knew it would soon be gone with the help of soap and water. Face painting was still a favorite activity at the girls' parties, but at the boys' parties, temporary tats were the rage.

He grinned at her, and pumped up his arm, flexing the blades.

She ruffled his hair, looking up at the expansive, moonless summer night sky. It was as clear as she'd ever seen, full of stars illuminating the sky.

"Look up, Colt. There are so many stars visible tonight; it hardly seems possible there could be room to fit any more."

Colt giggled as he skipped down the sidewalk. "How many stars do you think are up there, Mama?"

She beamed. "A lot, baby."

"Do you think Dad is riding on one of the stars, looking down at us?"

135

"I think he's always watching, protecting us."

"Me too." He placed his little hand in hers.

She smiled at him and swung her hand up, swinging his with it. She stopped abruptly, her back stiffened. She stood frozen, her eyes focused straight ahead toward their house.

Colt stopped, following her gaze. "Cool!"

"What in the world—"

"Mommy, who's at our house?"

She let go of Colt's hand. She didn't answer, taking off in a run down the sidewalk, her mind racing as she ran toward home.

They both arrived in front of their sweeping circular driveway at the same time. A white stretch limousine was parked in front of her house. Sue glanced in the dark windows as they proceeded to their driveway – the car was empty. Not even a driver.

"Who could be—" she started to say something but stopped, following her son up the front porch.

Sue walked inside, out of breath and sweaty, and froze in the foyer. Two men in suits lounged in the formal living room, in conversation with her father, all holding glasses of iced tea trimmed with lemons. Their conversations were low and strained.

They stood up as Sue entered. One of the men was tall, thin with spikey gray hair; the other was short, stout, wearing oversized dark glasses that kept sliding off his nose, revealing red marks.

"Ms. Logan, sorry for the late night interruption, I'm Cecil Pennington. I represent a group of investors interested in your company." He towered over Sue as he extended his hand. He was tall, very tall. He had to be close to seven feet. His crumpled suit and lengthy arms reminded her of a scarecrow.

She hesitated, and instinctively tensed, but shook his hand firmly. It was cold from holding the iced tea glass. Her eyes scanned the foyer to make sure Colt had wandered off. No doubt, he had joined his two sisters so he could gloat over his birthday goodie bag contents. She spotted a portly man through the window. He was in a black jacket, standing in her backyard staring at the golf course, smoking a cigarette . . . probably the limo driver.

The other man identified himself as Stuart Masson. He was stocky and tall but looked small next to Cecil Pennington.

136

Wilford stood up between his daughter and the seven-foot giant. "Sir, as I said, whatever your business is, it isn't appropriate to meet with Sue on a Sunday evening in her home. You should've called her assistant and scheduled an appointment." Wilford glared at the man.

Sue, on the same wavelength as her dad, stepped forward. She didn't want them in her home, but she was wondering what in hell this was about. "Please be seated. You should've made an appointment but, now that you're here, you have piqued my curiosity." She ushered them to sit back down.

"Thanks for listening," Cecil said. "We were admiring all your books and paintings."

"What brings you gentlemen out in the middle of a Sunday evening?" Sue asked, in no mood for casual conversation with these interlopers.

Cecil Pennington spoke first. "My colleague, Stuart Masson, and I work in our Indiana offices."

"Well, it looks like you've traveled a long distance. I have to say having you show up at my personal residence is a bit concerning to me. What could be so important about my company that you want to meet tonight?"

"We've been following the growth of Logan Designs and the success of several of your products in the marketplace. Our client, who wishes to remain anonymous at this time, would like to make you an offer to buy your company . . . a very attractive offer."

Wilford gave Sue a glance. She wiped the back of her neck under her long hair feeling drops of sweat. Her company was like a child to her. She had proudly watched it grow. Her employees were like family to her. She had an eerie feeling and stood up. "Wilford's right, this discussion can wait until Monday."

She brushed past the two men and opened a desk drawer, retrieving her business card. She handed it to the tall man. "This is my office number. You can call my assistant, Mary Jo, on Monday and schedule a meeting. But I'm sure you already know this." She looked at his cold and impersonal face.

He stood up, taking the card from her. "Ms. Logan, we respect that it is late in the evening, but it is imperative our client know if you are interested. Are you?"

She sighed. Wilford stood up. "This is bullshit! Sue is clearly not interested in discussing it this evening in her home. Now, gentlemen, please leave it. End of discussion. Let's call it an evening. She'll talk on Monday."

"Okay, we understand. This is a time-sensitive offer and, under the current circumstances, I would think Ms. Logan would want to hear our proposal."

"What do you mean by that?" Sue wanted to know if they knew about the lawsuits.

"The lawsuits are open to the public. We did our research."

"Then why would your client want to engage with my company under the *current circumstances?*"

"Just five minutes of your time."

His persistence winded her. "Look, Mr. . . ., Mr. . . . .," no one supplied the missing name, which put Sue at an immediate disadvantage. "No, not tonight." She took a deep breath and ran her tongue over her dry lips.

"I just want to talk about—" he never finished his sentence.

"I swear to God— just leave me alone!" Sue raised her voice and all three men were silent. His attitude had sparked off an uncharacteristic eruption of temper.

After an awkward silence, he said, "Okay, if you won't hear me out now, we'll get back with you tomorrow. Monday it is. Would you like us to leave the proposal, Ms. Logan?"

"Listen Mr. . . . ?"

"Pennington"

"Mr. Pennington, I wouldn't even entertain a business proposition until I know who I'm dealing with. I find it highly unusual that you won't disclose your client. *Under the circumstances,* this appears to be perilous ground you are treading on." She gave them a cold look. "I started this business from scratch and I've built quite a formidable presence in this marketplace. I recommend your client do his homework before assuming my business is even for sale."

The other man moved uncomfortably in his chair. Leaning forward, he crossed his arms in front of him. Good, she thought. I'd like to see them walk out of here with nothing to report back to their investor.

138

"Keep in mind that all businesses are for sale, for a price," Cecil Pennington said.

She would be damned if some scarecrow in a Hugo Boss suit was going to tell her that all businesses were for sale. *Well, not hers!* She spun around, staring into his beady dark eyes.

"Out, please. Just get out!" She pointed toward the door. Maybe it was her passion that gave her courage or maybe she had just had enough, but she just stared into his eyes with her deepest southern feminine charm and held back the retort that sprang to her lips.

"Okay, we're leaving. I'll just leave this behind."

If looks could kill, he would have dropped dead on the spot.

He opened the manila folder, hesitated before extracting several documents. "This gives the summary background and the recommendation for a buyout. The buyer wishes to reach a quiet, but amicable, decision." He laid it on the coffee table backing away like a seven-foot crawfish.

Sue didn't glance at the papers. "I don't appreciate this end run at my company."

"We do our best to take the company by surprise. That is our specialty." He gestured to the other man in the room.

The flat arrogance of his reply came close to unleashing Sue's simmering rage. She held it together by sheer effort of will. "This surprise approach is hardly a way to force my hand or to win my support."

"I know. Sorry for the intrusion." Cecil continued with a shrug of his shoulders and moved to place the rest of the documents down on the coffee table. He had the grace to look contrite for a second or two. The other man rose from his seat.

A smiled tugged at Cecil's lips. Looking anything but apologetic, he nodded toward the papers. "Please take a look at our offer. You may be surprised. We'll talk Monday."

Sue didn't see them out the front door. Despite the summer heat, her hands felt like she had just come in from a long walk in the cold.

THIRTY-ONE
Law offices of Triggs and Patterson

THE ELEVATOR DINGED and the door opened to the law offices of Triggs and Patterson. Sue sluggishly dragged herself into the familiar conference room, not even stopping at the lobby desk. The receptionist quickly summoned Bruce Barrows. Sue heard her whisper in the phone, as she plodded by, "She's here."

Bruce swung into the conference room less enthusiastically than the previous meetings. "Ms. Logan." He gave a nod toward her, placing on the table a stack of folders and computer printouts. "Have a seat, will you?" He straightened the knot in his navy striped tie and pulled out a chair.

Tired to the bone after three nights of shredded sleep, Sue sank into the leather chair creamy as if it was made of butter.

"I've prepared a summary of some statutes and case law that I thought would be of interest to you."

"Really?" Sue looked at Bruce with disgust.

"I'll explain. I don't expect you to read them. Just listen." He slid the stack of papers toward her.

Sue wore a crisp summer dress with a coordinating linen jacket the color of snow; her pearl earrings glistened like the beads of sweat forming on his forehead. "Okay, I'm listening."

"The complaint filed against your company is for alleged infringement for using the Yorkston toy photos and descriptions in your catalog."

"Infringement?"

"The Yorkston toys are copyrighted, so they have alleged that you are photographing a copyrighted product for financial gain—"

She couldn't bite her tongue, she interrupted Bruce before he could go on. "Bruce, you and I sat in *this* conference room several years ago and discussed the legalities of this product. *Your* firm rendered a letter stating the approval of my product. What has changed?"

She stood up and paced around the room. She felt a little queasy.

"It was an opinion letter. Nothing has changed. Yorkston allowed you to print edition after edition of the catalogs. We don't know why they have decided all of sudden to pursue a lawsuit.

But the fact that they have allowed you to sell this catalog knowingly for all these years plays well in a trial defense."

"A trial! Is that what we're talking about?" She shook the hair off her shoulder forcing it to fall straight down her back.

"Yes, we received the demand for a jury trial from the plaintiff, Yorkston Toys, this morning. An intellectual property lawsuit is no different from most lawsuits in that it begins with a complaint and concludes, if not settled or dismissed earlier, with a trial."

Sue slouched back into the chair. "I see." *Shit, a trial. How much will that cost me?*

"We have thirty days to answer the complaint." Bruce didn't look at her directly and glanced away often.

"Have you started our response?"

"Yes, and we've filed a motion for a change in venue to the Northern Texas district."

"What are the odds of winning that?"

"We feel very confident we can get the case moved. It is in our best interest to get the trial away from Indianapolis where the plaintiff is so well known. They'll oppose it for sure."

"Okay. But they're well-known in any jurisdiction," Sue said.

"Texas is better. It will save on your travel expense too. We have to charge for all the trips we would take to Indianapolis."

Sue turned her head toward him. "What about the lawsuit against me personally?"

Bruce twitched.

141

"Well?" She felt nauseated, as she waited for his response.

"My superiors have talked about this."

"And?"

"It is a tactic that Yorkston has used against you . . . a way to beat you down."

"I can see how this can be a beating both financially and mentally." Her voice was soft.

"It's like a boxing match with back and forth jabs."

Sue hung her head low. "Their gloves are coming off in this legal battle."

Bruce nodded, but didn't comment.

What else isn't he telling me? It felt like a boulder was crushing her.

"I have a feeling, based on the recent onslaught of legal filings, that I'm only in round one, and Yorkston is planning to chase me around the ring for fifteen more rounds. *Right?*"

"Yes. The lawsuit against you is a legal ploy that'll keep us busy responding to requests, but ultimately you, personally, won't be liable. We've filed all the appropriate paperwork to have you assign all copyright as the creator over to Logan Designs. Since your company is incorporated, you can't be held liable."

"Why would they waste money to pay lawyer fees to file against me personally? And won't the judge find this frivolous?"

"Unfortunately the plaintiff has deep pockets, so costs aren't a concern."

"Why do I feel like you aren't sharing everything?" Sue walked over to his side of the conference table, sensing his uneasiness as she moved closer to him. "Bruce, we've known each other for many years now, please lay it all out for me." He smelled like Old Spice, cologne her dad would wear. It smelled odd on this young lawyer.

He twisted in his chair. "The process we suspect Yorkston will take in the lawsuit will be a barrage of discovery motions."

She tilted her head to the right, uncertain of what he meant.

"Discovery is a request for information and it can be in the form of oral depositions of you and your employees and anyone that works or associates with you pertaining to the case. Discovery is used to bring all relevant information to the table so that both sides can prepare their cases." He paused letting it sink in.

"There's something else? Bruce, come on. Tell me everything, please? And don't sugarcoat it."

"Yorkston can deluge you with seemingly endless discovery requests and subpoenas. Your firm will be overwhelmed with the requests and you'll spend hours dealing with the lawsuit. We'll do our best to make it a smooth process. In the end, the plaintiff bears the burden of proving the infringement. We need to win."

"So what's our defense?" She felt like she was in a dream. *This is a nightmare.*

She watched Bruce as he talked. He didn't seem the confident lawyer she had met years ago.

"We have several affirmative defenses; suffice it to say that we have options in preparing our answers."

"Give me the bad news. What's the worst case scenario?"

"Worst case. We lose."

"What do I lose?"

"It could be a long, drawn out match. The Yorkston lawyers make a butt load of money with no risk at all. They get their dough, win or lose. Since they're paid by the hour, they've every incentive to drag out the proceedings in red tape and baseless legal proceedings."

"Uh-huh. What else?"

"You can lose the revenue produced from the product, plus have to pay their attorney fees and damages."

"Damages?" Her face felt flushed red from the neck up. "Damn it! Logan is helping their business. If it wasn't for our catalog, collectors wouldn't know a lot about the toys and their collectability. They should be paying me for boosting their business!" She glowed with anger. She was fragile and confused. "And we should be filing our own counter claims. I registered a patent on the numbering wristbands years ago," she said. "Bruce, you know I held patent registrations prior to starting my own business."

"I know. We've been through this. Our research had found the US patent office did have your design patent; however, the protection only lasted fourteen years from issuance."

"I know." She had been a young girl when it was registered. The design patent should've been renewed. It never was.

"We've discussed this type of pleading in the past."

"I know. It just irks me, because I was so close to that product and we had our patent, but I just didn't have the company and resources then to move it forward." Sue often wondered, when she first came to the law firm, why they didn't insist on reviewing her past intellectual property registrations.

A long silence followed her statement.

He shrugged. "I guess I don't see any advantage of bringing this up."

Why not? That question plagued Sue.

Twenty minutes later, Sue's high heels echoed across the parking lot concrete, crinkled jacket slung over her arm and the sun beating down on her. A punishing heat fell on her bare shoulders as she walked in the blazing sun. She ought to feel the embrace of the heat, but somehow the cold chill from her lawyer's office had followed her out of the building.

THIRTY-TWO
Sixteen Months before the Millennium
Francis TX

WILFORD LOCKES DUMPED another packet of white sugar into his iced tea. He twisted in his chair, spotting JC Bullock, his golfing buddy, weaving his way among the tables in the crowded dining room of the Francis Country Club.

"Great to see you Wilford," JC said, pulling his chair out.

"You too, JC." Wilford was genuinely glad to see JC.

A waiter appeared the instant JC spread a white napkin across his lap. "The usual gentlemen?"

"Yes," Wilford sighed reluctantly.

"You know it, man," JC grinned.

When the waiter was out of earshot, Wilford said to JC, "I still can't believe that my daughter's creativity might have just cost her countless years of legal battles." He shuddered at the thought.

"As your friend, and a fellow lawyer, I have to say Sue going into these legal dealings is like a medical doctor performing dental surgery. Sure, he's still a doctor, but he's doing an unfamiliar operation. She is a smart girl, but she is going to have her hands full with these lawsuits. Unchartered territory for her."

"This is bad stuff. I know I've knocked heads on more than one occasion with business folks who caused a stir in my otherwise peaceful existence, but shit and shiloh man, that was peanuts compared to Sue's monster, Yorkston." Wilford took a gulp of tea. *And what if she loses? She could lose her company, her livelihood,*

145

her future, my grandkids' future.

"This is a big deal and he's a big monster. I'm not sure our little town is a good backdrop for this voracious setting. This could be the biggest lawsuit this area has seen. I mean we live in a place where heads of cattle mow the town folk's lawns."

Wilford stared out the window. It was true; he had been born in the rural Texas town in the thirties. At the time, there were less than three hundred people living there, now the city limit sign boasted thirty thousand. His parents had moved to Francis from Scotland to farm.

"My pop used to say he remembered when the town was named Sorenson." Wilford recalled the story of the town's name. Ed Sorenson, a banker and a distant relative, had convinced the Lockes family members to move to Texas. The Sorenson farms once covered the area that downtown now occupied.

Stories were told that Ed Sorenson had promised to build a bank in the town if it was named after him. The town became Sorenson, but he never built the bank. Years later, the post office renamed the town because they thought Sorenson sounded too much like Sorsan, another town in a neighboring county.

The San Francisco railway system ran through the center of the city, so the name Francis stuck. The railway caused an influx of businesses; a number of cotton gins, grain elevators and home of the Farmers Coop Gin association.

"Your family reputation has a rich heritage here, Wilford. Does anyone you know have any leads into what's going on with these lawsuits?"

"Back when my family ran the depot store I was well connected."

A waiter placed a large burger in front of JC and a salad in front of Wilford.

"Wilford, this Yorkston group pursuing your Suzy is bad news." JC said, between bites of his oversized burger.

Wilford nodded, eyeing the burger. His wife had him on a new diet . . . no red meat. Last year's diet he could eat protein and no carbs. Blame it on that crazy Adkins guy. The good news on that diet was he could eat a stick of butter because it had no carbs, but the bad news was he couldn't eat popcorn. "What do you know about Yorkston?" Wilford said placing a forkful of salad in his mouth.

"My firm did some research and, honest to God, there are over thirteen thousand web sites that either mention or are devoted exclusively to the Yorkston stuffed toys. There are over twenty-six magazines, four collector books and a dozen periodicals. Jesus Christ, they'll probably end up as a children's cartoon series," JC said.

"So, what does this have to do with Sue's lawsuit?" Wilford didn't see the connection.

"Jesus, I just said there are over thirteen thousand other companies and individuals displaying photos of the toys." He chewed a large bite of his burger, leaving a drop of mayo on the corner of his lips. "Granted there's not a clear, crisp answer to fair use, and there are several guidelines her lawyers will need to present for their defense." JC chewed. "There's a list of the various purposes for which the reproduction of a particular work may be considered fair, such as criticism, comment, news, and let's see, teaching and there's research. You get the idea. The law sets out several factors to be considered in determining whether or not a particular use is fair." JC finished his burger, smiling as he munched the last bite. The mayo clung to the corner of his mouth, totally dispelling any attempt at maintaining a show of lawyerly credibility.

"This guy that runs Yorkston is richer than God or Gates. He is a successful businessman and investor, but he's no philanthropist and a most peculiar guy. He is one tough SOB. Wouldn't want him as my rival. What did your Suzy ever do to him?" JC said.

Wilford hated when JC called his daughter, Suzy. He busied himself by stirring another packet of sugar in his tea. Sue had stepped in a big brown pile of something squishy. "That is the question, my friend. Sue has never met him. Her lawyers have been communicating with their lawyers for years on the catalog."

"Well, there you go." He patted his mouth with a napkin. "Did her lawyers consider latches?"

"I haven't met with them yet." Wilford had no idea what his friend meant by "latches."

"Who's representing her?"

"Triggs & Patterson; her attorney is Bruce Barrows."

JC's lower lip jutted out and he shook his head. "Litigating cases involving Intellectual Property issues are complex. I know that outfit, and they ain't no IP lawyers. Barrows is a young pup just out of law school. The other two have no tact and are terrible supervising partners. I have bumped heads with them both many times. Won too." He flipped over the country club check and picked up a pen, signing his club number.

"Let me—" Wilford said.

"Save your money and get your daughter a real lawyer."

Wilford ignored the barb. "Who do you recommend?"

"Big Tex."

"Who?" Wilford knew he didn't hear him right. Big Tex was the name of the fifty-foot tall statue, the official mascot of the State Fair of Texas. Tex wore a size seventy cowboy boot and his hat was a whopping eighty-five gallon Stetson. He knew only one person in his past by that name.

"You remember Tex Thornton? He's the best IP lawyer in the state. Tell him JC sent you."

Twenty minutes later, Wilford exited Cotton Gin Road, his hands curled tight around the steering wheel as he maneuvered his Cadillac into Sue's neighborhood.

"Granddaddy!" the Logan kids shouted in unison.

"Hey munchkins, where's your mother?"

"She's in the study." Colt pointed toward Sue's home office.

Wilford walked into Sue's office. She sat with her back to him and the phone in her hand. He quietly walked over to the French doors leading out to the covered patio, the backyard and the golf course beyond. He saw a pile of dead crickets brushed against the windowsill. He made a note to hose them off later.

Sue hadn't noticed him. *God, she was beautiful. There isn't anything in this world he wouldn't do for his kids and his grandkids.* He didn't know how Sue did it. She managed a company and had a lot of love left for her kids and family. His little Suz had turned into an incredible woman. Now she was tied up in this mess. What had she done?

"Bruce, I did not receive a cease and desist letter. I only received the anonymous letter. This could've come from any kook out there," she said. "Uh, huh, right. Okay. If you think we can use it. Okay, thanks. Good-bye."

She hung up, swung around, and was startled to see her dad standing in front of her. "Hi Daddy," she said halfheartedly, sounding exhausted. "To what do I owe the honor of your presence today?"

"I just had lunch with JC. I wanted to stop by and talk to you about your case." He sat in a well-worn green leather chair across from her desk.

"How is JC?" Sue's eyes glowing affectionately toward her dad.

"He's great." Wilford felt tension between his shoulders.

"Mom will kill you if you had a burger."

"No. A salad with rubber chicken from the club." He picked up a knickknack off the side table toying with the glass sphere, fingering it idly as he talked. Sue watched with apprehension.

"Dad, what did you want to talk about?"

"I'd like you to change law firms."

"Why?" She pursed her lips.

"I know you've been with Bruce for four years—"

"Five," she interrupted.

"—but you need someone more knowledgeable in IP law. I've been told they aren't very experienced over at that freakin' firm. The whole bunch of them have no knowledge of copyright law."

He spun the glass sphere faster in his hand.

"Daddy, I know you have contacts, and I'm sure JC has his opinion of what we should and shouldn't do, but I really hate to switch horses now in midstream." Her eyes were focused on the little crystal paperweight in his hand. "You're going to drop it and break it to smithereens."

He set the paperweight down. "If it's costs you're worried about, your mom and I can help."

Her expression changed from annoyed to thoughtful. "It is a concern."

"How much have you spent already?"

"Thirty thousand."

149

"This can go on for years. Shit. Costing hundreds of thousands of dollars."

Sue bit the inside of her lower lip. "And I've invested every cent of Jonathan's life insurance money into the company."

"I know you have, sweetie."

"I need to get this over with so I can focus on my toy debut."

The kids laughing outside and jumping on the trampoline, made them both look toward the backyard.

"And your kids." Wilford said.

"I just don't know where else to turn for a respectable lawyer."

"I have a name. Will you call him, please?" He pulled a Swiss army knife from his pocket and began to clean his fingernails.

"OKAY, I know . . . I know . . . and I don't mean to sound ungrateful for all you and Mom have done. I'm not; it's just that . . . a . . . Jonathan always handled these matters."

She stopped staring at her dad, glancing at a framed photo of her and Jonathan on her desk. Tears welled in her crystal-blue eyes. His heart sank.

"Come on, it's going to be okay." He flipped the knife closed and slipped it into the pocket of his grey trousers.

"I don't know, for God's sake. I'm scared. What do I know about lawsuits? I designed a catalog, and now I wonder what I've done." She swallowed, fighting back tears.

He got up, went around the desk, and wrapped his arms around her. "What have you done? You have done nothing. Zero. Zilch. You created a successful product that thousands of kids love. You just happened to rub up against some . . ." he paused, searching for the right word, "dork. Is that what the kids would call him?" He smiled at her blushing face.

He wasn't entirely satisfied with their talk, but he felt more at peace knowing he could give his daughter some guidance—a new lawyer.

THIRTY-THREE
The Museum Store
Dallas, TX

"DON'T WORRY, MOM, this won't take long." Sue stepped out of her SUV. It was nine forty five in the morning when Sue and her mom stopped at the Children's Museum Discovery Store in downtown Dallas, on the fairgrounds. "No worries, honey I'm not going anywhere. I have my romance novel to read."

"I just have to drop off Hollis."

"I'm proud of you for donating that Yorkston hawk to the children's museum store."

"I hope it brings in more kids. See ya in a few. Lock the doors after I leave."

Sue strolled through the cobblestone paths cut into the grassy grounds. A helmeted bicyclist zipped past her, but other than that the fairgrounds were deserted for the most part, with a few people here and there, however the parking lot had been packed. She thought of her mom waiting in the car, and she knew her mom had been worried about her the last few months over the pending lawsuits. But then that's what mother's did, they worried about their children's well being. She knew she would be concerned if her girl's had legal issues.

She passed the Old Windmill Restaurant and the Cultural Center. She rarely visited her clients' stores any more. She turned the corner and stopped, staring at awe at the line of people wrapped around the museum store. The line formed off the sidewalk causing the grassy lawn to be squashed flat from the shoes of over a hundred fifty not-so-patiently waiting Yorkston evangelists.

She walked slowly, holding Hollis close to her chest.

"Hey, are you cutting?" A lady in hot pink velour shorts yelled at Sue.

"No. I'm an employee. I need to get to the door."

The lady seemed content with the answer, but kept her eye on Sue as she walked swiftly toward the front door, bypassing the line. She rushed up the cement stairs and almost slipped on the last step. Hollis was jostled from her hand and hit the ground. Sue promptly picked the toy up.

"Is that Hollis?" A teenage boy yelled and pointed at Sue.

Several people stepped out of line, all of them flocking toward Sue. She didn't stop. The crowd from the back wanting to see the commotion moved in closer, forcing Sue to push through the line by the front door.

"Watch it, lady."

"Hey, no cutting."

"Get back in line, pretty lady."

"Sorry, I'm an employee, trying to get to work. I need to get in before I'm late. Please move aside so I can knock on the door." Sue squeezed past a small man. He narrowed his eyes, grabbed Sue around her waist, and pulled her back. Sue bumped into the lady next to her. "Excuse me."

Sue turned to the man. "Sir, do not touch me again or I'll report you to Tom Powell, the manager of this store, and you will not be allowed inside. You're so close now to the door, I'd hate to see you turned away."

The man backed up a step, crossed his hands on his chest and crinkled his nose.

Sue pushed through the last few people and pounded on the glass door. Tom Powell appeared from behind a stack of boxes and unlocked the door. He escorted her through the double door. Once the door was relocked, he slipped the keys in his pocket.

"Sue Logan! So glad to see you. What brings you here?" Tom

gave her a hug.

"Hi Tom." Sue hugged the tall, gray breaded man. "I brought you —"

There was a pounding sound on the door and they both looked up. A lady smacked her purse against the glass. "Come on. Hurry up in there. It's ten o'clock." She pointed at her watch.

More people came from around the corner and pushed closer toward the store. For a few tense moments, it appeared that a near-riot might be added to the growing pattern of mania and mayhem attributed to the new release of the plushest of toy treasures, the Yorkston animals.

"Come over here. We are still unloading boxes of the new toys. Somehow a rumor went wild over the internet that we have all twelve birds."

Sue walked over to the counter where harried store employees were busy stocking the shelves. "What are you going to do?"

"I've called security. I'm waiting for them to come in and block the side walk with orange cones. If we exceed a hundred people in line they will turn the toy collectors away citing fire code violations."

"So that's why there's no parking spaces left. I had to park in the north lot and walk past the restaurant."

There were shouts and short tempers flaring from outside the store front doors. Tom looked outside. He appeared concerned.

"I'm sorry I chose today to stop by," Sue said quietly.

"No Sue. I always love seeing you. Since your company has grown so big, we hardly see you anymore. I remember when you first started the business, you would hand deliver the catalogs. What brings you here today?"

"I have a surprise for you." Sue held out Hollis to him.

Tom's mouth dropped open in shock. "Wow. Are you serious? Is this the real hawk?"

"Absolutely. I wanted you to have it for display. But promise not to sell it."

"No way. Did you hear the mint green elephant went for five thousand dollars last week at a collector's show?"

"For a green plush pachyderm?"

Tom smiled at Sue and gave her shoulder another squeeze. "It's really good to see you."

There was commotion at the door. An employee came over to Tom. "Excuse me, Mr. Powell."

"Yes, Shelia?"

"A lady and her little grandson left to use the bathroom and told someone to save their spot, but when they returned no one would let them back in line."

"This is just ridiculous." Tom walked over to the door and unlocked it. He stepped outside. "Listen up," he shouted. "I am the manager. We do have a new Yorkston shipment inside —" A loud murmur erupted from the crowd and the line went from straight to small bunches of people. A shoving match broke out between two men and toddlers were crying.

"Quiet please." Tom held up his hands. "We did not get the full bird line. We have some, but not all twelve. We are going to hand out numbers and let everyone in by your number order. So you are free to get out of the queue and walk around and use the bathroom or enjoy the art, eat at the restaurant. Keep stopping back to check where we are on the numbers. We will post the numbers of the people we're letting in the store on a large piece of paper in the window. Only fifteen at a time in the store."

A loud "aww" came from the crowd.

Three employees came out and started walking the line, handing out tickets with numbers on them. Tom returned into the store and walked over to Sue.

"The big-dollar animals have brought out the worst in some people," Tom said.

Sue nodded. "I hope I can sneak out of here. I should get back. My mom is waiting in the car."

"Please wait for security. They'll take you to your car."

"You sure?"

"Yes. Yes. Did you hear that last week, two San Antonio shopkeepers were clubbed with lead pipes by robbers who made off with a box of Yorkston animals? And a few days earlier, Houston police squelched a near-riot at the Gulf Coast Plaza, where a rare pink penguin plush was on sale. It is crazy. These are adults, but you get them here and they act like kids again," said a weary-faced Tom.

"Glad to see the customers are flocking here. A bit frustrating, but sales are good, right?"

"Fantastic."

A pickup truck with yellow flashing lights on top drove over the lawn, followed by three golf carts, each manned by park security in khaki uniforms and holstered guns.

"Reinforcements are here." Tom looked at his watch. "Opening time."

"It was great seeing you again, Tom."

"You too, Sue. Wait up I have something for you." Tom reached behind the counter and gave Sue a black plastic sack. "Here, I've been saving these for you."

Sue opened the bag and inside she saw three white Yorkston lambs. "Thank you so much. Maddie will love these." She gave Tom a hug.

Sue went out the front door and walked briskly toward the first golf cart. She climbed in the passenger seat and waved at Tom as he held up a large, white poster board at the crowd with the numbers 1-15 written on it.

THIRTY-FOUR

SUE UNFAULTERING TOOK her dad's advice to heart and consulted with Tex Thornton. His instruction to her during their brief phone call was to get her files from Triggs and Patterson. She would meet with him when she returned from Boston in a few days.

Her dad was right. It was time to move to a more experienced lawyer.

Jonathan's original choice for a law firm was old friends, but they didn't meet today's legal matters, which included experts in Intellectual Property law.

The house was quiet as Sue prepared to leave for Boston. Her parents had the kids at a nearby park. Sue picked up the blow dryer, directing the warm air at the few remaining strands of hair after her shower. She flipped her hair over, jumping as a shadow crossed the corner of her eye.

"Hello?"

Her shadow reflected from the light in her closet flashing at her. Her reflection stared conspicuously back at her from the bathroom mirror. She looked tired. Tired and alone.

Just as the blow dryer silenced, the doorbell rang. Her bare feet pitter-pattered across the cool hardwood floor, sidestepping a pile of Legos. A man in a blue shirt, striped tie and khaki slacks watched her approach through the textured glass of the front door. He was holding a clipboard in his hand.

"Can I help you?" She opened the door cautiously to the stranger.

"Hi, I'm with the post office. We're checking this street and

156

Billie's route. It's just a survey."

"Well, okay. Sure. Billie's great." Sue had known her mailman, Billie, for years. She received a lot of packages at her home.

"Have you been getting your mail before two p.m. every day?" he asked.

Sue noticed the lanyard around his neck with an ID printed *MPO*. A glance out front confirmed a silver gray sedan parked next to her brick mailbox.

"Um, yep. I guess. I haven't checked it today."

"Okay." He made a note on his clipboard. "Do you have any issues or concerns with your mail carrier?"

"No, not at all. I said he's great." Sue glanced at her watch. "Look, I hate to be rude, but I need to get going."

"Okay. No problem. Thanks for your time." He made a note on his clipboard. "I'm going to wait until he delivers it and make a note of the time. I just saw him around the corner."

"Okay. Bye." Sue shut the front door. She returned to her bedroom to finish dressing. She thought for a minute; *MPO*, Municipal Post Office, Main Post Office. Humph. His blue shirt didn't have the post office insignia on it. Sue shrugged her shoulders at her reflection in the mirror.

Fifteen minutes later, she was ready to leave. She grabbed her keys off the granite counter, passed the front of the house and noticed the mail truck across the street. It reminded her Shuhua Toys said they would mail a new prototype to her house. The rest of the samples would be delivered to the office. She decided to check the mail. She walked down the circular driveway to the mailbox. She saw the silver sedan sitting in front of her next-door neighbor's house. From her vantage point in her house, she was unable to see him sitting there. The driver was the man she had met fifteen minutes earlier. He waved, pulled out his clipboard and started writing. Sue waved, opened the mailbox; still no mail.

She would check when she returned from her meeting at the bank. She walked to the garage, got in her car and slowly backed down the driveway. The man in the car watched her as she left.

The mail truck pulled around the parked sedan, opened the

black mailbox marked *Logan* and placed a stack of letters and a small package inside. The mail truck made four more stops before leaving the street.

The sedan rolled up a few feet and the driver hopped out, opening the Logan mailbox. He reached in, pulling out a package covered with postage from China. He got back in his car and tossed it on the passenger seat. Without looking around, he drove off.

THIRTY-FIVE

SUE SULKED over the documents on Jennifer's desk.

Jennifer De Kreek, Sue's banker of eight years, leaned back in her chair. "I'm just saying, you used to be more sensible."

"I know, Jennifer. Please consider letting me draw more against my loan," Sue pleaded. "I have reviewed your detailed future sales projections for the next year. They seem solid. And your excitement in this product seems very sound."

"I know the short-term profit may not be very big, but I need to establish this product immediately in the market." Sue put her thumbnail between her teeth, feeling an unexpected surge of butterflies flaring in her stomach. *What am I doing? This is a big risk and I know it.*

"Here are the latest amounts." Jennifer pointed to a column on the bottom of the page. "You have about three hundred thousand remaining in this line of credit."

Sue followed Jennifer's fingers down the page.

She had thought it was crazy for Jonathan to enter into such an uncompromising financial commitment with the bank when they started the business. The bank commitment had Logan pulling from a line of credit over five years that totaled in the millions. They had been repaying the debt for years without any issues. This year was the biggest commitment yet, a million dollars, betting it all on the plush line.

Sue had opposed the terms at first, because she didn't want to commit to the bank that they would draw the large sums. Fortunately, her product ideas had taken off and, so far, they had been able to make all commitments. God forbid she would put her company in a financial situation that could cause harm later. But Jonathan had been reassuring and had an unwavering faith in Sue.

Jennifer smiled at Sue. "You know how I've always worked hard to get the bank commitment approved. And if it hadn't been for Jonathan's personal endorsement and guarantee back then, I wouldn't have gotten the loans approved."

Sue, concerned began to nibble on her thumb nail. "I knew he had guaranteed the restaurant, but after it was sold, we used other collateral."

"Well, the inventory, of course. And we have your personal residence as collateral."

"Of course." Sue was uncomfortably aware of the extent of the personal guarantees but, so far, there had been no reason to worry about it. She continued to pay the bank on time.

They finished up in no time. Sue kept eyeing her watch. Her mind was on Boston.

"Thank you again for donating the toys to my church for the children program. They were a godsend. You're the greatest." Jennifer walked her to the door. "See you later, Sue, and have a great trip to Boston."

"Thanks. I will." She wondered if Jennifer could see her eyes twinkle when mentioning the trip.

Sue was back at the house for a few minutes to pick up her suitcase. She had hoped to see the kids one more time before leaving. She found the house unnaturally quiet and empty, her children still at the park.

She saw a sheriff's car circle the cul-de-sac, twice, then come to a stop in front of her driveway.

"Shit!" She said, looking through the plantation shutters in the front living room, feeling as if she should run and hide. "Now what?"

A male process server in full uniform walked up her

driveway carrying papers and talking on his cell phone. She'd had enough of the servers. She wanted to duck out of sight and dodge his accusing stares. But, it was too late; he looked right at her.

Moments later, the doorbell rang.

She opened the door. "I guess you're not here to sell me Avon."

"Ah, no ma'am," he said. "Are you Ms. Sue Logan? CEO of Logan Designs?"

This guy obviously didn't have a sense of humor. Nor any compassion. She inhaled deeply. "Yes sir."

He was a medium-size man with a puffy nose that looked broken and pushed to one side. One of his eyes had a red, jagged scar running under it and his hands looked cut up. She wondered what the other guy looked like.

He pointed to the documents. "Sign here and here."

Sue took the pen with her shaky fingers. She hesitated for a minute, reading the first few sentences. Then started to sign.

He pointed to another line. "No, not there . . . here."

Sue snapped her hand back. She watched him stare past her into the large foyer of the house. A bright orange little tyke cozy coupe ride-on car sat behind her and other kids' toys were scattered throughout the hallway. He must think she lived with slobs. Truth was, it was rare for the house to be cluttered, but she hadn't been feeling her usual self lately.

"Nice house," the deputy said with sarcasm heavy in his voice. "Kids?"

"Yes. It's like a tornado blew through here sometimes."

He chuckled, though it seemed forced. "I've got the same problem."

Sue focused her eyes at the papers, not wanting to look at him anymore. She thought about refusing to sign the papers, but what good would that do? He had already handed them to her – the rest was a formality. She brought an unsteady hand up to her mouth covering her lips for a few seconds as she read. Her stomach began to roll inside, not a good sign. She decided to read the rest of the document before signing.

"Ms. Logan." The officer interrupted several minutes later. "I have three more stops to make. No one ever reads this crap. If you could just sign."

"Just give me another minute, please." She ignored the man's burrowing stare. "This is a deposition subpoena?"

He shrugged. "Dunno. I just deliver them Ma'am. I don't read 'em." He glanced at his watch.

She remembered her lawyer telling her this would be part of the process. Time for this guy to leave. She flipped through the pages, signing where he indicated. She looked up and saw her neighbor, Nelson across the street. She waved at him, though she didn't know why.

"First time you've been sued?" the server said, tearing off the bottom of the page.

She nodded.

He handed her the stack. "Thank ya, ma'am. Enjoy the rest of your day."

Sue slammed the door behind her.

THIRTY-SIX
Rural Indiana

PETE SHAPIRO SCOFFED at the idea that Yorkston Toys still employed him. It was going on six years now. He had never been with any one company or anyone in his sixty-eight years longer than three years, except his Siberian Huskies and his mom. And he damn near had a Husky that almost beat his mom's record, if the dog hadn't died at age fifteen.

He was the chief chemist at the giant toy company, but he didn't frequent the Yorkston offices; he preferred to work from his home lab, often not leaving his house for weeks. He didn't like to leave his beloved Husky alone.

Occasionally he went to Yorkston for meetings and once a quarter he had a visit from Anthony Romero. These meetings were always held at his home like the upcoming visit planned with Anthony this Friday.

"I want an update on the Pearson nomination." Dr. Shapiro had told Anthony on the phone earlier that morning. He knew Anthony was due back from Boston the next day and Anthony promised to drop off Shapiro's quarterly bonus Friday when they met. Then he would discuss the award with Anthony.

Dr. Shapiro looked around his laboratory, his eyes settling on his beautiful Husky, Henna. "I deserve that medal."

He moved his glasses farther up his nose and continued

163

talking to the dog, as if he was indoctrinating a new lab assistant. "I've been trying to get Romero to use his connections and nominate me for the Pearson Medal for at least a year! But no – he probably thinks it's too prestigious for me, like that old fart Sir Pearson earned it with his aniline dye, ooh-la-la, but he has done nothin' compared to me – after all these years!"

Henna looked up at him with sympathetic eyes.

He rubbed her behind the ears and went on grumbling.

"Damn, Henna, if I'm not qualified, nobody is! You know girl, I've published hundreds of damn articles," he clenched his fist open and closed, "and authored three books including that textbook on Organic Chemistry used nationwide. I have thirty-five patents, for God's sake! And the least to say, I've helped develop the most sophisticated tools that scientists use to measure chemical substances. I want that medal! I deserve it."

Shapiro sat down at the high top metal stool, alone in his home research laboratory. He recounted the day he discovered the exotic key to the famous blockbuster toy for Yorkston. His eyes behind his glasses were bloodshot, with the cavern ridges by his brows, and there was madness and revenge in them as he remembered several years earlier, when he was in his makeshift laboratory, his garage working on the experiment.

He skipped logging in his hours with the Yorkston Devine team because he was eager to follow up on his idea alone. He had been incubating the combination of the substances of the optical brightening agent and the DCDA crystallized powder with the red dyes for the last five days.

That day he would know the answer. That day he had blown off his chess game to wait for the results. That day would change his fate.

"Henna, even though this outcome may not win us the Nobel Prize for chemical discovery, this molecule combination will earn us the big payday," Dr. Shapiro said to the white Husky curled faithfully at his feet.

He removed the tray that held twenty Petri dishes from the incubator.

"Shit." Shapiro yelled after looking at the first dish. He kicked the metal dye vat under his lab bench, waking up his dog. The large Husky moved from Shapiro's feet hiding under a table.

"Give me a break, Henna. I haven't even completed the procedure. We've nineteen more samples here, old girl," he said.

"Don't you want to watch me win the big money?" With gloved hands, he picked up the first tray and set it aside.

"I, Pete Shapiro, am going to discover the answer to the mystery of the holographic substance suited for use as a dye in the form of lettering on fabric. It'll be suitable in an environment where children can play with it and stick the damn things in their mouths. Hell they can suck on it and use them as pacifiers, for all I care!"

He placed his safety goggles over his pewter wire-rimmed glasses. He picked up the second dish. With an eyedropper, he placed three drops of a clear liquid into the dish.

"The holographic substances have to be suited for use in environments where pH changes occur frequently, places where changes in pH are extreme," he said. Henna closed her eyes.

"The pH levels in saliva changes the makeup of the molecules. pH levels change during the day and night and from humans and animals."

He took the third dish adding three drops of liquid from another eyedropper. It turned the thick liquid in the dish from red to yellow. "Our test labs are skilled in performing site specific toxicity studies, but they don't have the adequate resources to test every combination."

He stopped to review his lab notebook. He rubbed his chin letting out a snorting laugh. "Of course! Curcumin is a halochromic dye! At high pH it becomes ionized and its color changes from red to yellow."

He snorted again. "Henna!" he said loudly. The dog looked up from a sleepy stupor.

He squatted down on the floor by his cherished pet. He was careful not to touch her in order not to contaminate his gloved hands. "We're almost there girl."

He returned to his workbench, glancing at the time displayed on the equipment monitor. It was almost noon. He set the timer dial for twenty minutes, took off his gloves and rubbed his face. "This is so profound to be tackled by just me."

"Holographic chemical substances mixed with certain saliva can go undetected alternating the acidity of substances, causing an exposure to carcinogenic attributes. It would take years to detect and it's hard to pinpoint the source especially after it's swallowed. I'm empirically able to emulate a site-specific protocol. My experiments with the dye samples include a broad range of acute and chronic tests using a wide variety of fresh youth saliva and rodent and dog species. Thank you Henna."

Sure, he had used his dog's and the rat's saliva for the testing, but he hated how other scientists used healthy animals for testing drugs. They made loving, healthy animals sick so they could test the drugs on them and then euthanized them after the tests were completed. Bastards! All of them!

He adjusted his goggles sliding forward on his sweaty forehead. When they didn't settle properly over his biofocals, he ripped them off, tossing them across the room.

He got up from his workbench, pacing the length of his garage lab. Henna followed close on his heels. He tired of this quickly. In order to pass the twenty minutes, he read his notebook.

I found the right chemical make up by complete accident! I ran the apparatus slower than it was intended to run and it took forty-eight hours to make a sulphonation. When the Shake and Bake was done, I had found it! I presented the holographic dye fabric samples to Anthony Romero before disclosing it to the Devine Team. He accepted that I had succeeded in discovering the safe dye but said the exotic dye was prohibitively expensive and it needed to be fulfilled using a safe, but economical substitution.

Shapiro snorted a loud laugh. An economical substitution, over safe, ha! Yes, it costs more to play safe.

"Hey Henna, maybe they can put a warning statement on the hang tag of their pint-sized stuffed animals; Caution, sucking on the tush tag when mixed with certain mouth bacteria can cause itchy skin, hair loss, swelling in the face, redness, trouble breathing, burning and an increased risk of life-threatening infections, and cancer in children and adolescents. Continued sucking on the tags could lead to hospitalization or *death.*" He boohooed, running a hand through his white hair. Shapiro noted the time, 12:20. He checked the digital thermostat's LCD display for the temperature & humidity. He clicked a button; the on-board computer monitoring systems showed him a read out.

"Henna, it's time."

He gathered up his goggles and gloves, put them on, and removed the dishes from the incubator. The dye's red hue tested perfect; the color of the Yorkston logo, blood red. The holographic lettering idea tied with the Radio Frequency ID transmitter had been incubating in Nathanael Yorkston's mind for the past five years. Shapiro knew when Nathanael Yorkston wanted something; he didn't stop until he got it.

He lowered the dish marked number five to his dog. "And the Oscar goes to… Number 5."

He stared at the dish, pontificating on the results in front of him.

"Look Henna, this is going to make us filthy rich but more importantly it is our secret ticket to winning the Pearson award!"

That had been four years ago. Then began the seesaw battle between the chemist and the Yorkston management. Shapiro felt he had done his part and discovered a safe, albeit, expensive solution. Nathanael Yorkston didn't want that solution. He wanted an inexpensive solution to contribute more to his bottom-line. Safe wasn't as important as success. Nathanael chose tainted tags in name of profit.

THIRTY-SEVEN
Atlanta

DANIEL STARED out the window of his dad's office. He was having a hard time concentrating. He was leaving for Boston later that afternoon and Sue had been on his mind all morning.

Communication with her the last few months had been practically non-existent. The times he heard from her, the messages were short and their conversations business-like, restrained. Maybe he had read too much into their relationship in China. He hoped not.

It was a busy season for his family. Of all the times in his life to find a woman he wanted to pursue, this had to be the absolute worst—especially because she was a business client.

"Daniel. Daniel, what do you think we should do?" His father, Harrison Winston, repeated while his older brother, Harry Jr., looked on.

"Sorry, Dad." Daniel concentrated on the conversation. He could feel the tension in the office. His brother usually handled the retail side of the business, but this was a serious matter and they had asked Daniel to join them. He shifted his weight slightly on the hard straight-back chair, hunching up his shoulder. He looked at Harry, his brother. "Has Taunya talked to all our sources there?"

"Yes, she talked to the Yorkston rep. He didn't have a good answer." The older Winston replied. "Shoot. I can't remember a time when the Winston Retail Stores were in the middle of a product crisis like this one."

Daniel and Harry exchanged glances.

"I agree. If we don't get that backorder soon we'll be in big trouble," Harry said. "I just don't understand why there's been a backorder of the Yorkston toys for weeks now. Our senior buyers have tried everything with the company to find out why we aren't getting them. All our orders are unfilled. We've even offered to pay COD. Taunya is ready to jump off a bridge."

"What are the damages so far, Dad?" Daniel asked. His father was in his seventies, but he still came to the office every day. His mom had encouraged Harry, Sr., to play more golf or take up bird watching, or anything to keep him out of the office. Harry Jr., Daniel's older brother, was sitting next to his dad. Both wore worried looks on their faces.

"Our store revenues are dropping at a rate of 10-15% per week," Harrison said. "And without the Yorkston plush toys, the customers are going other places to shop, causing a snowball effect in the decline of our other product sales."

"I'll see if I can meet with their reps at the Boston Toy show," Daniel said.

Harry and his dad looked over the spreadsheet.

Daniel's thoughts went to Sue again, ignoring his dad and brother for a minute. He had a personal life, but he had his rules. Rule number 2: Never date a client. But she was easy to be with. They had a lot in common and he liked her good looks. *Damn, why is she a client?*

"Dad, maybe we can do a store promotion to draw in the shoppers?" Harry Jr. asked. "We have the new Dream Fairies collection that has taken off. We could use that as a draw. I can have Taunya check on getting a special deal from Zenesco, their manufacturer."

"Good idea, son." Harrison smiled with pride expanding his face. He looked over at Daniel. "Daniel?"

"Sorry, Dad." Daniel realized he had said that twice in the last few minutes. His head wasn't in the meeting. He kept replaying his brief phone calls with Sue. *Why isn't she talking to me? Have I offended her? She was so standoffish. Why is she making me take laps around the oblivious pool?*

"Huh? Yep, Harry's idea is a good one. I agree with him. Let Taunya look into it." Daniel paused. "Look guys, I'm headed to

Boston. I need to grab lunch before I leave." He hoped they didn't see his anxiousness.

"Bro, you're agreeing with me? Since when?" Harry asked.

In many ways, Daniel's older brother was more controlling than their dad. He had been in the business longer than Daniel, but Harry still relied on the senior Winston when it came to crisis matters.

"Look I agree with the promotion and the Dream Fairies seem like the perfect lure." Daniel reassured them he wasn't playing games. Both Harry and his dad were watching him with amusement.

"Yes, and we could even include free tax." Harry threw out.

"Sure, whatever." Daniel glanced at his watch and began to gather up his briefcase.

"Okay, there you go agreeing with me again. You've never agreed with anyone so many times . . . let alone me . . . in your life." Harry smiled at his dad. "Don't you even want to know the sales and profits of the Dream Fairies?"

"What?" Daniel caught their exchanged smiles. *Why can't they just let me go?*

"When are you meeting with her?" Harry asked. Their dad smiled in the background.

"Who?"

"Sue. You are seeing her, right?" Harry said.

"Yes, tomorrow night. I'm meeting her at her hotel."

"And she's hot, right Daniel?"

"Shut up." Daniel said. As teens, it seemed all Harry wanted to do was break up Daniel and his girlfriends. Now as adults, all he wanted to do was marry him off. They seldom talked about Harry's sex life. Whenever he tried to picture Harry and his wife, Anna, all he saw was the two of them in bed wearing matching pajamas and reading glasses.

Their father just sat back listening.

"Tomorrow night could be the night you end up in bed with her." Harry teased.

"Look, she lost her husband years ago and I think a piece of heart too. She doesn't want to be exposed to that vulnerability again." But Harry was right, tomorrow could be the night. And that had

Daniel flustered.

"Well you better get going. You don't want to miss your flight." His dad stood from behind his desk. He came over and gave Daniel a hug. "Be safe, Son. Call your mom when you get home. Harry and I will handle this store crisis."

"Okay, Dad." Daniel nodded at Harry. "See ya— ya big schmuck." He kept his words clean with his dad watching.

Harry nodded and smiled to signal the end of this round. He mouthed a silent, "good luck."

Luck is what Daniel needed with Sue Logan because he was about to break his rule number 2.

THIRTY-EIGHT
Boston

THE BOSTON HARBOR hotel restaurant on the waterfront reflected the vibrancy of the ocean with its sophisticated, contemporary design, and was one of Sue's favorites. It was decorated in cool blue colors, inspired by the sea. Even though it was warm and windy, the bar patio out back was packed.

Sue, seated catty corner from the patio near the window, was early for her meeting with Daniel. She had spent the last three days at the Boston Toy Show. Every muscle in her body ached as if she had just finished training camp for the Dallas Cowboys.

She took off her three-inch heeled pumps, concealing them under her chair. She tucked her feet under her briefcase, hoping not to call attention to her aching bare feet.

A waitress, dressed in a short teal blue skirt and a white low cut ruffled blouse, approached her, rattling off the day's cocktail creations.

"Just ice water for now. I'll wait for my guest and order wine when he arrives."

"No problem. Are you staying at the hotel?" She chewed pink gum as she spoke.

"Yes, room 1709."

"Name?"

"Logan."

"Okay, cool. I'll start a tab when you're ready to order." She blew a bubble as she walked away.

Sue thought about her day, pleased with the show orders they had received so far. She had feared running into her arch competitor and now enemy number one, Yorkston Toys, while at the convention center, but they hadn't shown up. Over the last few months, they hadn't been at the toy shows.

She surveyed the room, waiting for Daniel to walk in. She was apprehensive about seeing him. She worried about how to discuss the letters and lawsuits. As her trade consultant, she didn't feel obligated to share with him the threats on her designs but, as a friend, she wanted to tell him. She had mixed feelings about seeing him, oscillating between excited and hesitant.

Sue glanced around the room again. She had always liked the hotel's location. It was a few minutes to the convention center, Faneuil Hall and Quincy Market.

The bubble gum waitress returned with a tall glass of water, placing it on a colorful blue cocktail napkin.

"Can you leave me a few extra paper napkins?"

"Sure, no problem, sweetie." She placed a handful of napkins on the table. "How's your room here? You like it?"

"Very nice. I'm on the top floor."

"Great views?"

"Breathtaking." Sue thought of Daniel, wondering if he would like the views.

The waitress nodded and smacked her gum. "I could sit and watch the Boston Harbor all day. Enjoy." She turned her attention to a nearby table.

Sue spooned out a couple of ice cubes from her glass, wrapping them in the blue napkins. She placed the makeshift ice bags over her toes, hoping to reduce the swelling and to ease the pain in her feet.

Daniel entered from the street door opposite of where Sue was sitting. The glare of the setting sun glowed behind him. Even so, she recognized him easily and raised her hand in greeting. He waved back and strode quickly toward her.

All the butterflies in her stomach fluttered as she watched

him walk across the room.

"Hi Sue."

"Hello Daniel."

He put his arm around her and gave her a friendly hug. His embrace was loose, casual. She looked into his green eyes as he sat across from her.

"It's so good to see you. You look great." His gaze wandered over her. "How do you do that? You look spectacular, even after a full day of standing on your feet at the show."

"Thanks, you look great too." She blushed.

The waitress returned to the table a few minutes after Daniel arrived. She shot an admiring glance at him.

"Two glasses of La Crema Chardonnay," Daniel said.

"That sounds good." Sue had a fondness for that vineyard.

Daniel broke the ice first. "How's the journey of a thousand miles going?"

"The proverb we discussed in China?"

"Yep. How's it going, Sue?"

"Okay. Product development is going well. I've had some other issues that have come up that have kept me busy lately." *That's an understatement.*

"I'm glad it's going well. But what issues?" Daniel asked with a puzzled look on his face.

She wasn't sure she could share her troubles with him. She wasn't ready. "Let's talk about the product first."

"Sure."

They chatted freely about business. She talked about her new products at the Boston show.

She became more anxious as the night progressed. She took a sip of her wine. "Daniel, there's something I've wanted to ask you." She bit her lip, shifting in her chair.

He leaned across the table. "What?" When she didn't reply he said. "You can trust me and you won't hurt my feelings whatever it is. Is there something in the product line we missed in China?"

"It's about China." After all the rehearsing, this was all she could say! She'd had many sleepless nights going over what to say regarding her lawsuits and the threats to her company. "When I left

Hong Kong I found an anonymous letter in my briefcase." She paused for a long moment, watching his reaction. The only reaction she read was a questioning look in his green eyes.

"A letter," he said. "What was it about?"

She didn't realize she had been holding her breath. She saw surprise in his eyes. "The letter was a warning to me that someone was trying to steal my designs and . . . ." She looked at him with sad heartfelt eyes.

"And you thought it was from me?"

"No, no."

"Oh, thank God. You look so nervous. Is that all?"

"Well, I know it sounds a bit silly."

"A little. Why even worry about it? It's probably just a prank."

"It wasn't a prank." She said in a low voice. "At least some of what the letter said has come true." She didn't know why she felt she had to confide that to him.

He sat up straight in his chair and moved to the edge of his seat.

Sue started to play with the blue paper napkin in front of her.

"What else did the letter say? What do you mean it has come true?"

Sue took a drink of her ice water, her heart in her throat. She thought about her kids. She thought about how the loss of her business would destroy her. Her business was all she had known, her only source of income for her family.

"There was more in the letter; a threat to sue my company." Her eyes welled with tears. "Daniel, I was sued the next week!"

He reached across the table and took her hand in his. "I'm pissed that someone would hurt you like this," Daniel said. "What lawsuit? Who would sue your company?"

Sue enjoyed the warmth of his hand entwined with hers. She felt better with just this single gesture. She tried to coax a smile to form on her lips; instead she ended up with a curve on one side of her mouth. "Yorkston Toys has sued Logan Designs," she whispered across the table to him.

He looked at her incredulously. He released his hand from

175

hers, said a few expletives under his breath and banged the table with his fist.

Sue smiled at his reaction. "Exactly how I felt." Her voice sounding hoarse and strained.

"Is it the catalog they're after?"

"Yes, copyright infringements."

"That's bullshit. There are hundreds of companies using Yorkston's toys in their printed materials and web sites. Have the others been sued too?"

"No, not according to my lawyers." She answered. "Please keep your voice down." Sue looked quickly around the room.

"Hey, don't worry. None of your customers are here," he said.

"I just don't want that news getting out and having clients cancelling their orders."

"Yeah, I understand. That could hurt your sales."

"The next three months are critical. We are on target to surpass last year's annual goals."

"Do you know for sure if there are any other lawsuits?"

"My lawyers have said they haven't seen any other suits similar to mine."

"And there are dozens of magazines focused solely on the toys."

"And they have more sales than I do. So I just don't get it, Daniel. Why me? Why sue me?"

"I can't figure it," he said.

"Who do you think left me the letter, Daniel?"

"Are you sure you got it when you were in China or Hong Kong? Could it have been hidden in your purse earlier?"

"I thought about that over and over. I'm not sure now. I had gone through my briefcase on the plane. But I don't know. I really don't know. I never really looked in my briefcase much that trip. I didn't take it out much. I guess it's possible."

"What are you going to do? Do you have a good lawyer?"

"I've had the same lawyers for years, but my dad thinks they are responsible for getting me into this mess. He wants me to change to a firm more experienced in intellectual property law."

"Sounds like a smart man. Is his daughter taking his advice?"

She looked deep into his eyes. *Does he have any idea how*

176

gorgeous he is? Warmth flooded her face. *What did he say?* She wanted his hand back in hers.

"Sue?" Their eyes locked. A big smile erupted all over Daniel's face.

"What?"

"Did you even hear a thing I said?"

"Yes, . . . you asked about my lawyer."

"Uh, huh, something like that. I'm glad you are hanging on my every word."

"I'm taking my dad's advice. I have hired a new lawyer." She teased back at him.

The next move he made took her by pleasant surprise.

Daniel stood up and walked over to her. Sue looked up at him with questioning, soft eyes.

"You need a hug." Without waiting for a reply, he leaned down and with his powerful hands he swept her up under her arms. He wrapped his arms around her small waist, squeezing her up against his body. Desire bolted through her; she responded by wrapping her arms around him.

"Thank you," she whispered. Her nostrils filled with the male scent of his skin. The brief embrace sent a sexual chain reaction in her body; from the softening of her eyebrows to the positioning of her toes curled under her bare feet and everything else in between. Aware that everyone could see them, she pulled away.

Daniel held her at arm's length and looked her over from top to bottom. The look on his face said his eyes were having a feast. Then he started to chuckle, spoiling the moment.

Sue pulled away and placed her hands on her hips.

"And what is so funny, Mr. Winston?"

He pointed at her bare feet.

Sue glanced down and giggled. Her toes were covered with a teal-blue color. The ice cubes had melted, causing the blue dye from the paper cocktail napkins to tint her toes a bright blue kaleidoscope stain. Her toes looked like they had been tied-dyed to match the restaurant.

Sue, embarrassed, didn't know if she should keep laughing or be mortified.

"I'll be right back." Daniel left the table.

Sue was seated when he came back. He had a shot glass in one hand and a water glass in the other; both filled with a cloudy liquid.

"Now is hardly the time for tequila shots." She smiled as he sat down.

"This is a special mixture that may work to return your toes to a normal shade fit for humans."

"What's in it?"

She took the bar towel dipping it in the glass.

"It's a special mixture of soda, alcohol and whatever cleanser chemicals the bartender uses to clean the bar."

"And if it doesn't clean my feet we can either drink it or clean our table." Sue bent down and started scrubbing her toes with the damp towel. She was surprised to see the clean white towel begin to turn a light shade of blue even though her toes seemed to remain the same.

Despite her klutzy behavior around him, she hoped he still thought she was a classy, smart lady. God, she was displaying so much vulnerability, something she hardly ever did. She was always in control. She was still smiling up at him as she managed to wipe her feet. She felt his warmth even across the table.

He got up, pulling his chair around the side of the table next to hers. "Here let me help."

Sue laid the lower half of one leg across his bent knees. She folded and carefully tucked the other foot under her skirt, not wanting to flash him.

"I hope you don't have sensitive skin and that you aren't allergic to bleach," he said. He took her petite foot in his hands. He seemed to be admiring her toes. Thank God, she had gotten a pedicure.

She braced herself for his touch, as he began rubbing her toes. He brushed her upper foot gently, but firmly and his fingers sent arrows of tingly sensations exploding up her leg.

"Not that I know of— ahhhhh," she grimaced, "cold."

The combination of his strong hand holding her leg and his other hand holding her foot as he gently rubbed caused a quivering sensation that ran up her, making her shudder.

He seemed not to notice and continued to rub the towel carefully in between and around her toes. Daniel's arm moved back and forth, as he worked to remove the stain.

"Shaving cream or nail polish remover may work to remove the color too." He looked at her.

"Okay," was all she managed to say. She could sit there all night. His gentle touch and his proximity stirred emotions she hadn't felt in a while.

She wasn't able to get him out of her head since their trip to China. Not that anything had happened, physically, between them on the trip but, emotionally, she felt close to him. But she was definitely attracted to him physically. She wondered if he felt the same way.

"I'm afraid your Smurf foot is only a bit lighter." He returned her foot to the ground. "Let me see the other, Ms. Smurfette."

She pretended not to catch the teasing tone in his voice. She shifted her weight and placed her other foot firmly, like a weapon, in his lap.

He laughed, turning his attention back to her foot. She watched him as he rubbed the liquid between her toes. She was glad he didn't make it an erotic incident; after all they were in public.

She glanced around. The bar was now dark, and the night crowd was filling it. She caught two solo women staring at them with approving jealousy.

"You better be careful, or we'll have all the women in the bar lining up for a foot massage."

"There's only one I want to massage." He didn't even look up as he spoke.

Sue loved the feeling of his hand holding her foot and the terrycloth material gently caressing her. It tickled, but in a sensuous way. When the silence became unbearable, she picked up where she had left off. "Well the letter may be just one of those unsolved mysteries." Hoping she sounded more convinced then she really was.

"It could be from a disgruntled employee." With the cloth wrapped around her foot, Daniel gave her toes one last squeeze.

"I suppose."

Sue's leg had fallen asleep with her feet contorted to

accommodate his position alongside her on the chair. She swiveled around.

"I guess I should get back to my hotel. Do you need help getting up?"

"Yes." She put out her hand.

She clung to his arm as he pulled her up. She stepped forward as soon as he did. They collided and were pressed up against each other for a few long seconds. A shot of adrenaline bounced through her. Between the two glasses of wine, the foot massage, and her girlish thoughts, she acted purely on instinct and pressed her lips up against his.

Damn, twice I've done that! Hell, I don't care.

Daniel didn't hesitate, his lips parted to welcome hers.

The sweet taste of this tender man was all she cared about as their tongues danced together.

Her knees felt weak again but his strong hands curled around her waist supporting her.

When they separated, Sue said, "I'm sorry."

"Don't be. I wanted to kiss you all night." When she didn't respond he kissed her again. When they pulled apart he said, "Should I stay?"

This was an open-ended question.

"I want to. I really do. But I should get some sleep. It's been a really long day. There's no need for complications." She answered not even convincing herself of the answer.

If he took her rejection hard, he didn't show it. "I understand. I'll call you tomorrow, maybe we can have dinner tomorrow night."

"I'd like that." Yes, she was excited at the idea of a date. "Thanks for being there. I'll be better company tomorrow. I promise." Sue smiled and touched his arm.

He gave her a quick peck on her cheek and walked away. He turned back around. "Try vinegar and salt to take away the stains."

Sue went into her hotel room, undressed and climbed into bed. She realized that having complete happiness required another ingredient, finding someone to love.

She had just turned down an opportunity to explore this possibility with a truly exceptional man she really cared for. Would another chance come along with him? Maybe tomorrow? Still, sometimes one shot was all you got. One shot. That was her last thought before falling asleep, her blue toes peeking outside the white cotton sheets.

THIRTY-NINE
Boston
The Next Day

"I DON'T GIVE A RAT'S ASS whether you understand, Daniel, I just want you to agree with me." Anthony Romero said to Daniel. The two sat in a Mexican restaurant with paint peeling off the walls, a hot sauce stained carpet, and an army of roaches. Anthony's voicemail to Daniel, saying they had to meet, had arrived while he had drinks with Sue.

"This isn't a business proposition, this is illegal," Daniel said. The muscle-thick Anthony sitting in front of Daniel was asking him to agree to a ridiculous proposal.

Anthony Romero was unimpressed. He rolled the unlit cigar in his mouth between pursed lips. He tapped his stumpy index finger on the paper in front of them. "There's nothing illegal about this. Yorkston Toys has a backlog."

"I see." Daniel crossed his arms. "A backlog. Sounds like blackmail."

"No sir. Just a backlog." Anthony laughed harshly.

"What does my consulting business with Logan have to do with our ability to receive products from Yorkston?"

"I'm just saying, Danny boy, if you agree to stay away from Logan Designs and their management staff, whether as a consultant or in any other *capacity* . . ." he paused, grinning when he said *capacity,* "whatsoever, we'll begin shipping product to your stores again."

"I don't believe this shit. For how long?"

"Until we say and until the lawsuit is settled between the two companies." Anthony stood up. "I take that as a yes?"

Daniel wasn't buying it. "You know, you look right at home in this sleazy Mexican cantina."

Anthony looked curiously at him and crossed his arms across his chest. "I can do more harm to Logan and the senior management. Are you willing to put her company at risk too?"

Daniel narrowed his eyes and his back stiffened. He was pissed, angry did not cover it.

Anthony leaned over and whispered, "Do you know what we can do to both of your companies?"

Daniel was furious, but this wasn't the time or place to settle with Anthony. He had other ideas.

"Well, are you in?"

Daniel nodded.

"We'll keep you posted." Anthony left the table, stopped and added, "And we'll know whether you are working with Logan or whether you've kept to our deal. Don't attempt to call or email. Avoid all contacts with them. You'll not get a second chance." He turned, picked up a toothpick at the hostess stand and stuck the sliver in his mouth as he left the restaurant.

Fifteen minutes after Daniel's meeting with the Yorkston hatchet man, he received a call from Winston's senior buyer. "Daniel, you're not going to believe this, I just got a call— we are getting a shipment from Yorkston this afternoon!" Taunya was ecstatic. "I've been begging them for weeks to ship us any product, but everything has been on backorder. I guess my bitching got through to someone there."

"Yes, Taunya, I think you got through to them." Daniel said softly, his heart stinging.

God, how was he going to not see her again? What would Sue think? It was probably better for her anyway. What did she say ...no complications?

Sue had returned to her harborside hotel after spending the last day of the Boston show with clients. She was thinking about her meeting later that evening. Just the thought of a date with Daniel gave her heart a jolt.

When she entered her hotel room, her heart got another jolt. There was a large vase with a dozen yellow roses. She was excited over the gesture . . . until she read the note.

Sue, sorry to cancel this evening. My office needs me in Atlanta. You're right, maybe we don't want complications right now. Good luck on your products. Always – Daniel

Her heartstrings tugged. Sue sat down on the couch, staring at the roses. Their sweet-scented fragrance filled the air around her.

She sat there surprised and despondent. He had blown her off. She went over their conversation last night. Maybe she shouldn't have burdened him with her troubles. But he had said he wanted to see her again. She hadn't detected any undertones of irritation when he said goodbye.

Well, she didn't need distractions or complications in her messy life right now. She needed to focus on her lawsuits… and her products.

Should I call him and thank him for the flowers?

She closed her eyes and his face popped into her mind. She smiled to herself as she felt the warmth of happiness when her thoughts went to him. A tingle ran through her . . . his emerald green eyes, his big, gentle hands, his sense of humor.

How did I blow it? Complications? What was I thinking?

She came to realize now, too late, that their times together made her happy and, darn it, she needed a little happiness in her complicated life right now.

FORTY
Texas
Law Offices of Tex Thornton

THE LAW OFFICES OF Tex Thornton looked like a government service agency. It was the sort of reception room that reminded Sue of her last visit to the Department of Motor Vehicles. She half expected to see a "take a number" dispenser as she and her children entered the lobby.

Instead, she was greeted with a tall cluttered counter with a sign indicating to her that she should call her party's extension on the white phone on the desk. No receptionist.

Before Sue could dial Tex's number, a plump lady with a double chin, sliver blue hair, and bifocal glasses came out.

"Good morning!" she bellowed out with a southern twang. "You must be Sue Logan." She extended her hand. "I'm Clara Dowell, Mr. Thornton's – you can call him Tex – legal secretary."

"Hi, I'm Sue Logan. Nice to meet you Ms. Dowell." Sue shook the elderly lady's soft but firm hand.

"Clara," she said. "And who do we have here?"

Clara looked past Sue at the two Logan kids huddled together directly behind Sue.

"I'm sorry; I left Mr. Thornton, uh, Tex, a voice mail this morning explaining that my babysitter was ill. I hope it isn't inconvenient, I can always reschedule." Today was her day to have

185

the kids at her offices, the unexpected lawyer meeting on such short notice left her without a sitter.

"No, not at all. I can take the two whippersnappers in another office while you meet with Tex. What's your name?" She looked at Colt.

Colt turned his face up, grinning a big toothless grin while his two dimples danced on his cheeks. "Colton Logan."

Clara shook his hand. Colt grinned even wider. "So very glad to meet you Mr. Colton."

"And what about you, princess?" Clara said in her most southern drawl to Maddie.

"I'm Maddie." Maddie's whole head of bobbing yellow curls flopped around when she shook Clara's hand. The way Maddie was dressed, in her crisp white blouse and red plaid jumper, reminded Sue of the diminutive charmer, Shirley Temple.

Maddie rubbed the back of her hand on her runny nose.

Clara pulled a pink Kleenex out of her pants pocket. "Here, sweetie." She looked at Sue. "It's clean."

Sue nodded. "Maddie, tell Ms Clara, 'thanks' ."

"Thank you." Maddie said softly and looked at the crumbled tissue. She blew her nose into it loudly and they all laughed.

"Sorry. She's had this lingering runny nose for weeks, it seems." Sue looked at Clara apologetically.

"Allergies, maybe. Come on. Let's get you two set up in your own office, shall we?" Clara winked at Sue. Maddie's little face brightened with a huge smile.

Sue and her two kids followed Clara. Elizabeth, the oldest Logan child, was at a friend's house all day.

They walked through a cluttered maze of cubicles where piles of file storage boxes sat everywhere and excess furniture was stacked in every corner.

"Do you like to color?" Clara led the children and Sue through the mess, undaunted by the chore at hand. She stopped once to pick up a legal-size folder that had escaped the file box's crowded conditions. She read it for a minute, scanned several nearby boxes, walked over and placed it on top of an overstuffed box marked, *Paula Smith, Plaintiff v. Parker County Board of County 1997.*

Sue looked around at the disorderly surroundings, which was a far cry from her former lawyer's offices. She wondered if this would reflect on her new lawyers productivity and success rates.

Clara and Sue got the two youngest Logans happily set up, coloring in a small office that appeared to be a storage closet for file boxes. Clara made no excuses for the untidiness of the offices. Her only comment was, "Lawyers and judges like to kill a lot of trees."

Maddie settled into a chair holding her favorite white Yorkston plush lamb.

"Maddie, sweetie, don't put that dirty lamb in your mouth."

Maddie gave her mom a look like; "Come onnnnn, Mom." Sue smiled and nodded. She winked at Colt. "Keep an eye on your sister. I'll be down the hall." Sue followed Clara down the hall.

"Here we go." Clara waved her into a large office substituting as a conference room. It was larger, but similar, to the other offices they had passed, sans the file boxes.

"Can I get you anything, coffee, Coke, water?" Clara asked.

"No, thank you. I'm fine."

"Suit yourself." Clara walked out in search of Tex.

Sue was nervous about the meeting. Her dad had offered to come with her, but she declined the offer telling him to save the time for when it was more than just an introductory meeting; maybe for the trial.

"Sue Logan?" Tex asked not gracefully interrupting Sue deep in thought.

"Yes, sorry, I didn't see you come in." Sue stood up to greet him. She saw where he got his nickname; "Tex" fit his cowboy-esque stature. He was over six feet tall by a half foot; his dark hair was peppered with a few strands of gray. He was dressed in a plaid shirt with pearl buttons, a pair of worn Levi jeans and scuffed up boots. The only item missing from his ensemble was a ten-gallon hat. Sue thought if she had met him in his office, she might find the hat sitting on his desk.

"Tex Thornton. Glad to meet you ma'am. Please sit down," he said. "What's the infamous Wilford Lockes up to these days?"

"My dad? He's retired. He sold the restaurant after Jonathan, my late husband, passed. I didn't know you two knew each other."

"We've mutual acquaintances. I reckon we've met years ago." He paused abruptly. "Let's get started. This meeting is costing you a lot of money and you didn't come here for small talk."

Sue decided she liked him already.

He took out a dictating tape recorder and placed it in the middle of the table. She glanced at it, about to protest, but before she did Tex commented. "I don't like to take notes. Clara can review the tape later if we need to. We don't usually refer to these tapes but it helps if we miss anything. Hell, we have storage boxes of these tapes everywhere. Never touch the damn things. Okay?"

"Okay."

"It also gets my new clients accustomed to answering in audible format for the recorded deposition. I know about the subpoena."

Sue nodded.

Tex turned on the recorder and quickly cited the date, the case and a few other legalisms.

He began with all the preliminaries, and brought Sue up to the present. He then proceeded to share with her Yorkston, the plaintiffs' next moves and their defensive retorts. His voice was toneless, almost bored, as he quickly ran through everything leading up to the present day.

"They'll file a motion for a preliminary injunction and a temporary restraining order, and we should win our motion for change of venue." Tex was stating the case like mere facts versus possibilities.

"What do you mean by a temporary restraining order?" Sue stopped him. She had heard of people getting a restraining order against an ex-spouse or a stalker, but why would Yorkston do that to her?

"A temporary restraining order is what the judge will probably grant Yorkston, if they win a preliminary injunction.

The judge will order Logan, and any of its associates and manufacturing reps to stop selling and manufacturing the catalogs that infringe on Yorkston's toys." Tex explained like he was teaching a business law class and he was the professor, Sue the student.

"Okay, gosh, can they do that?" Sue felt herself going pale.

"They can and undoubtedly will, in the next few days. Have you received a subpoena for a TRO yet?"

Sue shook her head slowly. She put her fingernail in her teeth.

Tex pointed to the recorder. Sue added belatedly, for the sake of the recording, "No I haven't seen anything relating to a TRO."

"Okay, good. But, you can count on it, you'll be asked to stop selling the catalogs."

Sue didn't hear much after that.

"Miss Sue?" Tex said. "Are you okay?"

"I'm sorry. Yes. I'm just a little shocked that I'll be ordered to stop selling the catalogs. They're doing so well." The realization made her sick to her stomach.

"I understand." Tex said.

"No I don't think you do, or that anyone can understand. That could devastate my revenues the next few quarters, especially until the new products start hitting the shelves and gaining acceptance," she shot back, the words coming unnaturally.

Tex nodded and looked up at the door to the conference room. Clara came in loaded down with files. She piled stack after stack of folders in front of Tex like she was building the wall around the Alamo to keep the enemies out.

Tex paid no heed to Clara and continued discussing the magnitude of Yorkston's potential to squeeze Logan Designs and ultimately massacre her and her company.

Tex reached across one of the piles, finding what he was looking for immediately.

"Nathanael Yorkston is one mean son-of-bitch." He read something in the folder and whistled. "Jesus, this industry is incestuous. It appears that Yorkston has sued ex-employees and several small companies. Some mom and pop companies claimed their products were stolen by Yorkston and sued, but it didn't come to much. Most of the suits are similar to yours; a David and Goliath match up."

"But I thought Bruce Barrows said there weren't many other similar cases."

"There are several out there." He put his hand on a tall stack next to him.

"These are cases where Yorkston is going after the little guys. I bet if I did some digging, there may be some commonality. They seem to pick and choose who they want to attack. It's not even based on revenues. I've seen two other publications like yours that have a larger subscriber base, and make more revenue, yet they are free to keep publishing."

Tex reached over and turned off the recorder. "Sue, can you think of any reason why this outfit would want to take you down? Can you think of anything? From the show circuit? From the past?"

Sue's brows closed together. "I've had my thoughts and even asked my other lawyers about it, years before this lawsuit. Their plush animal line uses a unique numbering system. I had patented a concept similar to this, years ago."

"I read something in the files about that. Go on."

She was pleased he read that part of her past, which was more than her other firm had done. "I always thought my parents registered the patent to conciliate me. But my dad told me years ago they really did it to help awaken my dreams; to keep me designing, and to never give up hope."

"But they didn't keep the patent renewed? Correct?" His voice was gentler now.

"Correct. I tried during college and afterwards to find an acceptable, fail-proof apparatus to mark the uniqueness of the doll's serial-numbered wrist bands. I guess Yorkston broke that code."

She explained to Tex about the soft tag sewn to the toys.

Sue perked up. "I have several next generation dolls coming out that are human-like but made of a special fabric. They were to incorporate the sequential wristbands. I call them my Millennium Kids of the World design."

"Millennium Kids?"

"Yep."

"I've seen your copyrights in the files for this product. It looks promising. When will you introduce it?"

"We've been showing the prototype to the sales reps. We'll begin delivering first quarter." *If Yorkston doesn't wipe me out before then, and I have enough cash to order the products.*

As if reading her mind, Tex asked, "Have you already ordered your products?"

190

"Some. But if I have to stop selling the catalog, I could lose enough revenue that it would limit my production of the plush kids."

Clara came in the room, interrupting them. She handed Tex a message. "Sorry to interrupt, but they insisted I pass this to you."

While Tex read, his brows moved up and down. "What the hell? I knew it. Those good for nothing low life weasels– predictable." He crinkled up the paper tossing it into the wastebasket from across the room. He stared at it, as it landed dead center in the trashcan.

"Those assholes are going for the preliminary injunction. I reckoned that Yorkston fella would jump to this quickly. Looks like you'll be served today with a cease and desist while they get a temporary restraining order. Damn them sonofabitches." He appeared to be talking to himself. He stopped after noticing the two women gaping at him.

Clara shook her pointed finger at Tex and both her double chins wobbled as she ranted. "Tex Thornton that ain't no way to talk around your lady client." She looked at Sue. "Sorry, he just gets so upset. I need to work to corral his maverick temper."

"Oh hell, Clara, she hasn't seen me upset yet." Tex looked at Sue and shrugged, "I'm just saying."

Sue actually appreciated the blunt exchange. She liked his unconventional style. She just prayed he could resolve this quickly and without costing her to lose her products . . . her company. "Damn them, is right. When will this end?"

"Sugar," Tex began. Clara gave him a warning look. He waved her off. "Sue, they're in for the long haul. It's like this. Yorkston's bank account is bottomless from the success of those funky stuffed toys. They're going to throw heaps of money at this lawsuit; and they plan on taking you down, crushing you, and squashing you like a cockroach. They won't give up until they've pounded every last cent out of you and your company. They'll use your Millennium Kids to wipe their floor. They are ruthless sons-of-bitches. And—" He stopped because Clara had firmly put her hands on her hips to protest his offensive pep talk.

Sue's hands trembled. The lump in her throat was so large she was afraid to speak because she feared her voice would be unsteady. She tried to will her tears away, but when that didn't happen, she let them fall.

"These goons don't deserve your tears," Tex said.

Sue swiped her palm quickly under each eye. "Sorry. I am a businesswoman. I always try to be professional but, shit, the thought of losing my company and all I've worked for has pushed me over the edge."

A few more tears slid out of Sue's eyes. "I should get going. I need to take Colt to soccer practice." She said it without looking at Tex.

"Plus, I'm afraid if I don't get out of this office quick I'm going to lose it." She brushed away the tears clinging to the corner of her eyes with her finger. They weren't a mark of her weakness, but of power. She used this to refocus her anger. She wanted to fight back. Losing her products and her business was a driving force; her company's welfare was no longer just a conscious thought, it was the weight, the shadow in her brain closing down over everything.

She inhaled and said flatly, "Let's do what we need to do to fight back hard. Tex, you have my full cooperation; my staff, designers, accountants, bankers, sales reps – whatever it takes." Her voice stronger, more composed.

"Now we're talking." Tex glanced at his watch. "I think you're right. We've covered enough for today. Clara will contact you about the list of items we need. And be prepared, you'll be getting a visit soon on the TRO."

He came over and gave Sue a big bear hug. "Ms. Sue, don't you worry, everything is going to be just fine."

It was such a huge, wonderful lie right now, that it wasn't even worth her arguing about it.

The kids were quiet on the trip home. Sue drove home mechanically; grinding her teeth the whole way. She couldn't comprehend it. She had sensed that no matter what happened, a discernible, suspicious presence was always there underlying all her legal troubles.

FORTY-ONE
Fifteen months before the Millennium

SUE'S DAYS PASSED in a blur of legal proceedings mingled together with creating her new designs and raising her kids. They won the change of venue and the case was moved to Texas. They lost the preliminary injunction and she and her reps were adjoined from selling the catalog. The temporary restraining order became a reality and the sale of her catalogs was frozen while the lawyers and judges battled.

The interested buyer for her company never disclosed its name, so she told the investors to take a hike. Besides she didn't want to lose control of her company and the buyout proposal clearly stated she would be left on in a designing capacity only . . . something that didn't interest her. Dee told her, "You need to run from that backwoods loser like he is trying to kill you."

Sue daydreamed, staring out her living room window into the cul-de-sac observing a hawk perched on a rusty birdhouse post. She reminisced back to Elizabeth's first day of kindergarten.

Elizabeth and another five-year-old boy waited under that birdhouse for the school bus. The bus driver maneuvered the large yellow transport filled with kids into the cul-de-sac. The two kids spotted a wandering armadillo, which came out of the dense bushes from across the street plopping off the curb. Elizabeth and the boy started chasing it. The bus driver waited. The two five-year-olds were giggling, squealing with excitement and chasing the armadillo as the armored mammal got stuck in the curbed cul-de-sac and couldn't quickly exit. Sue and the little boy's mom scrambled after the kindergarteners while the two children chased the armadillo, and the school bus driver, Mr. Willy, and the bus full of kids, sat watching and laughing as the chaos in the cul-de-sac continued for over five minutes until the armadillo escaped by forging ahead on a steeply-sloping bank by using its tail as a prop to keep it from sliding backwards after it lifted itself off the curb.

Sue grinned as she pictured the scene from years ago. She wandered into her office and sat down. It was already the end of October and she had three more months before announcing her new stuffed dolls to the world. Sue and her marketing company had chosen the New York Toy show in February as the official launch date. In the back of her mind she saw a countdown clock as she tracked the days to the New Year, the year before the new century, the new millennium.

She checked the mantle clock in her home office, six eleven. She still had a ton of work to complete, but she decided to take a break and check on the kids in the other room. Her parents were helping the kids with their Halloween costumes.

She wanted to talk to her dad before her call with her sister and her bother-in-law. Her dad had engaged them to snoop around Yorkston.

He had pleaded with her to have them look into the company. "I know there's more to this case. If there is something fishy going on, maybe your sister and her sleuth of a husband can dig it up. Either way, they could at least find out something about this guy, Nathanael Yorkston, so you can confront him to possibly make a deal. What he's doing to you just doesn't add up."

"Have you discussed everything with them?" Sue had asked.

"Well, as much as you've shared with me, young lady, especially the court decision to force you to stop selling the catalog. I suspect there is still more you don't want to tell."

"I know, Dad. I have my suspicions, but I am trying to confirm a few things."

"How can I help? This is deeper than a simple trademark infringement."

Sue slowly let out a breath as his words sunk in. Yorkston's lawsuits served as a springboard for them to subpoena the contents of Logan's computer hard drives and other records hoping to find anything they could use against her. Ostensibly, Yorkston was attempting to find any critical information on her company, but why?

"Smile, kids." Sue held her camera to her eye, clicking away. Elizabeth, Maddie, and Colt were dressed in the costumes their grandma had made.

"They look adorable, Mom." She walked over and kissed her mom on her creased cheek. "Thank you."

Sue's mom looked pleased at the results and her grandkids' reaction to the costumes. Colt came over and sat on his grandma's lap.

"Thank you, Grandma." Colt flashed a big grin.

Thelma tousled his hair. "You are welcome, sweetie." She lowered her voice so the girls couldn't hear, "Your costume was my favorite to make. I love green dinosaurs with long spiky tails."

He grinned up at her and in turn tousled his grandma's hair. Sue laughed at the exchange. Grandma Thelma tried to straighten her hair and a silver curl fell out of place. Thelma always wore her hair in a neatly styled French twist. Her blonde hair had been transformed over the last ten years into a silver-white mane. Sue admired her mom. She was a smart, dignified lady that loved her husband and family.

"Sue." Wilford called from the study. "Can you come in here?"

"Sorry, Mom, but Dad is helping me with a project. Colt, show Grandma what a skate-boarding dinosaur can do."

"Here's Sue now." Wilford said into his cell phone when she walked into the study.

"Patrick has found some interesting information on your Yorkston guy already. Here you talk to him." Before she could protest, he handed his cell phone to her.

"Hey Patrick, what's up?" Sue asked. Wilford watched her as she anxiously twisted her hair into a knot.

"This is a helluva of company you've got yourself messed up with. The boss man is like the lord to his serfs. If any of his people

195

desert the mother ship, they are bound and sworn by pre-employment confidentiality agreements. He has been known to sue his ex-employees for uttering his name at a bar mitzvah."

"I know, Pat. So what? He's a bad guy to work for. I get it. I can go to the internet and read that." Sue knew Nathanael Yorkston was a tyrant. She remembered reading blogs about disgruntled ex-employees. "What else did you find out?"

"He's been accused of witness tampering." Patrick announced like he had just released a juicy piece of gossip.

"Really? I wonder if Tex knows that."

"I can email you the case and what the judge found. I guess Nathanael Yorkston called and threatened a witness that she would lose her job if she said the wrong things. The judge found out the next day. Nathanael Yorkston himself had personally called the witness the night before a court appearance. I've plenty to email you about how he created his empire . . . the good, the bad and the ugly."

"Okay, thanks. I really appreciate what you and Dee are doing."

"You have a long battle ahead of you. Why have they picked your company to sue when there are companies that have exploited the plush toys to make more money than Logan, I can't understand. Our research found one company that gets over a million hits a day on their web site."

"What did you read about the lawsuits they lost?"

"One judge, while ruling against Yorkston, called the company liars and bullies."

"What about the ones they've won?"

"They've won more than they have lost. Hey, Sue I gotta run. Give the kids my love. Say hi to your sis. Bye."

"Thanks Patrick. Take care." Since the death of her husband, Patrick had been an avuncular figure to her and the kids.

"Hey, Sis. Have you been on any hot dates lately?" Dee's spunky voice asked.

"Hi, Dee," Sue scanned the room to make sure her dad hadn't come back in. She saw him outside with the kids and her mom, enjoying the autumn evening, his face buried in a golf magazine. "No, I barely have time to spend with the kids. Between the lawsuits and getting the new line launched, there's not a lot of time left for much else."

"Well maybe getting out on a date would help take some of the pressure off."

"If I had enough time to pull my head out of the vice it's been squeezed into the last six months, I might be able to meet someone." Sue liked teasing Dee back.

"So, speaking of that, what's the word on China boy?"

"Daniel?" Sue regretted sharing her feelings with Dee about him. And she hadn't shared *everything*.

"Yes, sizzling Daniel. Have you talked to him lately?"

Sue felt her cheeks flush. "No, not much. I've talked to him a few times." She lied. Since Boston, he hadn't called her back or returned her emails. She added, "About business."

"It's hard to kiss and tell, when you've hardly been kissed."

"He was helpful getting the plush kids launched, that's all. Besides, this is his busy season. His family owns a chain of stores in Atlanta. The holidays are their busy months." Sue almost believed her own lie.

"Well, maybe we should go gift shopping in Atlanta," Dee said.

Sieged with reluctance, Sue just sighed. She wasn't sure of the next time she would see Daniel. She knew he would be at the January show in Atlanta, but that was still several months away. Why had his not returning her emails been so devastating to her? It hurt that he didn't want to check in on her.

"Patrick and I have our marching orders from Dad. We'll keep you posted on what we find out."

"Okay, thanks." Sue pushed Daniel from her mind, looking out the window and watching her kids on the patio.

"Well give those darling kids of yours a hug from Aunt Dee and Uncle Patrick. We'll see you all in December, right?"

What was Maddie doing with her stuffed dog? Did she just cut off the tush tag?

"Sue? You still there?"

"Yes, we've got our tickets. I'll email you our itinerary. Colt wants to ski on those bunny hills you have in Michigan."

"Hopefully, we'll have snow by then. Hugs and kisses."

"Love you too." Sue hung up and walked out the French door from her study to the patio.

"Maddie, come here, sweetie," Sue yelled. Maddie, still dressed in her princess costume, skipped over to Sue.

"Do you like my costume?" She asked with a big flooding smile from ear to ear.

"I do. You make a beautiful princess." Since the death of Diana, Princess of Wales last summer, the popularity of the costumes had skyrocketed.

"What do you have in your hand?" Sue referred to a small child scissors.

"This is my scissors. It's safe, Mama." Her smile disappeared.

"I know, Maddie." Her kids were taught they can only use the blunt scissors with colored handles; the kid's scissors. "Why do you have it?"

Maddie looked uncomfortable. She started twirling the toile skirt.

"I used it to cut off the tag on my puppy." Maddie looked like she did when she was caught pouring her mom's favorite perfume into her artificial plants to water them.

"I can see that, but why?"

"Colt said, 'Orkston is mean to you and that we shouldn't have any of their toys'. I like my Orkston puppy, can I keep it?"

Sue pulled Maddie onto her lap as she knelt down by her. "Of course you can, honey." Maddie wrapped her little arms around her mom's neck, giving her a big kiss.

Later that night, while her youngest daughter slept in her pink canopy bed, Sue straightened Maddie's room. She picked up several stuffed toys and returned them to her daughter's shelves. She noticed some of the stuffed Yorkston toys were missing their soft tags. She examined all the toys made by Yorkston, and all the tags had been cut out of the toys' butts. One stuffed bear was cut so close to the seam it had poly-filled stuffing leaking out.

Sue smiled as she stood in her daughter's room. The irony; *if none of the Yorkston's stuffed toys had tags or identities, there would be no need for her catalog.* Without their cute names, release dates, random numbers, there would be no need for any catalogs to help collectors – or the secondary market, or the web sites, or the trader's magazines, or the mystique. It would be just a cute stuffed toy.

Sue stared at the shelf of Maddie's toys for a long moment. Many Logan toys, puzzle boxes, time capsules, kids games and other Logan products were piled on her shelves, mixed in with Yorkston's and other toy manufacturers.

If she had to give up on the Yorkston catalog forever, she felt confident her other gifts and toys would keep her business afloat.

And after her call this afternoon, it was uplifting to know that Patrick's snooping activities might help discover the reason for the sudden onslaught.

FORTY-TWO
Texas
Twelve and a half months before the Millennium

"CONGRATULATIONS, SUE," Mike Peterson said, as they settled inside the green taxi on Congress Street outside the hospital.

Sue pulled off her gloves, worn on a rare occasion in Texas. "Thanks." She smiled at Mike.

"The World Trade Center on Oak Lawn," he said to the driver. "Damn, can you turn up the heat? It is freezing outside for us thin-blooded Texans."

"I can't believe they are going to present the Millennium Kids to the hospital Board in a few weeks." She grabbed Mike's hand and squeezed it.

Mike Peterson was the CEO and president of the manufacturer rep group which had represented the Logan line for the last four years. He displayed her products in the World Trade Center.

Mike was a true friend to Sue. He was almost twice her age, but they got along like an old married couple. Mike had looks that intrigued women and there was something about his eyes that drew people in.

"Thank you for setting up the meeting," Sue said. "Mr. Weiner and Mr. Cole made a big difference in getting it to the board of United Hospitals for final approval."

Mike smiled at her. "Rudy Cole is a big shot CEO at United all right, but more than that, he is a political powerhouse in the healthcare industry. He can help you. But are you ready to announce the line in six weeks?"

"Yes, I'm almost ready to make the big splash." She regarded Mike intently. "And when this news about United buying the toys gets out, it will open a ton of doors. This success will help offset the lost sales on the catalogs." She had confided in her friend about the restraining order on the catalogs.

It was hard to believe it had been just eight weeks since Logan Designs was banned from selling the catalogs. As fate would have it, the December pre-show orders for the plush Millennium Kids line for next spring shipments had been astonishing.

"This was such a critical meeting. God, I loved hearing that the United group will commit to buying a record amount of my stuffed toys to give away to all babies born in January 2000. This news has a huge impact on my orders from China," Sue said.

"Our office pulled up statistics that predicts there'll be over four million babies born in the US alone in the year 2000. Damn girl, if you could capture just twenty percent of that market, you could sell close to a million units."

"The toys' designs would assure a follow up sale for children well into their school years. There's the build-your-own-doll in the third year after the product is launched. As children grow older and their hobbies evolve, they could go to my web site and design their next generation stuff toy." Sue felt comfortable enough in the confines of the cab to share the product line with him. Sue, her family, and only a few key employees knew of the research and development of the M Kids. Research information about the personality profiles of Millennia's was the basis for Logan's next generation plush toys.

"Do you have time for a celebratory glass of wine before you head back to the burbs?"

"Sure, it's only six o'clock. Plus I can wait until traffic dies down. The kids are going to an after-school holiday event."

"Perfect." Mike instructed the taxi driver to do a U-turn and take them back to Randy's, a high-end steakhouse, only a few blocks away.

The taxi pulled into the crowded parking lot and up to the front door, past the valet. Practically every Mercedes and BMW in the parking lot had a model number of 500 or greater. A white stretch limousine was parked near the entrance with a chauffeur waiting inside, his cap resting on his face as he slept.

While Mike paid the cab driver, Sue went into the dark bar. She was dressed in a white sweater and a short black wool skirt, both accenting her curves. Her black boots stopped short of her knees, leaving exposed a bit of her thigh. Sue scanned the crowd for a seat and opted for an empty bar stool near the entrance. Dozens of businessmen in sharp suits occupied the bar. A few heads turned her way.

"Wow, it is crowded." Mike slipped beside Sue. "What would you like? A glass of wine?"

"Chardonnay. Thank you."

They talked for a few minutes before Mike asked about the Yorkston case and the next steps.

"They've been awful to deal with. If I have to look at another legal document, I'm going to strangle someone." Sue sipped her wine.

"I bet."

"Mary Jo and I spent a full weekend gathering all the documents and information their lawyers requested. They had over a hundred and sixty items on their document request. Some were absolutely unnecessary, like three years' of phone bills. Seriously! And four years' worth of order history with all the clients' addresses filled one file box on its own. In the end, we filled over twenty-seven boxes. We delivered everything to Yorkston, all neatly organized and labeled."

"Wow."

"Yeah, wow is right. And in turn, do you know what they did for our discovery?"

Mike shook his head.

"They sent us a bunch of crap. My lawyers requested their files to do their preparation for the trial."

"Did they find anything useful?"

"No, are you kidding? Their lawyers only produced four file boxes and the papers were all randomly thrown in; like page one of a report would be in one box and page two in another. It was a total shambles."

"Those assholes."

"It cost me loads of lawyer's hours and money to go through the four boxes and, in the end, they couldn't find anything of value."

"What about the depositions?"

"Those were overkill too. They spent two days deposing me and another two weeks deposing a few employees and some of my manufacturing rep groups over the silly catalog. A damn waste of time."

"Depositions, document production, filings are all power struggles." Mike had downed several Jack Daniels. The more drinks he had, the more audacious he became. "You are up against a formable giant with a lot of power. Nathanael's wealth has given him an influence on the toy and gift industry far beyond his revenue numbers. He has made investment and business decisions that have opened or closed employment opportunities for many small businesses affecting many people. He has contributed money to political parties, to buy his way around the borders."

He paused and took a gulp of his cocktail. "Don't you find it interesting that his containers are never tied up in customs? And, he owns a few media companies. He controls the magazines. I've even heard the Yorkston technology staff run chat rooms to influence the secondary market of their plush toys. The more successful his products, the more wealth and influence Yorkston attains," Mike said, louder.

Nearby, a man with long salt and pepper hair, in a tweed jacket approached their table. He looked familiar. "Sorry to interrupt, but did I overhear you say you are with the Yorkston group?"

Damn, he heard Mike. "No, we are not." Sue didn't want to start a conversation.

"Hell no, we're not!" Mike added.

Okay, that wasn't needed. Who is this guy any way; a Yorkston toy groupie?

"Why do you ask?" Mike said.

Damn, Mike is trying to start a conversation. Sue was trying to think of damage control if Mike told too much. The last thing she needed was for her company to end up in tomorrow's papers; *Toy Giant crushes minuscule local company, Logan Designs.* This was her private hell.

"Well he and his group are here, so I thought maybe you were with them, that's all."

Sue's eyes pierced him. She almost spit her wine out.

"Sorry for the intrusion," he said.

Wait a minute? Did he say Nathanael was here? "Where?" Sue croaked.

"Here in the restaurant?"

Shoot, had she said that aloud?

"Yes, he's here in this restaurant." The stranger watched Sue as she slid down her bar stool onto the floor, the color going out of her just as fast. The man and Mike both grabbed an arm each.

"Sorry, my friend is recovering from the flu and is weak." Mike gave her a sideways glance. "Can you get her a glass of water?"

"Oh yeah, absolutely." The man hurried off.

Sue was visibly shaken. Mike tried to cheer her up. "Of all the gin joints, in all the towns, in all the world, he walks into ours." He said in his best Humphrey Bogart impersonation.

Sue smiled at her good friend. "I love Casa Blanca." She lost her smile as quickly as it came. "What the hell is he here for? The Dallas gift show isn't until next month."

"Here comes our new friend, let's ask him."

"Here you go." He handed a glass of water to Sue.

"Thank you." She took a gulp of the water.

"So how do you know this Yorkston fellow is here?" Mike asked.

"I was walking in earlier when his limo pulled up. I know his face; it's all over the news about those toys he created. The man is a genius coming up with that idea. Damn, wish I'd thought of it," he replied.

"I'm Mike Peterson and this is Sue Logan." Mike offered his hand.

"My name is Richard Speckman." He shook Sue and Mike's hands.

FORTY-THREE

SUE DAZED by the news the stranger had just delivered, felt her stomach filing with acid. *Maybe it's not true; maybe he thought he saw Nathanael Yorkston get out of the limo. Try to appear calm.*

One minute she was celebrating and just like that, lickety split, she was worrying about her enemy in the next room. Just like that, her spirit was melting faster than a speeding snowball.

She took a swig of her wine, feeling a knotting pain in her stomach. She brushed away several strands of hair that had fallen across her face; her cheeks felt flushed, despite the cold room. She tried to smile, to replace the expression that could easily be interpreted as utter confusion.

Mike reached over and patted her hand. "Sue runs a global manufacturing company and I represent her products. She has some impressive products herself, coming out in a few months."

The man turned his back to Mike to face Sue. "What does your company manufacture?"

Sue didn't want to discuss her business with this stranger; she wanted to talk to Mike and summon up enough courage to go talk with Nathanael. "Look, I hate to be rude, Mr. Speckman, but my colleague and I have some business to finish. Do you mind? We'd like to continue our meeting alone." She hoped she sounded polite but convincing enough.

If Mike was surprised by her comment to the outsider, he didn't show it. She felt a dark and angry mood settling over her.

"Sorry to bother you two. I would love to hear about your

205

business, but I can see you want to be alone. Maybe later?"

Neither Sue nor Mike responded.

He walked away.

Evan turned his back on Sue and her friend and walked over to the table he had been sitting.

Evan Taylor, alias Richard Speckman, had been in Texas with Naty. Evan had spent the afternoon trying to track down Sue. What a wild coincidence that Naty had his dinner meeting at this restaurant. Possibly Sue and Naty's accidental meeting might kill two birds with one stone.

Evan wasn't surprised that Sue wanted to be alone. He had just delivered explosive news to her. If she wasn't so damn cute, he would've enjoyed the misery he'd caused by telling her Nathanael was in the next room; it was like giving a bear a salmon to play with.

Yeah, her company was global and far-reaching and its secrets were deep, but he had to find out what she knew. His directive was clear as a glass of water. Nathanael Yorkston had given the edict to find out what Sue Logan knew. Evan had been trying to get information from her for months. Unfortunately, the lawsuit had kept her busy. This was a rare occasion to find her in a public place. He would approach her again later when Mike wasn't near, dropping a bombshell to get her attention.

Richard Speckman? What the hell was he thinking? *Shit, I could've chosen a better alias.* Wasn't Richard Speck a notorious killer who killed eight nurses in a Chicago hospital? He had better work on a believable cover if he was going to continue being Nathanael Yorkston's undercover reporter.

FORTY-FOUR

SUE WAITED until Speckman was out of earshot. "I'm sorry to be so edgy. I really don't feel like talking about my business right now to a stranger."

"You don't need to apologize. And you don't need to be embarrassed about your company. You've wonderful products and a successful growing company. What Yorkston is doing has nothing to do with it. You understand?"

"I know. Thank you." She touched his arm lightly. She struggled to find the words to explain to her dear friend without divulging that she suspected Yorkston was doing something terrible. She just needed more time to verify it. She decided against sharing anything with Mike. She was grateful he was as interested in her business as she was. She felt comforted to know he would be here at her side when she would finally confront Nathanael Yorkston tonight.

She read the time on her cell phone. It was after eight o'clock. She wondered how long Nathanael would be in his dinner meeting. In the background, she heard Nat King Cole singing, *Chestnuts roasting on an open fire.*

When she spoke again, her voice was scratchy and low. "I'm going to talk to Nathanael."

"Well if you want to, you better do it now." Mike nodded toward the entrance of the restaurant.

Sue saw an entourage of men in dark suits gathered at the front entrance, preparing to leave the restaurant. Nathanael Yorkston was in the middle of the pack, dressed in a custom-made Milan's

Caraceni camel wool suit. Sue was irked to think that his hand-folded silk hankie probably cost more than her whole outfit, including her Macy's boots. It was as if he was announcing with confidence. ' I can afford a ten thousand dollar suit, and you chumps can't.'

She stood up.

"Wait." Mike grabbed her shoulder. "What are you going to say?"

"I haven't thought . . . ." She gravitated closer to the group of men.

Mike and Speckman both stood, following Sue.

She was near the group when she saw two familiar faces leaving with the Yorkston entourage, Jeff Weiner and Rudy Cole, the executives from United Hospitals.

She stopped dead in her boots. *What the hell? Geez, this night just keeps getting better and better, doesn't it?*

Before she could regain her composure and shuffle another step, the group walked out. She forced herself to keep moving. By the time she reached the entrance, only the shorter man remained in the doorway. His concerned look settled on Sue, as she stood in front of him.

His face gave her pause. "You better watch yourself, Ms. Logan." He shut the door behind him.

In the white limo, Nathanael turned to Anthony. "What was the remark she made to you, Anthony?"

Anthony handed a glass of Scotch to Nathanael and held his friend's gaze, "We were mistaken. It wasn't Sue Logan."

Sue was still standing at the entrance of the restaurant when Mike reached her. "Did you say anything?"

"No, he was gone."

"Did the short man say anything?"

Sue hesitated. She could hear her heart pounding. "No," she lied. She felt her face flush as bright as the Texas sunset.

"Let me pay the bill and we'll leave."

In the background the hit song of the year played, *My Heart Will Go On,* the theme song from the movie of the ill-fated voyage of the Titanic.

In the taxi, Sue sat in silence. What was the hospital CEO doing with Nathanael Yorkston? It didn't make sense, especially so soon after her meeting with them. What had the short Spanish guy said to her? Watch her step? And he called her by her name. Who was he, another of Yorktson's smart-ass lawyers?

She shuddered when she tried to make sense of it all. She felt certain these people could take down her company and her with it. With her enemies circling, Sue would have to make choices that would affect her company and the people she loved.

FORTY-FIVE
February 1999
Yorkston Lawyer's Texas Offices

SUE RAISED HER HEAD, and her piercing stare found her rival's eyes, that were black and cold and deadly-looking as any rattlesnake. Sue Logan and Nathanael Yorkston were summoned together to mediate.

Sue smiled politely, acknowledging Nathanael's look, yet ignoring it. He held out his hand. Reluctantly, Sue shook his hand. Feeling his strong, rough calluses against her small, smooth palm, she felt weak and soft.

"Ms. Logan. Nathanael Yorkston, we meet at last. Pleased to meet you." His wicked smile didn't soften the cold blackness of his eyes.

Sue wondered if anyone else heard the condescending tone in Nathanael's voice. She nodded but couldn't utter even a hello. She sure as hell wasn't pleased to meet him. She was agitated and apprehensive, but secretly satisfied he looked older than his photos. She acted like he was important to their meeting today instead of her worst nightmare.

They were in the large conference room of the Yorkston attorneys' law offices. The downtown offices were opulent, but Sue could have been in the Taj Mahal and she wouldn't have noticed.

Sue gestured to get Tex and tried to make her voice sound calm, although she felt anything but. "Tex, are you sure this is the

210

best route versus a trial?"

"As we discussed last week, a judge has already issued a summary judgment in Yorkston's favor. The judge's decision was because there were no facts to dispute. Sue, you used their photos in your catalog and profited from their success. And as they see it, without their permission. Yorkston wins on the law without a trial. We are here today to mitigate your damages."

Sue twisted a loose strand of her hair between her fingers. "It's just so frustrating. I'm confounded by all the legalities. I hate that I had to give up the product, and now I have to pay them on top of that."

"If the district court hadn't granted Yorkston's motion for summary judgment, we could have taken a shot at trial. But a jury is bound to be sympathetic to Yorkston because of those damn popular stuffed toys. You made money off an infringing product and now they want you to pay." Tex put his arm around her shoulder and gave her a feeble smile.

Sue smiled weakly back at him. "Ok, today will settle it. After eight months of fighting Yorkston, I'm ready to get rid of them. It has been an exhaustive, costly, ongoing harassment from the get-go. Yorkston uses ruthless tactics, like the onslaught of deposition after deposition." Sue shuddered.

They rejoined the group.

Tex had explained to Sue both sides would meet and spend the day negotiating back and forth. The lawyers were there to support their clients, but the mediator was impartial.

The conference room was filled with five dark woolen suits; Sue and Tex, Nathanael Yorkston and James McDougal, and DJ Brentwood, the mediator.

DJ greeted them. "Hello. Good afternoon." He shook her hand.

"Hello," Sue said.

"Hey, good to meet you." He shook Nathanael Yorkston's hand.

He explained his goal was to help the two adversaries reach an agreement on a settlement amount. "A judge in Texas determined in a Summary Judgment that the catalog was infringing on the

Yorkston's plush by using photos of the toys," DJ said.

Sue wiggled in her chair. Tex gave her a look of sympathy. Nathanael looked smug. His lawyer looked at his yellow pad and checked off a list.

"I have been resolving disputes with some of the most publicized cases for over the last twenty years," DJ continued. After a brief summary of the mediation process, DJ turned to Sue.

"Would you like to present any opening remarks?"

"No thanks. I'll pass." Her eyes squinted at Nathanael.

"Any questions so far? No? Good. I hate questions. So don't be asking questions. A waste of time." DJ winked at Sue, laughed at his own joke and turned to Nathanael. "Mr. Yorkston, do you have any opening comments?"

Nathanael looked at Sue and grinned his row of perfect teeth at her. "No, I'll pass."

"Okay, good." DJ chuckled again as if he had an inside private joke. Sue felt no one wanted to show his or her hand.

"Let's get both parties settled in your own private rooms." DJ said they wouldn't see each other again, until the negotiating was complete.

Sue walked out of the conference room, and Nathanael stared at her every step of the way.

Sue and Tex sat in a tiny room, waiting for DJ to return from his first session with the Yorkston twosome. She looked outside at the cool bland February day. A foggy mist had settled on the horizon, like the fog in her brain. It was hard to tell whether it was the gray smog or the layers of gray clouds hiding the sun.

Time passed slowly. The clock on the wall read nine twelve.

At 9:45, DJ entered the room. Sue sat up taller. Was that a look of pity on DJ's face?

DJ sat down at the head of the table between Sue and Tex. He had a small folded piece of paper. He slid the paper to Tex. Tex opened it, read it, nodded and slid it over to Sue. Sue felt the whole process to be comical. The fate of her company was written on this tiny sheet of paper with one long number and the letter "S" with two vertical lines through it.

She read the amount. "You've got to be kidding, right?" She

turned to Tex and then D.J. "This amount is more than they had suggested when we were discussing settling outside of mediation." She was furious, but still calm. The mediation had cost thousands of dollars and it took another full day away from the office. "I mean, really? Tex? Twenty million?"

"Sue, it's a start," Tex said.

"A bad one." Sue crumbled the paper.

"I understand how you feel. It has been a long, costly process. Let me know where you were a few weeks ago, and we'll discuss a counter option," DJ said.

Sue and Tex spent twenty minutes with DJ. Each time they had a point in their favor, DJ responded with an argument against their point. It was obvious he had done his homework.

DJ took their counteroffer, written on a small sheet of paper, and went to the adjacent room occupied by Nathanael and his lawyer.

Sue and Tex waited in silence. They had both talked to each other until they were numb to each other's words on the settlement.

Twenty-five minutes later, DJ returned with another slip of paper. He handed it to Sue this time.

Sue opened it and straightened up. Fifteen million. She pounded her fist against the table, rattling the water glasses and the men's nerves. "This is a damn waste of my time."

"How much revenue did you make last year on this product?" DJ asked again. He had asked the question earlier.

"I told you, we have spent all that revenue. We reinvested in our company. I can't pay this. I will have to bankrupt my company."

Both men exchanged glances.

"That's their goal. Isn't it?" Sue shook her head and swallowed the lump forming in her throat.

"I will counter with one million." Sue wrote the number on the slip of paper feeling rather satisfied.

Another hour passed. Their offer, 10 million. Sue's counter, 2 million.

It just got crazier. On one of the counteroffers, Sue only raised her amount by ten dollars. DJ said Nathanael was amused by the gesture and lowered his counter by ten dollars.

Four hours, five tiny slips of paper, several verbal tirades and one outburst later, they decided to take a break.

213

"We are at eight million and ten dollars. Let's break." DJ told Tex.

"I agree," Tex said.

Sue and Tex went to a coffee shop in the building. They sat outside on the cement benches and ate their lunch. Sue felt the cool surface through her thin pants.

"I'd like to propose an alternate plan for you that we haven't discussed," Tex said between bites of his hoagie.

Sue's nerves were frazzled from the ping ponging of the mediation. She had felt them slowly unravel back and forth, back and forth, like her child's yo-yo. "Okay, what's the plan?"

"I would recommend you set up your new products under a separate company. Then settle. We'll structure a payment schedule to Yorkston under your old company. If Logan can't make the payments, then don't. If they pursue Logan for nonpayment, you can file for protection, bankrupting the company," Tex said.

Sue was silent for a moment, digesting his words. "So how did you come up with this plan, or is it a lawyer secret?"

"It is a secret, but you pay me well, so I thought I'd let you in on it." He smiled. "I wanted to wait until I saw where they were on the amounts before I recommended it."

"Seriously, this doesn't seem like it's legal. And if it is, I'd lose my company? I'd lose everything I've been working so hard for?"

"Yes. But we have started the process to sue your old law firm, Triggs and Patterson, for malpractice. That lawsuit could end well, since they gave you bad advice and let you knowingly infringe. We can ask for the amount you have to pay Yorkston."

"I don't know, Tex. So much has changed over last year. Just a year ago I was positioning my company for the new century with all my new products. I have always paid my creditors on time and I was in good standing within the industry. Now in less than a year, I've been forced to stop selling our hottest product, I'm being sued, and now I'm suing a law firm. And now, I'm contemplating not paying my debts and bankrupting my company."

"Just the Yorkston debt."

"I know. But shoot, I want to *grow* my company." She looked in her soda cup and twirled the ice cubes. "To file bankruptcy is a sad option," she said softly.

"This does happen, more than you think. I just wanted to let you know it's an option," Tex replied.

"There are no good options from where I stand. So this is what a year of legal battles will get me?"

"You've already spent a butt load of money on this lawsuit. I don't think these wild mustangs can be saddled any other way. So settle."

"They've spent a lot of money too. I don't understand what is motivating them." She recalled the Yorkston's man's words; *watch your step.*

"We've quit manufacturing and selling the catalogs and have made several creative offers of settlement, including shipping the remaining orders and giving them the profits from the sales. We didn't violate their rights intentionally; I went into this based on the advice from my lawyers." Sue thought about the annual sales results for Logan that she had reviewed again this morning. The two and one-half months of lost catalog sales had hit her company hard. To compound the lost revenue, she had lost many retail clients over the unfilled orders. One of her manufacturing reps groups had dropped her for this year and she had to scramble to sign up a replacement group for the spring shows. For the first time ever in Logan history, December sales had been flat, and her annual sales were at a decline overall from the previous year. The bank commitment had been met, but she had dipped into Logan's reserved funds to make the commitments.

"I understand; you had bad advice. You were wrong, but you didn't know you were doing anything wrong. You did the right thing by hiring a lawyer. It was Bruce Barrow that failed, and you are now in the middle of legal malpractice case against your old lawyers. I gotta hunch that this will go well."

"Frankly, I had never thought of suing anybody in my life."

"But look at the mess you're in now because of them. Besides, Triggs and Patterson is covered by malpractice insurance."

"I know. But still —" Sue shook her head and looked at her feet.

Then she let out a small laugh. "Yorkston sues my ass right

right into chapter 11."

She sucked her Diet Coke through the straw and mumbled into her cup. "Ultimately, this was probably their goal; to put me out of business. They'd be happy if I never make another product under Logan Designs again." *Well, they don't know me very well.*

Tex put his arm across her shoulders. "They can't touch your stuffed doll line. You aren't infringing there."

That's the issue. Their lawsuits are a warning to her. But why?

Tex looked at his watch. "Let's get back in there. Consider the settlement and bankrupt option."

The mediation continued the rest of the afternoon. At fifteen minutes to five, everyone miraculously felt like settling.

The amount was agreed upon…five million dollars!

"There's just one other item that Yorkston would like you to include in the settlement," DJ said.

"What else?" Sue was on guard, not knowing what to expect next. She reached for her glass of water to settle her nerves.

"They want you to agree to never manufacture or sell a stuffed plush toy." DJ looked like he was holding his breath, staring at her.

Sue set her glass of water down and wrapped her suddenly shaking hands around it. "No way! You mean my plush kids?" She had hoped her tone of voice had conveyed authority but the mediator's puzzled look told her she had revealed more than that.

"They are playing dirty. Her other products aren't in violation of the copyright infringements," Tex raised his voice.

DJ didn't comment.

Sue's whole body was chilled and she felt the color drain from her face. "My other products have absolutely nothing to do with this negotiation. All deals are off the table. I take my chances in court with these scum sucking bastards, if that's what they want."

Sue felt the grimness of a street brawler, belying her elegant business facade, and she let the two men in the room know she was serious. She wanted to demolish Yorkston. Who could blame her? Sue slammed her leather padfolio shut, holding it close to her chest, ready to leave.

"Sue, let's see what he has to say," Tex said.

She squeezed the black leather binder, leaving dents in the cushiony cover.

"Hmmp, Okay." She threw the binder back on the table.

"It wasn't part of the discussion all day, and Nathanael just brought it up when I told them you had accepted their final dollar amount," DJ said.

"We already have a substantial amount of plush kids orders to fulfill. This has absolutely *nothing* to do with this settlement. They do plush animals, not humans. We do plush humans, not animals."

SHE WAS FRANTIC. She was frightened as well, but most of all, SHE WAS FURIOUS with herself. Furious that she believed, even if only for a short moment, that Yorkston would ever settle and she would be free of them.

"Sue, you've been in business long enough to know what a ruthless businessman is capable of doing to another one. It is possible that they are threatened by your new products," Tex said. "A court would never ask you to stop producing a non-infringing product. This is an unorthodox request."

"Then we don't settle today, we have an alternative. Sorry, DJ, but it looks like we're going to trial. We appreciate your time." Sue stood up shoving papers in her briefcase. *You want a fight, you bastards, you'll get one.*

DJ left the room to give the news to Yorkston. He came back a few minutes later to announce that Yorkston wasn't going to negotiate on this item. That confirmed to Sue, *it's not about the money.*

She looked at Tex. "Come on. Let's get out of here."

They reached the lobby and Sue encountered Nathanael Yorkston once again.

She could see the muscles in Nathanael jaw tightening. He reached out his right hand toward Sue. Ignoring his gesture of civility, she turned and walked out, knowing they could never be friendly rivals, only deadly ones.

FORTY-SIX
Rural Indiana

ANTHONY ROMERO made his way up the decrepit steps of Pete Shapiro's run down ranch-style house.

Shapiro's home was typical tract housing, built during the seventies. The house was devoid of any exterior or interior decorations. Its decay and dilapidated condition made Anthony believe that the house could be torn down and the secluded three-acre lot would be worth more without the house. The house could be torched, probably doubling the value of the lot, Anthony thought as he knocked on the door.

There was a bark from inside.

Pete Shapiro opened the door. Shapiro wore jeans and his typical threadbare white lab coat with rolled up sleeves over his clothes, his white, wild hair uncombed. *Man, he looks like a mad scientist. What a kook.*

"Anthony, come on in." Shapiro led Anthony into his living room. There were no handshakes." How are things at Yorkston these days?"

"Fine." Anthony despised chitchat. He knelt down to pet the Husky. He tried to remember the name of the dog. It had something to do with its color. He made a mistake and asked Shapiro about the dog's unique coloring and, in turn, he received a thirty-minute lecture on the genetic effect of color, shading, and markings of the Siberian husky.

The dog was red, and its white undercoat contributed a

lightening effect causing it to appear the color of an orange fuzzy throw pillow, like something his ex-wife would use on a white leather couch.

Anthony stood, looking around the room. "Where's the other mutt?" Damn, he couldn't remember the name of Shapiro's other Husky either. He did remember it had bizarre eyes.

"I had to put Zeka down," Shapiro said in a sad voice, as if it had just happened.

"Sorry. She sure had strange eyes, that one did."

"She was bi-eyed, one blue and one brown, a genetic—"

"Yeah, whatever . . . listen, I didn't come to talk about your dogs," Anthony cut Shapiro off before he went into some genetic whoopee-de-do over the dog's eyes.

"I've got your quarterly bonus." Anthony handed Shapiro a two-inch thick envelope. "The usual, nothing's changed, all twenties and fifties, unmarked."

Shapiro took the envelope, setting it on the coffee table. Anthony wondered what the scientist did with his cash. He certainly didn't spend it on his house or his clothes and, from what he knew from having him tailed the first three months after they hired him, the guy had no social life outside his pet dogs. According to the men tailing him, he walked the dogs three times a day on his property but did nothing else.

Shapiro had never asked for unmarked dollars, Anthony just offered that up, as reciprocal collateral damage. He wouldn't want a lot of bills from any of their accounts traced back to them. Besides, they were already using unmarked money for Custom's bribes protecting against unplanned searches at the borders. It was easy for Anthony to skim off some for his scientist friend in exchange for Shapiro's loyalty. Shapiro received a modest paycheck from Yorkston for his toy testing research, but that was the only legit relationship Yorkston had with Shapiro.

"Aren't you going to count it?" The first four visits Shapiro counted every twenty, twice. After the scientist figured the Yorkston guys weren't going to dupe him, he quit counting. Still Anthony always asked.

"What about the Pearson award?" Shapiro asked in a

strained voice, his eyes dancing.

Oh shit, not this again. Nathanael had warned Anthony that this drivel from Shapiro needed to be kept under control. Month after month, Shapiro's badgering about the international medal was grating on his nerves. Yorkston didn't have connections at the Society of Chemistry, contrary to what Shapiro thought. Besides, there was no way Nathanael would let Shapiro have the limelight, as long as the secret project would be under the watchful eyes of the various agencies. It seemed that every year another US department got involved in toy compliance and regulations.

Yorkston's quality and regulatory team had a hell of a time keeping up with the agencies' mandates. Last week, the U.S. Consumer Product Safety Commission had announced one of Yorkston's competitors had agreed to pay a 1.3 million dollar civil penalty for violating a federal ban.

Anthony knew the truth was many toys have all sorts of dangers, but it was the high publicity of a recall that spurred congressional action.

Anthony knew it was the bad press that killed the products and the company, not the civil suits and fines. If a mother got it in her head that a product could be associated with a harmful incident, she would never allow her child to touch the product. Such was the case with the red dye scare many years earlier. Red M&M's were pulled from the market, even though they didn't contain any red dye number two. Red dye number two was found to cause cancer in laboratory rats. The bad press was enough to scare many buyers away from the red candies.

Anthony remembered his own mother not allowing him to drink red sodas, even though a child would've had to drink seven thousand cans of red soda to equal the same amount of red dye the rats consumed. Bad press killed products.

There was no fucking way Shapiro could be allowed to speak in the public's eye. Anthony liked him holed up in his secluded house.

"Pete, we are working on that." It was a lie Anthony believed he had used too often. He would have to come up with a solution to get Shapiro off the Pearson Award campaign. And soon. He had increased the dollar amount of the quarterly bonus a few times, but

Shapiro wanted the publicity.

Shapiro had told Anthony he dreamed of showing all his colleagues at the University and his former students that he had gained the most prestigious award the Society could bestow on a chemist.

"Anthony, I'm not going to wait another three years. I want to be the one at center stage this December when they hand out the gold medal." Shapiro folded his hands across his chest.

Anthony didn't like the urgency he heard in Shapiro's voice. The burly security chief faked a smile and nodded his head slowly. "I know, Pete. No one deserves it more than you do. That's what we keep telling the folks at the chemistry society. We're making waves. I can feel we're close." He noticed a change in Shapiro's body language. He isn't buying it. "Well, listen, I better get going."

Anthony moved toward the door. "You take care, okay?" He looked at the dog. "You too, pooch."

Anthony shut the door and stepped off the porch.

"Her name is Henna," Shapiro said, behind the closed door, as he knelt to scratch his husky behind the ears.

"I have failed," Shapiro said ruefully. "It's been years since I showed Romero a safe tag alternative."

He pushed back his couch and, kneeling on all fours, he lifted up a shabby piece of carpet. He pried a wood floorboard open and inside the revealed crawl space, he threw the envelope of money. It settled next to stacks of other overstuffed, yellowing envelopes.

Anthony left the house without a single soul having seen him.

His next stop was to an old friend's automotive shop; Andrew Fredericks' Autohouse. He was known as Andy the Arsonist in high school.

FORTY-SEVEN
Texas

"I STILL CAN'T believe they're willing to settle now." Sue sat in Tex office a few weeks after the mediation reviewing the documents.

"They are," Tex said softly.

"But five million? I can't pay that." Sue stared at the documents, choking back tears. "If my company were to miss a payment, Yorkston could pursue a garnishment against my accounts forcing my company into bankruptcy." She thought Yorkston was on a Logan witch-hunt. It was a huge amount of money; an amount she'd have trouble committing to each month. She knew it. Tex knew it. Her accountants knew it. Most likely Yorkston knew it.

"They may be settling because they know you can't pay. Maybe it's a tactic they're using to force you to bankruptcy to prevent you from making those dolls."

Sue stared at the Yorkston settlement papers as if they were a death sentence. She flipped through a few pages. "And there's nothing in here about the M Kids?"

"That's right. You're free to move forward with your plush doll kick-off."

"Ok. I'll sign the final consent decree." Sue reluctantly picked up a pen. She rolled it between her thumb and index finger.

"Did you bring a check?"

"Yes. I know. The first payment is due upon signing the decree. And monthly payments for a year. I can pay this first one, but then I'm not sure." She chewed on the tip of the pen, and reviewed the soggy papers, damp from her tears. Placing the pen on the signature line, she scribbled her name. *Susannah Lockes Logan, President/CEO Logan Enterprise.*

Sue stood close to the glass window, looking out at the pool. The setting sun radiated orange and pink hues across the water. Sue was so absorbed in her anger at Yorkston that the view of the outside world failed to comfort her.

The mantle clock chimed eight times. The house echoed after every ding.

She shook her head at her reflection in the window and shuddered. She turned and walked down the long hallway and into the kitchen.

A note from her mom said that leftovers were in the oven and that the kids were staying with them. At the bottom, in her dad's hand writing, *wine in the refrigerator.* Despite her sour mood, Sue smiled.

Her family was always there for her, always there to cheer her up. Forget about friendships. Forget about Daniel. Since their meeting in Boston, he hadn't contacted her once, avoiding her at the one gift show she had attended. Her emails to him went unanswered.

Sue was hurt over his rejection, but she still missed talking with him. She was so close on the designs and the big marketing splash, but he wouldn't be there to see it through like they had planned. It had been a deal, right? They had toasted each other over it.

Since the lawsuits, Sue noticed her happier outlook was changing for the worse. There was no denying that she had turned into a curmudgeon.

She poured a glass of wine, gulped half of it and went to her bedroom.

She kicked off her shoes as she entered her walk-in closet. There was the rack of Jonathan's clothes – a couple pairs of pants, a few shirts, a suit and a tie, below that a pair of his shoes.

She had donated everything else of his to charity years ago. She remembered how disposing his clothes and other things had broken her up. She found it hard to remember now why she had kept these last few items all these years. The smell of him was gone now, but it remained forever in her memory.

"We lost a battle today. But we won't lose the war," she said to the empty closet. She collapsed on the rich plush carpeted floor and began to cry. She laid there a few minutes before gathering herself and changing clothes.

She changed into jeans and a T-shirt, pulling her hair into a ponytail. She wandered into the kitchen and poured another glass of wine. She drank, not tasting it. She had no appetite.

She returned to her desk, picking up a copy of the last issue of her catalog. She turned the pages. Looking at the photos struck her. She would never be able to publish it again. *What am I going to do next?*

She yawned. The tiredness was overwhelming, after the day's events. She drained the wine, trudged to her bedroom, and collapsed into her bed.

She dreamed of a meeting, with a room full of stuffy Wall Street types. She was surrounded by a bunch of pin-striped suits, where she walked around with a smile and charmed them with a basket of millennium dolls.

She overheard one say, "She'll sell off everything she owns to get the money she needs to take back what was rightfully hers."

She felt teeny fingers poking at her. "Are you awake? Are you awake? Are you awake?" Sue pried open her eyes to see Maddie sitting next to her.

"Good morning, sweetie."

"Wake up, Mommy. Grandpa said you are taking us on a bike ride today."

Sue sat up to see Maddie dressed in sweats, holding her bicycle helmet.

"Oh my gosh, today is Saturday?" She tickled Maddie as she rolled out of bed.

"Granddaddy loaded our bikes on the car." Maddie said with

her uncombed, straggly honey blonde pigtails with loose tendrils in curly wisps around her jelly-sticky face.

She heard laughter drifting in from the living room. Sue tousled Maddie's hair. "Round up Lizzie and Colt and we'll head out, as soon as I change."

Feeling much better, Sue washed her face and threw on a running outfit and tennis shoes.

Thirty minutes later, the foursome pedaled their way around the perimeter of Fossil Park Lake. It was a beautiful sunny day with crystal-blue clear skies, a tad chilly, and not even a whiff of humidity in the air.

After one loop, the kids grew tired and were ready for the snacks their grandma had packed.

They sat on a blanket near their car, enjoying the picnic, with the lake in the background. Maddie had her favorite Yorkston white lamb. It was matted and yellowed from Maddie's constant touch. Sue had to replace it several times over the year. She would sneak in Maddie's bedroom at night, take the old lamb and replace it with a new one. When Maddie woke up, Sue would tell her elves had taken it to a hollow tree and washed it.

Sue looked around the park.

Sue caught a glimpse of a man dressed in khakis pants and a dress shirt, wearing a ball cap. They crossed gazes and he turned away, walking in the other direction. He stopped near a picnic table.

She noticed he was carrying a manila folder. She found this odd. Most people carried books or newspapers to read at the park. There was something familiar about the man. *Where have I seen him? Does he go to my church?*

The kids were chatting away on every subject from how gross worms were to what fast food restaurant they wanted to stop at on the way home.

Sue laid there for a few more minutes taking in the aroma of the fresh outdoors. She looked over at the man again, feeling uncomfortable. She stood up and tugged on the blanket. "Let's go grab lunch. Anyone for a Happy Meal?"

The three kids followed her to the car and helped load the bikes. She pulled out of the parking spot, but she had a nagging feeling something was brewing with the stranger who was still seated by the tables.

She drove past him, seeing a nasty smile on his face. For a split second, she remembered him from the restaurant last month. His long graying hair was hidden under the cap, but those bugging eyes; *what was his name? Richard Speckman?*

He was the man that told her Nathanael Yorkston was in the restaurant that night. What a coincidence, seeing him there in the suburbs.

Her stomach dropped like a stone to the bottom of a pond. Sue shuddered. *This wasn't a coincidence.* All the way home, Sue checked her rear view mirror, but the stranger was nowhere in sight.

FORTY-EIGHT

THE EXQUISITE SMELL of sweet gardenias and the chirping of birds filled her kitchen through the open windows. Sue had just returned from jogging and had her hands wrapped around a mug of fresh steaming coffee. She sipped the coffee while she watched a mother bird struggle with a worm. Another worm escaped the bird. Sue thought she should buy a bird feeder. It shouldn't be that hard for a mother bird to find food for her hatchlings.

In another ten minutes the kids would be downstairs, but she had time to finish decorating the cupcakes Maddie was taking to school. She had decorated the chocolate cupcakes with white icing, trimming each with a red candy heart since Maddie's birthday was so close to Valentine's Day.

Sue licked the icing on her fingers as she finished the final touches on the cupcakes.

Three phones rang at once.

Her mobile phone, which sat on the counter after her run, was vibrating. Her home phone was ringing, and she could hear her office line echoing down the hallway.

Sue grabbed her cell phone. The display said it was her sister, Dee.

"Hi Dee, I can't chat right now, can I call you back?" Sue panted in haste as she ran down the hallway. She wanted to see who was calling on her private home office line.

"Sue, turn on your TV!" Dee yelled.

"Crap, hold on, my office line is ringing." Sue put the cell to her other ear and picked up her private line.

"Sue Logan."

"Sue, it's Mary Jo. Are you watching the Today Show?"

"What? No, hold on." She looked at her portable phone sitting on her credenza. Her home phone caller ID showed her mom was calling.

She ignored her home line for a minute and got back to her cell. She searched her desk for the TV remote..

"Dee, what's going on?"

"Have you turned on your TV?"

"I'm still trying to find the remote."

"Hurry!" Dee yelled into the phone. "Turn on the Today Show now because—"

Before Dee could finish her sentence, Sue found the remote. The TV was already tuned to CBS.

She couldn't believe her eyes. She watched as the anchors, Katie Couric and Matt Lauer, played with several stuffed dolls, her plush Millennium Kids.

She dropped the phone on the desk, and stared at the TV.

"*Yorkston Toys does it again. This week they have been shipping a new stuffed toy line to retail stores just in time for the new millennium. The line of plush resembles kids from across the globe. The kids have been nicknamed the Y2K kids. Our sources say the marketing department of the toy conglomerate called the new line of dolls Y2K after the Yorkston 2000 Kids,*" Katie said.

Sue leaned against her desk, her legs weak, her gaze riveted to the Today Show announcers.

"*In addition to offering the toys for sale in specialty retailers across the country, the Y2K plush will be offered in a promotion with area hospitals,*" Matt said.

"*Spokesman Rudy Cole, of the United Hospitals group out of Dallas, confirmed an order of substantial volumes. He said there'll be over eight hundred thousand babies born in the year 2000 in the US alone,*" Matt continued.

Sue stood still, in shock, mesmerized. She stared at the television as if it had transformed into a powerful, evil robot, with laser beams shooting into her and assaulting her to the core.

What the fuck?

"I'd like to take this one home to my daughter." Katie held up a plush doll that looked identical to the one Sue had sitting on her credenza.

"I think that can be arranged," Matt said.

"Our next story after the commercial is about a family in –"

Wearily, she turned off her TV and stared at the phone . . . shocked at the news she had just heard. She bit her lip, trying to steady herself on her legs that felt as flimsy as a house of cards.

Sue had been unaware that her kids and the babysitter had been standing there, quietly listening.

"Yeah! Mommy's dolls are on TV," Elizabeth yelled.

Not knowing if that was a good thing or not, her younger two unenthusiastically yelled, "Yeah!"

"That's great Ms. Logan," the babysitter said.

Sue looked away from the kids. She didn't want them seeing her stricken look. "Dee, are you still there? Hold on a minute."

"I'm here," Dee said in a quiet voice.

Sue turned to the babysitter. "Can you take the kids to the kitchen to eat breakfast? I've got some important business to do for a few minutes. Thanks again for coming over so early to help get them off to school." Her voice sounded unstable, shaky, even to herself.

"No problem. Let's go, kids." The group trotted off to the kitchen.

Sue grabbed the office line but it was dead. She put the phone back on the receiver.

"What the hell is going on?" Sue said into her cell phone. She was stunned. "I can't believe this!"

"That nasty Nathanael Yorkston man is crazier than a shithouse rat. That's what is going on," Dee said.

Dee could always make her smile, even in a time of crisis, but Sue's devastated look quickly returned when she thought about what had just happened. "I can't believe they've beaten me to the stores!" Sue screamed.

"Calm down, Susie. We need to see the toys to see how close they are and then –"

"They are exactly like mine! The size, the styles, the

nationalities, the design and even the name of the toys! Millenium Kids and Y2K kids! Come on, sis! Who are they kidding!" she shrieked into her cell phone. What had Yorkston done to her sister this time? Damn bastard! She hated Nathanael Yorkston and all he represented . . . a Disney-fied likeable character on TV and a heartless son-of-bitch in real life.

Dee hadn't been able to give her the news about what Patrick had found out about the Yorkston chemist, Pete Shapiro.

It could wait, Dee thought. Sue had a lot on her mind right now.

FORTY-NINE

WILFORD WORRIED ABOUT SUE. She hadn't returned any of his or her mom's calls for the past six hours and she didn't show up at school for Maddie's cupcake birthday party, something completely uncharacteristic of his daughter. After he and Thelma returned from the elementary school party, he had let himself in her house with his key and done a quick search but she wasn't around even though her car was still parked out front and the coffee pot still brewing in the kitchen since this morning. His concerns now bordering on panic nonetheless he would widen his search to the garages before calling Patrick.

As he walked into the garage, he heard scuffling noises coming from the attic.

"Suze! Is that you?" He yelled up at the open attic door trying to sound calm against the building dread. *Why in God's name would she be in the attic?*

Sue tentatively peeked out the attic door to the garage below and smiled weakly at her father standing at the foot of the dropdown ladder.

"Well, you picked an odd time to clean the attic." Wilford smiled up at her. *Thank you God.* He glanced around the garage and just then noticed there were boxes stacked everywhere. Papers askew, left randomly thrown out of their file folders.

"Dad, can you give me a hand?" She yelled down.

"Sure, but I'm not climbing up those stairs. I don't think this ladder could hold me." He tried the bottom step again and was certain it wouldn't hold him.

"Suze, your mom and I are worried about you. And about a dozen other people have been calling you all day, and there's been no answer. And you missed Maddie's school party. Are you okay?"

"Yes, I know." She yelled down to her dad. "I've been up here since the *Today Show* airing that morning."

"I know. Everyone's been looking for you." He tried to sound calm and not controlling.

"I know, Dad. I checked my email once and saw that Jennifer DeKreek and a lot of my employees and my manufacturing reps had tried to reach me. I'm sure they want to know if I sold my Mkids to Yorkston Toys. I also checked my voicemail once, but didn't listen to the thirty missed calls, probably asking me the same questions."

"Can I help you?" He tried again a few of the bottom ladder rungs but was certain they wouldn't hold him.

"Dad, you don't have to climb up here. Just give me a hand with this box."

She scooted a file box to the edge of the case opening. With every ounce of muscle she looked like she had left in her, she lifted it through the opening and carried it down a few steps. He took it from there.

She climbed down the ladder. She was still dressed in her running shorts and a filthy T-shirt from the morning. Her hair, once in a tight ponytail riding high on her head, was now tousled with strands falling out of both sides. She wiped gray dust off her cheek and shook pink insulation specks off her clothes. His heart ached at the sight of her bloodshot, puffy eyes... a sure sign she had been crying.

"Well aren't you a sight for sore eyes. You have a hot date or did you dress up for little old me?" He teased, but he masked his worried eyes and looked caringly at her.

"Thanks, Dad, I love you too." Sue said without looking at him as she opened the box he had just set down.

"What the hell are you looking for?" He glanced around the garage floor, which was littered with opened file boxes.

She brushed dust off her shirt, lost in thought. It appeared she hadn't taken the time to replace the box lids, instead stacking them on the floor. Most of the cardboard file boxes were labeled DESIGN or MANUFACTURING. The dates went back seven years.

She stopped and stood up in thought. "Dad, do you and Mom still have my design kits from before I went to college?"

"I suppose your mom has them in storage somewhere. She never throws a damn thing out. Why?"

"Do you think you can find the box with the design notes from my patents? The early ones, I mean?"

Wilford felt a look of realization cross his face. "I may know exactly what box you're looking for." And he knew he did. "Now why don't you go shower before your kids get home from school."

She leaned over and kissed him on the cheek. Before she could see his approving grin, she was gone.

FIFTY

IN THE SHOWER, Sue let the hot water hit her hard, the burning inside her as scalding as the water on her back. Stunned and horrified, she shook as sobs wracked her body. She ran her hands through her wet hair, turning to let the water wash over her face and her tears, as she realized the enormity of the situation and the incongruous circumstance.

This move by Yorkston today said to her, *we know how to get at things that you really value, we can do more unless you stay out of the way.*

She thought of the anonymous letter, the warning. It had all come true! Someone inside or very close to Yorkston had known all along and tried to warn her. But who?

The clean water gave her a chill. She stopped crying but stared in the shower, as if to see the answer on the marble wall. Who would betray Yorkston?

This is someone I need on my team.

She tried to piece it altogether. She thought possibly an ex-employee, but Dee and Patrick had been able to check on all of the recent employees that had left Yorkston. Her sister and brother-in-law had talked to everyone on the short list, none had motive. Maybe their investigation could've missed someone or maybe the person was still working at Yorkston, or they don't work for them at all.

Yorkston was trying to get her to back off, to put her company out of business. They were taking their chances, probably already knowing that Logan didn't have the money or gumption to fight a lawsuit against them.

They don't know what I'm capable of doing.

She was a lot closer to exposing them for what they were than they ever knew. Or *did* Yorkston know?

She got out of the shower. Sue toweled her wet hair, looking in the mirror at her image, an older, smarter, more cunning person than she had been just a few months ago. She looked and felt as if she had aged five years since last summer. Her puffy, red eyes didn't help.

Sue finished dressing and headed for the kitchen. She realized she had skipped both breakfast and lunch, and she was starving.

Her dad was in the kitchen waiting for her. His aging face was still tan, creased deeply, with white stubble sprouting here and there.

There was a beat up brown cardboard box sitting on her kitchen island.

"You found it! That was quick." Sue smiled for the first time since she'd heard the Yorkston announcement that morning.

"Yes, I guess we've had it all along. Your mom had me bring over leftovers." Wilford scooped chicken salad onto a plate, appearing pleased that Sue was in a better mood.

"When are you going to fill us in on what's really going on?" He asked with a confident astuteness.

"Us?" She took the plate of chicken salad and dug her fork into it. She had suspected her dad would know about the past designs but she hadn't thought her mom would have any idea.

"Yes, us. Me, Patrick, Dee, your mother. We need to hear from you. Why this assault, this freakin' attack on you and your company? We have our suspicions. You do too, right?"

Sue put down the forkful of chicken salad. She shook her head slowly. "I shouldn't involve you guys. I do have a suspicion that his plush line has a horrible defect but it continues to mystify me. There is a lot more to it too. There are still some answers I need to find out."

Her dad walked over and put his arms around her, pulling her tight to his chest. "I respect your judgment, Suze. This isn't something we would handle carelessly. We want to help.

This son-of-a-bitch is going to ruin you and everyone around you."

"I could use some help about now." If anything, to release some of the burden she had been carrying inside of her for the last year. The thought that she might be one of the few to know what Yorkston had been getting away with kept her awake at night. But what did she really know?

She had to look through her research files to uncover the part that she was missing.

"Daddy, give me an hour. I've work to do." She nodded her head toward the box sitting on the kitchen island. "The kids will be home soon. Why don't you and Mom come back tonight for dinner? I'll get Dee and Patrick on the phone and I'll share with you all that I suspect is going on. Can Mom bring frozen lasagna? I haven't been grocery shopping. I meant to go today but—"

"We'll bring dinner. Now spend some time with your past." He nodded toward the box, both eyebrows arched. "Take your time. I'm sure it's there, whatever you're looking for."

Sue had spent the last forty-five minutes poring over the hoary documents of her past that filled the sagging box. She fretted over the reports, charts, graphs, drawings and even a few doll samples spread out in front of her on the kitchen table, not even taking the time to carry the box to her office.

She unfolded a smeared, dog-eared, fan-folded computer printout with shabby holes perforating its sides. This report wouldn't make sense to most people. Sue and a college friend had collected the data, and the information came back to her easily. She looked through every word, every number and every formula. The report was blotched with a dozen of additions, deletions and notes in the margins in Sue's curly, younger handwriting.

God, where have I missed it?

She was using her calculator, making notes when the kids and the babysitter came in from school.

"Hi Mommy!" They all yelled their greetings, running to the pantry for snacks.

"Maddie, how was the birthday cupcakes at school? I'm

sorry I got tied up at work." Sue was choked with guilt over missing Maddie's celebration. Normally she would be at her elementary school, helping pass out the cupcakes to the children, but today she had been preoccupied. *Damn Yorkston!*

Maddie came over to sit on her lap, wrapping her arms around her mom's neck and giving her a big sticky kiss.

Sue chuckled when she saw her youngest daughter up close.

"What do we have here?" Sue pointed to Maddie's hands. They were stained a bright red color around her fingers. She had red-stained lips and tongue.

Colt didn't wait for Maddie to reply. "Mommy, Maddie ate *all* the candy hearts off her leftover cupcakes in the car on the way home. She didn't share!"

"They were *mine*," Maddie yelled. "It's *my* birthday, not yours."

"Okay, okay. Enough, both of you. Maddie, you could've saved one for your bother."

Colt was about to punch his sister's arm. "Colt, I have two left over from this morning," Sue said.

"Yeah!" he yelled.

"They are in the laundry room, by the sink."

Both kids ran off to the laundry room.

When they came back a few minutes later, they both had big smiles on their faces and red stains on their lips and hands.

Sue looked at them both for a minute; she felt a knowing grin flood her face.

Of course! Why didn't I realize it before?

FIFTY-ONE
Indiana

A PURPLE PLUME OF SMOKE from Nathanael's cigar circled in front of him as he sat at his reserved corner table of the dimly lit gentleman's club. A bottle of Special Edition Scotch sat in the middle of the table. The club owner ordered the special reserve from Scotland just for Nathanael.

He swirled the glass under his nose, letting it rest there a minute, soaking in the aroma before dumping it down his throat.

Nathanael rested the cigar butt in an ashtray and watched a lone half-nude dancer center stage from afar. He had paid the club owner and the dancers handsomely to keep silent. There were no other clients in the club. His table was partly hidden from sight. He used a discrete door to enter the building that few people knew about. He hadn't run into the paparazzi or a toy fanatic at this private gentleman's club; he and the owner went to great lengths to keep it that way.

He saw Anthony enter the room through the back door. He was wearing sunglasses despite the darkness outside. Anthony stopped and watched the stripper as she twisted around a pole, then looked around, seeking out Nathanael.

"Naty." Anthony approached the table.

"Be seated." Nathanael pulled out a chair across from him. He picked up an empty crystal glass, pouring the Scotch into it. He handed it to Anthony. He topped off his own glass with the amber liquor and held it up.

"Salud," Nathanael said clicking his glass to Anthony's.

"Salud."

"Mmm. Very fine, very smooth—" Nathanael said.

"And very expensive." Anthony held the glass up.

"Worth every dime." Nathanael would easily pay thousands of dollars for a truly special bottle. "Thanks for meeting me here. Big ears and loose lips in the office, you know?" Nathanael wondered if Anthony's daughter had heard anything in the rumor mill. Victoria was Nathanael's snitch, like a jailhouse informer. She was paid well for being his mole. He always wanted to know what everyone around him was saying. He took a fresh cigar from the case and clipped the end with thought and precision, handing it to Anthony.

"Nothing is coming from the office, my man, take my word on that. Tori's got you covered." Anthony lit the cigar meticulously keeping the tip of the cigar above the level of the flame, puffing hard to get the ambers glowing and dipping the unlit end into his scotch and back in his mouth.

"What about 'C.' Did we get what we needed? What was her assistant talking about?"

"Yeah, we're working on that. There's been no more activity since she donated the bird to the museum store."

"Our prototypes have been presented to the public, but I still need to get my hand on an active chip."

"I know. That was a nice piece on the Today Show." Anthony gulped another Scotch. He chewed the end of his cigar.

"Keep on it. What's the word on the street? Anything from Fuzhou or the Devine team?" Nathanael asked. He had tried to stay far removed from the arrangements set up in China years earlier.

"Business as usual, production is going well. But we still have two possible leaks in the pipe. If we don't plug those two up, we could get wet. If you know what I mean."

Nathanael swirled his glass, emptying the contents into his mouth with a splash and a slow swallow. He loved the burn as it rolled down the back of his throat and stung all the way to his empty stomach. "Do they really know anything? What are you suggesting? Has anyone been to the plant?" Nathanael watched his longtime friend and protector.

He paid Anthony's private company well for all the in-house security they provide Yorkston Toys and its key individuals. As an added benefit, Anthony had ties into several government departments.

Anthony had been a former bouncer turned security guard. Nathanael thought Anthony was the one that needed a bodyguard to protect him from being mugged, since his pal always wore a few hundred thousand dollars' worth of jewelry at any given time.

A topless waitress with large breasts approached the table, retreating with a short wave of Nathanael's hand.

Nathanael knew Anthony was concerned about the lead chemist on the design team, Dr. Shapiro. They had christened Shapiro as the team's lead only to appease him.

Nathanael's business philosophy was to assign several individuals on their design teams. These teams included artists, creators and marketing employees. In addition to the design team for the new stuffed toy line, Nathanael had assigned an ancillary team that was code named the "divine team."

Since the toys were to be given to children, Shapiro was involved to make sure the dyes used were safe in case some kid sucked on it, but that didn't work out well Nathanael thought. He held up a freshly-poured Scotch.

"Salud." Anthony clicked the expensive crystal glass against Nathanael's glass.

Nathanael gave his head a quick shake after he knocked back the drink. "What are you planning to do to stop the slow leak, or should I ask?" He followed Anthony's eyes as he turned from him to the dancer. They both watched, as she took off her tiny top, circled the dance floor in her stilettos and black fishnet hosiery, then slid her legs apart until she was facing them in the splits.

After a long silence, Anthony gulped his Scotch and said, "Yeah, you probably don't want to know."

Nathanael nodded, expressionless.

"But I think my guys need to pay a visit to Texas first to see what the little lady knows . . . no harm, of course, just a fishing expedition," Anthony said.

"And the other possible leak?" Nathanael asked. "Any word on where he is keeping his money? Do you think he is planning on making a run for it, hoarding all his cash?"

"It's all unmarked, and there's no way of tracing it back."

"Good."

"We seemed to be leapfrogging over Customs just fine. Our contacts have been cooperative. I'll make sure Shapiro doesn't get too nosy," Anthony said in a whisper.

"This is a combustible situation we have here, leaving him on the payroll all these years since we never did see eye-to-eye on which label to use."

"Yeah, he took it hard when we didn't use his recommendation. But he has been paid well to keep it to himself. It may be time to cut him loose so there are no connections." Anthony turned his back to Nathanael to watch a new dancer on another stage. "It's all good."

"Yep, all for the good of the toys." Nathanael's obsession with an inanimate object had propelled him into both a genius and a madman. He was fine with both, and preferred it that way. "Time to toss Shapiro out like a used Kleenex."

FIFTY-TWO
Texas
March

SUE GLANCED AROUND Tex Thornton's familiar office, thinking about all the hours she had wasted in this small room, strategizing over her Yorkston defense. Well, now it was her turn to attack.

A week after the announcement of the Yorkston Toys new product, Sue was signing off on the paperwork to sue Yorkston for copyright infringements.

Tex watched Sue read through the paperwork.

"How does it feel to be the plaintiff against Yorkston this time, Ms. Logan?"

She was thankful Tex had agreed to take the infringement case on a contingency. After looking at the designs she had brought him of her dolls and comparing them to the Yorkston dolls, he had told her, "Damned if I can tell them apart. A jury won't either." He had agreed to take the case. She was starting to feel like his gravy train.

"I just want to get through this quickly. As long as they are selling their toys, my market share will be diluted. I'm the one that looks like the knock off!"

"I hear ya."

"When can we force them to stop?"

"It's not that easy," Tex replied. "We have to go through

the process; we'll file our complaint, and they'll file a reply. We'll go through discovery and oral depositions and gather the proof that they copied your design."

"How long are we talking about, Tex?"

"Could be eighteen to twenty four months for the case to go to trial . . . at least five or six months for a preliminary injunction in order to get them to stop selling the product."

Sue sank further in her chair, cussing under her breath. Damn! Their timing was horrible. What was it with this damn legal system? The Yorkston lawyers could sue her, force her to stop selling her product, and strongarm her into a ridiculous settlement that could bankrupt her in less than twelve months. And yet, when she had a product with an expiration date stamped on it, like souring milk, the legal process could take years. The timing sucked. Royally sucked!

"I'll miss the whole damn millennium mania retail opportunity." Her voice was toneless. She was on the verge of tears. The news made her feel weak, sick to her stomach. She wasn't sure how much more she could take.

She picked up one of her millennium dolls lying on the conference room table. She held her toy in her hands; it suddenly didn't feel like her design anymore, as if she had no right to look at her own plush dolls. All she could do was gaze listlessly at the creation.

"They'll sell their product for less until I'm starved out." Sue knew their price would be less, allowing retailers to sell the Yorkston dolls for a lower price. She had changed her manufacturing commitment to have her tiny tots made in the US just last week, while Yorkston's toys would be made in China. Sue had her reasons for changing manufacturing locations.

"I'm sorry, Sue." Tex handed her the complaint. "Take a look through this and let me know if you have any questions."

Sue read though the documents. She paused, rubbing her fingertips in circles around her temples. Crap on all the legalisms.

"Hell, skip through all that, you can read it later, take it with you," Tex said.

The complaint scared her. She was waking up a giant that

so far preferred its prey passive. Now she would be the hunter. This was all new to her; she wasn't used to dealing with copyright thieves, liars, crooks, and monsters. She had no idea what Yorkston was capable of, but she was going to do everything in her power to find out. The past year, since Yorkston had entered her life, she had been on a roller coaster ride that saturated her senses, an epic journey of dreams and betrayal, loss and hope. They had been stalking her like a pack of wolves tracking their prey, running her down until she was too exhausted to fight.

Sue thought it was their turn to feel some of the anguish. Their lawsuit against her was a desperate charade; her suit against them had merit and was just.

"Let's see how they like the sounds of the rustling of lawsuit papers!"

Once she did it, there was no going back.

FIFTY-THREE
Indiana

EVAN TAYLOR PULLED ON HIS PANTS quietly, not wanting to wake Victoria. It had been raining on and off for a few days now, and the last thing he wanted to do was get out of bed this early.

His car keys fell out of his pocket. Victoria stirred. She rolled to her side, her eyes fluttered open. "Whatssup? Come back to bed." she whispered hoarsely. "Why are you up so early?"

"Shhh, it's nothing." He continued dressing.

She kicked a long leg out from under the satin sheets. "Come to bed, baby."

"Go back to sleep. I need to go to the office early and check on that story." Evan rarely was in the office of the IndyStar newspaper before dawn. He wasn't normally an early riser, but today he had planned to read the research files of a colleague and he wanted to do so without the questioning eyes of the secretary.

"That story Scotty wrote?" She rolled out of bed and her naked body pushed past him to her apartment bathroom.

She returned quickly and gave him a kiss before jumping under the sheets.

"Hmmm, it's so warm in here. Come back. You'll read his article soon enough."

"I can't wait till then. I'm so pissed that someone else wrote the article. I'm usually the one that receives any assignments associated with Yorkston."

"But this isn't a human interest story."

"But still … my editor should have chosen me."

"I know, baby. But Scotty usually writes the article when people die."

Damn, I hate that too. "Let's meet later for lunch. Can you keep your ears open and see what everyone at Yorkston is saying about his death?" Evan gave Tori a quick peck on her forehead and was out the door.

He found the file folder on Scotty's desk, stacked in the inbox tray. He opened it, locating the blueline proof of the first section of this morning's newspaper. He took a whiff of the contents. He loved the smell of the printer's ink.

The first article on the front page started out *"as the millennium looms . . . ."* Evan was already sick of the hoopla around the new century. He kept looking.

He opened the front page of the crisp newly printed newspaper, finding the article.

Blaze Kills Longtime Scientist
IndyStar March 9, 1999 by Staff Writer Scott Morrow

The 911 call about a house fire came around 1:10 a.m. Tuesday.

Indianapolis Fire Caption Rusty Duran said the dispatcher asked whether everyone had gotten out of the house and the caller said he was on his way, but Pete Shapiro never made it.

The 68-year-old died of smoke inhalation, according to authorities. Duran said an investigation will be done to determine the cause of the fire that destroyed the home of Shapiro, who lived alone. Shapiro, a long time expert witness in scientific cases, worked as a chemist and consultant for many organizations. Chemical substances were stored on the property.

Shapiro was well-known by his students and he was relied upon by the Indianapolis chemist society to determine the makeup of unknown substance compounds.

A self-described "behind-the-scenes guy" for many local companies, Shapiro worked for Bradford Chemical, Glastap Pharma,

Yorkston Toys and Romero Security. He had aspired to the highest chemistry honor, The Pearson Award, and sources said he was to be nominated this fall.

Shapiro earned a master's degree and Ph.D. in chemical engineering from the University of Indiana. He held numerous patents and taught at Huazhong University of Science & Technology, China in 1994.

Shapiro's husky, Henna, also died in the blaze.

Realization hit him, and Evan felt a constriction in his throat. He took a deep breath. He glanced around the reporters' cubicles, which were still vacant.

He thumbed through several papers in the Shapiro file. It appeared to be all standard material. There were quotes from Shapiro's former students, a quote from a science teacher colleague, and a telephone number that looked familiar; Yorkston Toys. Evan wrote down the number and the extension on a slip of paper, stuffing it in his pocket.

He returned the file to the inbox and as he did, a photograph slid out, falling on the desk. How had he missed it?

It was a Polaroid picture of the torched house from the inside. He saw a pair of crumbled wire-rimmed glasses in the heap of rubble. Evan stuck the photo in his pocket.

FIFTY-FOUR
Texas

"HE'S DEAD!"

Dee had made this announcement to Sue on a phone call. She had called to deliver the results of the lab tests and the news about Shapiro. The test results weren't a surprise to Sue, but Shapiro's death was.

"Shapiro, the chemist?" Sue asked, trying to calm herself, her voice full of anxiety and fear.

"Yep. Dead as a doorknob. We located his whereabouts in a rural area of Indiana and we planned on paying him a visit in the next few days. Then I received a Hotwire alert that he was killed in a fire at his home."

Sue felt a rush of urgency over the news. She now had more at stake beyond the legal tangling.

"Do they suspect arson or what?" She couldn't believe she was talking casually about a criminal investigation, let alone a possible murder.

"Too soon to tell."

"Crap. Who are we dealing with? And the lab results? What did Patrick's CSI buddy uncover?"

"He found present a peculiar mixture of several suphadiade chemicals. This is a problem," Dee said.

Sue was surprised and shocked to have it confirmed. The tags submitted to Dee were taken directly from new toys Sue had purchased at a retail store. "What else did Patrick find out?"

"Turns out this is the same composition of a similar sample submitted from a plant in China where Pete Shapiro was doing research years ago. The chemical used was made up for Yorkston — you won't find that exact molecular makeup anywhere else. DMCY is a nasty toxic chemical and it has no place in children's toys. It's all in our report."

"Are you sure this is the exact traceability measurements?"

"Yes. It was measured at over 1000 parts per million on the tag. The allowed level is only 25 parts per million." Dee was rustling papers like she was reading a report. "These chemicals aren't necessarily subject to specific standards by the Consumer Protection Safety."

Oh my God, if this is true . . . .

Sue shivered at the thought.

"We tested and retested several," Dee said. "We even used a tag from my own pink Yorkston penguin, and the level of DMCY was 91%. Sis, you need to march straight upstairs and cut off all the tags on your kids' toys!"

Well, Maddie had already taken care of that. But she needed to make sure they were all thrown away. "Yeah, but the tags have the special serial numbers on them." Sue said absentmindedly, not realizing the ludicrousness of her own statement.

"I don't give a shit about the serial numbers! I care about my niece's safety. If I had my way, I'd throw every damn one of those toys in the garbage," Dee said.

"So the results are positive." Sue knew it; she just needed to say it aloud.

She stood up, walked over to her office door and leaned against it, as if she was keeping people from entering.

"As detective work, it's not homerun link evidence, but it is enough to concern a mother of a baby if the tainted tag theory leaked out," Dee said.

Sue sagged against the door. *Sonofabitch did it.*

"The results are conclusive; over time, the effects of the trace chemical used in the dye of the sewn tag you submitted, if digested often, could cause potential development issues. But, it could be years from now. It could start with a rash with redness and itchiness, and possible vomiting. It could be diagnosed as flu or allergies. Later . . . possibly cancer, but it would be a hard case to link," Dee said.

"Damn them," Sue said smacking her hand on the door.

"It would be especially damaging to children under age six, whose bodies are still developing. It causes nervous system damage, stunted growth and delayed development. It has been linked to kidney damage and affects every organ of the body. It can also be dangerous to adults, and can cause problems for —,"Dee continued.

"Okay, okay, I get it," Sue interrupted her.

"There's no way to know the extent of the damage this substance can cause without further lab results. The labs weren't set up for that type of testing, plus we are doing this under the radar."

"I know. Thanks Dee. I need to run." She was shaking and felt sick. Sue had to find the information and quickly. Without Shapiro, her plans would need altering. She'd be damned if Yorkston would get away with their nefarious activities.

"Where are you headed?"

"China."

"Be careful. Are you sure you won't bring the consultant with you?" Dee asked.

Sue only heard concern in her sister's voice. Not a hint of teasing, this time.

"No, he's busy, and can't make it this trip." The truth was Sue still hadn't talked to Daniel. Even though they hadn't talked since Boston, she couldn't get Daniel out of her head. She refused to accept that he was busy, and he wasn't interested in her.

"Okay. Be safe, Sis. Get what you need, call us when you do. Hugs and kisses." Dee hung up.

Sue had planned a follow up business trip to China, but now she needed to accelerate her schedule. The plant name was in the report Dee had emailed to Sue. She had to get answers, fast.

She needed proof.

It took Sue less than 5 seconds after she hung up with Dee, to jump to her feet and dash to Maddie's room on the second floor, she located the shelf of the Yorkston plush. She flipped the toys over frantically searching for their tush tags. *Of course, they're all cut off by Maddie.*

"Mommy, I said, I'm sorry I cut the tags off," Maddie's small voice said when she saw Sue examining all the toys.

Sue knelt down and hugged Maddie close to her. "Sweetie, I love you so much. I'm not worried about that, but what did you do with the tags?" Sue beamed at her beautiful little girl, who looked at her gratefully.

"They're here." Maddie reached behind a pile of Yorkston tiny critters and pulled out a zip lock baggie filled with Yorkston labels. The bag had child like colorings of a stick man with bizarre arms and a host of creepy facial features.

The red numbered tags made Sue ill to her stomach.

"Thank you, Maddie. I'll take these. And from now on, if you see any more of these toys in our house, let me know." She made a point to smile at her, even though inside she felt sick at the possibilities of what that bastard Yorkston was doing.

FIFTY-FIVE
China

"DO YOU WANT to share my car downtown?" Ken said to Sue. Ken, a friendly business man from Chicago, had been her seatmate in coach on the long flight to China.

"Sure, thank you," Sue replied.

He placed Sue's overnight carry-on baggage in the trunk. He looked around. "Is this all you have?"

"Yes, it's a short trip for me." Sue climbed into the back seat.

Ken climbed in next to her and said something in Chinese to the driver.

"I'm impressed you know the language."

"Don't be," he replied. "I know enough to get by, that's all. When was the last time you've been here?"

"It has been a year since I traveled to Hong Kong."

"A lot has changed."

"Yes, I see the new airport has opened. I was a bit lost when we landed."

"I love the new island airport."

"It is magnificent, but the maze of tunnels and suspension bridges connecting to the terminal were pretty confusing." Sue was tired and didn't feel like small talk. She tried to be polite.

"So you said this is a plant walk through of your toys?" He asked.

"Yes, a couple of business meetings, that's all." Sue thought this trip today was more treacherous than her last trip . . . a trip of desperation. She had arrived the year before with hopes and dreams. Now, all that was shattered by one mammoth predator.

"Great. How long are you here? Maybe we can have dinner." He smiled at her.

"Just one day here and then to mainland China and back to Texas."

"Wow, that is a quick trip."

Sue looked out the window. The beautiful architecturally stunning office towers now were startling to her. Every square inch of the island, all the way up the steep hills, was covered with buildings towering seventy stories high. It all seemed overpowering.

"Yes, it is." Her eyelids fluttering. "Sorry, I'm exhausted. I can barely keep my eyes open."

"I noticed you didn't sleep much on the flight."

Sue nodded her head and stifled a yawn. It was true, the long, last minute trip had been draining. Sue hadn't slept at all, stuck in a middle seat.

"Well, I hope your business is successful."

"Thank you." She turned her head and gazed out at the skyline, and the busy traffic on the harbor island. *Why am I here?* She questioned her own sanity sometimes.

She had the tags, but that wasn't proof enough. She had to prove that Yorkston was having them made here, tie the gap, and connect the missing pieces together. Her success was tied to their failure . . . but it was a lot bigger than that.

Sue met up with Li, her Chinese escort, before going to the plant in China. It had been easy for Sue to convince Li she wanted to visit the plant to review a special fabric tag needed for her Millennium Kids toys. Li wasn't curious; she just wanted to sell a lot of products.

The taxi dropped Sue at the Hong Kong offices of her China manufacturer. She spent the day going through her products, but her heart wasn't in it and she ended the day early. Sue checked into the same hotel she and Daniel had stayed at the year before.

Sue woke up the next day, excited at finally being able to face the maker of the tainted tags.

The trip to China was uneventful. She easily crossed through customs. She stared out the train window and thought of her last trip and being stranded in the village with Daniel; it seemed decades ago.

She caught a glimpse of her own reflection in the window and told herself, *I'll do what needs to be done!*

It was the end of the day before she made it to the secluded plant in Fuzhou. Having come all this way, Sue was petrified that she wouldn't find what she was looking for.

"The product must be stored in a dry, well ventilated warehouse." Sue's Chinese translator handed her a glass vial with the optical brightening agent.

"But the combination with the crystallized powder will make the holographic characters adhere to the fabric tags so the fabric printer can imprint the serial numbers?" For the third time, Sue repeated the question she had been asking the manager since she had first arrived in the chemical plant in Fuzhou.

"Yes, yes, this will work." Li translated the manager's words to her.

Sue took off her safety glasses and held the vial up to the light. She rolled it around to see the contents in the bottle. She nodded, and handed it back to the manager. "Okay, let me see the other fabric numbers with the non-brightening agent."

The manager retrieved a plastic bag of tags from a green metal container resembling a vintage tackle box her dad owned. The hinges and latches were rusted around the edges and there were Chinese characters scratched in the top.

Sue removed several tags from the plastic bag, and ran her fingers over the holographic serial numbers. She retrieved a jewelers loupe and examined the printing. "This is the lowest price alternative?"

"Yes, this the lowest price to make this."

"Can we test these samples?"

"Yes, we have a comparison for you. This way." Li and the plant manager escorted Sue to the laboratory.

On the way, they passed a loading dock. Sue spotted three large metal drums. "What are those for?"

Sue thought Li had translated her question to the manager.

She waited for a reply, but Li didn't look her way.

The laboratory for Lo He Dye was messy, with a crowded worktable piled high with reference books, fabric swatches, and an ashtray overflowing with cigarette butts. The plant manager set the metal box on the worktable.

Sue was nervous, as she reached a sweaty hand into her pocket to recover a tag she had bought from Maddie's childlike drawings baggie. Screening her left hand, she took her hidden tag and swapped it for their tag, like a magician practicing his craft.

"I would like to take these samples with me, after they are tested. I'll give you a check for the container." Sue knew if she offered to write a check for the purchase, she would get the red carpet treatment.

The plant manager smiled a devious slow smile, as one eyebrow arched.

Sucking in a quick breath, Sue knew she was about to connect the dots.

What will it be?

Sue knew from her earlier years of research in this area that the issue wasn't so much the apparatus as it was the chemicals used in the dyes. What made it more difficult was Yorkston used a red dye.

Sue remembered when she was a child growing up, she wasn't allowed to eat any red candies, due to health concerns over red dye number two. The dye was a suspected carcinogenic. When her parents heard that the FDA had safety concerns over it, she and Dee were never allowed to eat red sweets. Even red chewing gum was off limits.

Thousands of food products were made containing the dye, but it wasn't only used as a food color but as a natural dyestuff to color cotton fabrics. Though the FDA banned its use in foods, it still was used in fabrics. With this dye ruled out, manufacturers began shifting to substitutes. This pushed up the price of many consumer products.

Dee's research showed that the Lo He Dye Chemical Company had relied on the dye for up to thirty percent of their sales. After the loss of many of their US clients, the dye manufacturer had pursued alternatives. Dee uncovered that this was how the general manager, Kim Zhou met Pete Shapiro the chemist for Yorkston. Pete Shapiro and Kim met at Huazhong University of Science & Technology. Shapiro helped Kim Zhou with new chemical dyes. Shapiro had known Kim for years before involving him with the work he did with Yorkston.

For twenty minutes, Sue waited for answers, so impatient it felt like she would explode. They all sat quietly while Sue pretended to read reports—but inside she felt like she had swallowed a time bomb. She listened to the slow ticking of the clock on the wall, each second an eternity.

"Ms. Sue, here is the final report." Li handed over the printed report.

Sue read the traceability test results, her heart pounding.

"Is this for all the tags I gave you?" She stood up, pacing in a circle as she scrutinized the report.

"Yes. All of them, correct? This is good?" Li appeared puzzled by Sue's reaction.

"And this is the only place to make these with this serial number combination and the embedded software, everything we discussed?"

Sue waited for Li to translate the questions to the plant manager and his team of two.

Even though they talked in Chinese for a few minutes, it seemed like an eternity before Li said, "Yes this is the only plant to get this for your stuffed dolls. Nobody else can do this. The apparatus machine has a patent."

She stared at the report— the numbers on the report all matched, including the tag she had brought with her off Maddie's Yorkston toy. A jolt ran up her back and her knees went weak. The red lines in the report resembled the hospital flat line chart with no spikes. Her poisoned tag had not stood out. They were all bad.

Holy shit, that was it! She had found the smoking gun. Sue's chest swelled with excitement and fear.

She wondered if the Chinese workers were aware of the evil in which they were accomplices as they printed the tainted tags and sent them out to unsuspecting kids all over the world. The notion sickened her.

After a chilling long pause, Sue said, "Please make up a sample with my Millennium Kids with this same tag." She pointed directly to the one she had brought. "I'll need to get the proper toy registration." She watched the eyes of her Chinese associates, waiting for them to catch on to her ploy. But they didn't.

They talked in hushed tones in Chinese. Why whisper? She thought amusingly. Were they afraid that she would now understand their language? Sue tried to quiet her too-quick breathing. She waited with apprehension as they watched her.

"Okay, we'll give you this tag sample for your stuffed toy."

Sue's heart slowed its trip hammer pace; her concerns faded and were replaced by elation. One of her races was complete. Yorkston had lost. She now owned the track.

FIFTY-SIX
Texas

SUE HOME FROM CHINA for twelve hours, was up early making breakfast. It was a beautiful Sunday morning, and she'd been patiently cooking, waiting for the kids to get up, taming her urge to run upstairs and wake them. She felt restless. She had the Sunday paper spread out over the kitchen island. She read hastily through the business section and kept a watchful eye on the stove.

The bacon crackled and its aroma drifted upstairs to do its job.

Sue flipped a pancake over, watching the chocolate ooze from the bubbly batter holes. The bacon hissed and spit at her, showering her forearm with hot grease. She wiped the splatter off with a paper towel.

"Morning, Mommy," Colt said, rubbing his eyes as he walked into the kitchen. Maddie was right behind him, her cheerful blue eyes lighting up the room.

Sue put a chocolate chip pancake on the serving plate.

"I want that one." Colt stabbed his fork at the pancake.

"No, I do." Maddie stabbed the other half of the pancake.

Sue swooped in to separate them. "There's plenty more. Let's all wait until we sit down to eat."

Elizabeth snuck up behind Sue and gave her hug around the waist. "Thanks, Mama, for making chocolate chip pancakes."

Sue kissed Elizabeth on the forehead and went back to work preparing breakfast.

She poured a cup of coffee for herself plus three glasses of apple juice for the kids.

As she stacked the last pancake on the platter, she glanced through the kitchen door and saw two men walking up her front steps. They were wearing jeans and blazers. Her first thought was more process servers, but she knew they typically didn't work on Sundays. Plus they usually came alone, not in pairs.

She stayed in the kitchen, hiding behind the edge of a wall, knowing the men couldn't see her. The shorter of the two, a muscular man, bent down and adjusted a black strap under the pant leg of his jeans. The sun sparkled off the butt of a silver revolver tucked inside an ankle holster. He pulled his jean down and the gun disappeared from sight. *A gun!* Maybe they're detectives but she couldn't take a risk. Her instincts said to wait out back until they leave.

"Kids!" she whispered with a quiver in her voice. All three stopped talking and looked at her. "Let's eat breakfast outside today in the cabana . . . like we're camping."

The faces of her two younger kids lit up as if it was Christmas morning. But, it was Elizabeth who wasn't budging. "Why are you whispering, Mommy?"

"Shhhh."

Elizabeth took a plate from the stack of dishes sitting on the table. "It's hot outside. I don't want to eat in the cabana. I'm hungry. Can we eat in here?"

Sue ran her hand through her hair. "Um, I have a surprise in the cabana for all of you. But we have to play the quiet game. So everyone has to be silent and the first person that speaks loses and has to do the dishes."

She opened the backdoor, carrying a stack of plates in one arm, while scooting the kids out with the other. Her cell phone was in the bedroom in her purse and if she went to fetch it, she would pass the two men at the front door. The car was in the garage and her keys in her purse.

The doorbell rang. The kids stopped walking. "It's only a solicitor. Let's keep going. Follow me, this way." Sue coaxed the kids to follow her around the pool to avoid being spotted through the patio windows. They walked single file toward the cabana. She scanned the golf course fairway, searching for a golfer, a marshal, anybody. There was no one in sight.

Colt was the first to reach the cabana. His eyes scanned the wicker chairs and the glass tabletop. "Where's the surprise, Mom?"

"You lose!" Maddie screamed at him. "You were the first to talk."

"No fair!" he yelled.

"You have to do the dishes. You have to do the dishes."

"Kids, stop it. Be quiet."

The freestanding cabana was near the east edge of the property and had four brick open-air columns holding up a cedar roof. A gas grill and sink were tucked under the left side of the cabana, directly opposite of the bathroom and shower.

Sue rubbed her temples, eyeing the tall cedar gate along the side yard, cursing that she left the key to the padlock on the hook by the back door.

A five-foot-tall black iron fence separated the grassy backyard from a muddy creek that split the fairway and trickled past the property. It was home to thousands of buzzing mosquitoes and chirping frogs during the rainy season and usually kept golfers away from the yard as they approached the 18th green.

"Okay, here's a new game." They heard pounding on the front door. Everyone looked toward the house.

"Mommy, someone is still here," Maddie said.

"Okay, okay. I know." They were all looking at her as if she'd gone mad. "We are going to hide, um, I mean, sit behind the sink here. Like we're playing hide and seek. And I want you three to stay here until—." She scooped up Maddie and grabbed Colt by the arm, dragging them behind the brick wall supporting the sink, hiding them from sight. The kids followed the direction of her look to the patio doors.

"Look Mama, someone's in our house," Maddie said. Sue put her hand over Maddie's mouth as she watched a wide-eyed man open a kitchen desk drawer, while the other stood watch on the bottom step of the stairs leading to the bedrooms.

Elizabeth fell to her knees, crawling over to Sue and her sister. She covered her eyes, hiding behind her spread fingers, and watched the men inside. "Mommy, who's in our house?"

Sue surveyed the backyard, her heart pounding hard in her

chest. The trampoline was of no use unless she wanted to catapult the kids and herself into the neighbor's yard with the nasty pit bull that never seemed to stop barking, except, of course, today, when she really needed it to. The neighbors must be out of town. She thought about climbing over the wrought iron fence, but decided against it. Climbing would take too long with the kids in tow and the intruders might see them.

She snuck a quick look at the fairway – still no golfers in sight. It seemed like whenever she was sunbathing, a golf cart would pass by their backyard every ten minutes, but not today. There was no sign of anyone.

She checked her pockets. Nothing. Her cell phone, left in her purse in the bedroom. There wasn't a phone outside. Jonathan had planned to install a phone in the cabana, but never got around to it before he died.

She had heard of home invasions with horrifying endings. That only happened on TV, right? God, her kids! Elizabeth sat in the middle of Colt and Maddie with her arms wrapped around both of them, squeezing them to her chest in one big hug, like a three-headed centipede in pajamas.

Sue reached over her head and found the sink's cabinet drawer. She slid it open and felt around, searching frantically with her fingers, touching something wet and gooey. She touched a fork and a blade of a knife. She continued her search, feeling a small box with a rough strip on one side. She pulled it out, opened her hand to reveal a matchbox.

She opened the cabinet side door and found a cobweb draped over the middle shelf. She knocked the web out of the away, retrieved a brown cedar box and set it on the ground between her bare feet. She opened the lid. Inside were three cellophane-wrapped cigars and a half empty cigarette pack. The aroma from the cigars reminded her of Superbowl XXVIII, when Jonathan and his friends stood in this very spot, lighting up their Churchills during the half-time break.

"Kids, I'm going to fix something on Daddy's old grill. I need you to stay still and don't move or make a sound until I tell you, then we're going to run and hide behind the bushes by the big tree with Colt's fort in it."

They nodded, their faces pale. She checked the house again. The thugs were upstairs, knocking toys and books off the game room shelves.

She picked a cigarette out of the pack, tore the filtered end off the tube of tobacco and stuck the end of the cigarette into a vent hole in the gas grill's steel lid.

"I need you to take Maddie and Colt to the bushes now," she whispered to Elizabeth.

"No, Mommy, you come with," Elizabeth said, her baby blue eyes begging Sue to stay.

"I'll be there in a second."

Colt grabbed at her hand. "Please come with us."

"It'll be okay." Sue tried hard not to sound hysterical, patting his leg to reassure him. "I'll be right there. Whatever you do, *don't* move from the bushes. Stay down low. Promise?"

No response. Colt sat there, staring at his bare feet.

She took her little finger, wrapping it around Colt's little finger. "Pinky shake?"

"Promise," he said.

"On the count of three, you're gonna run to the bushes and I'll meet you there in a minute."

All three kids stared at her, their necks and faces white, and their eyes wide.

"One . . . two . . . three!"

The kids didn't move.

Sue closed her eyes for a second, then sucked in air and said, "You have to go." She pinched Elizabeth's leg. "Go now. Run!"

Sue watched the three kids dash across the yard to the bushes backing to the creek. The kids were hidden but Maddie's tiny pink toes hung out on one side. She wanted to yell at them, but she realized how deadly that would be.

She checked the house and saw the men in her bedroom looking in her dresser drawers – she ducked when one of them looked out the window, right at her. Her heart pounding, she looked toward the bushes where her kids hid. She heard a crash coming from the house.

Shit!

262

Sue had a brief vision of the two goons making their way to the backyard and discovering the kids hidden behind the bushes.

She opened the door of the stainless steel grill. The propane tank was on the inside with a rubber hose connecting the gas into the burners. She reached inside, turning the valve as far as it would go. The tank started hissing and she smelled rotten eggs. She fumbled with the matchbox, cursing that she didn't have the clicker lighter, spilling several matches onto the grass. She picked one up and struck it along the igniter strip on the side. The match didn't light. She tossed it on the grass and took out another match, rubbing it across the striking surface. Nothing.

Crap!

She rubbed all sides of the next match on the black surface until the red powder disappeared from the tip. She took out another match smashed it against the striking surface.

It lit! Thank God!

She put the cigarette in her mouth, lit the end, and took several puffs until the gray ash glowed red. She returned it to the hole of the closed stainless grill lid, the red embers facing up. The stick of tobacco was burning faster than she thought it would.

She stood up and ran to her kids, sprinting with every ounce of muscle in her legs. She could feel mud squishing between her toes as her bare feet dug deep into the lumpy sod. She plopped down, the kids crawled to her, and she tucked all of them behind the heavy foliage, pulling Maddie's toes under her pajamas.

The kids were still. She was silent. The cicadas roaring love song in the tree overhead was almost deafening. The back door flew open, smashing the wall. The bugs went silent.

Sue hunched over Maddie's trembling body. "Shhh," She whispered. Her knuckles were white from clenching her fist tight. She heard gravel crunch, and watched one pair of black work boots move swiftly past the bushes, toward the cabana.

Sue pulled the kids deeper into their hideout. Within a few seconds, she heard the back door slam open again and saw another set of black shoes walk by, the one with the ankle holster and denim-clad legs. She felt the skin crawl on her back. The boots stopped and returned in front of the bushes, as if he sensed her there. He started fanning open the evergreens. Elizabeth's mouth opened like she was about to scream.

"Hey Brick, come look over here. Maybe it's in the pool house."

The man's black boots disappeared from view, heading in the direction of the cabana.

She heard one of the men tell the other, "You look in the bathroom drawers. I'll check these cabinets."

"It looks like there was someone out here recently smoking a cig."

"Look under the sink cabinet—"

"Do you smell gas?"

The explosion vibrated the backyard like a cannon. The grill lid ripped off its hinges, flying fifteen feet in the air, and bits and pieces of bricks soared in all directions. The blast hurled one of the men near the pool. Sue hoped death was instantaneous, but was disappointed to see him roll over, his clothes on fire.

The other man had burns on his neck and face. He peeled himself off a pile of bricks and stumbled toward the gate, tripping over fiery debris scattered throughout the backyard.

Sue leapt out of the bushes and ran toward the man by the pool. She shoved him into the water, but not before his burning jacket scorched the back of her hand. She staggered three steps backwards, holding her hand close to her chest.

All three kids were standing, staring at her with their jaws dropped open. Elizabeth had her hands over her heart. Maddie turned to the side and threw up apple juice. The last corner of the cabana caught fire, right before the structure wobbled and fell to the ground.

Thelma Lockes, watering the roses on her back patio, looked across the parkway in the direction of her daughter's house.

"Oh my God!" she yelled. She dropped her watering can, putting her hand to her mouth.

"Wilford." She shouted as she ran inside. "The kids' house is on fire!"

FIFTY-SEVEN

WILFORD HUSTLED through Sue's busted backyard gate with several firemen rushing in behind him.

Thank God the fire station is close. The smell of burnt wood and gas hit his nostrils.

"Where are they? My grandkids? My daughter?" he asked a burley fireman who was covered from head to toe in yellow protective clothing.

The fireman pointed in the direction of the patio, and held his radio to his ear. "Call off truck number three. It's under control."

Wilford saw the remnants of the cabana smoldering. A fireman, holding a hose, kicked at some lingering embers and then sprayed water on them.

"Is Sue your daughter?" a fireman asked through his mask.

"Yes. Is she okay?" Wilford's heart pounded in his chest.

"She has some nasty burns on her hand. You may want to keep her away from cooking bacon on the gas grill. She could've blown up the house and herself, not just the cabana."

Wilford ran over to Sue and his grandkids.

"Hi, Daddy," Sue said calmly.

"Honey, are you and the kids okay?" He looked at her hand as she held it out to the fireman inspecting it. He gave her a quick, but affectionate hug. She reeked of the smoky odor of burnt wood and something else. Cigarettes?

"The kids are fine, but she should go to the ER," the fireman said. "She has second and third degree burns."

"I'm fine. I'm fine," she said.

"What the hell happened? Stay here, let me talk to a fireman," he said.

He talked to the firefighter for a few minutes, then walked over and studied the ashes and cinders around the cabana. The grill was burnt to a crisp. He recognized a metal meat fork curled up, its wooden handle burnt off in the fire. A polyester chair cushion was scattered on the ground in scorched and tattered fragments. He saw something peculiar; a dozen or so matches scattered across the grass.

Wilford stood there, rubbing his chin like he was checking his whiskers for a clean shave.

"She said the bacon grease dripped down and caused the fire," the older firefighter said after following Wilford to the cabana.

"If that's what she said, then thank goodness she cooked it outside and you guys responded so quickly."

"Her son was saying something about his mom starting the fire because of the men . . . is there a Mr. Logan?"

"No, she's a widow. I think you've done a fine job here. Thanks for your support and efforts. I need to take her to the doctor now." Wilford dismissed the conversation. The fire had been small, but its violence didn't escape him.

The fireman, seeming satisfied with Wilford's comments, began gathering up his team.

Walking back to the veranda, Wilford stooped down to pick up a half-smoked cigarette stub, planted vertically in the short grass like a spent cartridge case.

After the firemen left, Wilford tended to Sue's burns. The kids sat in the kitchen quietly. Wilford watched the kids unenthusiastically eat the cold pancakes. He noticed the house smelt like bacon. He hoped the fireman hadn't noticed.

"So," he whispered to Sue, "what aren't you telling me, young lady?"

"Did you see a car leaving when you pulled up?" She avoided looking into his knowing eyes.

"No, just the fire trucks and a bunch of concerned neighbors. Why," his eyes widened and he leaned in close, "did you have a visitor?"

"Let's just say some strong-arm men came looking for some answers. I didn't want to tell the fireman. I'll call the police. I think it was Yorkston men, since I found the dye plant."

"Shit. This is getting crazy. I'm calling the police."

"Daddy, I sent them away. I made the fire to get them away from here. One of them looked like he had burns on his face. We're all fine. I didn't talk to them . . . I didn't want to risk the kids overhearing anything . . . those men were trouble. Can the kids stay with you and Mom for a while until I figure this all out?" She wasn't making a lot of sense. "Geez, these burns on my hand are stinging and I have a pounding headache."

"It's okay, sweetie. I'll call the police and get this on record. Are you okay to talk to them?" Wilford held her burnt hand tenderly in his. "I suspected all along that you might be dealing with some rough characters. It pisses me off they came here, if it really was related to your discovery." He looked at the kids and lowered his voice. "I think you need to stay with us too."

"You think they'll come back? They didn't find anything. I scared them off." Her voice came out low and breathless.

Despite her injury, he was proud of the anger she managed to inject at the strangers and the courage to stand up for herself. She had fought them, and won, for now.

"I don't think they'll be back, especially since they now know you are on to them coming here. And they know you would have called the police."

"I can stay here. I'll be fine; more cautious, but fine. Just fine . . . ." Sue was drifting, biting her lip and mumbling.

He felt his brows wrinkling in concern. "They didn't find what you brought back from Fuzhou, did they?"

"No, Daddy, they took nothing that I'm aware of."

"We should tell the police."

"I know. But not yet. I can't. I need to finish something I started. I don't want this reported."

"Do you still have the Browning Sweet 16 automatic under your bed?"

"Daddy, don't be ridiculous," she said in a nervous trill.

"Yeah, I could use the shot gun like a sledge hammer on a would-be assailant, since it would take me forever to get it out of the leather carrying case, find shells, and load it." She smiled through clenched teeth.

His heart felt so heavy, like he needed a hand cart to tote it around. He stood up. "Let's get these kiddos dressed. Grandma wants to take all of you to the park while I run your mom to the doctor. Hurry up, skedaddle!"

For once, Sue didn't argue with him.

FIFTY-EIGHT
Texas
A Week Later

IT HAD BEEN OVER A WEEK since the fire, and Sue's hand healed slowly. She sat in the conference room, fidgeting with the loosely-wrapped gauze.

Patrick had told Sue he would look into possible individuals of interest regarding the invasion at her house that Sunday. Dee had offered to stay with Sue, bringing along her favorite friend, Pyca.

Pyca was an old black Colt revolver that Patrick had engraved for Dee. The gun's inscription read, "Protect Your Cute Ass."

Sue was more worried about protecting her company's ass than her own. This morning she had one thing on her mind; the settlement of her lawsuit against her first law firm.

Tex wasn't a malpractice lawyer, but he had agreed to represent her in the suit against Triggs and Patterson. He had persuaded her to mediate with their insurance company. It seemed ruthless for a lawyer to be suing their own, but Tex said their malpractice insurance covered a strict range of incidents, and fortunately their bad advice years ago, fell within the parameters.

Her mediation experience with Yorkston had left her with an acid taste in her mouth. Tex said, "This is different. You are the plaintiff this time. You'll call the shots. You can take it or leave it and continue or not continue the case to trial. Insurance companies are there to protect their clients from the courtroom. No one wants a lawyer being sued. It's bad publicity for the firm."

She had acquiesced.

Sue watched her dad pace restlessly, his boots clicking against the bare hardwood floors of the conference room. Wilford had insisted on going with Sue to the settlement discussion. He said he wanted to be there to support her and he would love to see one lawyer pulverize another. "It would be like watching a mother rattlesnake swallowing her young whole. I can't wait to be face-to-face with the jerk who gave you such bad advice."

He looked like he was ready to lunge on the bastard like a hawk on a jackrabbit. He was disappointed when he found out the insurance company representatives and the senior lawyer, Matthew Triggs, would be the only ones at the settlement discussions. But he insisted on attending anyway, even though Bruce Barrows, Wilford's chosen foe – the young whippersnapper, Sue's one-man destroyer – wasn't at the meeting.

Tex had permitted Wilford to attend as long as he became a fly on the wall and didn't partake in the discussions. Wilford slipped quietly into an overstuffed chair in the corner.

The negotiation with the insurance company progressed a lot smoother than her previous experience with the Yorkston group. They hammered out the merits of both arguments. No slips of paper with dollar amounts written on them were in sight.

They discussed the settlement like a business opportunity; lost revenues for the catalog, loss of clients due to not fulfilling the catalog orders, loss of other product sales because of the loss of clients. In addition, there was the costs she had paid in lawyers' fees to defend her against Yorkston.

At one point, the older representative asked Sue, "Can we ask you a few more questions?"

A small frown furrowed her smooth brow as the idea of more questioning crossed through her mind. She looked at Tex and he nodded. "Sure."

"Why did you hire Triggs and Patterson?"

"Well, as I said in my deposition, they were referred to my husband, Jonathan, through a friend. His friend used the firm for a family will and trust." Sue rubbed her forehead.

Wilford sat up taller in his chair.

"At the time you hired them, you felt they were capable of handling intellectual property?"

"That's what they represented to me. I presented the catalog idea to them and they gave me legal advice. I acted on what they told me." Her head began to pound. She rubbed the gauze on her hand. "We discussed this already."

"Why are we dredging up this old stuff?" Wilford yelped, the veins in his neck bulging. "She's been through this over and over. They ain't IP lawyers. They do family stuff, wills and divorces. You know those clowns represented themselves to be IP experts."

Wilford's eyes focused squarely on the senior insurance representative. "You have the opinion letter they presented to Logan. They were her lawyers, representing her and her ideas, and she believed in them. She didn't know an IP lawyer was skilled in a special combination of legal advice."

Sue felt a blush fill her checks. Tex rolled his eyes and shot Wilford a warning. Look you know that Triggs and Patterson gave their blessings on the Logan catalog, bad legal advice to my client that got her company sued by Yorkston. Your clients' mistake injured and harmed Logan in a way that can be measured financially. Our job here today is to decide on how much," Tex said.

Wilford chimed in again. He looked directly at Matthew Triggs this time. "Your young lawyer was dishing out bad advice. How the hell did he even get his license? If you ask me, it don't take much to become an attorney these days. Any boy from the farm just off the plow could take an online course, run by the law board, snatch a license and become a full-fledged attorney. The legal profession is becoming overcrowded with a bunch of incompetents."

Sue gave her dad a warning look. "Daddy, please let the lawyers handle this." She looked at the older gentleman and shrugged. "Sorry, he can get crazy sometimes."

"Oh, I'm fixin' to get crazy alright." He sank back in his chair, crossing his arms across his chest.

"It's okay, let's continue." Sue returned everyone to the settlement discussions.

Late in the morning, Sue felt woozy. Her hand stung continuously and wave after wave of nausea engulfed her like the tide at the sea's edge.

A blister had burst that morning, exposing another layer of raw skin. The large flap of pink dead skin still hung on her hand like a boiled pig's ear. She had taken a pain reliever on an empty stomach, increasing her queasiness.

"If you'll excuse me gentlemen, I need a break." Sue left the conference room before she threw up on them.

Tex met her after she returned from the ladies room. "Sorry, I feel queasy."

"Come sit in my office," Tex led her to an office connected to the conference room.

Tex had left the conference door a jarred. Sue could see the men still hashing out the settlement.

"Here, try this." Tex took out a small brown glass bottle from his credenza drawer.

Sue sniffed the bottle. "Smells like oranges." It looked like a bottle of vanilla she used for baking cookies.

"Bitters," he said.

Sue took a swig. "Yuck." She felt the liquid settle in her empty stomach. Despite the taste, she felt better already.

"I hated to be the one to draw the line in the sand," she said to Tex in confidence. "But mediation is like a tug-of-war game . . . the more I get, the less they keep."

"I hear ya. What do you want to do?"

"Well, at the end of the day, I'd rather be unhappy about the dollar amount, but have a resolution, than to risk a coin toss at trial." She felt they were railroading her into a lowball decision, but she didn't care. She wanted it over.

"I understand. Let me get back to the negotiations. Take your time."

Sue sat in Tex's office, drinking the orange bitters to calm the flutters in the pit of her stomach. Through the open door, she watched the team of insurance representatives, lawyers and her father fretting over this and that. She tried to gather her guts, courage and strength to return to the fight.

She caught the eye of the elderly insurance company rep. His face showed a look of pity as Sue sat alone in Tex's office and the men in the adjoining conference room argued the merits of her case. It was at that moment she knew they were going to make a deal.

They took a short lunch break. While she sat in the coffee shop with Tex and her dad, she saw two men lingering outside the building, their heads bowed in conversation. She couldn't see their faces. One had a bandage over the left side of his face and ear. Her heart fluttered.

Shit, is that the guys from that Sunday at her house?

"What's wrong?" Wilford asked.

"Nothing. It's nothing. I just want to get this settled. I have another installment due to Yorkston."

She had paid two installments and was planning to default on the remaining payments.

I really could use the settlement money. She stared out the window again.

Wilford looked toward the man. "Is that someone you know?"

The man left the coffee shop sidewalk and was gone when Tex looked up.

"No, I didn't recognize him." She didn't want to cause trouble now. She wasn't really sure, and she didn't want to look paranoid.

They returned from the lunch break. After five hours of negotiations, they had all agreed on an amount.

Sue was relieved to know her company would be receiving a settlement over the ruinous advice. Sue and Wilford thanked Tex for his negotiations. The feeling of achievement and the sheer exhilaration of just settling the case in her favor was monumental in her world of major setbacks and minor victories. However, there was little delight in the victory, because Sue found nothing enjoyable about winning a legal settlement, nor was she vindictive. All she felt was relief, which she hid.

The settlement papers would be drawn up that evening and faxed to her. She would review and sign them, and before midnight, she would receive recompense for the loss of the catalog sales.

FIFTY-NINE
The Oral Deposition of Nathanael Yorkston

IN THE WEEKS following the settlement with Triggs and Patterson, Sue had felt content, until today. There was an eerie calmness settling over Logan, like a gloomy rain cloud looming overhead waiting to erupt into a violent storm. Today the storm had arrived in Texas. Nathanael Yorkston was here.

On this humid, gray spring morning, Sue was an observer at the oral deposition of Nathanael Yorkston, in the case of her Millennium Kids versus his Y2K Kids. Sue thought about how hard it would be to keep a calm face around him. She thought the two of them sitting at the same table would be like two angry wild cats with only one tree between them. She hoped there wouldn't be a vicious confrontation.

She had watched him pull in the parking lot. She thought Nathanael was trying to go incognito, he showed up driving a rag top jeep – no white limo, no driver, no handlers, no escorts. He was dressed in an expensive casual blazer and tie when he entered the deposition room.

He sat in the same chair Sue had occupied the week before. She had spent nine hours with the Yorkston lawyers grilling her nonstop – now it was Tex's turn to interrogate Nathanael Yorkston.

Tex sat across from Nathanael, watching him closely. James McDougal, Nathanael's defense attorney, a man with a fancy reputation, sat on Nathanael's right. The egotistic nasty Naty Yorkston was engaged in a conversation with the court reporter who seemed to hang on Nathanael's every word.

Damn, even here in Texas, his celebrity status is evident.

Sue took a seat at the far end of the conference table across from Tex, avoiding contact with her nemesis. She couldn't even bear to look at Nathanael directly.

He's lucky I didn't bring Daddy's Sweet 16. I would give Yorkston a good ol' Texas welcome.

Her seat was out of sight of the camera, so she wouldn't be seen on tape. The aroma of the fresh-cut flowers on the credenza filled Sue's nostrils. The smell reminded her of a funeral parlor.

Nathanael stared directly ahead. He rubbed his left check. His fingers caressed the pit-like scars on his skin. His face looked like a lawn that gophers had left covered with pockmarks. For a brief moment, he glanced at Sue. His dark eyes met hers and he grinned.

Sue tried to read anything on his face. *Do you know, Nathanael Yorkston? Do you know what your product could do? Do you know the harm it could cause?*

The court stenographer turned on the tape recorder, and the video operator turned on the camera.

"For the record, Mr. Yorkston, please state your full name, your address and your place of employment," Tex said.

Nathanael answered, with no surprises there.

"Mr. Yorkston, have you ever been deposed?" Tex asked.

"Yes, all copyright and patent related." He squirmed.

Sue bet her sweet ass he had been. She wondered if this had relevance or if Tex just asked this at the beginning of a deposition because if the answer was yes, it made the deposed feel uncomfortable. She thought that might give Tex the upper hand, right off the bat.

Tex asked a series of questions. They seemed to follow a pattern, several easy-to-answer ones with a few tough questions thrown in. This continued for the most part of the first hour. Tex repeated the same line of questions that the Yorkston lawyers had used on her. At one point Tex asked him if he was the creator of the entire stuffed animal line.

Nathanael shook his head. To Sue he seemed excessively casual, as if he was stoned or really didn't give a damn about being there.

"I need a yes or no answer," Tex said.

"No."

Tex didn't look surprised. He made a few notes, his pen scratching on his legal pad.

"Okay, who are the creators and take me through how the products are designed."

"I used to be the sole creator, but I have a lot of other business ventures now, so we use design teams to assist in the product development."

"Who designed the Y2K kids?"

"I did." Nathanael's eyes blinked several times, like dust had swept into them.

This answer surprised Sue, and apparently Tex. Tex paused a minute, reviewing notes on his yellow pad.

"All right, so it's your testimony that you invented the Y2K kids?"

"Yes, sir." He glanced to his right and Sue caught a self-absorbed grin crossing Nathanael's face.

"I would like your testimony on how you made your designs. What are the steps of the designs and how do you get new ideas?"

Nathanael spent ten minutes explaining his design processes. A lot of his description sounded like the same process Sue went through when creating her products. That made sense. They were both playmakers, making successful playthings.

"After the initial sketch, I take it to China. I tell China exactly what I want them to do."

"Is there a particular individual in China that you work with?"

"Yes, sir."

"Who is that?"

"John Wong"

"Has Mr. Wong been in this capacity for a long time?"

"Yes, for as long as the company has been around. And I worked with him years before that."

"Is Mr. Wong an employee of Yorkston Toys?"

"No, sir."

"In what capacity is he related to Yorkston?"

"He is an independent contractor. I use him exclusively for

all my designs."

"When did you first approach Mr. Wong on the designs of the Y2K Kids?"

"1983"

Tex stared at Nathanael.

"No, 1985," Nathanael said.

Sue's chin went slack, her mouth dropping open. *He has to be joking. Shit, he was fabricating this story.* She thought her face must have lit up like a used-car-lot bulb because Nathanael Yorkston was gawking at her. She shriveled under his contemptuous stare.

In his curt, straightforward fashion, Tex fired question after question at Nathanael.

"Was there documentation of the dolls design in 1985?"

He glanced at his lawyer and then looked past Tex. "I don't recall."

"Were there any patterns?"

"I don't recall."

"Were there any drawings from that time?"

"I don't recall."

"Were there any prototypes from the earlier years?"

"I don't recall."

"Are you married?"

"I don't recall—" Nathanael stopped, correcting his answer. "No, sir, I'm single." He was sweating. He wiped his forehead with his hand.

"I see," Tex said. "Okay, Mr. Yorkston, are there any items that you have that shows you came up with the design during the time you specified?"

Sue thought about her Millennium Kids. She had notes. She had photos. She had patterns. She even had an old Polaroid picture of her when she was a teenager holding her original prototype. Her file on her doll designs read like a phonebook.

"No, but I told Mr. Wong. He would vouch for my idea in that timeframe," Nathanael said.

Sue swallowed hard, and intense anxiety swept over her. *Keep quiet. Don't say a word, not even a smirk.* She was relieved when Tex suggested a bio break.

She encountered Nathanael when she came out of the ladies bathroom. They were alone in the hallway.

He looked at her and said, "What do I need to do to get rid of you?"

Her heart jumped. "What?"

His dark eyes glared with hate, but he didn't reply. He turned and swaggered down the corridor, humming as he entered the conference room. She stood there with her mouth hanging open.

"There you are." Tex strode up to her. He put his hand on her arm. "Are you okay?"

"Nathanael just made a rude comment. He said he wants me to go away."

"Well, you'll go away after we sue his ass. And win. How do you think it's going in there?"

"He's lying," she whispered to Tex, still staring at the hall where Yorkston disappeared. "You need to prove it. A company their size doesn't develop a full line of new products without having any dated material to show for it. I suppose he'll say they magically lost all of their records. The jerk. He stole my idea."

"Yep, he's lying like a cheap rug," Tex replied. "I'll get him. Calm down. You look like you've seen a ghost."

"Not a ghost . . . a monster." She looked down the hall. "I think he's threatening me."

"I'll talk to his lawyers."

"I want this to end. And take him down." She felt like a piñata, loaded with surprises and waiting for someone to give her a strong whack to let it all rain down on them.

She regarded Tex. The last year of working on the Logan lawsuits showed on his tired face. She could see that his hair was now flecked with a few more strands of gray.

"Make sure you ask him about the fabrics and the tush tag. Find out what China plant makes which items, specifically ask about the tush tags with the serial number." Sue was ready to trap her prey.

She knew how he could get rid of her. Where he was going, she wouldn't be there.

When she returned to the conference room Nathanael was seated. He watched her like a hawk as she slouched in the seat.

For the next several hours, Tex took Nathanael through a myriad of questions. At one point, when Tex was trying to get the Y2K kids straight with the different exhibit numbers, Nathanael impatiently blew up at Tex. "I don't have time for this!" Yorkston said.

Sue caught a glimpse of a quick smile from Tex. He turned his head away from Nathanael, as if to sneeze, but as he covered his mouth, he looked at her and winked where Nathanael and his lawyer couldn't see him.

"Mr. Yorkston, how did you come up with the name Y2K Kids?" Tex changed his line of questioning.

"We wanted an acronym to depict a new era of stuffed dolls, since the dolls have unique functionalities that other toys don't have. The acronym stands for Yorkston 2000 Kids."

"When did you come up with this name?"

"1995."

Tex scribbled on his notepad, then shuffled a few papers and placed several in front of Nathanael.

"Mr. Yorkston, let me show you what we've marked as Plaintiff's Exhibit 38, which is stamped Y2K0123 and Y2K0124. Do you see that?"

Nathanael looked at the documents. "Yes."

"What is this document?"

"It's an invoice from our China toy manufacturer for the costs of the Y2K Kids."

"Uh-huh. And this is for the product you offer for sale now?"

"Yes, sir."

"What was the manufacturing cost of that particular product?"

"Of the Y2K Kid?"

"Uh-huh."

"The manufacturing cost is approximately $2.90."

"And on this document, Plaintiffs Exhibit 38, why is this cost higher?" Tex asked.

"Without using a calculator, I'd say it looks like it is the costs with freight added to the unit price to come up with the landed costs. There's no import duty on toys."

"Do you pay agent fees for clearing goods through customs for you?"

Good. This is good. Sue thought. *Keep going Tex. Keep digging.*

"I object to the question. I don't know what all these 'goods' means. He may pay fees for some goods and not others. It's unclear," James McDougal said.

"Okay, let me rephrase it," Tex said. "Do you pay agent fees at customs for the Y2K kids?"

Nathanael hesitated glancing at his lawyer, seeming unsure whether he should answer or not.

James nodded.

"Uh-huh," Nathanael said.

"Do you pay agent fees at customs for your stuffed animals too?" Tex continued.

"Yes."

"James, I need to have . . . I don't necessarily need the invoices for the agent fees, but I do need the addresses of the customs agents, or the agent list or something like that. How about it?" Tex asked Nathanael's lawyer.

"I've no reason to withhold that from you. We'll have Mr. Yorkston's administrator get that to you," James replied.

Sue smirked. *Now we're getting somewhere.*

"Mr. Yorkston, you testified earlier that the full line is made in China, at Mr. Wong's plant, is that correct?" Tex said.

"Yes."

"Do you have all parts made there? Like the dolls themselves, their clothes, the hang tag and the tush tag?"

"I object to the question. First of all, it's compound; and secondly, I don't know what 'all parts' means," James said.

"Okay I'll rephrase it," Tex said. "Are the dolls bodies made at Mr. Wong's plant?"

Sue's nerves were strung and drawn tight as the strings on her daughter's guitar. She bit her lip.

"Yes," Nathanael replied.

"Are their clothes made at Mr. Wong's plant?"

"Yes."

"The hang tag?"

"No."

"The Tush tag?"

"Uh — no."

Bingo. Sue's excitement pounded in her. She could now validate this against her last trip to China. Nathanael, himself, had just given her another weapon. She wondered if he could read the triumph on her face.

SIXTY
Seven Months Remaining

SUE CAME HOME to a dark, empty house. The phone sitting on the kitchen counter was ringing, displaying Dee's number. "Hey, Dee. Do you know what time it is?"

"No, not really. Is it too late to call?"

"No, the kids are staying at Mom and Dad's." Sue had planned to see them on her way home from the office but it was after ten, which meant they would already be asleep.

"What did Tex tell you about the payments?"

"He said Yorkston would probably reopen the case, locating Logan's assets to satisfy judgment."

"Damn him! Sorry to hear. I can't believe they can do that," Dee said with a sigh. Sue could hear the frustration in Dee's voice.

"They can do it, according to Tex. And they will. I have been so wound up. I haven't been able to sleep. And I'm missing my kids. I even miss running. I haven't jogged in days."

"Hey, why don't you take thirty minutes to yourself and go for a quick run."

"Again, do you know what time it is?"

"Hey, I gotta go. Patrick just got home."

"Tell Patrick, 'hi'. "

"Hugs and kisses. And cheer up!"

Sue changed into her running clothes and trotted out the back of her house, entering the golf course through the iron gate. Dee was right. She needed to unwind.

She never ran on the course during the day because she respected the golfers' rules but occasionally, at night, she jogged the path running the length of the eighteenth and seventeenth holes which was dimly lit by the backs of the houses.

She ran to the north. She looked into the starlit night, remembering when she and Jonathan would sneak out on the golf course and lie on the hill behind the green, looking up at the sky full of crystal stars. She had felt happy and safe.

Now, she had never felt so alone in her whole life. No one to talk to. Daniel was still ignoring her calls. Sue refused to believe that Daniel would just blow her off, even though she had more than turned her cold shoulder at him after receiving the letters. And then to blame him was a horrendous mistake. *Thank goodness I have my family and my company and my employees to worry about right now.*

And then there were the lawsuits. A full time job. She felt Yorkston was always stalking her, like a hawk circling overhead waiting to dig his razor-sharp claws into her.

Sue jogged carefully down the cart path, focusing on each step. The houses were on her left and the fairway and the creek, made incandescent from the moon's reflection, was on her right. The creek spilling into the pond on number eighteen resembled a sterling silver chain ending with a silver locket.

She skirted past two holes. Over the years, she had stumbled upon skunks, opossums, rabbits and field mice, and once shared the path with a coyote.

"This feels so gooood!" The jog made her happier than she had been all day.

She neared a turn off from the course cart path and onto a lit parkway ahead. In her peripheral vision, a silhouette of a man emerged onto the curved path ahead, startling her. She thought he was a neighbor walking his dog, but then saw there was no dog.

Should I just run by him? She could detour and take the path to the right. That would push her deeper into the golf course, and away from the backs of the houses. The threat of encountering an ominous critter made the unlit path not a wise choice. Her other choices were to run quickly past the stranger, or to turn around and go back the direction she had come.

Damn. She had never been concerned before about passing a neighbor. Why now?

She watched the ghostly shadow take a few steps forward. She was closing the slight distance between them. Twenty yards, fifteen yards, ten yards . . . .

Something isn't right!

Trusting her instincts, she stopped dead, turned around and sprinted in the direction she had come. Her breathing was desperate, the path darker, the silence unbearable.

She felt like she was running in quicksand. Nothing worked properly. Her spine was made of rubber, lactic acid burned her legs and she couldn't swing her arms. She didn't dare risk losing a second by turning around to check on whether the stranger had followed her.

A neighbor's dog started snapping and barking behind her.

She made the last turn toward her house, a straightaway and, with a gasp, flung herself full out into the final stretch. She heard pounding steps behind her.

Don't panic.

She ran like it was life-or-death who won this race. She was accustomed to the path and adjusted her footing in the dark.

She looked to her right and saw the backs of her neighbor's houses zipping by. She could not risk stopping to locate any of their gates in the dark. Besides, she knew many would be padlocked. Her back gate was unlocked. If she screamed, she would use what little energy she had left on an empty, echoing golf course. The trees she passed behind her neighbor's houses were now jumping at her, their mangled limbs reaching out to grab her.

They ran on, Sue and the stranger.

He was close enough for her to hear him. His deep gasps echoed across the fairway. He sounded like he was in considerable distress.

"STOP." She heard the man yell.

A neighbor a few houses back in the trees turned on a porch light.

Thank God.

She listened. Was he still there? Could she outrun him?

I'm a runner; I know how to deal with discomfort.

Sue felt tears stinging the corners of her eyes. She had a vision of a hand reaching out for her ponytail and yanking it back as a sharp cold blade slit her throat. Her imagination was running faster than she was, and she didn't like it.

Tears slid down her cheeks. She wiped them away with the back of her hand. She had to force herself to not panic. She used a runner's technique; she formed the mental image of reaching a goal, her gate, her refuge. She focused her mind on her iron gate ahead. She was dizzy. Melton . . . Thompson . . . Curtale . . . Jardines . . . neighbors' houses whizzed by her, dark, unwelcoming.

She wasn't sure he was still there. She didn't want to stop and turn around to find out.

Maybe he gave up. She was accustomed to this distress. Her familiarity with runner's pain but that in no way lessened it during the half-mile sprint.

She thought of a trump card.

There was a dip on the cart path between the Drake house and her house that was a constant puddle. Standing water was never a welcome mat. She had avoided it going out on her run by jogging off the path and onto the fairway. The wet patch wasn't filled with water, but it was slimed over with algae built up from the standing water. The golfers and Sue had constantly complained to the groundskeepers about the puddles. Tonight she was thankful it was never dealt with. If her assailant stepped unknowingly into the algae, he would most likely end up on his keister.

She spotted it ahead.

She planned to swerve off the path to the right where the mud was thick but not as heavy as it would be on the left. Ten feet ahead. Her sneaker caught the first part of the slime before she veered off the path. After two steps, the mud was sucking at her shoes. She shot out of the mud and back on the path in four long strides.

She heard the fall. She automatically turned her head over her shoulder and saw that the dark figure had lost his balance and had fallen head first into the slippery algae.

She didn't drop her stride, but her panic dropped a notch and a dizzy giddiness rushed her.

Her iron gate was in sight.

She sprinted away the last strength left in her. Fifty yards straight ahead – her calves, thighs, arms, back, shoulders, chest, and knees all battling numbing pain. She felt every step of the last yards, until she was there. She had beaten him.

Inside her locked house, she staggered down the hallway to her bedroom. She fell on all fours, lifted the lacy dust ruffle and slid under her bed grabbing the Browning. Sue backed against the wall, next to the bed, taking deep breaths, listening to the silence, hefting the shotgun in her hand.

She cradled the heavy gun against her, curling her knees up tight to her chest, like a baby in the womb. She laid there on the dusty hardwood floors, blubbering and whimpering like a forlorn child. She decided to wait a few minutes, catch her breath, and then call the police. As the minutes ticked by, surrounded by the silence of the night, her heart slowed and steadied. She fell into an exhausted sleep before she could dial 9-1-1.

SIXTY-ONE

SOMEWHERE IN THE DISTANCE, Sue heard her cell phone ringing. She sat up and looked at the red numbers on her digital clock, 3:30.

This can't be good.

She picked herself up from the floor next to her bed wondering how she had manage to crawl out from under it and almost fell over. The lactic acid built up in her legs the last four hours caused her to be immobile for a moment. She felt like a semi had run her over.

"Hello." She cleared her throat.

Her mother's voice came over the phone, a worried note in the tone. "Honey, Colt is sick. He's been throwing up all night. He keeps calling for you. I hate to wake you –"

"No, Mom, Mom, it's okay. I'm glad you called. I'll be right over."

"We can bring him there. I think he misses his bed."

"NO!" Sue screamed in the phone, bile rising in her throat.

If her mom was surprised at her response, she didn't show it. "Okay, Honey, we'll see you in a few minutes."

Sue slammed down the phone and rushed to remove her crumpled jogging clothes. Her stiff muscles ached, making the simple task of removing her sweat stained T-shirt difficult. Throwing on a golf shirt and flip-flops, she grabbed her purse and walked unsteadily to the garage.

She shuffled past the dark family room windows which

showed the now-menacing golf course beyond. Goose bumps covered her arms and neck. She wondered if the stranger had left or was still out there waiting. She tried to slow her wildly beating heart.

When she entered the garage there was a manila envelope propped against her windshield. Her heart skipped a beat.

"I have a gun and I know how to use it!"

She didn't have a gun. Not even a knife. The Browning was hidden under her bed.

She tiptoed to her car, grabbed the envelope and tossed it on the passenger seat like it was a poisonous snake. She closed the car door, locking it before starting the engine, then opened the garage door and backed out.

Once down the driveway, she surveyed the street. There wasn't a car or person in sight.

"His temperature is normal, but he has been vomiting," Wilford said, staring at Sue.

She figured she must look an awful mess.

"Thanks, Daddy, for watching him." She rested her hand lightly on her son's back. "At least he's sleeping for now. I'll sleep in here with him in case he wakes up, so you two can get some sleep."

Sue was in her parent's small living room, now doubling as a bedroom. When the grandkids visited overnight, which had been a lot the last few months, Thelma had the girls sleep in the guestroom. She had turned the living room into a boy's retreat for Colt. The only feminine furniture left in the room was Thelma's mahogany secretary, filled with Limoges porcelain boxes and Hummel figurines.

Her father's collection of WWII artifacts covered the walls, including a bayonet that she had once hated, locked in a glass case. Sue now took comfort in the sharp blade mounted above her son's daybed.

"No, sweetie, sleep on the couch. There's no room in here to sleep," Thelma said, followed by a yawn.

"I'll be fine. I'll make do on the chair. Please, go back to bed. I'll watch him." Sue kissed her mom on the cheek. "Thanks for calling me." She slouched into the cracked, creaky leather chair, closing her eyes.

"Are you okay, honey?" Wilford patted Sue's shoulder . . . a nice fatherly gesture. "You look like you've seen a ghost."

"I'm fine, Daddy. Just tired." She was sore and exhausted. Every muscle in her tense body ached. She was spooked from the run on the golf course and she was anxious to look at the contents of the manila envelope. *Could her parents tell by looking at her that she had freaked out tonight?*

"Honest, I'm fine. Good night. See you in a few hours." She watched her parents wander down the hallway toward their master bedroom suite.

She waited until the last of the muffled conversations in the house had stopped before turning on the Tiffany lamp on the secretary desk. She reached in her purse and retrieved the envelope. She ripped it open without looking it over.

Meet me at Main Street Café, 9:00 am. We must talk. I have information you need.

She stared incredulously at the typed words on the paper. Meet her stalker? Or who? Unbelievable.

She thought he was bold to leave a note on her car in her garage. Where else could he have been? What could he want from her? She decided not to waste her time wondering. It made no difference now.

She waited in the chair for Colt to awaken, drifting in and out of sleep. She dreamed vividly.

She was running. One man after another was passing her. They were all dressed in pinstriped suits, carrying briefcases. One passed her, carrying a handful of plush dolls. She slipped and fell in the slimy mud. They stepped on her as they continue to run—

"Mommy, I'm not feeling well."

Sue snapped her eyes wide. She saw the orange glow of daylight peeking through the transom windows. She could hear the early morning train whistle in the distance.

Colt was sitting up in the trundle bed.

"Hi honey. Are you hungry? Or do you feel sick to your stomach?"

"I'm not sure . . . my tummy doesn't hurt like last night . . . I'm hungry, I guess."

Sue glanced at her running watch, six o'clock.

Her dream had left her within seconds of waking.

"How about toast and Seven Up?"

Colt's eyes lit up. "Soda for breakfast? Yeah!"

"Just a small glass. It's good for an upset stomach. We'll see how you hold that down. Now let's be quiet so the girls and Grandma and Grandpa can sleep."

It had been a long night for everyone, and it was going to be a long morning.

SIXTY-TWO

IN THE DAYLIGHT, the run on the golf course and the fear she was being chased by a stalker didn't seem real. Still, she decided not to shower at her house. She'd run home to grab a change of clothes and to check on the house. Everything looked normal, and she returned to her parent's house to spend time with Colt and the girls. She needed to feel she was in a safe spot – like her parents' home, with her dad's old worn leather chair and her mom's homemade muffins.

She was getting out of the shower when she heard her cell phone ringing. By the time she reached her phone, tucked away in her purse, it was quiet. She checked her watch, seven-thirty. The girls had been up for a half hour and they were watching cartoons in her parent's family room.

"Where's Dad?" Sue walked into the kitchen, looking at her cell phone. The caller ID indicated a missed call from her bank. It could wait. The aroma of cinnamon muffins and fresh brewed coffee filled the air.

"He left early for the club, mumbling something about a breakfast meeting," Thelma replied, handing her a delicate blue Danube tea cup balanced on a coordinating saucer.

"Mom, can you watch the kids this morning before the sitter comes? I've a meeting at nine." She sipped the coffee, placing the cup on the shiny clean counter.

"Sure, but I have a hair appointment at one. Are you working on a Saturday?" Thelma eyed Sue's outfit, a knee-length chiffon navy skirt with a lavender paisley print, and a navy velveteen blouse with a lavender leather vest. Her long blonde hair fell across her shoulders and contrasted elegantly against the dark blue fabric.

"Katy will be at the house by noon. I should be back before then anyway. I'm meeting a potential rep for our new line," she lied. Her stomach leaped when she said it.

Who am I meeting? What information does he have that I need?

She kept her eye on her watch, looking at it every fifteen seconds and hardly hearing a word the kids were saying to her. She twisted her hair as she waited.

"Honey, have another fresh muffin." Thelma watched with a concerned look.

Sue was tired and edgy. "No thanks. It's time for me to go."

Sue pulled her black SUV into a parking spot in front of the Main Street Café. She glanced around, watching the people in the parking lot. Everyone looked like they belonged there. No one suspicious caught her eye . . . until she caught a glimpse of a man sitting in a blue Taurus, smoking a cigarette. He didn't see her looking at him. He was wearing a golf hat. He removed it and scratched his head and she saw a Band-Aid on his forehead.

A Band-Aid! The jogger following her last night had slipped forward. His forehead could've hit the cement cart path. Sue's heart raced, as if an icy wind blew through her.

She sat in the car for a few minutes to calm herself. Taking a deep breath, she got out of the car.

A smell of bacon and coffee greeted Sue when she opened the café door. The place was packed. She scanned the red-checkered tables looking for anyone she would recognize. Not a one.

"Table for one?" A mousy hostess with red hair startled her.

"Yes, um, no, I'm expecting someone."

"Okay, table for two. Follow me."

Sue followed the redhead mechanically. She led Sue to a small table in the back corner. Sue's eyes darted around . . . no exit nearby.

"Can I sit closer to the door?"

"There's a table near the front but it's noisy and the wind

blows in."

"That'll work."

She maneuvered Sue back to the front of the café. "What's the name of the party meeting you?"

I wish I knew. "Um—I think he'll see me when he comes in."

The hostess shrugged and whisked away.

Sue recognized him when he walked in the café. Even though his hair was shorter and he had a beard, she knew him.

"Ms. Sue Logan?"

Her stomach dropped. "Who are you? Richard Speckman? Who . . . who sent you here?"

"May I?" he asked, pointing at a chair.

Sue nodded.

He took a seat across from her, his back to the door.

Her mouth was dry. Her hand shook when she reached for her water. She saw two familiar figures walk in the front door, her father and JC Bolluck. The man sitting in front of her didn't see them enter, but did he see the two take a seat at the table adjacent to Sue?

"Ms. Logan, you are one hard person to talk to confidentially. I'm not Richard Speckman. I'm Evan Taylor, a reporter." He slid a press ID badge across the table to rest in front of her.

Sue picked it up and looked it over. It had a photo of the man in front of her, with longer, darker hair. It looked more like the man she met at Randy's restaurant. *Evan Taylor, Reporter, IndyStar.* It looked official enough. She shoved it back over to him.

"I'm listening," she said curtly.

"I have some business information that you may be interested in. I've been picking up bits and pieces for a long time."

A chubby male waiter rushed up to the table. "Sorry to keep you waiting. Are you ready to order?"

"Just coffee," Sue replied never taking her eyes off Evan. She was feeling more relaxed knowing her dad and JC were in the restaurant.

Evan looked at the waiter. "Same, please."

Sue waited for the waiter to walk away. "What is it you want to tell me? And why lie about who you are and follow me?"

"I had to be careful. I work for the IndyStar. I know

Nathanael Yorkston well. He considers me one of his friends."

Sue's mouth contorted in a grimace. Yorkston – just the mention of the name caused her stomach to twist up like a pretzel.

"Does he know you're here?"

"Hell no!" Evan said.

Sue relaxed some but she didn't trust the man in front of her. The waiter returned and placed two cups of steaming coffee in front of them. "Will you be ordering food?" He hovered over them.

"No."

"No, thank you. Not now. Check back later," Evan replied, watching him walk away.

"Where were you last night?" Sue asked, giving him her most wicked glare.

"I went to your neighborhood and waited for you to come home. I was sitting a mile away on the parkway. I parked and walked out on the course to have a smoke. Then I saw you running up towards me. At first, I wasn't sure it was you until you got closer. I was going to speak to you when you approached, but you turned around."

"You chased me!" She said, raising her voice. She glanced at the nearby table and saw her dad and JC looking at her.

She ignored their concerned looks.

"I tried to catch up with you. I yelled your name once. You were so deeply engaged in – shall we call it – the encounter, that you didn't hear me."

Evan's earnestness sent chills creeping along Sue's nerves. The encounter? Hell, he was chasing her, right? And had he really called out? And she didn't hear him in her blind panic? He really could've caught her if wanted, couldn't he?

Evan took off his cap to expose the Band-Aid.

No mistaking it. He had a big knot on his freshly-bruised forehead. "It's pretty obvious that I don't know the path as well as you," Evan winced. "I finally realized if I did reach you, you would scream, and I would be shot by one of your Texas buddies. So, I stayed back a bit. I wanted to make sure you made it home.

"Since I didn't have a chance to talk to you last night, and I had tried several other times, I finally had to resort to meeting in public. If Yorkston's men see me – well, it doesn't matter anymore."

"You were at the park a few weeks ago? And Randy's restaurant?"

"Yes, and other places, but that can wait until later. This is a lot to absorb right now."

Sue exhaled. "Why not just call me? Why all the secrecy? Why play an imposter?"

"At first I was sent by Yorkston, to—um, find out more about you . . . um, an interview." Now it was Evan's turn to stutter. "But there was a mix up. I couldn't call you. I didn't want to risk an unsolicited call to you. Plus they are monitoring my calls, and probably yours."

What? Sue couldn't believe what she had just heard. Why would they want to hear her calls? "Why?"

Evan surveyed the restaurant. He saw her dad, and grinned. Sue wondered if Evan knew her dad.

He leaned closer across the table and whispered to Sue. "They really want to know something about your designs – your stuffed kids, everything, particularly, the tags."

A shiver ran through her.

They know.

SIXTY-THREE

JENNIFER DE KREEK glanced at the memo again to make sure she had read it correctly.

National Bank received a Writ of Garnishment for the accounts of Logan Designs, Inc. in the amounts of $1,969,000 payable to Yorkston Toys, Inc. ordered by some judge in the Northern district of Texas.

Jennifer knew, as the bank officer responsible for the Logan account, bank protocol required her to call her client. Her computer clock displayed ten fifteen. She had called earlier around seven thirty, but she hadn't left Sue a message.

Breathing deeply, Jennifer sat at her desk. She picked up her cup of pencils, rattling them in the tin holder that her daughter had made, a soup can wrapped in orange construction paper. She blew out her breath, picked out a pencil and used the eraser to poke the numbers on the phone.

After the fifth ring, it went to Sue's voicemail.

"Good morning, Sue, this is Jennifer DeKreek from First National Bank. Can you please call me as soon as possible? Girl, it's very important. I'm staring at a Writ of Garnishment on your company's account. It's payable to Yorkston Incorporated," she said. "Sue, this is an unpleasant situation, since the bank also holds your note. Please call me. Thanks."

Jennifer hung up the phone.

She read Sue's office number on her pad but before she could dial it, her phone rang. Crud. It was her boss.

297

"Hey Marc," she said. Damn it, she didn't want to answer to him yet.

"Did you see the Writ on the Logan accounts?"

"Yes, I just left a message for Ms. Logan."

"Did she ever tell you that they owed Yorkston nearly two million dollars?"

"No, but based on the withdrawal activity, there were some sums paid out to Yorkston in January and February."

"Interesting."

"Logan Designs also received a substantial wire deposit from LMLIC in Russellville, Iowa."

"LMLI— what?"

"It's a private insurance company. My research shows that this company insures lawyers; Lawyers Mutual Liability Insurance Corporation."

"How much was the deposit?"

"Five hundred thousand."

"Whew! How much—"

"They had a balance of just over two hundred twenty-three in all of the combined accounts as of three this morning."

"Not good. And their commercial demand note is due this year."

"Marc, are you monitoring my client's accounts now?"

"Just doing my due diligence. There's a possible investor out of Indiana looking at taking over the bank."

That was news to Jennifer. "Let me refresh my coffee and I'll come upstairs to your office."

Fifteen minutes later, Jennifer was holding her coffee cup in one hand and the Logan file in the other. She was staring into the deep-set, brown eyes of her supervisor.

They discussed several clients, but when the discussion of Logan came up Jennifer saw Marc's mood darken.

"Jennifer, Logan's loan is a demand note. We can call it due with no default."

"All demand notes have that fine print clause and we never exercise it," she said. "In all the years I've managed this account, there hasn't been one late payment. It is a solid business. I think you're rushing to conclusions on this garnishment."

"We need to start the process. You need to talk to the client."

Jennifer was speechless. Marc's eyes registered finality. That garnishment, like an octopus, would grab hold of Logan's assets, and that could bury her.

Thunderstruck, she left his office.

Minutes after Jennifer left, Marc typed an email to Anthony Romero.

LEI accounts garnished this morning. Balance $223,000. Note demand in process.

He shook his head. It's a shame that her commitments were tied back to Romero's circles. The garnishment could leave her company ruined or, even worse, in the hands of Yorkston, her presumed archrival.

SIXTY-FOUR

EVAN TAYLOR LEFT the café an hour after meeting Sue. He had a new appreciation for the young entrepreneur from Texas. She seemed nice enough, normal. And, boy, did she have gumption.

He laughed to himself, reminded of how she had gotten up from the table after one too many worried looks from her father, walked over to his table, and asked him to leave.

According to Sue, Wilford had found Evan's note that Sue accidently left on the desk and, wanting to make sure she was okay, he had followed her to the restaurant. Sue assured him that she could handle the meeting and she would explain later.

Evan recalled their earlier conversation.

"Now that my bodyguards are gone, tell me who your boss is."

"I don't have a boss; I'm a freelance reporter."

"Does the name Anthony Romero mean anything to you?"

Evan laughed. "I don't regard Romero – or any of the Yorkston clan, including Nathanael himself – as my boss."

"I want to believe you, but trust is something I don't have yet."

"I know that. I didn't believe a lot of what I heard until I saw their new product announcement last month. It's a lot like yours."

Sue bit her bottom lip. "You followed me!"

"I'm sorry for that."

"You lied to me and Mike at the restaurant?"

300

"I had my reasons. I had to find out more about your products."

She crossed her arms in front of her in disgust. "I'm not buying it."

"Look, I didn't give Yorkston the information I found out about you and your products. I could have, but I didn't."

"Oh, is that an olive branch you're holding out to me?"

"Look, lady, we want the same things here. Maybe for other reasons, but we both have the same goal."

"Why, exactly, are you here?" She asked.

Evan peered across the table at her. "I know what you've been looking for. I've found it too."

Sue squirmed. She looked like a jackrabbit ready to jump up and run out the door. "What did you find out and how?"

"I snoop. I have ways to get inside intelligence."

"What do you think you know?" Sue took a sip of her water, peering over the glass.

"What they're doing is complex but, to the normal consumer, it just looks like a successful product. But I know things. What if you could follow a toy or any product?" he said.

Sue gave Evan a blank stare and slowly nodded her head. "Yep, if you could follow a product, you could discover so much about it. Based on information gleaned from tracking the product, you could develop pricing and placement strategies to create a high demand product."

Evan paused and reached in his pocket for a small tattered notepad. "In college you wrote a program for an apparatus to work with unique serial numbering software. Correct?"

Sue leaned back in her chair, rubbing her fingers back and forth across her lips. "Correct. I configured a system that ties together unique serial number designs with superior intelligence that could monitor and control the supply and demand of products."

"And what makes the Yorkston toys appropriate for this technology is when you add in the low costs, a cute collectible and the children factor, viola; you can discover the formula for a wildly successful product like the Yorkston plush." Evan put his hand on top of the notepad. He didn't need to refer to his notes, but he wanted Sue to believe he had facts. But what he really needed was Sue to help fill in some blanks. I need her help. *Shit, she's gorgeous and smart. How did she get into this mess?*

He shook his head. "I really didn't think this would work. Can it really be done?"

Sue tucked a wisp of hair behind her ear. "Yes. Some people suspect the toys have a hidden bar code or Riff ID tag associated with the number but I know—"

Sue was cut off by Evan. "Wait; hold on. A what? A Riff ID?"

She grinned, but her smile changed as she thought about it, and a haunted expression crossed her face.

Evan wanted her to keep talking. He flipped a few pages in his notepad. "Oh, it's the tracker."

"Yes, it's a radio frequency identifier. RFID. Think of it as a bar code or a tiny chip that transmits radio signals."

"Wow, this is so next millennium technology, but I said to myself, you did this years ago. Nice."

Sue shook her head. "The technology isn't new. When you think about it, this technology is in use all around us. We use identification microchips for our pets. A cat could have one embedded, in case it got lost. Or when you use an EZPass through a toll booth, or if you pay for gas with speed passes, this is the same technology. So no, I didn't actually come up with the idea. I just worked to use it differently."

"But it's a great idea in a toy. Think about it. I buy a Yorkston black bear while here in Texas and the RFID tag tells the checkout system the costs and the item details. If I use a credit or debit card the software knows what, where and how much I bought. Yorkston's marketing intelligence system knows that I bought the toy and if I take it to Indy for my little niece's birthday, they have a report of where it ends up. Most new devices coming out are connected to your home wireless system, which is connected to the internet," Evan said in a dismissive tone, as if stating the obvious.

"Yeah, so in theory a product can transmit where it ends up. They can monitor the household income level, and strategically price items through internet blogs, driving demands up," he continued.

As Evan explained the intricacies of the product, Sue looked like she had seen a ghost.

"So this machine you had designed in college allowed an RFID tag to be printed and embedded on the soft tag sewn into the dolls." He stopped and took a sip of his coffee. "Am I right so far?"

Sue was speechless. She nodded.

He flipped a page of his notepad. "The software can track a lot of useful information. It can decide what stores to ship to, based on what the software has told them about inventories and sales. It can decide on the price based on sales intelligence.

"Ms. Sue, you are not only a toy designer but a computer geek." He grinned at her. For a brief moment, she regarded him with an ill-concealed look of pride.

"But what I keep missing is the answer to why aren't all toys using this?" Evan asked.

"Costs," Sue said softly.

"Uh huh. Because that minuscule chip costs too much and if you sew it onto a toy tag, it has to be safe and consumer tested and approved. If pulled off it could be a choking hazard. It would not work stuffed inside the toy. It may need to be on the outside, depending on the toy stuffing, to catch the radio frequency," he explained to Sue. "The more I investigated, the more I found it amazing. I just thought the toys were cute."

"That definitely helps," Sue said. "Without a cute design, the control of the supply and demand would be easy: no demand, therefore no supply needed. The toys would just be traced to garage sales and the dollar stores. But instead, they are cute and they are fetching over a thousand dollars for one bear that probably costs less than a dollar to make because of the tag. It's like Nathanael is printing money."

"How does Yorkston make any money if the item costs a lot to make with this technology when they sell them for a retail price?" Evan asked. He knew the answer but wanted to see how much she knew.

"I want to discuss this, but I'm not sure how much I should share." Sue's face and neck flushed bright red. "There's a reason I kept the designs undercover, and I never did anything with the technology after I was out of college."

Evan nodded, his stomach twisting.

"I was lucky to have had some really smart lab partners in chemistry those years. I engaged my lab partner in some simple calculations for the disguise of the chip in the wrist band tag for the arm of the dolls," she hesitated before she went on. "There is a way to use a holographic ink stamp, a special dye, on the label to hide the RFID in the design. The costs of the chips are coming down; some could be bought for less than fifty cents now. But the lower priced inks ... um ... the dyes used on the labeling ... not good for toys."

Evan nodded again and understanding dawned. "They're caustic."

Sue eyes focused around the room settling back on Evan. She shook her head.

"Sue, I'm done with riddles. Tell me what I need to know. Aren't you done with being pushed around by Yorkston? Don't you want vengeance?"

"The technology can't be used on the toy's tag because it's harmful." Sue's voice was almost inaudible as she mumbled.

"It's poisonous." Evan declared. "God, these are toys!"

"What I'm saying is that the dye that did work in the printers was not cost effective, but it's . . ." she paused and then she leaned forward and barely whispered, "safe."

Evan nodded his head slowly like he was finally realizing something. "The dye is costly to make, but it's safe, while the cheap dye is caustic."

"How can they do this? With the safety commissions monitoring? Are the bastards switching tags?" Sue asked.

"I was hoping that chemist, Shapiro, could shed some light."

"I heard about him," she murmured, her brows furrowing, her face sad. She took a deep breath, picked up her coffee and asked, "Can you fill in the gaps without him?"

"I suspect they send the safe, expensive tagged toys to the consumer safety department for the correct toy registration numbers because they don't care what those cost. Then they send the cheaper one into the hands of kids. Occasionally they ship the expensive tagged toys as loss leaders when there's a surprise inspection."

Sue nodded.

Evan frowned. "What are we talking here on the hazardous compound? Could it be traced?" he asked.

"I have been looking through my old reports, and the formula's make up can be so scant that the traceability is near impossible to detect. Besides, no one is looking at the tags. Toy makers have been using safe inks on tush tags for years. No one thinks about the RFIDs or the software technology," Sue paused.

Evan added, "Only you and me."

"And my family," Sue said.

"Crap!" Evan yelled. "The hospital order Yorkston just announced for the New Year plush kids . . . ."

A few people looked over at Evan. He lowered his voice. "They could potentially be putting a toxic stuffed toy tag in the mouths of suckling babies across the US."

She screwed up her face as if she had just swallowed bitter medicine.

"It looks like we have some work to do," Evan said.

Evan was troubled, but worried about Sue. She might have been discrete, but if someone had been following her footsteps, they would have discovered all of her research.

He had some information, but he needed more. He needed dates, times and places of the product testing, lab reports, formulas, even pictures. He wondered how much she would share.

"Keeping quiet all these years had to be challenging for you," he said.

"I really didn't know exactly until recently. And now you know. Do you think Yorkston will try to buy your silence? I'm sure they've paid off many. Are you trying to get money?"

"Don't I wish. But no. I'm not here for money, like Shapiro probably was. I mean, yeah, sometimes I think, why should Yorkston and Romero get everything? I stay in a crummy rental house while they live in luxury. I drive a beat up Taurus. A Taurus! While they drive around in a limo."

Sue leaned in close. "If you took their money, then what? You'd always be looking over your shoulder. How could you live with yourself knowing the damage this may cause? This secret can impact the lives of so many." Sue stopped and shuddered.

"I agree. Yorkston Toys is only about profit. The role of children is a clear one; they are cash cows to be milked. I've seen their security team working with headsets and computerized inventories. It's still incredible to me Yorkston can trace the toy animals across the borders. They doled out their products according to unethical methods."

"Why do you think they are doing this?" The tension around Sue's eyes had vanished.

"Money. Fame. Yorkston's greed led him to burying his head in the sand, ignoring the dangers. It just got out of control."

"I knew they thought I had something on them. Shit, it's been like a hurricane of lawsuits flying at me. Well, Nathanael's whole scam is about to blow up on him. I'll make damn sure of that! Are you ready? I could use the help," she said.

"I'd like to."

"Really?"

"I mean, I don't have kids or anything, but I don't want anyone to get sick or worse."

"Yeah. And it doesn't hurt you to scoop the story."

He pointed at his chest and gave her a look like, "Who, me?"

Sue added, "Oh come on, everyone knows that media loves to focus on bad news to attract eyeballs."

"If it bleeds, it leads."

"So you'll help?"

"We're in it together."

Evan lit up a cigarette as he drove north. He had a new appreciation for Sue Logan. She cared about family and people, and she knew people were more important than dollars.

He held up the napkin with her scribbling on it and began the long drive across country toward Kalamazoo to meet with Patrick and Dee McCray.

SIXTY-FIVE
The Offices of Logan

SUE'S HEART QUICKENED with each step as a sense of inevitableness came over her, as she walked down the long office hallway to the warehouse. She encountered Vernon, her accountant before entering the warehouse.

"Good morning Sue. You look radiant today. Calm and beautiful."

"Thank you Vernon. I may appear calm, collected and confident but inside I'm a mess."

Her hair was pulled tight in a golden French twist, revealing her grandmother's pearl earrings. She was the epitome of style, dressed in her navy business suit.

"I can't even imagine. I've watched you grow a small company to where we are today. And now we're discussing bankruptcy."

"Bankruptcy. Oh God, to think I should ever hear myself speaking the word." She shook her head sadly.

"I was outraged when Jennifer called me a few days ago about the garnishment. This is a new low for Yorkston."

"It's unreal. But we'll close Logan down and start fresh with the new company, with our new M Kid products leading the pack." She had made her pitch several times to investors. Vernon had found one that wished to remain anonymous, but appeared to be legit. She was assured the investor was in no way, shape, or form related to the Yorkston Group or any of its subsidiaries. Still, she felt she was giving in, and that really infuriated her. It was heartbreaking.

"I'm glad you agreed to stay on in the chief management role. I want you to know I support you. There are no recriminations." Vernon put a hand on her shoulder.

"Thanks Vernon. No one wants to see our new company take off more than me," Sue said solemnly.

Sue nodded to the closed door leading to the warehouse. "What's the buzz amongst the troops?"

"The gossip is all over the place. They've heard the company is closing, they're going to be laid off, or they'd be asked to work with lower pay."

Sue shook her head. "No way." But what did she really know? She wasn't sure what the new owners would do.

"Let's go address the troops."

He nodded. "Show time."

Sue walked into the warehouse and glanced around to see all her employees gathered. Dozens of bewildered faces watched as she approached them. She walked up to a few men sitting on stools. They rose and she shook their hands. Other employees were sitting on mismatched chairs, forming a half circle. Stacks of unshipped catalogs sat shrink wrapped on the dock.

It was warm in the warehouse. She walked over to the middle of the chairs, reminded of the many monthly company meetings she had conducted in the exact spot. She noticed the black skid marks on the warehouse floor from the forklifts. Usually, AJ kept the floors polished. Today, they were not.

"Good morning, AJ."

"Good morning, ma'am." AJ said, eyeing her warily.

"Hi, Darlene. How's the grandbaby?"

"Good, Sue." Darlene's smile was frozen on her face.

Mary Jo came bouncing through the double doors. "Good morning." Sue smiled. Mary Jo was radiating excitement. Or was it anxiety? It was difficult to tell.

"Good morning and good luck." Mary Jo handed Sue a steaming mug of coffee with cream and winked.

A pity wink, Sue thought. "Poor girl is losing everything," is what Mary Jo was probably saying to herself.

Sue scanned the crowd. A wave of utter misery swept over her, compounded with fear over the plan that was now in full swing behind Yorkston's back. It was what they deserved. She had witnessed firsthand their gluttonous pursuit of power.

She let out the breath, unaware she had been holding it.

She looked at her warehouse manager, Jamie, sitting at the workbench near her. He doodled on a soggy paper towel his water glass rested on. The ink stains ran like purple varicose veins. They exchanged looks. His eyes were dark, wide, flashing with fear. Sue felt like her heart was in a vice.

She walked over to the open metal staircase along the sidewall that zigzagged up to a second story warehouse office. She climbed a few steps and paused at a landing half way up.

"Can everyone hear me?"

Several employees nodded at her. Sue smoothed her hand over her hair and took a deep breath. She wanted to keep it short. No lectures, no should-haves or could-haves. What was done was done.

"I appreciate all of you gathering together today. I'll be the first to admit there's been a lot of rumors flying around lately that can seem confusing. This face-to-face meeting was necessary to clear the record."

All eyes were on her.

"First off, it is true, we have sold the company."

There was a burst of noise from side conversations, everyone talked at once to each other. "Who's the buyer?" AJ yelled out.

"And what about our jobs?" Darlene asked rising from her chair. She was a short lady, and she needed to stand up for Sue to see her.

Sue held up her hand. "If we can hold questions till the end, I may answer most of them with my comments.

"As many of you know, the company has been involved in a few lawsuits regarding infringements and malpractice." Sue saw a few nodding heads in the crowd.

"These lawsuits have left us with no solution but to split up the company." Sue stopped and took a sip of her coffee. Mary Jo caught her eye and mouthed, "Good job."

Sue looked over at her accountant and he smiled. "Vernon

and I have been in closed-door negotiations with an investor's accountants for the last several weeks." She paused, worried about how far she should go with this. She decided not to discuss the garnishment of Logan accounts by Yorkston, or First National Bank calling for full payment of her loan causing her no choice but to bankrupt the company.

"We have a new boss, Wayne Montague."

The crowd was motionless.

"What the fuck?" AJ said softly, but everyone heard him.

A few ladies giggled at his slip up, others smiled.

"It's okay, AJ. I haven't met him, but he has a strong retail background."

"But I bet he's no match to you."

"Thanks. I appreciate that. I will be staying on . . . ." Sue paused, thinking carefully about her next sentence. She cringed at the thought of not knowing all the details of her employment. She wanted to be President, not Wayne.

"And I want you all to be reassured, we will run business as usual. And I'll do everything I can to make certain our new designs and products grow the new company twofold over the next few years as we move into the new century."

Sue looked at the blank, anxious stares. Many of their eyes gave it away. Sadness? Pity?

Crap. Could this get any worse?

She and Vernon answered questions for the next twenty minutes.

Sue dismissed the group and said she would have another meeting next week to discuss any updates. Several employees thanked her and shook her hand.

Sue grabbed her briefcase from her office and rushed through the lobby toward the front door. On her way out, she encountered Mary Jo.

"Why the disappearing act?" Mary Jo gestured to the briefcase strapped over Sue's shoulder. "Early lunch with a new man?"

"No, not a new man, but a young man. Colt has a science fair and he is presenting his project to the entire school," Sue said. "See ya, Mary Jo."

"Tell the little prince hello from me. And Sue,—"

Sue stopped and turned to listen to Mary Jo.

"I'm proud of what you've achieved," Mary Jo said.

"Thanks that means a lot. I'm proudest of my role as a mother to three amazing children — that trumps everything else I've achieved." Sue nodded, and closed the door behind her feeling the enormity of the loss of her company sinking in.

Sue reached her car, her hand shaking as she put the key in the ignition. Once the car started, she leaned against the seat, swallowing past the lump in her throat, as tears streamed down her cheeks.

SIXTY-SIX
Indianapolis

EVAN TAYLOR STARED at the blue screen on his Mac with his hand unmoving across the keyboard.

"Taylor!" His editor yelled across the room.

"I'm working on it." Evan sat, waiting in frustration for the inspiration to leap from his fingers, realizing part of his writer's block came from the fact that he wasn't actually ready to write the story.

"Our deadline is tomorrow." Tom, the managing editor, walked over to his desk.

"I know, Tom. I still need some specific details to pin down or you won't approve it."

"Damn right, I'm not approving the story until the information is verified." Tom stood behind Evan. "I made certain this story would make top play. I need copy over to layout. Jessie can check dates and names for you and other facts."

"Get out of my face so I can finish." Evan sulked at the screen. Tom walked away, shaking his head.

Evan reviewed his notepad and began typing. He stopped and stared at the screen. His assistant walked over to his desk. "This Fed Ex just arrived for you." She placed a box on his desk.

"Thanks, Ariel."

He watched her walk away, staring at her nice ass. He read the return address, Texas. His heart raced when he tore open the box, dumping the contents onto his desk. A card and a pack of his favorite cigarettes fell out.

Evan ripped open the envelope to find an ivory note card with a cursive "L" embossed on the front. He opened the card and read the hand written line.

You really should lay off these - but when writers block sets in and all else fails, take a walk, watch your step and enjoy a smoke.

Evan picked up the Fedex box and turned it upside down again, shaking it. Nothing. What the hell?

Damn, she decided not to expose them. He couldn't disclose the secret shit without concrete data.

"Evan, if you broke the story, it would be a way to bring the issues to the limelight," Sue had said, at the café.

Why hadn't she helped him with the story? Maybe Yorkston finally got to her, scaring her off. She was a mom, which should be her reason enough to want to do this. Why the hell did she chicken out? Screw the malicious rivalry she had with this bastard. Screw her ongoing lawsuit with Yorkston.

With or without Sue Logan, his conspirator, he would write a story. There'd be lawyers in heaven before he ever let Yorkston get away with this.

He logged off his computer, crumbled her note and threw it and the Fed Ex box in the trash. He put on his coat and stuck the cigarettes in his pocket. He left the office, miserable and upset.

SIXTY-SEVEN
Texas

SUE LOGAN AWAKENED to a familiarly empty bed. She heard the birds chirping outside as the sun rose over the fairway's winding creek. She stared at the ceiling, thinking about her day ahead; a meeting with her new boss, a meeting with Tex, and planning for Colt's birthday party.

She rolled out of bed and tromped into the kitchen in search of a cup of coffee. Her mom was at the kitchen table, folding towels.

"Coffee's made. Can I pour you a cup?" Her mom fluffed a green plaid dishtowel, carefully folding lengthwise and then in half. She stacked it with the others.

"No, no, Mom. I can get it." Sue retrieved a cup from the cabinet, poured herself coffee and walked over to refill her mom's empty cup. "How long have you been here?"

"Just about an hour. I stopped by to drop off Colt's goodie bags."

"Thanks for helping, Mom. I hardly have time for anything nowadays." Sue padded over to the wood shutters in the kitchen and cracked them open. The warm sun flowed through.

"Do you like your new boss, Wayne?"

"Wayne Montague? He's okay. He really knows the retail gift business. He was humble when he took over the reins of my company and he lets me call some shots."

"I would think so. As the former owner and founder of the company producing the plush kids, he needs you!"

314

"No matter what title's on my business card, being a manager of design and manufacturing enables me to work in the trenches at the most basic level on my new product designs…which I love."

And I'm contractually obligated to stay on with the company for six months.

However, being able to continue designing attracted her. Had anyone predicted a year ago what she would be doing, she would have shuddered. She had been flourishing. She had worked at a company she knew and loved. Now she was working for someone, and she didn't call all the shots.

Her mom placed her arm around Sue's waist. "Honey, I know this isn't easy for you. And your father said the salary wasn't much, and that you were concerned. Do you think you'll sell the house?"

"I dunno. Since Yorkston locked up my accounts, I'm having trouble making my commitments to the new company."

"You know your dad and I would like to help… but we just can't, right now."

"No Mom, that isn't necessary. You both do so much. Who knows, maybe I'll get promoted. Wayne said he is really impressed with me."

"And he should be. You're the only one there that knows how to cut and sew the new doll designs, you know how to price them, how to market to the manufacturing reps, and what packaging worked. Heck, you even know a lot about the safety and country of origin labeling to satisfy the law." Her mom winked at her.

"I know, but for the first time in my life, I'm not the boss. I'm still working for someone else." She twirled her ponytail into a knot.

"We all love you, Sweetie."

"I know. I love you, too. Thanks for the pep talk. It's good to hear, once in a while."

"Hey, what about Daniel? Any news from him lately?"

"Nice way to change the subject." *Speaking of love.* Her mind wandered to Daniel. She had only talked to him once in the last few months, and even then, it was very cool and cordial.

"I had a brief encounter with him during his deposition

with Yorkston's lawyers." It had been an unpleasant meeting for her, one that left her anxious. She didn't know what to think of his lack of response other than no interest on his part to assist her on her new toy line.

"And what did he say?" Her mom's eyes were bright under her tortoise shell glasses.

"Mom, we had small talk. Nothing new. I'm too busy with my business to worry about romance, that's all." She had to get Yorkston out of the way. If she didn't, her business would tank. Too many people were depending on her to make her dolls a success and to make the business grow. How couldn't he understand this? How couldn't he understand her?

She had run into him by the elevator at the lawyer's offices, for a few brief moments. They exchanged a few cordial words before the elevator doors had shut. The last impression she had was his emerald eyes burning in her.

"You do need to slow down after the dolls are successful."

"I will, I promise." She kissed her mom's cheek and headed to the shower. It was true, she was putting in ten to twelve hours a day, six and sometimes seven days a week. Through her work, and her children, she found strength, fortitude, and conviction that life goes on – after crisis, after tragedy, after heartbreak.

SIXTY-EIGHT
Indianapolis

EVAN HAD BEEN UP since four a.m.

The search for the missing pieces of his story led to more questions. A pile of crumpled papers were scattered in the corner of his bedroom around the trashcan.

Evan decided to take a walk. He stepped out into the chilly spring morning, then dashed back inside, grabbing his coat from the hall closet.

He walked along the pavement, reaching into his coat pocket for his cigarettes, and pulled out the new pack. As he shook out a cigarette, he noticed something shiny inside the pack.

What the hell?

He examined the pack and saw three cigarettes and a flash memory stick. He hadn't used this technology yet, but he knew others in his office had mentioned it before..

He grinned. Of course! The cigarettes Sue had sent him. *When writers block sets in, a walk always helps.*

After a few phone calls, he was able to secure a location where he could take the memory device to read its contents.

Evan stared at the screen in front of him. The files contained spreadsheets with possible infected toys and their associated serial numbered tags. The files also contained the source of import entry and a list of custom agents working the imports. Another document disclosed the name and contact at the dye plant, Le Ho Dye chemical,

317

and even a scanned diagram of the printing apparatus . . . everything Evan needed. The common denominator? Yorkston Toys.

The search for answers had ended. He was ready to start a fire and Sue had just given him the gasoline.

He was impressed with the minute details his Texas conniver provided. This information, along with what Patrick's buddy in the lab had discovered, was all he needed.

He picked up his cell phone and dialed Nathanael Yorkston's private number.

Within hours, that same day after Evan found Sue's gift, Sue met with Tex, and received a surprise gift of her own.

"I'd like you to review and approve the draft of an agreement Yorkston lawyers had drawn up, proposing that *both* lawsuits be dropped." Tex looked pleased as punch to be saying those words to Sue.

"Dropped? Just like that?" Sue was shocked. She almost slid off the edge of her wood chair.

"Yes, dropped. Canceled. Done." Tex smiled.

Sue jumped out of her chair, ran over and hugged the tall man around his neck. "Thank you. Thank you. Thank you!"

"Don't thank me. I was just as surprised as you to get a call out of the blue today." Tex said. "After I talked to him, I received an email from James McDougal, Yorkston's lead council. Now, we have it in writing. Yorkston wants to call a truce. Imagine that, Sue. Just like that." Tex rubbed his chin in puzzlement. "James told me that he had received a call from Nathanael asking him to close out all legal activities with Logan, as quickly as possible. McDougal didn't mind. He and his team were up to their elbows suing other small businesses, and they didn't care to be on the defending side."

Tex slid the pages in front of Sue.

Sue took several minutes to read the paperwork. A smile formed around the edges of her mouth. She was too excited to read any more. "In layman's terms?"

"Yorkston agrees to drop pursuit of the garnishment and their lawsuit against you that was reopened after you failed to make the payments, in exchange for you dropping your lawsuit against them."

Sue squared her shoulders taking in a deep breath of exhilaration. "What about the money we've already paid them? And the money we lost on catalog sales? Does this mean they can continue to sell my plush kids knock offs? Their Y2K kids?"

"They'll reimburse all funds you've paid Yorkston, plus all your attorney's fees. The lost catalog sales can be discussed when the lawyers for both sides meet to adjudicate the matter of the product similarities and to decide on a recommended settlement."

"Then let me know after that meeting. However, this is a great start to a settlement. I'm excited to put this all behind me." A fantastic start! God was she excited! She wanted to jump up and down and had to resist the urge to start cheering.

When Sue left the law offices, she felt as if she had shed a punishing burden. She felt a relief that was indescribable, unlike any she had ever felt before.

Sue hadn't heard from Evan in weeks, but her meeting today confirmed Yorkston had received the news. The shoe had dropped! She wouldn't be the one to yell "uncle" this time. It was Yorkston waving the white flag.

SIXTY-NINE
Indiana
Five Months Before the Millennium

DURING THE HOT SUMMER, most of the country was experiencing a drought and heat wave. The small farming town outside Indianapolis where Evan Taylor lived was one of the areas hit hardest.

Evan sat in his home office with an oscillating fan directed on him, perspiration on his brow. One of the headlines in the papers littered across his desk grumbled about the record precipitation deficits resulting in huge agricultural losses and drought emergencies declared in several states. In addition, wildfires had developed where too little water was plaguing much of the southern Plains and Southeast.

The heat wave, the millennium frenzy, and the Yorkston recall were headline news most every day. Despite the drought and the Y2K computer threats, the media coverage had shifted a helluva lot of attention to the massive toy recall stories. Evan loved it!

He looked at the papers. "Yep, that's what I'm talking about!"

Yorkston Announces Largest Toy Recall in its History

By Evan Taylor, Staff Reporter

Just one month after issuing a recall of their birds and bears stuffed animal toys, Yorkston has announced a second, even larger, recall. This time, the recall targets two other types of the stuffed toys. First, 5,100,000 stuffed toys with serial numbers named on the following charts are being recalled because they have been found to contain DMCY. Like the toys from the previous recall, these tainted toys were made in China. Yorkston states that it was trying to prevent harming children with its products by moving production to Chinese facilities that it owns and controls, instead of having the toy tags made by Chinese subcontractors . . . .

He studied the articles, like a new dad in the maternity ward staring through the glass at the bundle in the bassinet. Proud, but wondering what had he started?

His private line rang.

"Taylor," Evan said.

"Hi is this the award-winning investigative reporter, Evan Taylor, himself?" Dee McCray teased Evan.

"Not only award winning, but now nationally-syndicated journalist," he replied.

"Congrats, great job."

"The media fury the last few weeks over the Yorkston recalls has just monopolized the news."

"I know. It seems like every newspaper, every radio station, every television newscast covers the list of serial numbers that were suspect. To think, we started it all."

"Thank goodness, the threat wasn't as eminent because we disclosed the contamination early. It seems as rapidly as they became popular, they became a ghastly fading craze," he said.

"I hear their sales have plummeted faster than the Titanic."

"Once the story was out, there was no turning back; it was like squeezing toothpaste back into the tube. The recall has killed Yorkston's stock."

"Patrick said the guys at the Chicago lab have been very helpful," Dee said.

"They've been great. They helped label the tags in various priority levels."

Evan took a puff of his cigarette. "Hey Dee – how's Patrick?"

"He's doing great. I called to give you some more good news. Eric, his friend from the lab. You remember him?"

"Yep."

"He said that at the Senate hearing yesterday in Indy, they

passed some new legislation that gives the Consumer Product Safety Commission more power. This will allow for a faster recall to get dangerous products off the shelves."

"Dee, my God, I'm glad to hear that. Hell, it's about goddamn time." Evan was shocked how much red tape was involved to remove dangerous toys from store shelves. Legally the Yorkston toys could have stayed out on the shelves for many years. Fortunately, his news stories were enough to scare parents away, but unknowing consumers might still be able to buy the contaminated products. It would have taken months, maybe years, to get the Yorkston toys removed from the market and prevent them from causing further pain, suffering and damage.

"Great work you and your Texas team have done on this," Evan said.

"Yeah, it's amazing the safety board never does those tests—"

"—Unless there's a reported incident," Evan interrupted Dee.

"Their procedure is to wait until a child is hurt before they can even start investigating a potentially dangerous toy."

"It's amazing that those assholes on the Yorkston executive team wouldn't issue a recall voluntarily." The morning he found Sue's data, before his story broke, Evan had gone to Nathanael but he denied any allegations, refusing to make any statements.

Evan began looking over the stack of articles he had authored, barely listening to Dee.

". . . we had to get the freaking legislation to be passed to move the process for recalls along faster. I think we're only seeing the beginning of some massive recalls," Dee said.

"Yorkston's marketing and PR guys are wishing they were hiding out like Nathanael and Anthony," he said.

"Speaking of those two, did you find what you were looking for at the scientist's house? Or did he take his secret to his grave?"

"It's been vacant for four months, but I'm headed there to look through the debris. I know from a close inside source that Yorkston paid a special bonus to Shapiro. I just don't know where he keeps the files." Through all the Yorkston betrayals, Victoria Romero had maintained a close alliance with Evan. Their rendezvous continued through secret meetings at hotels. Evan and Victoria couldn't risk her father finding out about their relationship, especially now.

"But all our investigations of his bank accounts came up empty. His only family member, a niece, found nothing but useless chemical notes in his safety deposit box."

"I'll keep you posted if I uncover anything. The house was almost gutted, but the firemen were able to save the structure and most of the roof. The auction is Saturday, so I have a preview later this afternoon." Evan was eager to snoop through the dead scientist' house.

"Keep me posted."

"Tell Sue hello," Evan said.

"Okay. Patrick said hi too."

They hung up. Evan wiped the perspiration from his forehead and moved his face closer to the fan, scanning several of the articles he authored:

RED DYE PROMPTS YORKSTON TOYS TO RECALL MILLIONS

CONSUMER PRODUCT SAFETY COMMISSIONS URGES ALL TOYS BE TOSSED

THE HOT TOY THAT MAY BE TOO HOT FOR YOUR CHILD'S HEALTH

TOY GIANT LOSES SALES AND ATTRACTS SUITS

ARE BABY BIBS SAFE USING THE RED DYE, DMCY?

Volumes of printed articles and TV news reports herald about the financial losses of the families and collectors as well. The Yorkston craze was at its peak when Evan's warning came out. The craze stopped dead in its tracks and collections were invaluable, but Yorkston didn't care because they had made their fortune. During the whole Yorkston hoopla, Nathanael didn't care who got hurt both financially and physically. Many families were now stuck with thousands of Yorkston plush as their values dramatically decreased overnight for less than a dollar each.

Evan saw teenagers wearing T shirts with the Yorkston insignia on them that read *Bankrupt by Yorkston* and others that read *I lost my ass on Poison Plush*. Even the famous celebrity, Ben Stiller did a satire on Saturday Night Live about being addicted to the cocaine like eyes of the Yorkston plush. For weeks, Jay Leno and other night time comedian talk show hosts made Yorkston the butt of their jokes, not trying to be mean-spirited due to the nature of the recall, but nonetheless funny antidotes.

As he reviewed the articles, he reread the last disturbing article attributing a death to the Yorkton fiasco.

Lo He Dye Chemical Company, a contract manufacturer based in southern China, was responsible for producing the tags for the toys. The tags contained excessive levels of caustic chemical dye cited as the cause for the first recall. Yorkston stopped accepting goods from the contractor and, last week, the Chinese government revoked Lo He Dye's export license. The manager of Lo He Dye, Xu Guan, committed suicide by hanging himself in a factory warehouse last Monday, Chinese officials have confirmed.

He replaced the clipped article in his folder and picked up a photo. "Where are you hiding it?" He reviewed the picture of the burnt remains of the Shapiro home. He looked at his watch. It was time to journey over to the former residence of Dr. Pete Shapiro.

SEVENTY
Rural Indiana

THE DUSTY BLUE Taurus came to a rest in front of the scorched house. The outside showed streams of black burn marks circling the roof edges. The windows that weren't boarded up were shattered with cracks.

Evan's shoes crunched as he stepped on the shards of glass sprinkling the front porch.

Lifting the metal lockbox hanging from the doorknob, he exclaimed, "Shit, that's hot!" Juggling the sun-baked box, he quickly dialed in the combination and the bottom popped out. The house key tumbled onto the porch.

He picked up the key, scanning Shapiro's property. It was a heavily wooded, unkempt tract of land, isolated from neighbors.

He inserted the key, pushing against the door to force it open. The inside of the house was in shambles. A musty, moldy, cellar-like odor filled his nostrils as he wandered into the living room. He was surprised the stench hadn't dissipated over the months.

He surveyed the room. Smoke and water had destroyed much of the front half of the house, however the walls were in decent shape. The garage and the back half of the house didn't fare as well. The house would have to be torn down. The value of the property was of no interest to him because he did not want to buy it, as he had told the real estate agent.

According to the police report, the cause of the fire was

325

being recorded as Undetermined – Probably Accidental by the Indianapolis Fire Marshal's office.

Accidental, my ass.

Evan slipped under the sagging yellow tape put up to secure the scene many months earlier. He had read that Shapiro and his dog died from smoke inhalation and were found in the farthest room from the fire.

He shuffled through the ashy soot in the living room to the garage, leaving a trail behind him. Once in the garage the smell was sharper, pungent . . . like vinegar. It reminded him of dyeing Easter eggs on his kitchen table when he was a kid.

He looked into the black, collapsed interior of the garage, spotting in the third bay a burnt-out VW bug covered with debris from the collapsed roof. All other items and furnishings were charred beyond recognition, making it impossible to determine whether Shapiro kept files or not in the makeshift laboratory.

Evan covered his nose with his hand, returning to the front half of the house. The stagnant air held an unfamiliar odor like burnt chemicals or burnt human remains. His foot caught on the drooping yellow tape. He stumbled and then plummeted to the soot-covered living room floor.

"Damn it!"

Picking himself up, he felt a few loose boards under the worn carpeting. He took off his shoe, tapping it on the floor as he crawled, hearing an echo from a crawl space underneath the boards.

He heard a noise behind him. He turned around and jumped when saw a rat clinging on the twisted and gnarled slip-covered couch.

"Shoo!" He waved his hands at the rat. It didn't budge. Pissed at the rodent, he hurled his shoe at it. Startled, it scurried under the couch. The shoe landed on the floor and rolled under the couch as well.

"Fuck." Evan stood up and walked over to the couch. He shoved the couch to the side cautiously not wanting to disturb a family of rats. He knelt down to pick up his shoe.

"What's this?" He saw a buckled board bulging through the threadbare rug. The board ran under the tattered couch. It made a solid thud when he smacked his heel on it. It wasn't hollow.

Even though his shirt and pants were glued to him, bathed with sweat from the heat, he started shivering when he pulled back the frayed rug. Concentrating on the rotting wooden floor that had buckled, he pried the warped board up with his bare hands. The smell of mildew threatened to overpower him as he removed the rotting wood plank.

He stared at its contents.

A fuzzy gray and black fungus was threaded over the top of a pile of graying envelopes. He became flushed, as he felt his temperature rising. He saw stacks of twenty-dollar bills protruding out of the envelopes amassed in the crawl space.

He opened an envelope. "Holy Jesus!" There in the crawl space under the hardwood joist was a pile of crisp money, undamaged.

After three trips to the trunk of his car, Evan discovered a thinner envelope under the stacks of bills. He opened the envelope and read the first few lines of the document inside.

He pounded his shoe on the floor. "Damn it! Yorkston should've done a total recall voluntarily; they knew those damn tags were poisonous. Their own scientist had proved it." And what about Shapiro, was this his hush money? Shame on him. "You can't get in bed with the devil without having some of it rub off."

The information he held in his hands would keep Yorkston's lawyers busy for years. In addition, this evidence would reopen Shapiro's house fire case and get a closer look from authorities.

He had just finished loading his Taurus when a car rolled around the corner. The silver Mercedes with black tinted windows came to rest next to his car.

Evan was paralyzed, watching the car. Now that he held evidence that could involve Yorkston in Shapiro's death, he would have to be cautious. After all, if they were capable of torching a scientist's home and making it look like an accident, it would take next to nothing to make a midlevel reporter at the IndyStar disappear.

The driver's door opened and his heart skipped a beat until he saw a tall brunette in a halter top, a tight short skirt and sandals exit the car.

"Are you Evan Taylor?" Her chest bounced as she walked over and thrust her tanned, petite hand at him.

"Yes. Ms. Leavitt?" He extended his sweaty palm.

"Oh sweetie, call me Jenny. Ms. Leavitt sounds like my ex-mother-in-law and, in the real estate business, that's not a good thing." She flashed a generous perfect-toothed smile. "So, what do you think?"

"I'd say it's pretty much a total loss, based on the damage and debris."

"Would you be interested in the lot?"

"No, I have an uptown luxury apartment in mind." Evan grinned as he made a quick glance at his closed trunk.

"Good luck." She took the key from Evan.

Luck is only half of it.

SEVENTY-ONE
Texas

SUE WATCHED the nine o'clock news from the corner of her eye as she helped her mother finish cleaning the kitchen. The kids were tucked into their beds upstairs. It had been a long week, and it was only Wednesday.

"Mom, you and Dad can leave. I'll clean up the rest of the dishes."

"No, Honey, I don't mind. Besides, your father has been snoozing on your couch for the last thirty minutes. I hate to wake him."

"I'm beat too. I have an early meeting tomorrow."

"How is it going with Wayne?"

It had been a few months since Sue had let Logan Designs go defunct. She was now the head of design for the new company which sold the products from her old company. She didn't mind the demotion, but what she really missed was the freedom to make the design changes and choices.

"It's fine. He's a good man to work for." Sue didn't like the feeling of utter hopelessness that had settled over her these days. Before her mom could reply, they both paused to listen to the TV newscaster.

"Listen up parents, if your kids are cuddling up to a Yorkston bear or pony tonight, you may want to watch this next segment. New laboratory tests have found that additional Chinese-made tush tags

329

on the stuffed toys appear to be contaminated with a dangerous red dye . . . ."

Either the news caught Wilford's attention or he had been pretending to snooze on the couch. He opened one eye, watching as well.

Sue took several deep breaths and schooled her face into a careful mask of indifference. For weeks, the headline news had centered on the Yorkston recall.

The recalls represented far more than just a cause; it was the final exclamation mark on a yearlong evolution for Sue's company, from an upcoming frontrunner providing hot new products into a reinvented ancillary under new leadership.

Sources said that a reporter close to the Yorkston group, Evan Taylor, spurred the national attention. Sue's family was aware of the truth behind the press.

According to the media, Evan was a friend of the mysterious Nathanael Yorkston. The press believed someone within Yorkston had given Evan some crucial evidence against Yorkston, tying the company back to the illegal tag cover up. Some commentators wondered aloud if Evan had stumbled on the cover up when he began investigating the toys for a story on Chinese manufacturing plants.

Evan had always driven to Texas, and he told Sue he had paid cash for gasoline. There were no airplane records of him traveling to Texas, no record of his meeting with her . . . no phone calls, emails . . . not a thing.

Because of the cryptic aura around Yorkston, no one suspected Sue's involvement. Her lawsuit against them was locked away from the public in confidentiality agreements.

Wilford yawned and stretched his arms. "That damn, greedy bastard," he grumbled.

Sue looked at her mom. "Here we go again."

"Well if there is a bright spot in all of this, it's that Sue's stuffed plush kids have made a huge splash as a sweet aftermath of the Yorkston fiasco." Thelma took off her apron.

"My Millennium Kids are doing great. Thank you very much." Sue bowed. Her parents exchanged smiles.

"It's because the world has become suspicious of toys manufactured in China. And our smart daughter made the fortuitous decision to have all her plush made here in the US," Thelma said.

"I don't think it was luck." Wilford winked at Sue.

"All I care is they are flying off the retail shelves." She had canceled her orders with the Chinese plant she and Daniel had visited. It had cost a lot to break the contract, but the decision to oversee the manufacturing in Texas made it necessary.

A few months ago, Sue would have been delirious with joy over all the Yorkston recall news. Now, the fact that she was making a successful product for someone else's business overshadowed everything. There were nights where Sue stayed in the plants all night, overseeing the employees, watching to make sure the dolls were made properly, and helping where she could.

"Thelma, we need to be heading home, before I take up camp here on Sue's couch." Wilford bellowed to the kitchen.

"I'll get my handbag," Thelma replied.

Thelma left the room. Wilford walked out to the kitchen. "Any word from the terrible twosome?"

"Nathanael Yorkston and Anthony Romero?" Sue narrowed her eyes.

He nodded.

"The last news reports said they were vacationing on a private yacht somewhere halfway around the world."

"Yeah, yeah, what does your source say?" He added air quotes around the word *your*. Sue knew Wilford had never trusted the Indy reporter, even though, in the end, Evan had taken the heat off Sue's company by totally obliterating Yorkston's power.

She carefully considered her next words. "Dad, as I mentioned before, I don't have a source into the whereabouts of Yorkston, or any of his doings."

"I understand. I just don't think he's finished breaking this story." Wilford pointed towards the television.

Sue realized he was referring to Evan knowing much more about the scandal.

"Nathanael Yorkston let greed, power, and ruthless business acumen forge his success. If there's more evidence that can conclusively link Yorkston and Romero, it'll come out."

Yorkston marketing personnel were handling the press. No official charges had been filed on any of the Yorkston executives. Many executives were unavailable for comments.

"Good night, Sue." Her mom returned to the kitchen.

Sue eyeballed her dad, signaling the end of their conversation. "Good night, you two."

She embraced them both, and linked one hand under her mom's elbow, escorting her to the front door. They had been her rock through this horrible journey, the stability she had turned to in the difficult times.

She locked all her doors, set the new security alarm, and crept upstairs to check on the kids.

Sue smoothed Maddie's sweaty curls. What a cutie pie. She peeked in on Colt. He was sleeping diagonally on his twin bed. She kissed his cheek. She checked on Elizabeth who was reading a book.

"Lights out in ten minutes," Sue said.

"Okay, Mom." Elizabeth kissed her mom on the cheek.

"See you in the morning, seven a.m. wake up call."

"Mom?" Elizabeth called to Sue as she exited the room.

"Yes, Sweetheart?"

"Now that Yorkston is in trouble, will you be getting your company back?"

Sue kept her tears at bay, crossing the room to sit on the edge of her oldest daughter's bed.

She placed her hand on Elizabeth's arm. "Honey, I'm still doing what I did before. Whether I'm the boss over everyone or not, that doesn't change the fact that they are my designs," she choked, holding back a sob. Even as Sue said the words to her daughter, she knew this wasn't exactly true. She had to get approval on minor changes to her own products. She no longer had the power to make decisions. For the first time in her life, she couldn't control every aspect of her business.

Wayne meant well, but he seemed more concerned with the ego reasons for the job than the excitement to take the company to the next level, which was the right reason to take the job. The preponderance of his excitement rested on things like the size of his office, studying the sales figures and balancing the checkbook. Sue knew those could exist, but he should have balanced that with things like working with his new employees, rising to the impossible challenges, and rolling up his sleeves and getting something done. He'd rather manage the books, not the products and people.

"I love the new trivia game you showed me," Elizabeth said, content with her mom's response. "You sure can think of awfully terrific toys."

Sue couldn't speak past the lump in her throat, so she nodded and patted Elizabeth's cheek.

Once back downstairs, she checked her email one more time before retiring to her bedroom. Surprised to see one new message, her heart did a flip-flop when she recognized the email address, *Daniel.*

SEVENTY-TWO

DANIEL'S EMAIL sat blinking at her as she melted into her desk chair. She slowly read every word. His email was short. It said he was in town tomorrow for a meeting with a new manufacturing line and he wanted to buy her lunch . . . to catch up.

To catch up? She hadn't seen Daniel since his deposition in Atlanta. They barely talked then. And now he wants to catch up? She thought of the pain his lack of response had caused her. It ripped a piece of her pride away, and left a scar.

For months, she had longed for his reassuring words. Now, he was back. Well she wouldn't let him back into her life that easy. His desertion had destroyed her faith in him and their future. If he wanted her trust again, he'd have to earn it.

The P.S. said he would be showing a new line, and that he had hired Mike Peterson's manufacturing rep group to represent it. They would be sharing the same rep group.

Sue focused on the screen. She took several deep breaths, trying to still her galloping heart. She should want to strangle him, after his lack of support, but instead she found herself typing a quick reply:

Yes, I'll meet you for lunch.
Lulu's Grill. Noon.
Sue.

She stifled a yawn, powered off her PC and went to bed.

The next morning, Sue stood in the elevator, making her way to the restaurant. She was apprehensive about seeing Daniel. The elevator seemed to take a century to arrive.

Lulu's was located at the thirty-second floor of the WTC Hotel. Sue had chosen the restaurant because it was walking distance from the World Trade Center.

Many of the retail manufacturers' reps and vendors held power meetings at the elegant restaurant. The food was sublime, the atmosphere – while divine – was businesslike, and diners could enjoy the panoramic views of Dallas and the river.

Sue stepped off the elevators a little before noon.

SEVENTY-THREE

DANIEL, SITUATED AT A TABLE in the restaurant for thirty minutes, was excited to see Sue. He felt himself flush as he thought about how it had been necessary to walk away from her. There wasn't a day that went by that he didn't think of her. He had been worried, but she was a fighter. She had gone through so much alone and taken care of herself just fine.

Daniel had read Evan's articles and watched the television reports of the massive Yorkston recall. He had scoured the newspaper reports voraciously, looking for any information that would point at Sue or her company. Evan Taylor had done a great job of uncovering the news, without one bit of a hint of Sue or her company's involvement. Her reputation was intact.

He saw her approach the hostess stand and exchange a few words. The hostess smiled at Sue, directing her toward his table by the window.

Sue walked through the restaurant and Daniel watched as every male, and several females', eyes followed her. Sue looked like she had just returned from a sun-soaked destination with her golden legs and tan, sculptured bare arms. She was wearing a tangerine colored dress that accentuated her perfect skin and honey butter hair pulled back in a loose ponytail. Several strands had already tumbled out of the coifed style, making her appear as youthful as a senior in high school.

For the first time in far too long, he actually felt something real for a woman, something deeper.

He felt it with shocking depth for this pony-tailed, hard-driven, but adorable woman with unconscious warmth and an innate sexiness, and a set of blue, haunted eyes. Perfect combo. The complete package.

Every sense in his body was on high alert. He realized how much he had missed her; more than he wanted to admit. She walked toward his table and a realization came over him. He really did care about Sue. A lot.

"Hello, Daniel." Sue extended her hand.

He stood and took her warm, soft hand in his. God, how he want to pull her into his arms and embrace her, to taste her lips again.

She looked at him with resentment for a moment, and then she softened. But when she sat down, she appeared guarded, not knowing what to expect.

Daniel had dressed in casual slacks and a golf shirt that fit his frame well. He had spent the last few weekends on the golf course and was sporting a deep, summer tan.

They made small talk about the views of the skyline while they ordered their food.

"I'm glad we could meet up. How is the business going?" Daniel restrained this time from quoting any Chinese proverbs.

Sue didn't reply. She sat there as if she was contemplating what to say.

Daniel read something in her eyes. Before she could answer he said, "I'm sorry to hear about the change in your business."

"How . . . ?"

"Mike told me."

"Of course. You and Mike Peterson are friends."

"Despite the new management," he said with a wry grin, "how are the products going after the Yorkston blowup?"

"As you probably know, the retailers have been ordering the Millennium Kids line by the truck full," she said. "Kid-n-Kidoodle ordered four pallets in time to stock their shelves for the holidays. Reading that faxed order was one of the most thrilling moments of my year. It validated all my years of work."

"That's fantastic. I'm so proud of the hard work you have done on this line." Daniel knew, if the early buzz was to be believed about her dolls, they could be headed straight for the million-dollar club.

She discussed her designs, and then a cloud came over her blue eyes, concern on her face. "Daniel, can I ask you something? Personal?"

Daniel shifted in his seat.

"Why did you ignore my business requests?" she asked.

"I didn't ignore you on purpose."

"Then why did you quit communicating with me?"

"It's complicated."

"I have nowhere to go right now. I'm listening." She sat back, folding her arms across her chest.

He felt his face flush under his tan. "Yorkston had stopped all their shipments to my family's stores. I was threatened by Romero, Yorkton's muscle, to stop communications with you and Logan Designs or our stores would never get another Yorkston product." Daniel watched her expression turn to one of unbelieving. Even as he said the words, he realized now how shallow they sounded.

"So you listened to them, versus helping me?"

Daniel's mouth tightened. "It wasn't that simple. Yorkston's products represent a substantial percent of our company's revenues."

He hoped she could believe him with respect to his family's business. Wasn't that a similar fear that had driven her? Her future and fate had been tied to Yorkston in a crude way.

Her blues eyes glinted like steel. She swallowed and said softly, "But I thought we had a business deal that you wanted to see through to the end."

"So did I. You're the one that changed manufacturing from China to Texas."

Sue look surprised and hurt. "I didn't do that to insult you. I realized that you had worked hard to help me secure the Chinese manufacturers, and I can imagine what that must have looked like, with me going back to the US plants. But I had my reasons."

Her eyes softened, the sunlight casting them in ocean shades. "Daniel, the change of product manufacturing wasn't because of anything you did or didn't do. I had other reasons, they—"

"I know more than you think I do."

338

"But . . .," her mouth opened and closed, "why didn't you—"

"I was afraid to reach out to you. "Daniel leaned across the table, taking her hand in his. "I wasn't really afraid of Yorkston hurting my company. I was afraid of what they would do to you."

He saw Sue blush. A strand of hair fallen loose from her ponytail rested on her cheek. He resisted reaching across the table and tucking it back. He felt warm. He wasn't sure if it was the sun shining into the windows as much as the feeling of her staring at him with her intense eyes.

"I've learned how tough they can be. Once you get in bed with Yorkston, you don't get out again," she said.

"Or at least not on your terms," Daniel said.

"It has been a horrible year with them in my life. What is it with this guy? Did Romero really need to hire muscle to rough us up and keep us quiet and to keep all their secrets safe? The problem is once these hooligans are in, Yorkston couldn't get rid of them, and so guys like the ones that came to my house looking to find out what I knew are the dirty part of their business."

"They came looking for you?" Daniel refrained from being visibly upset at hearing that they would bother her or her family.

Sue rubbed a pink, fading scar on her right hand. Daniel reached across the table and took her hand in his.

"They were afraid of what I knew and wanted to make sure I kept quiet," she said softly.

"You also sued Yorkston. It doesn't take much to get him riled up. I'm so glad to see they are out of the picture." He lightly touched her fading scar.

"Let's hope so."

Daniel had suspected that there would be more product recalls. Sources said that Evan had exposed only a small percentage of the serial numbers of Yorkston's bad products. He figured the reporter would milk the story for as long as he could.

"How do you like working with your new president; is it Wayne?" Daniel asked. He hoped Sue didn't see the glint of something in his eyes when he mentioned Wayne.

"He's difficult."

"Seriously? How so?"

"He tries to micromanage everything I do. Our first trivia puzzle did okay, but not great. My gut was to test a new product, a trivia game and he was dead set against it."

"Really?" This came as a surprise to Daniel. He had no idea her ideas were scrutinized. That would kill her creativity.

"Yes."

"So what did you do?"

"I did some designs, tested them out on my kids and some of their friends."

"And?"

"You know Elizabeth. She loved it! She said, 'Mom you sure make awfully terrific toys' ."

Daniel loved watching her beam as she talked about her work and her kids. Her true loves. As a beautiful and vivacious woman, Sue had defined herself in the retail world as a tower of strength and power she hadn't realized she possessed.

"So what did Wayne end up doing?"

"I gave him an ultimatum. I said, 'You can tell your boss, Mr. Investor, either buy me out at fifty cents on the dollar or I buy you out.' I just can't work like that. I knew Wayne loved telling me what to do but he wouldn't actually have the creativity to do the work himself. And he never interacts with the rep groups."

"Well, I always say, its people, not just product. Sue, you have done a great job of rallying marketing reps and distribution behind you and your products. A company can have the best product in the world, but if it doesn't have the distribution to get it out there, it'll flop."

"Yes, I have the contacts, but now that I had to hand in my YPO membership card, I don't feel I'm in control."

"YPO?"

"Young Presidents Organization," she said. "Oh well. Maybe it's time to put this ol' horse into another race to make my money back before I retire." She said it with a smile; a facial gesture that surprised Daniel, because he knew all too well she was serious. He had heard rumors that Sue was looking at leaving to start her own company again.

"You can't give up on this one."

"We'll see. I've lost a lot of things over the last year."

Including me, she is saying. Daniel hated the fact that he hadn't been able to reach out to her over the months. It had almost killed his soul. He buried himself in his work. Now that Yorkston was too busy to worry about some little Texas company, maybe she could start over; after all, she had her designs. But would she leave it all? And start fresh? He wore a concerned look.

"Would you have dinner with me tomorrow night?" he asked. "To discuss a business idea?" Daniel could move on, now that Yorkston was out of the picture. He was free to choose his own business associates.

"I'd like that, but let me check the kids' schedule. I'll let you know what time works."

He tried to calm his gut, which was churning like a blender. "Okay, then I'll see you tomorrow."

SEVENTY-FOUR
Michigan

DEE ANSWERED her cell phone on the first ring.

"Do you and Patrick still work out at the gym on Sycamore Street?" Evan asked Dee.

"Evan?" Dee replied.

"Yes . . . this isn't a social call. I want to give you something," Evan said.

"Me?"

"You, Patrick and your southern renegade."

"No need to thank us. You're the one writing the articles. You're the one with the talent. The stories are enough of a gift."

His unrestricted articles about Yorkston's tainted toy tush tag now broke in weekly sessions. The Associated Press seized every morsel of information Evan disclosed as if it was a bikini clad cellulite movie star in the tabloids. The nighttime talk show comedians had a field day. Who could blame them? Yorkston had been a mysterious billionaire and the success of his toys had interested the world. Disclosing their marketing secrets came with the package.

"Well, I think it's time you get back in shape. Back to the gym," Evan said.

Dee laughed. "Thanks, we like you too. Couldn't we all lose a few pounds?"

"Do you have a pen?"

"Yes, what do you have? Do you have a new case for us to research? Do you need some PI muscle behind you?"

"Locker 32, got it?" Evan was nervous that Dee wouldn't take him serious.

"Yeah, that's it?"

"Combo 11-04-68"

"Hey, that's my birthday."

"I know."

"What's in the locker? I know those lockers at the gym are too small for a body—a secret note?" Dee said.

"Yeah. A thank you note." Green notes, Evan thought.

"Now I'm curious."

"Guess you need to work out then."

"I may just do that."

"Dee, thanks again."

"You too, Evan. Be safe."

They hung up.

Fifteen minutes later, Dee was sitting in Patrick's unmarked crown Victoria at the Y on Sycamore Street.

She held the thank you card in her trembling hand. It said only two words.

Unmarked – Enjoy.

Sitting next to her on the front seat was a black gym bag filled with twenty-dollar bills.

Shit, Evan, what the hell did you discover?

Evan had told her he had solid evidence that Yorkston had been paying Shapiro under the table to keep his mouth shut.

She wondered if anyone else knew about the hush money. Well, she would have to keep this in a safe place until they could get to the bottom of it. No need to get our new friend in trouble.

Dee pulled a twenty-dollar bill out of the bag and stuffed it into her pocket. She zipped up the gym bag.

She rolled slowly out of the parking lot whistling absent-mindedly to the tune of *God Bless America*.

SEVENTY-FIVE
Texas

WHEN SUE RETURNED to her office, she had received another surprise email, this time from Wayne. He said the silent investor finally wanted to meet her, tomorrow. The meeting was scheduled for ten am.

She was excited to meet the investor. Sue spent the rest of the day tidying up her office, reviewing all her designs.

When she had lost her shares in the company to the new investor, she had lost a lot more. She could oversee launches of the new products, but she couldn't run the company. This hurt her feelings. This had been a family business. Her family.

Wayne never fit the mold as a president, at least not the mold of the nineties. He wasn't leading-edge savvy, and always stuck with the tried and true products, never wanting to take risk for high rewards. This aggravated Sue the most. She had a passion and knack for creating new designs. With that stifled, she felt it might be time to move on to something new.

Wayne worked often from his remote offices and had yet to move his family to Texas. He had planned to be in the Texas office tomorrow.

Mary Jo entered Sue's office. "Well, take a look at your office. Isn't this looking exceptionally tidy?"

Sue heard Mary Jo's sarcasm and laughed. "I'm finally getting a visit from the new investor."

"You mean the silent investor?" Mary Jo walked into Sue's office.

"Yes."

"Well it's about freakin' time. Are you going to ask him about what's-his-butt?" Mary Jo stood with her hands on her hips, referring to Wayne Montague.

Sue smiled at Mary Jo. The change in management had been hard on everyone. "I'm sure we'll discuss everything."

After an evening with the kids, Sue was exhausted when she crawled into bed. She thought of her meeting the next morning, but most of all, she thought of her meeting with Daniel.

She remembered his gaze, every word he spoke, every nuance, every expression. Just his presence breathed sensuality. Her whole body was responding to that sensuality; the palms of her hands that were tingling, her breasts felt suddenly sensitive, even her pulse was beginning to race.

Son of a bitch, she was falling for him.

Go to sleep. It's not going to do any good thinking about him.

She had a big day ahead of her. She pulled the sheets up to her chin and closed her eyes.

Don't think about him.

She did, as she fell sound asleep.

SEVENTY-SIX

AT A FEW MINUTES BEFORE 10 a.m., Sue looked more like a regal monarch than the Manager of Development standing tall, wearing a crisp cotton lavender dress and matching jacket, as she and Mary Jo waited in the lobby for Wayne to arrive. Her blonde hair was wrapped in a braid around her head, her blue eyes matching her dress.

Wayne's email said he would arrive in Texas that morning and pick up the investor at the airport at nine, meeting at the offices by ten.

The white stretch limousine drove in front of their warehouse office and parked diagonally across the parallel spaces out front, taking up four reserved spots.

Sue's heart pounded furiously in her chest when she saw the limo pull up at ten o'clock sharp.

"Oh. My. God," Sue said. She rubbed her hands down her neck. Didn't Yorkston drive around in a stretch white limo?

"But it couldn't be . . . ." Sue stared out the office window, her mouth dropped open, feeling her heart pounding in her chest; surely, Mary Jo could hear it standing next to her.

"Sure, I'm not impressed that Wayne hired a limo to bring out some bigwig, but it is his money. What's the big deal?" Mary Jo said.

The driver walked around the car and opened the back door. Sue caught a glimpse of wing-tip shoes coming out of the limo. It wasn't Wayne Montague.

The man exiting the limo wasn't Wayne, but he wasn't Nathanael Yorkston either.

In fact, he wasn't anyone Sue recognized.

He was an older gentleman, probably in his early seventies. He was a tall, distinguished man. He had silver hair with streaks of dark brown still lingering around his temples and scattered through the sides.

He entered the office and, with a spreading smile, he walked over to Sue and took her hand with both of his hands. Sue liked him before he even spoke.

"Sue Logan, we finally meet. I'm Joseph Harrison."

"Mr. Harrison, nice to meet you." *Relieved to meet you.*

Sue stared into his green eyes and felt warmed by them.

"Call me Joseph."

"This is Mary Jo. She really runs the place." Sue pointed to Mary Jo.

"Nice to meet you, young lady." He shook her hand. "I've heard great things about you both from Wayne."

Something in his voice and mannerism seemed familiar to Sue. "Speaking of which, where is Wayne?"

"He had another engagement. Can we go to your office and talk?"

"Yes, absolutely. Would you like a tour of the warehouse first?" Sue had forgotten her manners. "And how about a soda or coffee?" She was puzzled not to see Wayne with the owner.

"Coffee would be nice. Let's talk first, and then we can take a tour."

Mary Jo set off to get the coffee.

Sue felt extremely comfortable with the older gentleman, Joseph. She had prepared for a battle this morning, a war she intended to win. She had invested too much in her company to let it fall into the hands of the likes of Wayne. She now felt her proposition would be easier to present to this man in front of her.

They stood in the foyer of the office. Sue noticed the driver of the limo, still leaning against the back door.

"Should I invite him in to wait? It's terribly hot outside."

Joseph appeared uncomfortable. "Well, before we go any

further I do want to discuss with you Wayne's replacement."

"What?" Sue couldn't believe her ears. He was replacing Wayne already, and he hadn't even considered her for the president position? "You know, if you are making a change in management, I'd like to talk to you about me," she said.

"I've already made a change."

Crap. Sue didn't see that coming. She was prepared to discuss her company options, but not prepared for another new president. Her eyes watered up.

He reached over and took her hand. Sue glared at him in surprise.

Joseph had a slight grin on his face or did Sue see a grimace?

"I'd like you to meet him now," Joseph said.

"Now?" That's just great. He replaced the two-month-old president and now he wanted her to train another one. *Now!*

Joseph led her outside. The limo door opened and out stepped a tall man. Sue couldn't see his face because he was holding a bundle of long stemmed yellow roses in front of him. Her heart skipped a beat when he lowered the roses. Daniel handed the flowers to Sue.

"Hello, Sue."

She fought down the emotions swirling around inside of her. She brushed off a tear that slid down her cheek.

"Oh, Daniel. But how . . . ?"

Sue turned and looked at Joseph and back at Daniel. Daniel, a couple of inches taller than the older man, with emerald green eyes and gold trimmed irises, dressed in a blazer and slacks. Joseph, dressed impeccably in a designer suit, with his soft emerald green eyes with golden flecks, staring at Daniel with admiration meant only for a father to his son.

Daniel embraced Sue, her moist eyes meeting his.

He stepped back. "Sue, I'd like you to meet my father, Joseph *Harrison* Winston."

"That's impossible. I never thought, you . . . ." Sue couldn't think straight. She just stared with her mouth open. "All this time . . . ?"

Sue let another tear slide from her eye as she shook her head.

Daniel had a charming grin on his face, and those wonderful teasing emerald eyes. She stood, looking at both of them, tears streaming down her cheeks.

Mary Jo stepped outside balancing two cups of coffee. She surveyed the two men and the chauffer, all staring at Sue, as Sue stood by crying.

"What'd I miss?" She asked with a surprised smile.

All four laughed.

Mary Jo took Harrison, as most people called the elder Winston, on a tour of the warehouse while Sue and Daniel met in her office.

"Why didn't you tell me?"

"It wasn't appropriate. We both had a lot to lose if Yorkston would have found out. Wayne had been my father's accountant –"

"I knew he didn't fit as president," Sue interrupted.

"Wayne secretly arranged the buyout with your lawyer."

"You know Tex?"

"Yes, we met yesterday."

"Yesterday?"

"Sue, we have a lot to catch up on. We have no intentions of running your new company. I had a vested interest because of Yorkston. We wanted to make sure he didn't corner the supply side."

"Is that the only reason?" Sue hadn't been able to stop thinking about Daniel since lunch yesterday. She didn't look away from him. Her stare was intense. Did he know what he was doing to her? From the gleam in his eyes, as his gaze met her own, she guessed he knew her thoughts.

Daniel stared at her face for a long moment before he smiled. "Do you know there is no one in the world like you? God, I've missed you through all of this."

Sue felt melting warmth flow through her. He stepped in closer, within inches of her. Bittersweet emotions raced through her.

Despite her "no complications" warning signals blaring in her brain, she let him move in closer. When it came to a choice of her brain over the complex cascade of sweet emotions, this time, she truly wasn't in control. Her cerebellum lost out.

Without a fight from Sue, Daniel cupped her chin in his hands and pressed his lips to hers. Their kiss deepened. A roaring fire burned inside of her.

"You are incredible."

"So is this why you bought my company? Fringe benefits?" Sue said.

For an instant, he looked surprised, and then he chuckled. "Sue, you're an amazing designer; you have a knack for what is going to sell and what isn't. You belong at the head of the company. This company."

Sue's cheeks burned. "Are you serious? Do you really want me to take it back?"

"You didn't read your card." Daniel referred to the yellow roses lying on her desk.

She opened the envelope and found a membership card for the Young Presidents' Organization inside.

"We have worked out a proposition that I think you'll be happy with. That is, if you want to take the company back?" Daniel asked, looking a bit concerned. "Yesterday, I was afraid you had already committed to another venture, another start up."

In the past, Sue would write out the pros and cons, and take a logical approach to her decision process. But the shift in the fabric of her life had made her realize that she should go with her heart rather than her head.

The feelings that raced through her were so strong they yanked her from passion, respect, and admiration to terror and back again. One thing was for sure, these feelings scared her. Knowing he expected her to jumped at the offer in front of her, she relaxed and stared at him, hiding her triumph, as she saw him give her a puzzled look.

"So do we have a deal?" Daniel was still looking at her as if she would turn down the business.

"Deal," Sue said. They sealed it with a handshake, like they had in China so long ago. As she shook his hand, the burst of excitement she thought had been gone forever rose again in her chest.

She could be a successful entrepreneur again. She could

concentrate on what she was good at; designing products, instead of stressing over lawsuits and competition and the things she couldn't master. She had won! At last, after a year of the most despicable and manipulative fighting she had ever witnessed, Yorkston was out of her life and Daniel was back in it.

She could work with Daniel again, who had as much heart invested in her designs as she did.

"After all, Elizabeth said you make awfully terrific toys," Daniel said. "What will you call your new company; Logan Designs II?"

"No, I'm thinking I should name it *Awfully Terrific Toys*."

Sue knew it was time to move forward.

Epilogue

THE GOLF COURSE route at sunrise was Sue's favorite run. There were no groundskeepers or golfers this early. She set out from the back of her house and chose the route backing up to her neighbors houses.

The highlight of the run was when she turned east and the sun crested over the undulating fairways, dramatic bunkering and the scenic wetlands. Some mornings, the early dew would settle on the perfectly manicured grass, looking like a bride's veil of lace. The grass blades radiated with the early sunlight reflecting millions of dewdrops bound to every faceted edge.

She jogged, avoiding the scattered webs of the grass spiders, their funnels perched perilously among the plants, the perfectly-formed web holes bursting flashes of color, like a horizontal rainbow at her feet. The sun's refraction off their webs was magnificent, and Sue thanked the grass spiders for their unintentional genius.

Sue watched her step and avoided their webs. A hawk roosted peacefully in a tree. She smiled when the first sunrays kissed the sky hello as it peeked over the horizon.

She saw his silhouette in the newly-built cabana as she neared her house. Her heart raced even faster than her feet, and she slipped through the iron back gate.

He handed her a cup of coffee.

She gazed into Daniel's face.

He wrapped his hands around her waist, pulling her into his embrace, infusing her with his strength. He dropped his head toward her upturned face. His lips met hers and they exchanged a long, soft kiss. Locking their arms about each other's waist, they walked toward the house.

Twelve hours later and twelve thousand kilometers away in the South Pacific Ocean, the Le Grand York cruised toward Gisborne, New Zealand.

A three hundred and ninety foot private yacht, The Le Grand York was, one of the finest in the world. It had been made especially for an American businessman last year— Nathanael Yorkston.

The yacht moved swiftly, powered by its twin 3,800 horsepower engines. Its two passengers were on the top deck, enjoying the serene weather.

The Le Grand York was a beautiful sight to observe on the open sea. The media knew little details of the yacht since its owner, Nathanael, was so protective of his privacy.

Nathanael, tanned and spouting a gray beard, was standing on the main deck that led to the custom-designed pilothouse.

Anthony approached Nathanael, carrying a black satellite phone. "McDougal. He said it's urgent." Anthony handed Nathanael the receiver. Anthony's natural olive skin had tanned to a darker brown, making him look more like his father's ancestors from southern Spain than his mother's Italian family.

"James, what brings this urgency?" Nathanael barked into the phone, without saying hello to his chief lawyer.

"The Indianapolis police said they have received a document that your chemist, Shapiro, left behind. Nathanael, it isn't good. They asked you to return to Indy."

"Why?"

"They believe Shapiro may have been murdered."

Nathanael's eyes settled on Anthony, giving him a despicable, hateful glance.

"You need to return immediately," McDougal said.

"We are headed to Gisborne now."

"Okay, we'll book you out on an Air New Zealand flight."

Nathanael hung up the satellite phone. He turned to Anthony. "We aren't going to Gisborne. Tell the captain to turn the boat around. Now." He picked up the satellite phone and threw it overboard, contemplating his next move as he watched it plunge to the sea below.

About the Author

Pamela Laux was the owner of a toy and gift manufacturing company. She holds dozens of product patents and trademarks.
She loves traveling and attributes her creative inspiration from it.
She has published several catalogs, calendars and guide books.
This is her first novel. She resides in Dallas.

Go to www.pamlaux.com and enter the drawing for a chance to win prizes.

COMING SOON!

www.ingramcontent.com/pod-product-compliance
Lightning Source LLC
Chambersburg PA
CBHW020823180626
46814CB00001B/87